Pup

LEDA

AND THE

SWAN

LEDA
AND THE
SWAN

Anna Caritj

RIVERHEAD BOOKS   NEW YORK   2021

RIVERHEAD BOOKS
An imprint of Penguin Random House LLC
penguinrandomhouse.com

Library of Congress Cataloging-in-Publication Data

Names: Caritj, Anna, author.
Title: Leda and the swan / Anna Caritj.
Description: New York : Riverhead Books, 2021.
Identifiers: LCCN 2020024988 (print) | LCCN 2020024989 (ebook) |
ISBN 9780525540144 (hardcover) | ISBN 9780525540168 (ebook)
Subjects: GSAFD: Suspense fiction.
Classification: LCC PS3603.A7496 L43 2021 (print) |
LCC PS3603.A7496 (ebook) | DDC 813/.6--dc23
LC record available at https://lccn.loc.gov/2020024988
LC ebook record available at https://lccn.loc.gov/2020024989

Printed in the United States of America
1st Printing

BOOK DESIGN BY LUCIA BERNARD

For Mom

A sudden blow: the great wings beating still
Above the staggering girl, her thighs caressed
By the dark webs, her nape caught in his bill,
He holds her helpless breast upon his breast.

How can those terrified vague fingers push
The feathered glory from her loosening thighs?
And how can body, laid in that white rush,
But feel the strange heart beating where it lies?

A shudder in the loins engenders there
The broken wall, the burning roof and tower
And Agamemnon dead.
                              Being so caught up,
So mastered by the brute blood of the air,
Did she put on his knowledge with his power
Before the indifferent beak could let her drop?

—"Leda and the Swan,"
William Butler Yeats (1924)

LEDA

AND THE

SWAN

1

Saturday, October 31

Leda tied her neon-pink running shoes while angels, astronauts, and superheroes began their first rounds of trick-or-treating. They passed her on the front step of the Psi Delta sorority, adjusting halos, dragging polyester tails, running (or being advised, *no running*), or simply being carried: an amazed bumblebee, a pod of peas. In astronomy class, Leda had learned that the world was 4.5 billion years old and that humanity had barely wrinkled the cosmic scheme. Life was small, she knew. But it felt big in moments like these—hearing children's high voices, the *tit* of masked chickadees, and police sirens singing somewhere, almost sweet. It felt big when she could just open her door and witness the dogwood's last red leaves, the crisp sunlight, and the white abacus of clouds overhead, shifting. Here was Leda, with the world around her, ringing. Then, here was Leda wondering, as if the day were a threshold, if today might be the beginning or end of things. Something, she sensed, was slipping.

The children were headed to the college Lawn—a grassy, terraced quad surrounded by ten pavilions and fifty or so upperclassman rooms whose residents, Leda assumed, were already handing out candy from their stoops. As a kid, Leda had come to this festival, too. When she'd caught her mom pilfering a piece of her candy, her mom had joked, chewing, that she was checking for poison.

Now, Leda was too old for trick-or-treating. She stretched wide legged in front of the house, the crown of her head reaching down. She smelled brick moss and dropped leaves. Upside down, she watched a band of pirates cross under the stoplight at the corner of Memorial Road and University. She watched a T-bone steak dash for a neighbor's kiddie pool, which was full of melted ice and unopened Natty Light. The steak's parent (a cow) wrangled the kid and carried him back toward the sidewalk through dewy red cups.

Leda stretched, and her skull grazed the ground. She looked up at her freckled legs, short shorts, and beyond—an arrow of honking geese, the wind pushing clouds. Her guess was: morning. Though the time didn't matter, really. It was Saturday. She yawned, upside down, and covered her mouth. Funny, covering her mouth when no one was around.

She jogged to the nearby Varsity Field for calf stretches. It had a classical Roman theater aesthetic with gray columns and concrete seating, and that crumbly vibe, that dilapidated energy that made students feel comfy enough to pass out there, or leave their used tampons there, or have sex, even though this seemed *uncomfy* to Leda—there was broken glass everywhere. The arches and colonnades were part of the look her university had gotten off on for two hundred years, though the architecture was less cared for here. It was off-grounds and surrounded by Greek life (aka drunk people everywhere).

Bland, brick dormitories stood at the far end of the field. Beyond the dorms, Leda could see O-Hill (*O* for *observatory*), one of her two preferred runs. The trail went through dense woodland and ended at the university's refracting telescope. Her other run took her to a Civil

War–era graveyard, downtown. Though this one was shorter in miles, it always took longer than O-Hill because she'd made a habit of wandering among the graves, searching, half-consciously, for family names. She never found anything. The grave that mattered—her mother's—was forty miles away.

Leda turned her back on the mountain, put her toes on the edge of a step, and stretched her heels down. Someone had spilled glitter here, making the grit shimmer. Overhead, five pairs of panties fluttered from a string, tied between two pillars of the Doric colonnade. Across the street, the sun peered over the Kappa Chi fraternity. Greek letters and the tags of secret societies decorated all sides of the building. A girl in a sequined shirt sat on a porch keg in front of a painted chi. The white *X* sprang from behind her like wings.

In the yard, a fleshy mask drooped from the end of a stake. Inside the frat, something like feedback cracked. Leda picked up her feet, ducking the panty flags, about to start running, when piano spilled from the fraternity. Two doves, like firecrackers, lobbed into the sky. The sequined girl looked after them as the music wobbled—synth now, and again piano. It could have been a warped LP, or it could have been Leda's ear misinterpreting the sound: major chords staggering into minor, an unclear key. Then the piano flared again, then the dizzy singing:

You can dance . . .

A train clattered along the far edge of the athletic field, drowning "Dancing Queen." By the time Leda had shuffled her feet—a groggy dance—she could barely hear the music. The train flashed behind diamonds of chain link, repeating black, red, and gray geometry. Leda usually waved at the conductors of trains—a silly habit from childhood—but she didn't see a man in the engine window today.

See that girl . . .

The sequined girl disappeared as Leda turned the corner. She passed more frats and a few sororities. She crossed Beta Bridge, layered in generations of paint, where already a long stretch of silence thwacked in the wake of the train. A sedan passed, and the air stirred behind it. Down the sidewalk, a tiny Power Ranger walked with his mother. Leda ran. She leapt over a patch of broken glass—gravelly, smashed—and crossed to the other side of the street, where there was also glass. The Rotunda rose in the distance, but she turned down a side street and lost sight of it. Overgrown shrubs blocked the sidewalk. Disney Princess towels hung on a sorority's porch railing: Jasmine, Belle, Sleeping Beauty.

Down Fraternity Row, she passed another girl running. Then another. She passed a dining room table jutting into a holly tree, its surface covered with fake cobweb and orange beads. She passed three Styrofoam containers holding something that didn't look like food. She passed four boys sitting on a fraternity's roof, drinking from red cups and eating bunless hot dogs. Only one wore a toga, but all four held themselves like small-time gods. One threw his sunglasses off the roof and shouted something. Leda ran, steady. She didn't want to give them the pleasure of being noticed. She hummed, *Young and sweet* . . . The street widened. Behind her, the gods howled from the rooftop, appalled at how little attention they'd gotten.

"Cunt," one called after her. "Bitch."

Leda saluted. In her three years of college, she'd been called worse things. The names found for women, men—anybody—were like the names of plants and animals: just a method of convenience, a dumbing down of the world's endless manifestations. Because, before all this naming—before she could remember, really—she had been a child holding a plastic pumpkin: tiny and wondrous and growing into today. Same as anybody.

She yawned again. Covered it, sparing the world the sight of her tongue and teeth. She'd heard that a girl had fallen off one of these frat roofs recently. Not a god, she guessed. Not an angel. Just some wasted chick.

A church clock struck the hour as Fraternity Row came to a T with a busier street. Here, there were still more runners: more short shorts, more neon sneakers. A bus wheezed and knelt in the crosswalk, and Leda waited for it, face bobbing in the dark grime of the windows, red ponytail bouncing. She hummed with the engine noise, looping the same "Dancing Queen" verse. The church bell kept hitting. It was not morning, actually. Surprise: Leda had slept in. The clock on the bank read 12:00 p.m.

Children flocked to the Lawn. Behind them, parents toted pumpkin buckets and lunch boxes. In the midst of all of this, Leda could make out university students, dressed as extravagantly as the kids. She ran past three in fencing garb—their masks lowered, their white gloves flaunting foils with wobbling thrusts. She ran past the anthropology building, where animal busts glared from the stone frieze: a walrus, a tapir, a rhino, and some openmouthed beast.

Leda took the Rotunda's wide steps and jogged the terrace, level now with white pediments and southern magnolia canopies. Her shoes squeaked on the marble. Her reflection, no more than a slip of color, darted in and out of the Rotunda's windows. She rounded the building, passing beneath trunk-thick columns and brimming capitals. A balloon sailed overhead—one, and then three, and then uncountable.

The world was awake; the day had started without her. Over and over this happened to her: the future hit, as if the world she'd left on the other side of the Rotunda's steps (the ginkgos shimmering, the stone chapel, the stacks visible through library windows) were a curtain that could be thrown back. Revealing . . . nothing awful, obviously. It was just surprising. Here, she turned an ordinary corner and met a slap of face paint, sequins, and braided wigs. Voices rising. Joyful screams. Jack-o'-lanterns in the midday sun, grinning.

No one else looked surprised. No one else seemed to notice Earth's endless, incremental turmoil. But Leda had to stop. Take it in. It was as if time had cracked, letting some of the past spill out and the future seep in. Year after year, the festival did not change. Her mother could be here, even now: the red clogs, the Nikon around her neck. It was easy to picture the reading glasses in her hair, the wool purse, and these same white columns around her, roped in orange streamers. But her mother herself—her actual face—she had trouble imagining.

Leda reached out and held on to a railing.

From the grass, a voice called, "Lee!"

Near one of the Lawn's massive trees (a maple, by the red of the leaves), silver balloons reflected people—gnawing on Sugar Daddys, pulling up tights, sheathing and unsheathing plastic knives. In many cases, it was hard to tell the difference between the college students and the kids. Leda held the railing. Some of the balloons reflected the white curtain of sky. Here was the world: bright, buoyant, and yet swollen with vacancy.

The voice in the grass kept on. "Leda the slut! Ho bag. Lee!"

Of course, the balloons weren't really empty. Just because she couldn't *see* the helium and whatever else, didn't mean it wasn't there.

"Yoo-hoo, *Lee*!"

Leda blinked. Below her, a blond witch brandished a carved pumpkin. A Reese's slipped from the pumpkin's mouth, and a skeleton—a man in a full, boned bodysuit—snatched up the candy, showed his skull to Leda, and disappeared into the crowd.

The witch adjusted her boobs. "Leda, where's your costume?"

"You're looking at it," Leda said, coming out of it, meeting her friend and fellow Psi Delt Carly at the base of the steps.

"Funny. Will you hold this for me?" Carly loaded the pumpkin into Leda's arms without waiting for an answer. Carly was Leda's "Big"—short for "big sister," i.e., her mentor when Leda had first joined the sorority—so Leda, Carly's "Little," was used to the servitude (joking-not-joking). Now, Carly adjusted her pointy hat and combed a plastic spider out of her staticky hair. "I should have just done a plastic pumpkin, but I thought this would be, like, witchy. Now I think my arms are going to fall off my body."

Somewhere, recorded maniacal laughter was on repeat. Leda shifted the pumpkin, damp and heavy. A ghost in a white sheet rushed by, excusing himself by saying, "Ladies," while a boy in a too-large football helmet stood before Leda, singing, *Trick or treat.* Leda lowered the pumpkin, and the boy took a Reese's.

"Thank you," the boy said, and placed the candy in his pillowcase.

"I thought I would unload that thing in no time," Carly said. "But the kids here are so frickin' polite. They use two fingers to pluck out one tiny piece. What happened to stealing the whole bowl?"

"I think that was just you." Leda moved her feet.

"Also, it's not even night. Part of the fun was going up to some stranger's house, right? And there'd be someone sitting on the porch in the dark, like, dead or asleep, with the candy bowl in their lap and you'd have to sneak over and you'd have to reach . . ."

"Trick or treat!"

Leda lowered the pumpkin for a fairy trio. The girls each took a piece of candy, shivered their wands at Leda, and ran off, legs flinging.

"It's a fucking tragedy," Leda said, coming to herself again. "A war on Halloween."

"Someone should do something. Plus, ninety percent of these costumes are stupid."

"You're a witch, Carly."

"The witch is classic. Untouchable. It's historically interesting."

"Have you seen Mary?"

It was an innocent question, but Carly seized on the opportunity to dis their former sister. "Oh my god." Carly rolled her eyes. "Mary's wearing black wings. She told me what she is, but I can't remember. It's not even pretty. She must be drunk or something."

Mary lived on the Lawn this year. Her door opened straight onto the long, grassy quad. This was an honor—you had to be in high academic standing in order to live here. But lately Leda's sorority sisters were saying that Mary had gotten weird.

Carly applied lip gloss. "Would you take that for me?"

"What?"

"The pumpkin. The candy. I can't even lift my arms, Lee."

"Love to, but I'm running O-Hill."

"No, you're taking my pumpkin to go say hi to Mary, whose single redeeming quality is her suite's proximity to Ian Gray, who is, this very day, wearing but a loose toga over his magnificent chest."

Leda tried to veil her interest. "Sounds like an event."

"He is so cute," Carly said. "And he likes *you*."

Ian was in the A School, which stood for *architecture*. He was blond and a swimmer and had this tuned-in, blue-eyed face that said something like, *I listen* or *You're beautiful*.

Leda said, "Says who."

"Lee." Carly gave her the round-eyed *duh* look. "It's obvious. Please."

Carly was not the only one who had been talking about Ian lately. The Psi Delta volunteer leaders were always gushing about his work building homes in this or that village, about how he wanted to learn how to *build* structures as well as design them. This past summer, his appendix had apparently ruptured on a volunteer trip, and he received an operation in a field tent under only local anesthetic (though the details changed slightly, depending on who was telling it). After recovering, he went back to building the house he had started.

He is so *dedicated*, Leda's sisters went on, ad nauseam. *Not to mention gorgeous.*

Someone shouted, "Move!"

The fencers were coming through, crossing foils. One leapt down the Lawn's first small hill. The grass was terraced, so Leda, from where she was standing, could see the mountains over the rooftops of the Lawn rooms, domed pavilions, and Bell Hall, which faced the Rotunda on the far side of the quad. The fencer landed lightly on the brick path tracing the base of the hill, two more pursuing. A pack of miniature Ninja Turtles charged after them, shouting.

"Since when have you even seen us together?" Leda asked Carly.

"I don't have to."

"We're in the same astronomy class with, like, two hundred other people. We don't even sit on the same side of the room."

"Well, (a) you already know where he sits, and (b) I heard he texted you."

"So?" Leda could feel her face flush. Yes, he had texted, and she had coyly not responded. She was just crushing, honestly; it wasn't like she loved him. Even so, it was no small thing to be seen, to be noticed. She felt pleasantly disoriented, as if with that one text, her whole map had shifted.

"I'm just saying it's ungrateful." Carly hoisted the bust of her dress. "You should be acting at least marginally enthused. I'd be bowing down if I were you."

A smile escaped Leda's lips as she took Carly's pumpkin toward Mary's room. Of course Carly would never have sent Leda over here if Ian hadn't lived next door to their former sister. Typically, Carly and the other Psi Delts behaved as if Mary no longer existed. *Sister*, Carly had said once, drunk, *is just a word.*

But Mary had been Leda's first college friend. She didn't say this to Carly, obviously, but less than a year after Leda's mother's death, Mary had been the first person to fill in (even if only a little bit) that deep aloneness.

Mary's door was open, like all the other Lawn rooms. The quad was her yard, essentially. And the covered brick walkway and endless colonnade was her patio, mobbed with squealing children today. Mary sat on her stoop, letting a pride of small lions pick their candies. She wore a velvet dress and sparkling green eyeshadow. Fake blood dripped from her mouth. A succubus, she said, when the lions left. It *was* pretty. Sexy, even. The costume just wasn't Psi Delta approved.

"Carly said you had wings," Leda said, popping one of Mary's candies.

"Carly's drunk."

"That's funny." Leda unloaded Carly's pumpkin, glancing toward Ian's room. "Carly said the same thing about you."

Ian's Lawn door had dark shutters, which had been lashed open with bungee cords. Next to his stoop, his university-provided rocking chair was cable locked to the building's exterior beside a stack of university-provided wood. The inside of the room, Leda knew, would be identical to Mary's—one window, one fireplace. A loft-style bed, a rolltop desk. They were all singles—scholarly and austere, a fantasy for life-of-the-mind dorks like Mary.

Mary saw her looking. "I think Ian went to buy more candy. These kids are wolfish."

Leda toed Ian's woodpile. "They're not taking Carly's."

"That's because Carly comes off as a real witch."

"I'll tell her you said that." Leda smiled, tapped her own lips. "What's with the blood?"

"Well, I'm a demon, right? It's messy, sucking men's . . . reproductive strength, let's say." Mary grinned gorily. "And don't even say what I know you're thinking. This stuff is fine. It tastes like cherry."

Leda zipped her lips, innocent. For all her smarts, Mary was afraid of blood. Or, more accurately, Mary couldn't deal with the fact that she had a body. If she hurt herself—a paper cut, a splinter, or just a safety pin grazing her thumb, not even breaking the skin—she would wrap her injury in paper towel or hold it balled in her fist until she found someone else to look at it.

"I blame Sleeping Beauty," Mary said. "She pricks her finger and what? Dies? Am I remembering correctly?"

"Well, we don't want any little girls getting jabbed by strange pricks . . ."

Mary slapped her forehead. "I have never even *thought* of Sleeping Beauty like that. Seriously. Why aren't you an English major again?"

A standard Mary nag. Leda had taken a few core English requirements with Mary, only to choose a major in Spanish. She ignored the comment, drifting casually in front of Ian's open door. A fire burned in the hearth. His desk was cluttered with books and drafting paper. There was also a skeleton next to the closet.

"Oh—" Leda stepped back as the skeleton came forward. A man, that is, dressed as a skeleton. Leda couldn't see his eyes, but he was about Ian's height. "Sorry. Ian?"

The skeleton stepped toward her, breathing loud against the nylon covering his nose and mouth. He touched his forehead in acknowledgment, ducked out of the room, and slipped into the throng.

Leda went back to Mary, pointing. "Did you see that?"

"What?"

"There was a dude in Ian's room."

Mary was checking her fake blood in a mirror. "I think the swim team's here. A bunch of them were doing handstands on the grass in, like, Poseidon costumes."

"This was a skeleton."

"Cool. Original." Mary unwrapped a Tootsie Roll from her own trick-or-treat bowl. She offered one to Leda.

"No, thanks. I'll take a lollipop, though." Leda unsheathed the thing and crunched it between her teeth. "You going to the bubble party later?"

"I'm fairly certain bubbles have never been a part of All Hallows' Eve or Samhain or, now that I think of it, *any* tradition."

Mary had been saying shit like this lately.

"*Shut up*, Mary. Come to the party."

Mary shook her head, smiling, as Leda let the crowd sweep her into its glitter and paint and sulfur-smelling bodysuits. She glanced once more into Ian's empty room, taking the last few crunches of lollipop and reciting in her mind, as if casting a spell, *Come to the party.*

The masses swept her away, flowing and halting alternately. Leda stopped for three giraffes, cantering in an endless ring. A wailing Cinderella in blue puff sleeves bumped into the backs of Leda's knees. At the next opportunity, Leda ducked down an alley, passing between walled gardens, jogging away from the Lawn. Her shoes crushed blond pebbles and fallen leaves. Pebbles became asphalt. Columned buildings became brick dorms as she moved away from the heart of the university. She passed the gym, where she did her work-study. The job involved sitting at a desk and watching students and profs swipe their IDs. Sometimes she had to lock doors. Sometimes she had to clean things. On slow days, she gazed out the big, interior windows behind her desk at the Olympic-size pool, two floors below.

Oddly enough, she never used the gym's facilities. She didn't like exercising indoors, didn't like running in place, didn't like wheezing up at some arbitrary point on the wall (e.g., the thermostat, the television's volume buttons, the defibrillator instructions). She needed obstacles to leap. She needed wind, rain, ice, or heat. She needed to feel as if she were running from something. *Chase me*, she used to beg her mother, terrified, delighted. *Chase me.*

She passed the football stadium and turned into a neighborhood of off-campus housing, the slap of her feet the only sound echoing off the concrete. The trailhead was just up the road a bit. She sprinted for it, watching what she thought was a bird, then a big leaf, and then what turned out to be a padded bra draped over the chain across the entry.

The sun was still high, but she didn't have as much time as she would have liked. Yeah, it was Saturday, but she still had to get home and practice a song for choir. Then she had to finish astronomy homework, read a play for Chilean Lit, and then try to memorize Martí or Paz or some other difficult poet. (It was now or never; tomorrow, she'd be hungover.) Then there was a pregame at the Cathouse across the street before Moonie's bubble party. It wasn't a brothel or anything—just a lot of girls in one place, not unlike Leda's sorority. Still, Leda had never been; the Psi Delts made a point of never socializing with non-Greeks. But tonight a few of her sisters had agreed that a Cathouse pregame might be spooky, Halloween-y. Plus, booze was booze. Though there was almost zero chance of Ian at that party, Leda figured it might be good to show a little late for the bubble party (per the law of scarcity).

The pavement turned to dirt. Now there were roots to dodge and stones to navigate. There were tiny birds in the trees, bitching and singing. She breathed. The sun clinked through the brittle canopy. She ran switchbacks. She could feel her heart in her thighs, in her feet. When the trail was level enough for her to look up, she could see where the sun lit the bald cap of the mountain. She ran faster, blood pumping, and broke out of the trees. Old goldenrod stalks batted her calves as the meadow gave onto mowed grass and then, eventually, the observatory.

The observatory was a white eyeball, staring up at the sky. Leda ducked the gate, ran past the building, kicked the base of a rusted water tower, and bounded back down the little mountain. Above her, two ravens surfed on air currents. She sped up, watching the black birds on blue air. Stars shone behind that blue curtain; she couldn't see them, but that didn't mean they weren't there. A raven croaked, *Ian.* She laughed out loud—light, unburdened. It was one of those rare moments in which she felt she was right where she ought to be. She knew where she was going. Gravel skidded under her feet, her breath hot, her heart happy to find itself beating.

At the road, a pickup had parked outside the gate, its engine ticking. The windshield reflected opaque white light. Leda dashed by the passenger door. The cab was empty. In the back, four hounds had their heads stuck out of a diamond-tread dog box in the bed. She gasped, and the dogs lunged as well as they could, barking. In Dice County, where Leda had grown up, trucks with big tires, gun racks, and hunting dogs were common, but here in town not so much. She fled—the dogs gnashing and howling, their owner nowhere. She sprinted through the goldenrod toward the lip of the forest. It was weird—this fear was nearly indistinguishable from the excitement she had felt moments earlier. Her nerves were tight enough to pluck. The hounds bellowed. She only just resisted the urge to scream.

The Psi Delta house was off-grounds in a renovated plantation-style building, divided up into a kitchen, common room, and fifteen bedrooms. The house was small-ish, by Greek standards, and of course you didn't *have* to live in the house to be a chapter member. Leda, though, had wanted to. It sounded cheesy, she knew, but she'd wanted a home. A family.

Room-wise, she had gotten lucky. While most of the rooms were shared, Leda's was one of a handful of singles, awarded by lottery. The room had a porch, too, shared with her sister Naadia, a fourth-year, Pakistani poli-sci major. Naadia was smart and serious, though her life outside of school seemed regal. During summer break, she'd taken pictures of herself on yachts in the UAE, wearing literal gold bikinis. There was a map in her room with pins stuck in all the countries she'd visited. Leda couldn't imagine having the funds for this, though there was something attractive in the idea of packing a bag and peacing—to Colombia, maybe. To Greece. To Egypt.

It was a nice dream. But Leda was *here* now, stinking and sweating. She dashed upstairs and into her room to strip. In the closet, she had to push her mom's old Chinese dragon off the hamper to fit the damp clothes in. Her mom had bought the dragon at an estate sale, and instead of taking it to her rented ten-by-ten space in the antique mall—a mildewed warehouse where Leda had spent uncountable childhood hours—her mother had brought it home and hung it up. Its body had paper scales like a snake. Its head had great, lidded eyes that could be clapped open and shut. Leda had been (and still was) a little afraid of it—the big, blunt teeth in its fishy mouth; the coked-up eyes; the hollow insides.

Her mother had made up all sorts of theories about the dragon. The dragon was wise and all-knowing: it knew when to dig up the potatoes in the garden, and it knew whether or not Leda had brushed her teeth. It loved popcorn (with Milk Duds) and American cheese. It traveled whenever they left the house, touring the globe, the galaxy.

Now, the dragon lived in the farthest reaches of Leda's closet. Three years since her mother's death, and Leda still didn't have the courage to get rid of it.

In the shared bathroom, Leda gulped water from the sink while the shower got hot. She stepped in, scrubbed the salt off her skin, and came out smelling like Froot Loops, red and sopping. She dressed and sang "Adam lay ybounden," music stand raised, pencil in hand, marking surprise rests and tricky rhythms. The setting was slow as a Gregorian chant, the chords designed to rise and fill an empty space with ringing. It would be performed a cappella in a select group, for which Leda had auditioned. In concert, she and the other members of this group would have electric candles hidden in their robes. They would twist the bulbs of their candles until they lit. In the same instant, they would open their mouths, their voices reaching out.

Their conductor was known for theatrics. He was known for climbing onto his desk and shouting, *We are communicating!* among other things. This particular phrase came more often as admonishment than praise; we're *supposed* to be communicating, he meant.

What are you saying? he'd scream. *What are you SAYING.*

Now, Leda sang, *"Blessed."* She sang, *"We moun singen."* Her voice filled the space. As always, the bed was unmade. Her two comforters were all wound and separated. From the corner of her eye, they looked like bodies. She sang:

> *Blessed be the time*
> *That apple taken was,*
> *Therefore we moun singen.*
> *Deo gratias!*

Her conductor, on the little desk in her head, shook his fist. What *was* she saying? She took a guess: What beauty, what art, what reverence emerges from sin! Gracias, god! Though she wasn't sure about this. Plus, does sinning always create sublime art? Probably not, she guessed, thinking of some local graffiti of fried chicken with human breasts and angel wings, thinking of the "poems" her sorority sisters composed on the common room whiteboard (e.g., *Roses are red / Titties are pink...*). No, Leda didn't want to hear *everybody's* mournful singing. But, most people plucked the apple, didn't they? And, whether she liked it or not, everybody had something to sing.

Of course, it was possible to eat an apple and then not say anything. It was easy to "sin" without really paying attention. Plenty of people did it, like Mary not wanting to look at her own bleeding. And it wasn't like Mary was crazy; even Leda's first reaction when she cut herself or smashed something or slept with somebody was to look away. They were terrifying—these bites of reality that reminded her that she *was* her body. She would look up at the ceiling, holding the hurt part away. She would close her eyes, as if to find that other Leda (the "real" Leda) that was not composed of nerve endings, not woven tissue, not bones and blood and organs somehow pumping, somehow miraculously keeping her living.

There must be a real Leda, right? An essence, a soul, a spirit. Though it always confused her when people referred to it—"your true self" or "the real you."

Downstairs, Leda's sisters sang along to the kids' song "Witches' Brew," shouting in unison, "Alakazamakazoo!" They were eating Halloween candy, probably—overindulging as only children are supposed to do.

Leda watched her bed's twisted sheets, singing, *"Ne had the apple taken been . . ."*

Her voice went flat. She sang it again. She opened a window. The world smelled like soured recycling. A mourning dove wept under "Witches' Brew" and a surge of jackhammering. The house next door had been demolished recently, and the construction (or destruction, rather) was progressing slowly. Or regressing. Or something. A concrete walk was being broken up today, revealing underneath raw, red clay.

Beyond the demolished lot was a regular neighborhood—a few sorority houses, old mansions divided into rental units, and the occasional professorial abode. There were also shared houses with no Greek affiliation—just clots of oddball undergraduates storing their Pop-Tarts in the same kitchen. The Cathouse was the closest of these, full of girls with tattoos and painful-looking piercings, who majored in things like women's studies and philosophy. They threw long, noisy parties. But at least they could. At least they didn't have to go a-wassailing like Leda and any other Greek-life girl. Alcohol was verboten in any sorority on campus. Parties, too. The ban came from on high—the national chapter heads made those decisions. Maybe it was an image thing. Maybe it ensured lower insurance premiums. Or maybe, as Mary said, it was just good old sexism.

Without meaning to, she'd stopped singing. She was eyeing her phone on the windowsill. She checked it. Nothing. But by the evening (by the time she finished singing, finished a few homework assignments—Poesía Moderna, astronomy . . .), she was rewarded with a text from Ian.

Hey, Leda, sry I missed you.

Something lit up inside her even as she wondered, for the first time, how he had gotten her number. Then someone knocked. She spun, threw her phone onto the bed, and opened the door wearing (she could feel it) the stupidest grin.

In the doorway, Mary flinched. "You look sick."

"Who let you in?"

"Carly. Believe me, she resisted." Mary came in, the fake blood smudgy around her lips. She said, gravely, "I've decided to come to your party."

"Gee." Leda shut the door. "Don't sound so excited."

"Just being back on Psi Delta territory gives me the heebie-jeebies." Mary wrenched off her shoes and flopped onto Leda's bed, toeing a nest of discarded sports bras and leggings. "I don't know how you do it, Lee—all this spandex. All this posturing."

"Spandex is comfier than jeans," Leda countered.

"Be honest. Do you own pearls now, Lee?"

"They're fake." *But pretty*, Leda didn't say.

"Well, at least you admit it." Mary shifted. From under her butt, she extracted Leda's thrown phone and keyed in the passcode. "You know, the only reason I'm coming to this party is because you asked me. If anyone inquires, tell them I'm a nun. Tell them celibacy is part of the outfit."

"English majors don't have parties?"

"They do. But your meat isn't, like, graded before they let you in."

"You're just worried the fratties won't think you're sexy."

"I'm worried they *will* think I'm sexy. And speaking of sex." Mary held up Leda's vibrating cell. "Ian's calling."

Leda snatched the phone, looked at the screen, and pocketed the thing.

"You're not answering?"

"Are you kidding?" This was Boys 101, completed freshman year by everybody (except Mary, apparently). "It's supply and demand, Mary."

"And you're the commodity?" Mary sat up. "Leda, you are totally baffling."

"Yeah, well, your mouth is smearing."

Mary went to the mirror. Leda thumbed through her closet,

looking for a costume, peeking at the missed call on her phone while Mary wasn't looking. The dragon stared through sundresses at her knees. Downstairs, the kids' music had been replaced by howling synth.

"I'm just going to wear all red." Leda held up a dress. "Then I'll let other people tell me what I am. Are redheads allowed to wear all red?"

Mary fished a tube of red liquid eyeliner from her makeup bag and offered it.

Leda said, "That's hideous." Still, she sat on the bed and let Mary pry open her eye. After the first eye was finished, she asked, "What's Ian?"

"His costume?" Mary bit her lip. "Zeus or something."

Under Mary's fingers, Leda felt her eyeball move. "Carly said he's wearing a toga."

"Well, Zeus wears togas, doesn't he?"

Leda giggled. "It seems stupid to picture gods wearing anything."

Mary stepped back. "Keep your eyes open."

"Maybe I could be a goddess." Leda dabbed at her eyes, blinked. In the mirror, the eyeliner was the color of Twizzlers. "Or I could be a pious mortal in whom Zeus takes a special interest."

"You and a thousand other mortals," said Mary. "Also, I'm not sure how that would translate to a costume."

Leda swung her feet. "Maybe, at the very least, Zeus would come down and bless me."

"Maybe, Lee." Mary paused, lipstick in hand. Their eyes met in the mirror. "Maybe you'll fall in love, on the off chance, and everything will be peachy."

"Um." Leda's heart beat. "Who said anything about love?"

Love wasn't the goal, was it? It seemed too big, too risky.

"Okay, not love, but if you *like* him, I would just say something. Don't you think? You can't just pray that this 'immortal' will keep texting you, unprompted. Zeus requires sacrifices, doesn't he? You've got to kill some sheep."

Leda went to the closet and tugged on her dress. "Sounds a little obvi."

"Then don't." Mary capped her lipstick. "I'm an atheist; it's the same to me."

Mary had always been smart. It didn't irritate Leda the way it had other Delts; she didn't mind being challenged intellectually on any little thing. She was used to it, maybe; Leda and Mary had been assigned the same dorm hall first year, and they had become friends almost instantly. Maybe it was because they shared a sense of humor, or because they were both readers, or because they'd both felt adrift at college and were searching for some kind of anchor. Mary's parents were professors at a West Coast university, and she'd been so homesick that Leda was able to convince her to rush the spring of their freshman year. It would be a home away from home, she'd told Mary.

Now, it was obvious that Mary thought Leda should leave the sorority. That it was beneath her or something. But Leda needed a home. Needed a family. For her, *sister* was not just a word.

Outside, the sun dipped. Orange machinery poised next door like stiff livestock, backlit. Leda and Mary loitered on the porch a moment before leaving. Growing up, Leda and her mom had often sat on their porch and watched the neighbor's cattle like this. It had been comforting, knowing that the animals would always be out there, pushing through darkness. They never seemed to sleep. Sometimes, if she listened carefully, she thought she could hear their stomachs; she thought she could hear the sand and clay compress under their feet.

Now, loud pop music blurred in the distance. The windows of the

Cathouse, just across the street, jerked with bodies. Mary squeezed Leda's hand. They got going. Downstairs in the common room, Glock the sorority cockatoo squawked, "Drunk ass!" when they came in. Some of Leda's sisters hugged her, some sang her name, asking if she was *actually* planning on going to the Cathouse pregame.

"Be careful," one of them said.

"Who *are* they?" another pried. "We don't even know them."

And another: "I heard they do heroin."

Mary lifted her eyebrows, like, *Are they serious?* In the past, she had been vocal about this, their sorority's suspicion of difference. Their mistrust could be triggered by pettiness—a different style, different interest—or by something serious: a different skin color, different gender, different social stratum. Sometimes their fear seemed subconscious—an almost-innocent phobia of newness. But other times, like now, it was explicit. Ridiculous.

Still, Mary was being ignored. Her look went unnoticed.

"It's *Halloween*," Leda said, trying to keep the peace. "It's supposed to be scary. Plus, I don't know Moonie, either, and I'm still going to *his* party."

Mary said, "Yeah, and remind me why we're going again?"

"Alcohol." Leda opened the mostly empty fridge. "True love's first kiss or equivalent."

"Oh, that's right." Mary picked at her phone. "So men can revive our unconscious bodies with kisses."

"Excuse me?" Genie, a nearby Psi Delt, looked horrified.

"Like Sleeping Beauty." Mary qualified. "Or Snow White."

This seemed to satisfy Genie, who was busy tugging a mermaid tail up over her feet. Glock beat his xylophone in the corner and chanted, "Drunk ass," flexing his crest and flapping his wings.

In the fridge, there was milk, block cheese, and a crusting jar of pickled beans. Leda took out the beans and struggled with the lid, facing Carly's *How Am I Feeling?* dry-erase chart—a grid of emotional, yellow smileys that she had bought on a self-help website. Every morning and evening, Carly consulted the chart, circling the smileys that matched her feelings. Today she had circled Blissful, Hungover, and Innocent. Not an unusual reading for Carly.

What would Leda circle? The In Love smiley looked like it had been punched in the face. The Undecided smiley had one eyebrow raised. In her purse, Leda's phone whirred. The jar of beans popped open.

u going to moonie's?

Leda swallowed her butterflies—sick, ecstatic. She typed, maybe, biting a sour bean.

"Mortal or immortal?" asked Mary.

Leda twirled the rest of the bean, taunting.

"Leda, who is it? I heard you do that little gasp."

Leda grinned, shoved her phone down the neck of her dress, and ate the bean. "I don't know about you"—Leda twirled in place, curtsied—"but I'm about ready to get wasted."

It was a little early, but that was what pregames were for. Leda tugged Mary out the front door.

The neighborhood was already swamped with reverb and bass. Headlights flickered between trees and buildings like trick candles—blowing out, sparking, lighting. A dude peed in a hydrangea. Girls in spike heels struggled down level sidewalks. A group of witches stumbled into a blue-lit campus safety monolith, featuring a blue button that said CALL, and a red button that said EMERGENCY. Someone had spilled a bag of candy corn at its base, like an offering. Leda and Mary crunched through as the witches held one another, fighting to remain upright. Mary and Leda shared a look, doing their best not to laugh.

For Leda, the pursuit of alcohol was basically an extracurricular activity. Because alcohol was forbidden in sororities, you had to be resourceful and diligent. Sometimes there were only so many parties happening, and you couldn't afford to be picky. That was how Leda occasionally found herself drunk in unsavory locations—in unknown neighborhoods, in alleys, in fraternities where she didn't know anybody. Bars were too expensive, and often the scenes there were just as shady. So, the Cathouse, in Leda's eyes, was not the worst place to get tipsy. Plus, the buddy system was in place. Leda and Mary would look out for each other, barring unforeseen circumstances, i.e., Ian. (Surely, Mary understood this.)

Not to mention that the Cathouse was in theme with Halloween. The house was dark and low-ceilinged. There was dyed hair. There was sinister, undanceable music. There were costumes that were not in any way pretty, and some that concealed the wearer entirely. It was a little disconcerting not being able to see the person inside the suit. It made Leda remember that some of her least pleasant encounters, sex-wise, had been with people whose faces she hadn't taken the time to internalize.

But college was not a convent. It was not a time to stay shut up in one's room. And for Leda, alone time was actually the scarier option of the two. When you were alone, the drag of time caught up with you.

Mary elbowed Leda, shouted something, and then sucked into the party, as if caught in a riptide. The crowd swept Mary past an old box TV, which was tuned to *The Nightmare Before Christmas*, that old Tim Burton movie. In front of the TV, people seemed to be drinking on the words *pumpkin* and *Halloween*. At this point in the film, corpses and vampires were singing: "*This is Halloween; this is Halloween. Halloween! Halloween! Halloween! Halloween!*"

Someone shouted, "Waterfall!" which meant "drink until further notice."

This wasn't so different from a frat party.

Leda pushed into the room. A girl with waist-length hair demonstrated some kind of tai chi move, pulling an invisible orb toward her belly. A goat demon ate grapes. People played Jenga on a coffee table. The tower wiggled as a girl in a Viking helmet extracted a block. At the end of the sectional couch where the Jenga players were sitting, a winged Nike (wearing all Nike swooshes) dipped her hand into a condom basket. A handwritten sign read *Be safe. STDs are SCARY.* Leda was not on birth control; she had tried it, and it had made her at best emotional, at worst deranged. She picked a condom as a drink appeared in front of her. She took the cup with the hand holding the square gold wrapper, turning, ready to make a joke about it, but it was not Mary beside her.

Ian said, "I know you."

Leda pretended to laugh, holding the drink and the condom between them. *What are* you *doing here?* she wanted to know. Instead, she said coolly, "I know you, too." She tried to put the condom back, but she fumbled and missed the basket.

Ian had this little half smile. They both looked at the fallen contraception. He picked it up and gave it back with a gallant flourish. Leda returned it to the basket. Ian put his hands in his pockets, cheeks flushed. Somehow the blush, on him, looked more like confidence than embarrassment.

Not far off, the Jenga blocks crashed. The players howled. A girl wearing a white dress and white boa had collapsed the tower.

One of the players shouted, "Everybody wins but you!"

The girl put her hands up in defeat. "I lose."

Ian was watching the girl, too, so Leda smiled the way that she and her sisters sometimes practiced in mirrors. Ian looked at her now. Leda sipped the drink he had brought her. Too sweet. She thought about saying, *Do you know someone here?* or *Sorry I threw a condom at you.* Ian drank, too. He looked good in a toga. She thought about saying this, too. It was strange, not knowing what to say. It was strange, feeling your heart reach out of your own chest—so vulnerable suddenly, so out in the open.

Still, neither one of them had spoken. They looked at each other. Someone turned on synth pop music. Sometimes music was helpful like this; it was too loud to say all the boring things like, *How's the semester going?* or *What classes are you taking?*

Instead, Leda shouted, "I have a question."

"What?" Ian leaned in, not hearing.

She said it louder. "I have a question." She sounded calm, she hoped, even though she was shouting. His ear was an inch from her mouth. "How did you get my number?"

"Ah." Ian tousled his hair, which looked damp. His biceps flexed. "Was that creepy?"

Leda shrugged. She touched her own hair, which was staticky. "Could be."

An enormous figure moved between them, wearing what appeared to be a gorilla suit. It took a moment for it to get through. Jenga players restacked blocks across the room. The girl who had collapsed the tower watched it rebuilt. Her black hair stood out against her white costume. She was Chinese, Leda thought. Not far off, Leda spotted Carly in her witch costume, buttressed by a squad of Psi Delts doing their best not to look unnerved.

The gorilla passed, and Ian shouted, "I wasn't supposed to tell you."

Leda lifted an eyebrow.

Ian hesitated, then cupped his hands on her ear. "Carly."

Leda looked back at Carly, who was now watching her, too. Carly and the Psi Delts sent a silent cheer across the room. This hadn't happened since high school—back when everyone seemed to understand your romance more than you. Leda blushed. Even at this weird party, she felt safe, loved. It was a little scary, actually, like those trust falls during rush. You stood up on a table with your back turned to your sisters, your heels at the edge. And you were supposed to cross your arms and fall like a dummy, trusting that your sisters would prevent you from cracking open your head. And they had, with their great cradle of arms, and Leda had stood up again. Since then, Leda believed that whenever she fell, she would be caught by some net, even in her mother's absence.

"So . . . why would you want my number?" Leda asked Ian.

"That's easy." Ian smiled. "I like you."

When Ian glanced away, Leda mouthed to Carly, *You're dead.* Carly made a face remarkably similar to her emotion chart's Innocent smiley, the mouth a pious line, the round eyes looking up and away from life.

Then Carly's face was replaced by Ian, suddenly close. He smelled like chlorine.

"Then you're not a stalker," Leda said to him.

Ian smiled. "Not yet." His hand touched her wrist, and Leda felt her pulse lunge up at him. They stayed like this—inches apart—for several moments until the Jenga tower crashed again. The players dispersed, filtering out into the rest of the room, parting Leda and Ian. They left the blocks where they'd fallen.

Mary appeared with two drinks and gestured at the cup in Leda's hand. "What's that?"

Leda pointed, but the crowd had swept Ian back. In his place, a girl in a grim reaper's hood stood before her. "Are you the devil?" the girl asked.

Leda pretended that the girl wasn't talking to her, but the reaper was waiting for an answer.

"You're wearing all red."

"No." Leda's eyes focused (the reaper's blond hair trailing out of the hood) and then unfocused again. "Sorry."

"Fire, then," the reaper guessed.

Leda took a step back. "Nope."

"Fire *engine*. Fire alarm. Alert. Emergency!"

Still moving backward, Leda bumped Nefertiti and Superman taking a selfie. Superman's phone flashed, and Leda blinked. Was this a haunted house or something? She felt the wall behind her. She felt somebody's arm. Mary's face came back into focus, and Leda clung to her. Somewhere, someone scream-laughed.

In Mary's ear, Leda shouted, "Bathroom."

But the reaper was there again, pointing her scythe up the stairs. "I'll show you."

Reluctantly, Leda followed. Upstairs, the girl stopped in front of an open door. There were people in the bathroom. A boy huddled on the closed lid of the toilet. Beside him, a chubby girl in a slutty nurse costume was on the phone.

The reaper asked, "Is he still tripping?"

The nurse shrugged, barely looking up. "Sorry, Mom. I can't hear you. The library is super busy."

Leda asked the grim reaper, "Was that him, screaming?"

The reaper shrugged. "Probably." In the light, Leda could see that half of her blond head was shaved. "We've asked around. Nobody knows him."

"No, Mom." The nurse held her phone like a walkie-talkie. "I'm *studying*."

The boy, unprovoked, tumbled off the toilet and grabbed the grimy bath mat. He moaned, long and low.

The nurse checked her teeth in the mirror. "How's Daddy?"

"Never mind." Leda turned to leave, when the boy met her eyes. He had beautiful gray eyes—swirled like the Milky Way and bright with reflected overhead light. He held her gaze. Leda took a step back.

The nurse said, "But *nobody* has gout, Mommy."

"Hey, by the way," the reaper called after Leda. "Are you the girl with Ian?"

Leda paused. She didn't know what to say. *No* was the answer, obviously, but her lips couldn't form the shape. The boy's gray eyes clung to her. What was he seeing? Tears began to leak down his face. Then he opened his mouth and, like a child, shrieked.

Leda fled for the stairwell, the grim reaper literally cackling behind her. How did that girl even know Ian? And what had that boy seen in Leda that had made him scream?

Whatever. Halloween was supposed to be spooky. At the base of the stairs, Leda stepped out and forgot about it. Something about walking down steps into a crowded room felt like a reset. She could imagine, say, "Dancing Queen" coming on the stereo. She could picture Ian taking her hand, spinning her into some choreographed dance. *Was* she the girl with Ian? She stepped into the room, believing it for a moment, feeling a Disney Princess spotlight trail out behind her like a bell-shaped dress as she spotted Ian near the front door, talking to the girl who had collapsed the Jenga tower.

Then Mary was there, her fake blood smeared.

"Moonie's?" Leda proposed, thinking of supply and demand, thinking that she'd do well to make herself scarce at this party.

They pushed through the crowded room. "Dancing Queen" played in Leda's head, the verses truncated, the chorus looped. She pushed people aside to get through, feeling her pulse thrusting up where, moments earlier, Ian's fingers had been.

The few Psi Delts in attendance seemed to take the hint, ready for any excuse to jump ship. Genie hobbled up, looking impressively natural wearing shells over her boobs (though her mermaid tail seemed to inhibit most waist-down movement). Still, Genie lifted her arms in the threshold as if she might dive. Leda had that feeling, too—that she was about to jump from a rock into a river without first testing the temperature of the water. Her feet tingled, urging her. But before she reached the door, an object landed in her palm, bringing her out of it. The gorilla was passing out condoms and had pushed one through Leda's fingers. She almost laughed, seeing the same gold wrapper. In that instant, something clicked. Leda looked up. Someone beside the door had a camera lifted. Leda frowned into the black lens. The camera lowered. It was the Jenga girl. White dress, white boa. The girl who, just a moment ago, had been chatting with Ian.

The girl said, "Do you want me to delete it?"

Leda shrugged. "Whatever."

"It's for a class," she said. "It might not come out."

Leda slipped the square of foil into her boot, half listening. "Cool." She felt the package sink. Then Leda and the few Delts who had braved the Cathouse fled the premises.

It felt good in the air. The world swam pleasantly now, as if Leda were in the river, letting the current take her. Mary caught up, and Leda said to her, "Now, the real party."

Genie twirled in the street between the Cathouse and Leda's sorority, her mermaid tail just allowing her to shuffle her feet. As she twirled, more of Leda's sisters dispatched from the sorority, wearing slightly different iterations of the same costumes—cats, policewomen, bunnies.

"How was it?" they asked, and, "Is everybody okay?" as if eager to hear that the opposite might be the case.

Carly made sure they hadn't left any women behind at the Cathouse party, shouting, "Buddy check, everybody!"

Fraternity Row was like the Sahara, like any wild place, and the buddy system was supposed to be how you stayed safe. Of course, the system became less effective as both buddies became increasingly intoxicated. But, for now, Leda slipped her arm in Mary's, and they massed toward the bubble party.

Mary said, "I feel like a lemming."

Leda ruffled Mary's hair and kissed her cheek. She glimpsed Ian, a little ways behind the group. He must have followed her from the Cathouse, as she'd hoped he would.

In front, Carly chanted Eminem lyrics, something she only did when she surpassed a certain level of drunkenness. "Sit your drunk ass—" Off beat, Carly shook her ass. Somewhere in the course of the day, she had lost her witch hat.

Leda's crowd turned onto Memorial, which was already a thoroughfare of intoxicated students. A guy jogged down the center yellow lines, covered in what appeared to be fresh, purple paint. A new Psi Delt (Mallory or Mel or Melanie . . .) crutched by in a shiny policewoman getup. She wore a giant cast on her leg. In passing, she called Leda a slut.

Leda said, "Excuse me. What?"

But the girl kept going, joining the Psi Delts in front. Leda thought about calling after her, but the girl hadn't even looked back. Was it possible that Leda had just imagined it? Anyway, the moment passed. Ian's arm brushed hers. He'd caught up to her. Leda stepped over a spilled pillowcase of candy—a casualty from that afternoon's trick-or-treating. She grabbed a pink Starburst from the carnage and popped it.

The purple guy had left purple footprints, and Leda's group, bulging into the street, followed them. A Honda revved around them, blew a stop sign, and shattered a pocket of short-skirted girls in the crosswalk, wearing some of the very same outfits as Leda's friends. Watching them, Leda almost walked into a little memorial—a platter of wilted flowers, a name on a cross that Leda didn't read and had never read despite the hundreds of times she had passed it. As she stepped around it, something black flew over her head. Her mother would have pointed—*Look!*—as if a piece of the world's meaning might be sewn into that night bird's wings; into the scent of beer and urine emanating from the fraternities; or the veins of leaves cracking at Leda's feet.

Leda did not look. They were approaching G Kap, its yard circled in grand boxwoods and orange construction fencing. The tall windows writhed, the gutted house (fraternities always felt gutted inside) risen-up, zombie-like: alive. Bodies spilled from the front porch and onto the lawn: chick firefighters; three girls dressed as salt, tequila, and lime; a gumball machine with a crotch-level twenty-five-cent coin slot. Two dudes wearing sheep horns grappled in the grass. A priest threw books into the yard.

No one was controlling entry, so Leda's group siphoned through a section of trampled fencing. Carly rushed ahead, flickering blue in a campus safety bulb for an instant before disappearing inside. Leda paused, watching Eve hold on to a tree swing, retching. Leda had been there, sure. But that didn't make it any more likely that Leda would go and comfort her. The vomit was just part of the experience, wasn't it? The vomit just as much as the laughter.

Psi Delts streamed past Leda toward the party, sprinkling her with *love you*s and kissing her cheeks. It was nice, wasn't it? She was lucky.

"Lee?" Mary touched Leda's shoulder.

"You go ahead," Leda said. "I'm coming."

Mary went, shivering. The cold didn't bother Leda; her legs and arms had numbed already. Eve gagged, dangling from the swing. Leda bit her lip, watching. *Why am I here?* she wondered briefly.

Then, as if in answer, Ian came to stand next to her. He looked her up and down. He guessed at her costume. "Cupid."

Leda shook her head, smiling a little.

"A lollipop." His shoulder bumped hers, jostling her. "Cough syrup."

This was why she was here, wasn't it? This boy—this Ian. She wondered if she would soon be obsessed. It had happened first year, too. She had *wanted* so badly, as if a boy were a toy or a piece of candy. The problem was that she had wanted without really understanding the object, without understanding what *wanting* meant. At that point—the beginning of her first semester at college—she had never had sex. Now, three years later (and, yes, having lost her virginity), she still wasn't sure what *wanting* meant. Still, something with Ian felt different. Perhaps this not knowing was the thrill of it: the mystery, the risk.

Leda followed Ian in, moving between two shirtless guys harassing a line of tiki torches. One said, "None of them will freaking light."

The other, chubbier boy wore a tiger suit peeled to the waist. He had his phone out, reading aloud from something. "'The wick you are lighting has to be soaked in the oil, or it will just light and burn out.'"

Ian gave her a look. *Pretty please*, she thought, jumping and begging that night bird or her mom or whoever it was that could hear her. *Pretty please with sugar on top.* Though she wasn't sure what she was asking for.

"You wanna feel this thing?" The first guy flicked the lighter. "It's soaked, man."

"That's what she said," the tiger, inevitably, responded.

On the porch, Ian placed his hand on Leda's elbow and navigated her through a group of shirtless men with hand marks on their chests, puffing cigars. Leda held her breath.

The frat smelled like a fog machine. White spiderweb decked the front hall, stretching in cotton nets over their heads. Fake spiders littered the floor or clung to the web. Through the web, Leda could see a hangman dangling from a high rope where a chandelier might have been. A grand, L-shaped staircase led up to bedrooms. (Once or twice, Leda had been up there.) Along the big stairs, someone had taped printed-out portraits of dead men and women—eyes rolled back, jaws slack. Halfway up, a few girls took a picture with the hangman behind them, sticking their tongues between peace fingers, eyes fluttered not unlike the dead portraits across from them.

Ian bro-hugged a dude in devil horns wearing a very nice suit. Behind him, people took off their clothes and tossed them into a pile before stepping through a narrow door marked BUBBLES. Just before the door shut, she glimpsed a set of basement steps, leading into yellow light.

Ian shouted, "Drink?"

"Please!" Leda's voice sounded strange to her, like somebody else's.

A strobe light went off in the crowded living room, and the bodies sucked Leda in. Where had her sisters gone? she wondered briefly before dissolving into the dancing. Before her, two girls sandwiched one guy. One danced low—dick height. He held her head. Her breasts were nearly exposed. Even so, this was nothing out of the ordinary. This was the beauty of college, of frat parties. This was a safe environment in which you could be anyone, try anything.

And anyway, Leda's dress was revealing, too. She didn't deny it. It wasn't like she was going to be Mother Teresa for Halloween. Though once, in elementary school, Leda had dressed up as an archaeologist. She and her mom had decorated a safari hat with fossils and tools, which she had worn with a vest, khaki shorts, and explorer boots.

The year before that, she had been a timber wolf, because that had been her fantasy. That was what she had wanted to be.

Now, she was waiting for someone else to tell her what her costume might be. Now, she was busy dancing. The floorboards bucked. The strobe halted over twisting bodies. She wasn't even drunk. She looked behind her for Ian, but he still hadn't appeared with her drink. The music veered, and everyone jumped. In a room full of jumping people, it took more effort *not* to jump. So she jumped—buoyant, like a baby bounced on a knee. In front of her, a girl's brown hair floated as she jumped and screamed soundlessly under the bass, heavy as an embrace.

With every jump up, Leda could see an illuminated kitchen. She swam for it now, hardly moving until the strobe light flicked off and the crowd spat her before a keg and punch bowl. A shirtless guy with a blue circle painted on his chest held a ladle. He served Leda a Solo cup of what tasted like juice. Leda drank, thirsty. Then the dude took out three purple balls and literally juggled.

Leda said, "Are you, like, Cerberus or something?" Though that wasn't right, was it?

The boy smiled, not hearing. "How's it going?" He put the balls down and poured Leda a shot to go with her drink. "Are you having a good time?"

Frat boys always said something like this. No matter how hard they had spiked the punch, they always started with something polite. Leda took the shot. "You're good at juggling."

"It's just a hobby." He poured another shot. "What year are you?"

"Third." She took that shot, too.

"Cool," he said. "Me, too."

He would have said, *Me, too*, to anything, she knew. She thought about what she might get him to agree to until Mary came out of the kitchen, saw her, and towed her away.

Leda raised her glass—"To the underworld!"—and drank.

Mary tugged Leda's elbow earthward, examining her drink as if she'd be able to see the roofies. "Do you know him, Lee?"

"He's just Hades's guard dog." Leda waved her free hand dismissively. "Either that or a jester. What have you been up to?"

"Oh, someone just asked me to take a picture of her nipples. You know, the usual."

"Did you do it?"

"Lee, of course I didn't."

A new song came on, and Leda couldn't help but slip out of Mary's grip. Orange and black swirls projected onto the wall. The spirals turned into rainbow fractals. Behind her, Mary shouted into her ear. Mary disappeared. Leda danced. Soon, she felt hands on her hips. A body behind her. It felt good to be touched. She danced with whoever it was. He ran his hands up her body. She could feel him through his pants. She imagined it was Ian. But, when she turned around to face him, he was tall with dark hair. South American? Italian? It didn't matter. She put her arms around his neck and moved into him. The boy said something very close to her ear, but his voice didn't break the surface of the music. It was Girl Talk, and somewhere Carly called out the artists as they cycled through.

"Elton John," Carly cried. "Biggie! Ying Yang!"

Somehow, Leda's lips were now close to his lips. She knew that, in a song or two, they would kiss. It wasn't because they liked each other; it was just that the world had hurled them together. It was liberating, really, giving in to it. Then, abruptly, the music ended. They bumped each other, like strangers. On the wall, a picture of a cat overlaid the rainbow fractals. Leda wondered if she should say something. Like, *Hello.* Like, *My name is . . .*

But he didn't say anything, so she didn't. His dark hair was lit with rainbows. Then someone hugged him from behind, and he turned around, surprised. He and a girl started talking. They appeared to be friends. Leda drifted away, her body cold, her cup empty.

Don't you feel alone? she could hear Mary saying. *Isn't it lonely dancing with people you don't even know?* Or maybe that was Leda's voice. Anyway, before the thought could grow, the music restarted, and she felt herself press against another warm body. Not alone, suddenly. Not alone.

After a few songs, Leda tried to escape. She spotted a boy carrying Genie through the crowd, her neck hung with what looked like pounds of party beads. It seemed Genie, in her mermaid tail, was tired of walking. She saw the girl with the camera again, wading through the masses, her white boa trailing. The girl came close. Their bodies probably touched for a moment. Then she lifted her bulky camera over the dancing, and nobody noticed the flash that, for a split second, exposed them. Leda was just over the girl's shoulder, and she saw the tiny image appear on the screen: Carly grinding with a skeleton. Leda pushed through the crowd and grabbed her friend, but Carly only draped her arms over Leda's shoulders and grinned.

"Lee-Loo, Ian was looking for you."

The skeleton drifted away, pumping his arms. He wore glow sticks on his wrists.

"Carly, are you safe?" Leda spoke with a tone of authority that really just betrayed how drunk she'd become. Carly didn't hear her, and Leda repeated the question. It was ridiculous. If Carly were to say no, what could Leda do? She could barely find her own way out of the living room.

Carly took Leda by the hand and towed her into the hallway. Walking was more difficult than Leda thought it should be. She stumbled against a rise in the floor, and her body tipped like those falling blocks until she hit something solid: Ian. He held two red cups. Leda apologized, standing herself up. Ian gave her a drink. So forgiving.

Down the hall, Carly stripped to her underwear, threw her witch dress into a pile of clothes, and opened the basement door. She descended the soggy carpet and disappeared into something bright and filmy. Leda followed her sister through the threshold, but stopped when she got to the bubbles. They reached halfway up the basement steps in lemony crests. Leda stared down into them like a child, her mind wiped, until Ian closed the door behind them. She looked up at him. Warm air gusted up from the basement. He came down the steps, stopping when her head was level with his chest. His hand found her wrist, but Leda lost her balance. She felt for the handrail, pulling free from his grip.

Downstairs, buff frat boys were assembled in a kind of greeting committee. They were shirtless, wearing only boxers, bow ties, and sunglasses. Their fixed smiles were surprisingly convincing. Leda felt good being smiled at in this way as she waded in. They slapped Ian's back and squeezed Leda's hand so politely it was almost menacing.

"Hey!" they said. "Hey!" As if they were all friends already.

They gave Leda an open can of beer with an umbrella stuck in, even though she already had a drink. A human skull on a table wore sunglasses. Fake eyeballs floated in a punch bowl. She glanced around for the skeleton, but didn't see him. She felt safe down here with Ian in this faux heaven. There were white clouds of soap foam. There was yellow-gold light. There was mercurial glinting, like stars, from shiny cans of Natty Light.

Happy hip-hop played, and the frat boys sang to it, like cherubim. One cherub bent his legs and made a choo-choo motion with his fist. He wore a curly-straw beer hat. Bubbles clung to the hair on his chest and belly. Beside him, Cerberus pumped a giant foam hand. The blue circle had smeared on his chest. They sang. The song was about a hungover guy riding his bike. Some of the boys pretended to be on bikes, hands on handlebars, coasting. Some of the boys manned the indoor Slip 'N Slide, spraying almost-naked girls with Dawn soap and a nozzled hose.

The room was too sticky for Leda to be wearing a dress, but she didn't remove it. She plucked the umbrella out of her beer can with her teeth, spit it out, and took a drink. Heat pumped in from somewhere. Under the smell of lemon soap was sweat and BO. She couldn't tell how many people were down there; the bubbles (which ranged from about three to five feet deep) made it unclear where the basement began or ended.

Ian beat the backs of other shirtless men. A tarp dripped on Leda's head. A corner had unpeeled from the ceiling, revealing old ductwork and pink insulation covered in moisture beads. *Isn't it lonely?* Mary hadn't said; Leda herself had posed that question. Still, she pushed it from her mind, moving toward the Slip 'N Slide. Carly skidded by in her underwear. She was the perfect angel—chubby and well proportioned. She careened off the end of the runway and upended, laughing. There, a girl cracked a beer—"Cheers!"—and shook it out on Carly, who tipped her face up into the amber stream.

Would Mary be horrified? Probably. Even Leda was beginning to have a soft-drink feeling in her throat, as if she might sneeze or vomit. Maybe it was just the lemon soap. Somehow it had gotten in her mouth. The boom box said, *Sum-sum-summertime* and *lovey-lovin'* and then started this happy, high-pitched whistling. Girls poured beer into each other's mouths. It made Leda thirsty. She pinched the tab on the already open Natty Light and drank, but it tasted like a punch in the mouth: bloody. She blinked. The light was too bright down here, plus she probably had soap in her eye. She took another drink. Oddly, there was something satisfying in the blood taste, like how whenever she bit her lip, she couldn't stop tonguing it.

Ian took up the Slip 'N Slide hose and a bottle of soap, preparing the runway for the next slide. Leda rubbed her eyes. A stage light hung a few feet from her face, its yellow filter slipping. The volume rose. She turned and bumped into somebody. It was Cerberus. He had the *#1* foam hand on his head like a rooster comb. He danced into her, slower than the bounce of the song, and she danced with him. She almost wanted Ian to see them. She let him dance against her ass as she watched another couple across from them grind beside some exercise equipment. The girl's short red dress rode up too high on her hips, her underwear showing in glimpses. Leda pushed her hair out of her face—it had gotten sticky—and the girl mimicked the motion. She was dully surprised. She turned away from the mirror and faced the boy, her pelvis drawing into his.

He said, "What's your name?"

But Leda was taken aback by this. She didn't want him to know her, and she didn't want to know him. She just wanted to dance, anonymous. Plus, she didn't mind the idea of piquing Ian's jealousy.

Thankfully, it seemed that the boy did not require an answer. "I'm Moonie." He touched the blue circle on his chest, and it smeared under his finger. "See?"

"Moonie?" She wanted to start laughing, but she felt too sick, not to mention that he was very close to her suddenly, removing his sunglasses. His eyes looked like cotton balls. The *#1* foam hand loomed overhead as his mouth found hers. He tasted like Winterfresh gum and corn chips.

Is it lonely? went Leda's voice in her head. She pushed Moonie off and left.

Her escape, however, was not smooth. She stumbled where old bubbles had flattened into whitish goo. The basement steps were soaked. Had Ian seen her? She didn't know. She climbed the steps, using the handrail like a rope. Moonie, thankfully, didn't follow. At the top, her soapy hand slipped on the doorknob. She used her dress to get it open.

The house was cold. The front door was wide open. Lumps of something tan and pulpy trailed down the hall. She stepped over a glob of it, trying not to look; she didn't want to know.

She found a bathroom, crouched over the toilet, and peed. There was no TP. The floor was tacky. In the mirror, she saw she had smears of Moonie's blue moon on her dress. At the sink, she scrubbed the dress and rinsed the dried soap off her face and neck. Some of the untouchable, cloudlike feeling peeled away with it. She rubbed at her red eyeliner with a damp finger. She looked deranged and sleepless. She thought of her childhood costumes, wondering if this was today's timber wolf, wondering if her costume revealed some sort of hidden fantasy. Or perhaps this was no fantasy; perhaps she *was* the blood-shot girl in the red dress, wanting a stranger to kiss her out of fear of both love and loneliness.

Mary was waiting for the bathroom when Leda came out. Leda collapsed into her, blinking.

Mary cursed, held her. "Leda, you are really disgusting."

Leda nodded. "I met Moonie."

Mary pulled back, fake excited.

Leda shook her head. "He kissed me."

"Ugh—" Mary cooed and hugged her again.

"It was gross. He had a circle on his chest and a big orange thing on his head."

"I know . . ." Mary rubbed her back, soothing. "But you really do look terrible. You should take it as a compliment."

"It must have been my personality," Leda said into Mary's neck.

"Sense of humor," Mary added.

"Yeah. That must have been it."

The music in the other room cut out for a moment, leaving a blab of voices. Even as Mary squeezed, the night slackened. Leda felt lost suddenly—bereft.

"Leda." Mary spoke quietly. "Why do you do this?"

Leda peeled back, looked at her friend. Of course she couldn't answer this. Wouldn't.

Mary didn't make her answer. Instead, she pulled her down coat out of the clothes pile and gave it to her. It felt like a blanket. Leda wanted to go to sleep in it. She wandered outside in the coat while Mary got back in line for the bathroom. The air felt good. On the porch, two black guys in thick-framed glasses compared iPhones. An enormous white dude cradled a twiggy girl, who looked frigid in the blue campus safety glow. Everyone else was backlit by the porch's one, moth-swamped bulb. Leda batted a moth out of her face, and it hit the black leaves of a holly. Winter, she hoped, would kill the bugs soon. Thinking this, though, made her chest go hollow.

Existential puke, she'd heard someone call it. All at once, with no warning, your sadness and dread bubbles up. She took a few steps. Breathed. Tried to ward it off.

The yard was damp. Leda could feel its cold through her boots. Above, she could find no moon. The sky was dark except for a low shelf of unnatural lavender. Leda looked back at the house and listened for something. A bird, maybe. Maybe those mourning doves she had heard weeping. Instead, someone hurled a disco ball from a window. It happened too quickly for Leda to duck or wince or otherwise react reasonably. It sailed past her, glittering, and everyone howled when it shattered in the yard a dozen feet from where she was standing. She looked at it, went down the walk, and stopped on the other side of the boxwoods on the sidewalk.

Mary, she knew, would want to leave. A part of Leda did, too, but the other part of her didn't want to return to an empty room. It was more pleasant here, outside. Overhead, the clouds glowed. Leda had learned the word for this in astronomy—*nocti-something*.

Down the sidewalk, another girl stood squinting at the sky—the girl who had lost the Jenga game. The girl in white. She balanced on the edge of the curb, camera dangling. Then she noticed Leda, lost her balance, and stepped into the street.

"Hey, I just saw you," the girl called. "You're the apple."

"What?" Leda went closer. The girl had white glitter in her black hair.

"The red apple. Like in Snow White."

"An apple." Leda considered this. "Maybe you're right."

"Maybe?"

"I don't know what I am, honestly."

The girl kicked leaves. "Halloween is such bullshit."

"What are you?"

"A swan. Well, sort of."

Leda saw it now. The white boa was like a swan neck, with something like a head, a beak at one end. This meant that the girl wasn't a swan, exactly, but a girl wrapped in one.

"That's funny," Leda said. " 'Cause I'm Leda."

"You're joking." The girl laughed thinly, the sound swallowed by wind. "Leda and the Swan. We could have made a great costume together."

Leda was surprised the girl knew anything about the Greek myth, the poem. Leda herself had only read the Yeats poem once, just a few minutes before a quiz in Intro to English Lit. She said, "You must study English."

"Shit," the girl said. "Is it that obvious?"

Leda hugged Mary's coat. "I don't know what my mom was thinking when she named me that."

"Yeah: raped by God. You should ask her about that."

The girl touched Leda's shoulder. It was so fast that Leda missed the actual moment. The girl had breached the distance and then, just as quickly, receded. Leda paused. She didn't know what to say about God—Greek or otherwise. She didn't know what to say about the poem. Her mom. She did know that in the small span of this conversation, her mother's death had become a secret. Something she didn't acknowledge. What good did it do, mentioning it? But, at the same time, it was weird lying about it, weird letting this girl believe (letting *herself* believe, if only for an instant) that she, Leda, had a mother that could be asked anything. A mother that could be called, spoken to, seen.

Leda found herself saying, "She died, actually."

The sentence was sharper than she thought it would be. It had been three years, but in those three years she hadn't talked about it, really. She hadn't even gone back to the cemetery. It was pointless, she thought, to visit a stone, a patch of grass, a name on a plaque. Going there would be pathetic. Sad. And now, just thinking about it, Leda was pissed with this girl for bringing it up, for making her face it. This girl didn't understand, Leda thought. She didn't understand . . . what? Life? Death? Four point five billion years flecked with their little lives: flaring and burning like meteor dust. As if Leda understood any of it.

The girl, Leda realized, had said, "I'm sorry."

"It's okay." Leda's voice was strange.

A block away, headlights turned the corner. Even after the floodlights had dimmed, Leda's eyes were still hot. The car pulled up, a gray Honda. The driver leaned, opened the passenger door, and the interior light struck him: the skeleton, his mask peeled to reveal a normal-looking boy.

The girl went to the passenger side and looked at Leda over the roof, her face dimmer now. Different. She said, "You know, you look familiar."

Leda shrugged. "You took my picture earlier."

"No. From further back." She looked at Leda harder. "Do I look familiar?"

"Not really." Leda realized she was still drunk. She was trying, and failing, to think. "Another life," she tried.

"Another life." The girl nodded, though she looked disappointed.

The girl got in, and the interior light blackened. Leda felt the condom drop farther down her boot. The car idled. Leda glanced back at the party. A circle of fairies had linked arms around a keg in the yard. Behind them, the windows stirred, as if the house were full of moths. The music moaned. When Leda turned back, the Honda had already driven halfway down the road. The engine noise combined with the low bass of the party—quieter, quieter, quiet.

Ian was inside, wanting her, she realized. Leda decided that she wanted him, too. She walked back between lit tikis, shedding Mary's jacket. She was alive, she figured. This is what the living do.

Behind her, the clouds crumbled, showing a bright, blind moon. Behind her, the street was empty. It was like magic: the girl had been there one moment, and then she wasn't. Back inside the fraternity, Leda almost collided with, again, a skeleton. There was more than one. Of course there was. Behind the skeleton, she found Ian, standing under the tent of fake spiderweb. His body looked oiled. The hem of his toga was stained punch red. He smiled at her, and the universe expanded. He was peeling the black wax paper off one of those shapeless, nameless candies that Leda, as a child, had never been allowed to eat.

2

The Monday after Saturday's Halloween parties, the trash truck woke Leda up early. She buried her head, trying to smother the splintering of unrecycled glass. All around the block, she heard the clunk of trash cans and the squish of garbage. Her neighborhood was arranged in a loop, so the truck seemed to orbit Leda under her comforter. At the moment that the truck reached its quietest, it was already getting louder.

Could a hangover last for twenty-four hours? It didn't seem possible, but Leda's head still hurt. Her eyes watered as she sat up, squinting against a direct blast of sun. She blinked, seeing only red pulses. Beneath the trash truck, she heard police sirens. She pushed her head down under her pillow again, waiting for them to pass. They didn't.

Sunday, she had done little more than sleep, rising only to the smell of afternoon brownies in the kitchen, of which she had eaten three. Then she had worked to change her ringtone to "Dancing Queen" before going back to sleep.

Now, Leda's fracket (that is, *frat jacket*) stank beside her in bed.

She sniffed it. It smelled a bit like beer. A bit like smoke and semen. That was it. It hadn't taken any serious hits. It used to be that if something really bad happened to a fracket, you could take it to the dry cleaner's and act like it never happened. But these days the cleaners had gotten strict about what they would wash and what they wouldn't. The rule was that if a garment came to them in a bag, they would ask you to open it. If you wouldn't open it, they wouldn't wash it.

This was just beer-semen; it was no biggie. So why did she feel so shitty?

She checked the time on her phone, opened her email. It had become rote—this mechanical clicking and scrolling before she had even fully woken. In her inbox, the most recent message had been sent only minutes ago: *Security Alert from the University Police.*

Her thumb hovered, about to scroll away. But she stopped herself. She opened the message. Her headache nearly dissolved as she read the brief email.

> The University Police Department is seeking information that
> would help locate a missing person. Charlotte Mask, a 22-year-
> old student in the College of Arts and Sciences, was last seen
> two days ago on October 31st at the Gamma Kappa Omega
> fraternity . . .

Leda looked up, squinting against the sun. The world, again, blotched red. The trash truck squealed. She tried to think. Gamma Kap. The fake cobwebs, the bubbles in the basement, Ian. Did she know anyone named Charlotte?

> Mask was seen wearing a white dress and white knee-high
> boots. She has black hair and brown eyes. She is 5 feet

8 inches tall and weighs approximately 130 lbs. To view a
photograph of Charlotte Mask, click on this email's attachment.

But Leda didn't click on the thumbnail—a tiny image of this missing girl. She didn't want to look. At least she didn't know any Charlottes, she reminded herself. She stood up without reading the end of the email.

Out the window, it appeared to be a normal day. The smell of her sister Naadia's jasmine vape wafted from their shared porch. The birds chanted. The trash truck had gone, finally. But, oddly, the sirens had landed like buzzards. Minutes passed, and still they remained.

And then there was Naadia's voice on the phone, saying, "No, I wasn't there, Amma. And it was just the one girl, okay? There was no mass anything."

It was only 8:00 a.m. Did everybody know something Leda didn't? She went back to her phone, glimpsing the last lines of the email (If you have seen Charlotte Mask or have knowledge of her whereabouts . . .) before clicking the photo.

Alone in her room, Leda covered her mouth. She shut her eyes before facing, again, the girl who had collapsed the Jenga tower, the girl who had taken Leda's picture, the girl in white. It was the girl who had spoken to Leda outside the bubble party before the rest of the night had warped and blurred. Not a swan, she remembered, but a girl wrapped in one.

The room seemed to flex around her. She took a step and her feet got tangled in something—her red dress from Halloween. *Cupid*, Ian had guessed. *A lollipop.* Leda sat on the floor in the middle of the room. Up close, the dress looked sweat stained. Her knee-high boots were down there, too. She reached a hand in, remembering the gold condom, but the boots were empty. Funny. She read the email again.

> . . . last seen two days ago on October 31st at the Gamma
> Kappa Omega fraternity.

She had been right there, hadn't she? She had watched this girl, Charlotte Mask, get in a car with a boy dressed as a skeleton. She had watched him drive her away from the place where, according to the email, she had last been seen.

But who had been the last to see her? Not Leda, surely. The skeleton would have been the last. He had driven her somewhere; *he* knew where she had gone after Gamma Kap. Of course, he would come forward, straighten things out. Of course.

The dress under Leda's legs stank of alcohol and, strangely, wood smoke. There was something else, too—something clean, chemical. She pulled it out from under her—the seam under the arm was loose—and tossed it toward her hamper. She reached into the boots one more time, feeling for the condom. Nothing. She noticed that her feet were oddly dirty. She sat back, trying to remember. But since Halloween night, she wasn't even sure if she'd showered.

It occurred to her that she might have been the only person to see Mask get in the skeleton's car. A Nissan. A Toyota. A Honda maybe.

But then what had happened after? She honestly couldn't remember.

Leda stepped outside, hoping the air might wake her, telling herself that the skeleton would come forward and thus prove that she, Leda, was not the last to have seen this missing person.

Naadia was still on the porch, head bowed over her phone. At her lips, a vape pen glowed. She didn't look up when she spoke. "Did you know her?"

Leda heard the girl, Charlotte Mask, say, *You look familiar.*

"No," Leda said. "I don't think so."

Naadia arched an eyebrow at Leda, as if to say, *You don't* think *so?*

Machine noise pounded from the neighbor's construction pit. Leda squeezed the bridge of her nose. The air wasn't helping. She went back in.

The bathroom had two doors, connecting Leda's and Naadia's rooms. Leda locked both and sat on the toilet while the shower heated, about to message Mary about the disappearance. But then she paused, noticing Mary's most recent text: Are you alive?

Followed by Leda's crabby response: Why wouldn't I be?

This was weird. Leda didn't even remember this exchange, which had been time-stamped around 4:00 a.m., the night of the bubble party.

But Leda didn't have time to probe into a weekend of drunk texts. And besides, it was this girl, Charlotte, whose life or death now seemed most urgently in question.

In the shower, Leda let the water run into her eyes. She washed the grime off her feet. She scrubbed her body twice. After, she blow-dried her hair and did her ponytail in front of the mirror. The routine was comforting; it fooled her into thinking that today was just another Monday. She did her makeup, humming a bit of Eminem that Carly had gotten stuck in her head.

She put on lip gloss and said to the mirror, "I'm here to save you, girl."

She wore a fluffy white towel, monogrammed with the Psi Delta pitchfork and triangle. Above the towel, she wore an uneven necklace of hickeys. She inspected these, almost proudly. From Saturday, she was guessing.

Charlotte Mask, she thought occasionally, just hearing the name, not yet connecting it to anything. The reality of it (a disappeared girl; a maybe-raped, maybe-murdered girl) just missed her. Even her own involvement—the fact that Leda had seen the girl leave with a boy, in a car—seemed somehow peripheral. The whole thing was jammed in her periphery, actually; even if she tried, Leda couldn't look at it directly.

Leda ran the sink, getting a washcloth hot to dab off any smeared makeup. Naadia had already showered, so Leda could take her time. Though she was probably pissing off Genie, who had the room under hers. The pipes in the building were old (and disintegrating from all the Drano the girls poured into them on the daily), and any water Leda ran upstairs plunged like a cataract through the walls. Downstairs, there were water stains everywhere. Plus, Leda was bouncing on her feet, the boards under the linoleum squeaking.

"Lo siento." Leda wrung the cloth, pouting, giving Genie her fake apologies. "Disculpe."

There was a deep crack in her lower lip, rose colored and glassy. She dabbed at it. She had noticed it yesterday, too, in that bleary hungover haze, but she'd figured she had just bitten her lip. Now, she saw that it was surprisingly deep. Still, it wasn't horrific, and it only stung when she touched it.

There was no way to cover up a lip gash that she knew of, so she proceeded with the normal routine. She patted concealer under eyes, applied mascara, and rewrapped her towel. When Leda was growing up, her school bus serviced a suburb that had been full of this pillowy, monogrammed baloney. It had taken only a few playdates, a few birthday parties in this neighborhood to make Leda indignant. Dust didn't seem to exist in the suburb. Bugs didn't get in. Her mom had said that it was the antique business; antiques were old (*this just in!*), and sometimes they smelled like mothballs or motor oil or mold. Sometimes they came packed in dead strangers' towels with centuries-old insects folded in. Sometimes Leda had feared that every object in her childhood home was haunted.

Today, it felt good to be wrapped in something without a history. It felt good to look clean and pretty. Leda pursed her lips in the mirror, and the gash started bleeding.

You know, you look familiar, Charlotte had said. *Do I look familiar?*

It did seem extremely likely that Leda had been the last person to see her and perhaps the only person to see the boy—a suspect, maybe. But how could she be sure? Whom could she ask? Mary? Ian? She remembered going inside to find Ian. She remembered going home with him, vaguely; the memory was dreamlike, hazy. In his Lawn room, she wasn't sure what had happened. And she had no clue how she'd busted her lip or how she had gotten back to her room.

"¡Qué tragedia!" Leda sang, bouncing on the balls of her feet.

Spanish was useful in times like these. She had decided to study Spanish both because she found it easy, and because anything she said in it didn't quite sound real. If one of her classmates asked about her family, her mother, por ejemplo, she could respond painlessly:

"Se murió."

And Charlotte, too, she thought. *Se murió.* Though that wasn't true. She was not dead, but missing. Something more complicated, maybe. But Leda didn't know how to say that in Spanish—*missing*. She thought through the words she knew: invisible, unknown, lost, absent, undecipherable.

She is not here, she could manage. Or, *We don't know where she is.* Both sentences were so sufficient . . . and insufficient. Still, it was nice to be able to say something without having to feel it.

If Leda's mother came up in Spanish class, Leda's classmates usually lacked the linguistic skill to respond as they normally would, in English. Usually, her compañeros either didn't understand or weren't listening, too busy calculating what they would say when their turn came. ("I have a mother and a father and two siblings and one dog," or "I am a student, and I have a family.") Maybe Spanish felt less real to them, too. For Leda, it was a play language—one to be poked around like a stick tool. Of course, some people would get it and say sorry—*Lo siento*—their bad accent making their sympathy sound as fake as it was.

Me acosté con Ian, Leda formulated now, triumphant. I slept with Ian. At least, she assumed she had slept with him. The condom was gone. And all day Saturday, she had been anticipating it, wanting it. Hadn't she? But now that it had happened (now that she *thought* it had happened), it confused her a bit. Her heart throbbed like it had when she'd sprinted down O-Hill—jolted with equal parts fear and exhilaration.

Leda leaned close to the mirror and tongued the welt on her lip. She whispered, "Superman ain't saving shit."

Back in her room, Leda wandered around in her towel, packing her books. There was a quiz in astronomy today, and she wondered whether she should try to speed-study. She would probably get a mediocre grade either way. The subject didn't come naturally. Still, she liked the class. She liked the expansive head feeling she got when she learned that, e.g., while Earth's rotation period was twenty-four hours (-ish), Venus's was two hundred forty-three days. *That* was how long it took for the sun to rise and set. It made her mind stretch as she imagined it. By the end of each class, her brain was elastic.

Also, it didn't hurt that Ian was in the class. Yes, she sat light-years away from him. But, however distant, she always made sure to sit in his line of sight. It made her sit up straighter. It made her at least appear to be listening. She didn't take notes in most classes, but she did in this one. If she couldn't achieve perfection at close range, she wanted to at least appear perfect from a distance.

Somewhere in her room, her phone vibrated. Leda jumped, flung her towel onto her bed, and padded around naked to find it, thinking, *Ian? Ian? Ian?*

But it was Carly, initiating a Psi Delta group text, offering support for anyone especially affected by Charlotte Mask's disappearance. Eight billion Psi Delts were already responding: Hugs for Charlotte; so much love to Charlotte; PRAYING! Leda picked at her lip as she read them, and then typed her own message, on a whim, asking if anyone knew where Charlotte Mask had lived. She said that she wanted to leave flowers. Other than this, she did not join in.

Back in the day, she had gotten to live in the sorority house by 100 percent joining in. She had known everyone's full name, hometown, birthday. She had volunteered for everything. She had gone to every party. Back then, if she were to have received a group text like this, she would have been *the most* sorry. But this semester, she was losing energy. She didn't fill her schedule with "playdates." She didn't go vineyard hopping, didn't go to every football game. And today, it felt as if some pearly filter—creating the illusion of sisterhood, of family (the very things she had wanted when she joined the sorority)—were slipping away.

Even if the other girls hadn't detected it (Leda didn't necessarily want to advertise it), Leda feared that she, like Mary, was getting weird. What's more, she feared that her strangeness might run deeper than Mary's eccentric taste in eyeshadow, her developing obsession with the Middle Ages, and that one fateful evening in which Mary called *The Little Mermaid* (to a roomful of Psi Delts cuddled up with popcorn and Disney-patterned Snuggies, about to watch the anniversary edition) "trite, misogynist bullshit." Even Carly had made a big stink when Mary got a nose piercing, printing out copies of *The Unofficial Psi Delta Style Guide* for everybody.

Still, they had fun together, Leda and her sisters, even as it became clear that they barely knew one another. But if that were true—that they didn't "know" Leda—then what were they missing? Who *was* Leda, really? How could she expect such knowledge from her sisters if Leda herself didn't have an answer?

Eventually, Naadia texted Leda with Charlotte's address. No one else in the sorority, despite the heartfelt declarations of grief, seemed to have known Charlotte personally. Leda replied with an emoticon of praying hands. Thx!!

Leda got dressed. Downstairs, she borrowed someone's straightening iron in the shared bathroom. She had time before class, and she wanted to run, wanted to sweat, but she didn't want to look apestosa— pestilent. While she waited for the iron to heat, she poked her head into the common room, where a few girls gazed into their phones and picked at cereal. Glock patrolled his xylophone. Three girls embraced beside the bird, one with tears on her face, saying, "I was *right there*. I was *at* that party."

Carly was in the adjoining kitchen, filling her thirty-two-ounce thermos with coffee. On her emotion chart, she had circled only the Brave smiley. We will not stay silent, she had recently texted.

Leda said, "Job interview?"

"I know." Carly thumbed her feminine lapels. "I'm so Comm School."

Leda fooled with her bangs. "¿Por qué?"

"Did you get my texts?"

Leda's phone vibrated in her shorts pocket. "I'm still getting them."

"Well, I'm getting organized. Even the weirdos across the street are mobilizing."

While many terms in the Psi Delta vocabulary had complex definitions (a single word could range from derogatory to affectionate), *weird* was never ambiguous. It always meant freakish. Leda went to the front windows to look. Carly was right. The Cathouse girls were gathering, wearing all black, their shirts tied above their bellies. A girl painted red letters on their skin. Some said RAPE ME. Some said KILL ME. A dingy sheet hung out of the window, printed with the words FIND CHARLOTTE.

"Freaky." Leda headed back for the iron.

"I didn't think I'd say it," Carly said in the kitchen. "But they're right. We've got to do something."

"Huh?" Leda called.

Carly said something else that she couldn't hear. Or maybe Leda's hearing was slightly selective this morning. She was trying not to think too carefully, trying not to invite another absence into her life too eagerly.

"I said . . ." Carly appeared beside her in the bathroom mirror. "Where were *you*?"

The iron hissed Leda's bangs straight. For an instant, Leda's eyes met Carly's in the reflection. She lowered the iron. It was a strange question; they had gone to that party together. Did Carly not remember that night either?

"I was there . . ." Leda looked for some glimmer of recognition in her sister's face. "I was at Moonie's, too."

But Carly just cooed and squish-hugged her. Carly didn't seem bothered that she herself did not remember the night entirely. So maybe it was silly for Leda to worry. Everyone had been boozing and hooking up. Maybe it didn't matter that she couldn't remember whether or not she and Ian had slept together. Maybe it didn't matter that one of her last conscious glimpses had been a now-missing girl.

Back in the common room, Leda googled the address that Naadia had given her. She recognized the neighborhood, but she wrote the address on her hand just in case.

"Flower run?" Carly asked her.

Leda nodded, though it wasn't. She didn't buy flowers for her own mother's grave. *Perdóname*, she thought. *Disculpe*. She just wanted to see the house for some reason. She was just curious, curious about this girl who had taken her picture, who had said she looked familiar.

But Carly interrupted her thoughts, pushing cash toward her. "Buy some for me?"

And then there were more girls around her, pooling their money, telling Leda to buy as many flowers as she could carry. They group-hugged, and for some reason the gesture struck Leda as repetitive, flimsy.

Outside, the sky was impossibly, insensitively blue. Leda ran. Everything appeared to be business as usual. Students came out of Starbucks with whipped cream on hot drinks. People crossed the street while texting, bundled in scarves and bunchy layers. A busker played harmonica—a repetitive, choppy melody that Leda heard almost daily. A large rubber kitchen mat, hung to dry on a balcony, slipped and slapped the brick sidewalk below, hitting nobody. Leda froze for an instant, looked at the mat, looked up to see no one on the balcony, and kept jogging.

Up West Main Street, Leda could hear music from Wild Wings before she could see the building. The bass thumped through an empty stretch of dead cornflowers and scrub trees—a remix of "Girls Just Want to Have Fun." She passed the old U-Haul, where a hotel was going up. She passed Sweetie's Cupcakery, which had recently installed itself in an old tire shop. Its garage doors were rolled open, its pink awnings flapping. Leda glanced at the address on her hand. She would just run by, she told herself. She was just curious.

She crossed the train bridge, her step matching the now-full-volume remix (*Oh, girls just want to have*—). A passenger train wheezed into the station, which shared the same building. People got on and off. Street traffic moved and then stopped. A girl with dreadlocks whizzed down the center yellow line on a bike. A man in dingy fluorescents swept around parked cars' tires.

It would be stupid to say that the train held its breath. Stupid to say that the fluorescent man swept the curb in an anticipatory way. Leda ran past the man. He smelled like Skoal and coffee. It was probably just a Leda thing: Leda on the edge of something, Leda anticipating catastrophe.

—just want to have fun!

Parking meters ticked past. A man on the train platform looked like Ian. She craned her neck, looking back. He didn't, actually. Not really. When she looked ahead again, she almost smashed into two white women with yoga mats on their backs. Then more yoga mats passed, and she bumpered between them. Like most of the city, this stretch of West Main was newly occupied by boutiques—an organic butcher that bottled its own iced coffee, a vegan cake shop, a gastropub. In the middle of this, leftover from the old days, there was a diner with silver two-way windows, reflecting a brief, dashing Leda. Above her, one cloud packed like gauze into the dazzling blue.

The flower shop smelled like lilies, like a hospital. It made Leda's sweat suddenly chilly. There was a sale on yellow roses. She put the cash on the counter, and the shop clerk chose stems with remarkable slowness. Leda swallowed, closed her eyes in the stench. Her sisters' money alone bought nearly three dozen roses. She left with the thorny stems pressed to her belly, trying not to breathe in.

She couldn't run with the roses, so she walked the rest of the way. Her turn came at the Baptist church, where the doors stayed open all Sunday. On those days, you could see little girls in wedding cake dresses, men so closely shaved their cheeks might have squeaked, and women in tremendous hats—periwinkle, shamrock, tangerine.

Today, the doors were closed: no joining hands, no prayers, no singing. Not that Leda was religious. She just liked the idea that if you sang loud enough, someone might listen.

The railroad tracks crossed behind the church parking lot. Then the road dipped. She looked around the flowers at the address on her hand. She had just wanted to jog past. She had only been curious. Now, these roses turned her curiosity into a big production. The next few houses had NO TRESPASSING signs. She felt conspicuous. She passed a house with boards instead of windows. She passed a sedan with its back window busted. An older, shirtless man sat on the curb beside it. Leda went around him, and though his eyes were open, he seemed not to see her or the roses.

The next porch dripped with wind chimes. The next yard was filled with bleached toys—a plastic playhouse, a Barbie car soupy with old pollen and fallen leaves. Leda, when she was a kid, had desperately wanted one of these.

Charlotte Mask's house was on Nalle Street—a faded blue Victorian with potted herbs on the walkway and a chipped porch swing. There was a misshapen garden in the front yard, but, since the frost, no one had pulled the now-dead things.

Leda hoisted the flowers. Gravel cracked under her feet. She had expected it to be busy. She had expected it to look like TV—crime-scene tape, news crews, police—but the road was empty. The house had its windows open, revealing nothing but screens. It would have looked abandoned if there had not been some air about it—some sense of the living.

The windows glared down at Leda in her sports bra and short shorts, long-sleeve college tee tied around her waist. She took the flowers to the front door. A letterbox beside the entry was marked with three names: *Flora Blackshear, Charlotte Mask, Angel Carter*. She placed the roses at the top of the stairs, cupped a hand and squinted through the front door's glass. A plain, dusty vestibule. A yellowing plant. A big, black duffel beside a sagging staircase. She stood back, staring at the three names on the mailbox. With one finger, she opened the lid.

The letterbox looked empty. But just as she eased the lid shut, she noticed a card. A postcard, maybe. She glanced through the front door glass again. The house seemed empty. She peered back into the letterbox at the card. Wasn't it illegal to open other people's mail? But this was a postcard; there was nothing to open. She blew warm air into her cupped hands, eyes cutting back at the empty street. No one was there. No one was watching.

The front of the postcard pictured a generic Appalachian stream. Autumn leaves. The other side of the card was addressed to Charlotte. There was no one to stop her from reading on.

Dear Charlotte, I'm dropping out soon. Maybe I'll think more clearly after. Maybe I'll find something out there— down there—and someday I'll tell you about it. Take care of yourself, friend. SAVE YOURSELF. Love, Pia

Something beat, like a clock ticking. Leda stared at the signature. *Love, Pia.* It wasn't clear from where the card had been sent. She flipped the postcard again—a pretty river.

The pulse drew nearer. Footsteps. A shape moved behind the front door glass. Now, Leda could hear the house's floorboards. Her calves stiffened, ready to take off. But it was too late. She stayed glued to the porch, shoving the postcard into her sports bra as the door opened.

A girl with short, pink hair stood there. She saw the flowers. "Did you bring those?"

"Yes." Leda stepped back, her hands empty. "Sorry . . ."

But the girl was quicker. She seized Leda's shoulders and hugged her. "That is so, so sweet."

Leda stared at the letterbox over the girl's shoulder, its lid still open. The girl squeezed her tighter, hugging for too long, sniffling. Was she crying?

"I'm sorry," the girl managed, clinging. "It's just—Charlotte loved roses."

"I didn't even know," Leda said, still apologizing, the postcard jammed between their bodies.

"It is just *so* nice." Finally, the girl stepped back, crying freely.

"You're . . . Flora?" Leda guessed, glancing at the names on the mailbox.

"Yeah." The girl wiped at her face. She wore glitter on her cheeks. "Don't worry about me. I've been crying all morning; this is my new normal."

Flora gestured inside, and Leda followed her awkwardly. Despite the open windows, the house smelled musty. It felt both busy and empty, like a frat house after the party.

Flora leaned against a hall table, the tears still rolling. Beside her was a stack of postcards like the one stuffed in Leda's bra.

Flora saw her looking. "Charlotte was out of town for a couple weeks." She tapped the stack, as if this adequately explained what looked like two dozen cards. "Before she went missing, I mean. But I'm sure you knew that already."

Leda nodded, though of course she hadn't known it. She asked, "Are they all from the same person?"

"Oh . . ." Flora wiped her face. "I've never read them because, you know, privacy. But I guess they're probably important now. Now that Charlotte . . ." Flora's throat caught. Eventually, she managed, "Do you want tea?"

Leda shook her head. Really, she just wanted to leave. The house felt hollow. Haunted, even. Though Flora seemed to be the only person home, the building creaked. But Flora looked ready to start on a new round of crying, and Leda couldn't just leave her here, weeping.

Leda said, "You and Charlotte were housemates?"

"We were best friends, basically. We met hula-hooping, first year on the Lawn. We'd both signed up for Hula Club. It turned out we were the only ones." Flora smiled weakly. "This year we got into photography. Charlotte had no barriers, right? No boundaries. She was always trying new things. Knitting. Climbing. Making cheese." Flora took a gray tissue from her jeans and blew her nose. "I'm sorry. I'm blabbing. I have chamomile tea. And valerian, actually. I haven't even asked how you knew Charlotte, but it's okay if you don't want to talk about it. You're probably in such a wounded place, emotionally."

"I can't really stay." Leda stepped back, eyeing the postcards again. A big black camera sat on the table beside them. "Were you guys in a photography class?"

"Yeah. I'm a gender studies major, but I always try to do an art class. It's an intro class, but Charlotte is *so* good. Was." Flora glanced at the cards. Took a breath. "She was *so good*, wasn't she?" She no longer seemed to be talking about photography.

They hit a silence. Leda pulled on her long-sleeve shirt. She was cold. Besides the cards and the camera, the only thing on the hall table was a toppled woolen figurine—a goat or a sheep.

"Well, I don't want to bother you," Leda said finally. Even though Flora had done most of the talking, Leda was beginning to feel like a liar.

"You are not *at all* bothering me, but I totally get it. Our door is always open. Literally." Flora tried laughing. "This is a community house, so it's, like, part of the philosophy. Anyone who needs a place to stay is welcome. Besides, I think both Angel and me lost our keys.

And, if Charlotte comes home . . ." Flora left off, wiped her nose. "I want the door to be open."

Outside, the yellow roses looked tacky. At the bottom of the porch steps, Leda turned around before Flora went back in. Flora was peeking in the now-empty mailbox. Leda's fingers itched. She wanted to touch the postcard that she had taken. *Stolen.*

"The flowers aren't from me," Leda admitted. "They're from my sorority. I didn't know Charlotte that well, really."

Flora shut the mailbox, nodded. "There's always more to know." The glitter on her cheeks shimmered—either a smile or a grimace. "No matter how much time you spend with a person."

Leda nodded perfunctorily. She took the sidewalk quickly, slipping beyond a telephone pole, her shirt tugging for an instant on a raised staple. When she glanced back, Flora was still in sight. Flora waved. She hadn't even asked for Leda's name.

In astronomy, Leda slid the postcard out of her bra and looked at it. She had brought only this and her phone to class. After chatting with Flora, she hadn't had time to go home for her backpack and a change of clothes.

> *I'm dropping out . . . Maybe I'll find something out there— down there . . . SAVE YOURSELF.*

No matter how many times she read it, she still had no idea what it meant.

On her phone, she browsed her university's course offerings, finding only one Intro to Photography. What else had Flora said? Hula-hooping? Valerian?

At least Leda was not the only one distracted. Her whole class bombed the routine five-question quiz. They answered on expensive remote controls that recorded, tallied, and graphed their responses, so they saw instantaneously how everyone did. Today, the class average was 40 percent. Leda, still in her running clothes, had gotten two lucky guesses.

It was fine. Ian wasn't in class today, and this, among other things, made it difficult to focus. Leda had hoped that seeing him might jog her memory. Maybe seeing him would recall that first kiss—in the frat, perhaps, under the fake cobwebs. (Had her lip already been bleeding then?) Maybe she would remember the walk to his place. (They had walked, hadn't they?) And maybe she would be able to convince herself that she had not seen Charlotte again, that there was nothing she could have done to stop what had happened.

Even her professor seemed distracted as he reviewed the answers to the quiz, discussing the developmental stages of a star as the news streamed audibly in the lobby outside the lecture hall. Cell phones and laptops gleamed, showing articles and images that anyone seated behind them could see—CHARLOTTE MASK: MISSING. The girl in front of Leda, for example, didn't once close NBC. The girl clicked through photos of Charlotte Mask—Charlotte in jean overalls, Charlotte in front of the Rotunda, Charlotte holding a duck. Eventually, Leda put the postcard away, took out her own phone, and scrolled. Every so often, it vibrated with a new Psi Delta group text: Won't give up; Still can't believe it; MWAH! We love you, Charlotte.

After class, people clumped around the lobby's televisions, a to-scale model of their solar system dangling in the atrium above them. The crawl at the bottom of the screen read 22-YEAR-OLD CO-ED VANISHES FROM PARTY. The newscasters said that Charlotte was a fourth-year English major. (*Shit*, Charlotte had said. *Is it that obvious?*) She was on the Dean's List. Her father was American, her mother Chinese. She had grown up, like Leda, in Dice County.

"What?" Leda spoke out loud inadvertently, seeing the map of her own county highlighted in green. But the news moved on, and no one in the crowd seemed to notice that she'd said anything. A box containing Charlotte's personal details appeared on the screen:

HEIGHT: 5′8″

WEIGHT: 130

HAIR: BLACK

EYES: BROWN

AGE: 22

RACE: ASIAN

TATTOOS/DISTINGUISHING CHARACTERISTICS: NONE

It was scary to see how normal, how unexceptional the girl seemed to be. Give a few tweaks to weight or height, and Charlotte Mask could be anybody. She appeared, holding a duck, on the screen: the girl everyone was now forced to know, and whose story would now irrevocably color their own.

The front doors of the lobby opened and closed. A chill slipped into the building. Every so often, Leda glanced over, thinking, *Ian?* What did *he* remember from that night? What had happened after Charlotte got into the car with the skeleton? Leda had watched her get in, watched the interior light blacken. Then she had walked back inside, thinking of Ian, finding him.

And then?

The next thing she remembered was the dried blood on her lip. The smell of fireplace and semen on her clothing. The missing condom (which at least suggested that she and Ian had used protection). There were also a few unhelpful shards of memory—Ian's hand in hers, an ivy-covered wall.

Charlotte Mask's car was also missing, the newscasters said. Which struck Leda as odd. Why would *Charlotte's* car be gone if the skeleton had picked her up and, ostensibly, taken her off?

The same photographs shuffled across the television. The crowd around Leda thinned.

Her astronomy professor was the last out of the lecture hall. He came and stood beside Leda, watching the screen. Then he asked what everyone seemed to be asking, in one way or another: "Do you know her?"

Leda looked at her county, highlighted on the TV. She thought of how she had answered this question to Naadia, and then to Flora. She felt the hidden postcard against her skin. "Maybe," she said. "I sort of did."

"I'm very sorry," her professor said. He glanced up at the solar system—the monster sun, the little bead of Earth—and left the building.

Leda touched her face, as if to make sure it was still there, still together. When her hand came down, her fingers shimmered. In that long hug Flora had given her—a hug between strangers—Flora's glitter must have rubbed off on her.

3

The sidewalks surrounding the Lawn pumped like arteries early Wednesday morning. The long quadrangle of grass stayed wet with dew even after the sun clipped the pavilion roofs, so students flowed up and down the brick perimeters—colorful jackets blinking behind the white colonnade, footsteps trickling until they dispersed at either end of the walkways, forking out to the limbs of the university.

It was the perfect time to ask people for money. Students flowed toward quizzes, presentations, and meetings, remembering that they hadn't eaten just as they passed the bake sale tables. It had been Carly's idea—a joint fundraiser between all the sororities to "bring home Charlotte." Leda wasn't sure where the funds would go, exactly, but, all the same, she and her fellow Psi Delts had made cupcakes, muffins, and brownies yesterday. Today, Leda arranged the baked goods on trays and shook an old cheese puff jar, rattling with quarters.

"Bring home Charlotte Mask," she said, over and over again. "Bring home Charlotte."

A second-year Psi Delt in suede barn boots kept up their social media presence, posting photos of whoever bought a baked good with digital hearts and stars around their faces. She captioned one of the photos *Heroes*, which Leda thought was pushing it. Buying a fifty-cent brownie didn't make anyone a hero. But everyone was exaggerating lately, to the point where words were losing their meaning. I'm devastated, one of Leda's sisters had texted that morning. A few other girls, though they had never met Charlotte, had eaten their cupcakes while discussing the stages of grief, and Leda had had to bite back something remarkably mean.

To Leda, words were becoming increasingly baffling. There were the words *love* and *friend*, the words *crush* and *sex* and *loss* and . . . If Leda really thought about it, she didn't know what anything meant.

Por ejemplo, first year, when she lost her virginity at a party, she had called the boy her *boyfriend* for an embarrassing twenty-four hours until Mary, gently but firmly, set her straight.

Well, Leda had asked Mary, *if he's not my boyfriend, what is he?*

Now, Leda knew not to ask that question, even though she still wasn't sure she had an answer. If she were to see Ian, she'd have to play it cool. She'd have to act like she already knew.

So, for now, Leda just sang with the others: "*Bring home Charlotte Mask. Bring home Charlotte.*" They were all selling basically the same baked things (with the exception of the Sexual Assault Hotline chick, who had nothing but vaguely vaginal coin pouches and pamphlets). There was also a fraternity, handing out Koozies and energy drinks.

To tell the truth, Leda hadn't particularly wanted to do this. She didn't want to shout Charlotte's name as if it were a commodity, as if any of these passersby could buy her back from wherever she'd been taken. She didn't want to listen to girls who had never known Charlotte discuss grief, while that girl Flora described crying as her "new normal," and while she, Leda, was afraid to even speak the word *grief,* afraid she might actually come to understand its meaning. But, here she was, wearing a cute knit hat and a bunchy scarf, like everybody else this morning. Here she was, smiling, singing, *Bring home Charlotte*. Here she was, glancing up and down the Lawn, half looking for Ian, whom she still hadn't seen or spoken to since Halloween.

A black-haired girl dropped a dollar in, slipping back into the crowd before Leda's sister could snap her pic.

"Oh my god." Barn Boots pointed after the girl. "She looked so much like Charlotte."

Leda said nothing to this. Was she serious?

Leda unwrapped a cream cheese cupcake and bit in. Nearby, a blond girl chalked enormous hearts in front of the Sigma Kappa table. A few of Barn Boots' friends stopped and donated, chatting about their prayer group and how they hoped to get five hundred people praying for Charlotte. *If you sing loud enough, someone might listen,* Leda thought, though now she believed it less for some reason.

She tried to tune the prayer girls out, taking out her phone. Just seeing the screen light up made her feel slightly less alone.

Charlotte's Facebook was jammed with new posts, including links to updated articles. One news agency reported that Charlotte's car had been found. This was good news, but, for Leda, it was alarming, too. The car had been found about forty-five minutes from town, not far from Leda's childhood home. It had been parked along a country road that Leda knew well, leading to the Dice County reservoir, the National Forest, and a connection to the Appalachian Trail. A local man had noticed it parked there Sunday morning. He'd looked in the window yesterday (Tuesday) when he noticed the vehicle hadn't been moved. The keys had been in the ignition. He'd called the police. According to the article, the plates were registered in Charlotte's name.

After skimming other news reports, Leda realized that no one else had seen Charlotte get in a car with a boy. And it seemed that the skeleton, whoever he was, had not come forward. Every article still indicated that she'd last been seen inside the fraternity. It was suspicious, obviously. But what did it mean? Had the skeleton picked Charlotte up in her own car? Had he driven her out to the middle of nowhere?

It was all a bit over her head, admittedly. Leda supposed she could just call the police. She could say, *I think I was the last person to see Charlotte Mask.* She could describe the boy and the car to the best of her ability. The problem was that then she'd have to admit that she didn't remember anything after that. She'd have to admit that she had blacked out. That's what had happened, if she was being honest. Calling the police wouldn't solve anything; it would just be embarrassing.

Leda bit her busted lip, staring down at the screen. It hurt—intense and brief. Where had she, *Leda*, gone after the bubble party?

A naked bagel appeared in front of Leda. She looked up. One of the prayer girls was holding it out to her—some sort of offering—asking if she was interested in joining their group prayer on Friday.

"Oh." Leda put her phone away, not taking the bagel. "I'm not religious. Sorry."

"That's okay!" the girl exclaimed, bagel still extended.

Leda ignored it. "Is the idea that God is more likely to hear more people praying?"

The girls nodded, though, to Leda, the concept seemed foolish when put this way. It was hard to believe that anyone was paying attention up there, much less listening.

"Thanks," Leda said finally, shaking the cheese puff jar of dollars and quarters. "But I'm just not interested."

Reluctantly, the girl retracted the bagel. Before they left, they all joined hands with Barn Boots while a mass of frat boys emptied their pockets of change in exchange for pink sprinkle cupcakes. The girls let their eyes shut, backpacks piled in the middle of their circle. The one who had offered the bagel spoke, almost rhythmically, and though Leda strained her ears, she couldn't hear. The other girls smiled, as if they were being told a secret.

"Bring home Charlotte." Leda kicked the leg of the table, shook the jar. "Bring home Charlotte Mask."

The sky was tense and cloudless. Hundreds of boys passed, and every one of them was not Ian. She wanted to see him. She thought that seeing him might help her remember. Not to mention that she liked him and wanted to know what they were. Boyfriend-girlfriend? Friends? Strangers? She wasn't naive; she knew that just because they'd had sex (she *thought* they had, at least), didn't mean they'd get married. Like a lot of college girls, she'd slept with boys whose names she no longer remembered. It was all part of play-pretending adulthood; you had to figure out who you were, what you wanted, and then what you would do. It wasn't as simple as everyone made it out in childhood, how they asked you what you wanted to be, as if *that* were the only decision you'd be making. They never told you about the in-between choices. They never said you'd be deciding if and how much to drink; deciding where to draw the line between flirtation and harassment, between fun and scary; deciding whether or not to trust somebody.

It was all remarkably tricky. And, for Leda, what made it worse was that she had no one to ask, *Is this okay? Am I on the right track?* Without her mom, she had to figure it out through trial and error. On the subject of Ian, a few moments were beginning to stand out to her: their interlaced fingers, his eyes meeting hers, the way he'd touched her hair as if it were precious, as if *she* were precious. No one had looked at her like that—no one since her mother.

Outside these brief moments, she had nothing else to go on. So, here was another one of these adult situations for which no one had prepared her. If you *think* you had sex, how do you make sure? Or, put another way: If you black out, is it worth looking back? And what if you look back . . . and find that something awful happened?

Mary stopped by on her way to Shakespeare II as the Christians dispersed. She had made Leda take Shakespeare I with her last year (still trying to convince Leda to study English with her), and though Leda had liked it, it had been demanding emotionally. It had made her consider things—Yorick's skull, the living statue of Hermione— that she'd rather not dwell on, really.

Now, Mary took hold of Leda's own skull, pushing Leda's hair back, examining something.

"Um," Leda managed. "Excuse me?"

"What happened to your lip?" Mary said.

"I don't know." Leda pulled out of Mary's hands. "Dry skin."

"That is not dry skin."

"It's not like I'm bleeding."

"You *are* bleeding."

"Oh, shit." Leda touched it. Her finger came away red.

From her satchel, Mary extracted a Kleenex. "At the risk of being too much of a mom, I also have Neosporin."

"I'm fine." Leda took the tissue. She was only bleeding a little bit. Still, her friend looked concerned, her brows knitted. Her eyelids were glitter dusted. After her nose piercing, this eyeshadow had really provoked sororal hostility. It was stupid, but these little beefs were relatively common, concerning, e.g., when you could wear sweatpants or how often you shaved your legs. Glitter lids were out of bounds, obvi.

Leda stepped away from the table and dabbed at her lip. "I thought you were afraid of blood," Leda said.

"It's your blood," Mary said. "That's different."

They bumped shoulders, moving away from the bake sale table.

The Lawn pumped around them—a dude on a long board, a girl juggling a violin, textbooks, and coffee. Three cadets hurried over bright sidewalk chalk as the chapel bell marked the hour.

"You're late," Leda told her friend.

"Today's *Romeo and Juliet*," Mary said. "Not my favorite. Plus, I just wanted to make sure you're good. I haven't seen you since Halloween when you, like, vanished on me with Zeus."

"Sorry . . ." Leda scuffed her foot.

"That's not what I mean. I want to make sure nothing, like, happened."

"I mean . . ." Leda hesitated. Was this the moment? Was this the friend to whom she could say something cringeworthy? But for some reason, she resisted. Maybe she just didn't want to feel vulnerable this morning. She answered smugly, "We had sex, if that counts as something 'happening.'"

"And was it . . . good?"

Leda raised one eyebrow. "What do you mean?"

"You don't have to go into detail, Lee. You just sort of disappeared. I want to make sure I don't have to kill somebody."

"Mary . . ." Leda hugged herself. It was too humiliating to admit that she didn't know what had happened, especially to this always-smart, always-sensible friend. She didn't want to admit that she was at once confused, nervous, and still somehow infatuated with Ian. So she said, not untruthfully, "I can't stop thinking about him."

Mary looked genuinely surprised. "Seriously?"

"I guess I shouldn't, probably." Leda tried to sound normal. "He still hasn't called me. And he hasn't been in class, so he might be avoiding me . . ."

"Look, Leda," Mary interrupted. "I was wondering because something sort of weird happened, actually—"

But Carly's voice cut in, calling, "Lee!" Back at the Psi Delta table,

Carly had come to relieve Barn Boots. She was loaded down with fresh muffins and caffeine. Once her hands were free, she tapped a nonexistent watch, shouting, "You're on the clock, Lee-Lee. Seriously."

In reality, Carly probably didn't like Leda talking so visibly to their ex-sister, Mary. Sure, Carly hadn't been above exploiting Mary for strategic, boy-proximity purposes, but now, in front of all these other frats and sororities, Carly was probably worried about the "impression" this little convo might leave.

To Mary, Leda whispered, "Sorry."

"Go." Mary gave her a little push, though her brow was still knitted. "No worries."

Mary went to class, and Leda returned to her post. She was scheduled for two shifts in a row, so she took a muffin and a coffee. The sun climbed. The day was warming. A few tables away, girls clapped and shouted. They were offering colorful strips of paper to fold into origami "prayer stars." Already, these tiny stars had half filled a gallon jar.

"You should do a star," Carly said. "They're so fun and, like, pertinent."

So it seemed Carly was no longer concerned whether or not Leda was "on the clock." Whatever. Leda joined the chanting girls and accepted a thin strip of orange paper. You were supposed to write your prayer on the paper and then fold it. She stared at the blank strip for a moment, wondering what it was that Mary had been about to say.

"We're doing prayers for Charlotte," one girl prompted.

This much was obvious. The table was cluttered with photographs of Charlotte Mask. Leda left her paper blank, folded it, and dropped it in the jar.

"You're so cute," Carly said when Leda came back. "I saw you praying over your little star."

Though it shouldn't have, this comment annoyed her, just like the invitation to the five-hundred-person prayer circle had annoyed her. Maybe it was the implication that she was the kind of person who needed other people around her to feel even slightly significant. And of course, she *was* that kind of person. That's why it bothered her. She loved sitting in lecture halls, loved knowing that, for an hour and a half, she was exactly where she was supposed to be. She loved going to choir, braced on all sides by voices and bodies.

She glanced back toward her star, indistinguishable now, surrounded by hundreds of others.

Or maybe she was just irked that Carly had caught her in a moment of uncertainty, vulnerability—the very thing she'd been trying to hide from Mary.

A British guy came by the bake sale, wheeling a road bike, and bought two currant muffins. "Cheers," he said before leaving. Carly giggled. She swung her spandexed ass and shouted to anyone who would listen about Charlotte. She stopped a group of EMTs. She scratched a professor's schnauzer's belly. Leda had to forgive her—she was so bubbly, so full of energy. Plus, she had brought Leda coffee.

Along with the muffins, Carly handed out T-shirts. From what Leda could see, the graphic featured a pair of comic book–style lips, screaming.

"What are those?" Leda asked.

Carly said only, "You'll see."

The British guy came back and bought four more muffins. "They are so good," he said. "It's uncanny." He wore pale-framed glasses and a bike helmet. He was—Leda admitted it—enormously attractive.

"You've bought, like, six muffins," said Carly. "I think that makes you a philanthropist."

"Hardly." The British guy flushed. "I'm just a lowly PhD candidate, scrounging for some kind of nutrition that isn't made of text and parchment."

"That sounds pretty desperate," Carly said. "What do you study so I know to avoid it?"

"Philosophy," he said, chewing. He looked like he could model for Burberry—the chiseled face and the tousled I-went-to-bed-in-this-eight-hundred-dollar-sweater aesthetic. When he removed the dweeby helmet, Leda had to stop herself from gasping.

"Wow." Carly turned to Leda.

"Wow," Leda agreed. "Philosophy."

Carly gave the guy her number, casually, in case he wanted any more philanthropic opportunities. He typed it into a flip phone, saying, "I'm an absolute wally at texting, so I might actually *call* you. Fair warning."

He swung his leg over what might as well have been a steed and rode away just as Genie arrived with more muffins. Leda, in a squeaky British accent, said, "I'm an absolute wally—"

"Shut it." But Carly couldn't keep from grinning. "He's royalty, and you know it."

Leda hoisted her backpack. It was almost time for astronomy. "Maybe in a grandpapa kind of way."

"Oh my god, are you blind? He was only, like, twenty-eight. And British accents are so sexy. Admit it."

"Who's British?" asked Genie.

Leda teased, "He was wearing *tweed*."

"Um, that was cashmere, bitch."

"*Who?*" said Genie.

Leda stepped away. "The guy with the monocle and the watch chain."

"What's a monocle?" Genie looked around.

"An STD."

Carly punched Leda, surprisingly hard, actually. "His name is Benjamin, and he's the love of my life, probably." Then she told Leda to stop by the table after class, even though Leda had worked both her shifts already. Something might be happening, she hinted, around noonish.

Leda said, "Cryptic."

"What can I say?" Carly slipped on her Ray-Bans. "I'm a subtle lady."

Again, Ian missed astronomy, and Leda spent the class convincing herself that it was no big deal. He wasn't her soul mate or anything. He was just this dude with whom she had had sex. (Probably.) He wasn't a god. He was just smart (smart enough to live on the Lawn, which was saying something). He was just handsome (he had a six-pack, plus the blue eyes, plus the tousled hair, plus the high cheeks). And he just liked Leda (or he had *said* he liked her, at least).

Usually, Leda didn't get attached to flings. But she couldn't help obsessing over the bits and pieces she remembered from the evening. They had stopped in the gardens (she was pretty sure of it), kissing (possibly) against the ivy. Judging from the wood smoke on her clothes, he'd probably built a fire in the fireplace. From the little that she could recall, he had been romantic, persistent.

Now, he was avoiding her. Either that or (perhaps worse) he had forgotten about her.

Still, it was whatever. It was almost noon, and she had things to do. She needed to finish the reading for Poesía Moderna (class was later that afternoon). She needed to petition her astronomy prof for extra help, or to at least let her retake the last few quizzes. She needed to swing by the Lawn to see Carly, her subtle lady, whom she now found in the middle of a crowd, shouting.

Among others, the crowd included about fifteen Psi Delts in matching neon shirts, the ones Leda had seen Carly hand out. The phrase YOU HAVE A VOICE was printed under the screaming mouth. The backs of the shirts were cut out like blinds, revealing tanned backs and elaborate, neon bra straps.

Carly, also wearing one of these shirts, announced that she had been born with a talent for making noise. She had squalled through infancy. She had thrown tantrums as a toddler. She had cried and slammed doors and thrown massive, breakable objects through childhood, adolescence, and into adulthood. (Is that what they where? Adults?)

"My ancestors were Scottish immigrants," Carly said. "And they yodeled—literally yodeled—to communicate between mountains in the Allegheny."

Leda spotted a Cathouse girl in the crowd, looking out of place—tattoos swarming her collarbone, head half-shaved.

"Now, compared to my ancestors, we're mice," Carly cried. "We never raise our voices. It's unseemly to be a woman shouting. But, in my humble opinion, who gives a flip? When something is wrong, we need to stand up together and scream. We need to *say* something."

A few Psi Delts did a silent cheer, like, *Go, Carly!*

"So." Carly clapped her hands. "I'm gonna scream. It's really loud, so just, like . . . be aware of that. Plug your ears if you're a sissy."

The crowd backed off. Some people raised their phones, recording. Leda watched from the back of the crowd, wishing Carly had run this idea by her. She wasn't sure how impressive a scream could be. Even movie-grade screams were, like: okay, duly noted; something's scary. And then that something usually *wasn't* that scary. It was an alien. It was the swamp thing. These days, the horror in *horror movie* came from silent creepiness—contagions, brainwashing, a hunky tech guy who emotionally abuses androids or something. Leda had thought that even psychopaths, even murderers were passé . . . but movies were not real life, were they?

Carly's chest expanded. She seemed to grow two inches taller. She stared at a spot in the Lawn and opened her mouth. Light broke from the clouds. A ribbon of sparrows snapped from a power line and shattered into the sky. The scream was terrifying. If Leda hadn't known it was Carly, she would have immediately called the police. People gasped, covered their ears. The scream sounded as if it had been kept under pressure for years, shooting from Carly's body like blood shoots from a horror-flick stabbing.

The crowd applauded dizzily, but Carly was still screaming. Leda made an effort to clap, too, but her hands were too stiff. She tried to relax. Still the scream hit and hit, and she had to brace herself against it. It battered the Rotunda and echoed. Surely they could hear it on Memorial Road, crashing through the windows of fraternities, swirling around the copper statue in front of the art museum: a woman without any arms or legs, though she appeared to be running. The scream seemed separate from Carly. It was living.

Carly's mouth closed, but still the scream echoed. The crowd swayed. The whole Lawn had stopped. The sparrows had been obliterated. Carly looked like a fat Buddha, beaming as the crowd blinked.

"It's not just a matter of self-defense," Carly called to crowd. "It's a matter of self-respect. Every woman has a voice, but not every woman knows how to use it. Who's next?"

The crowd murmured, looked around. Leda wondered if she was even capable of screaming. If a scream wasn't good, then it was embarrassing.

Carly stamped like a child. "Don't let fear and inhibition keep you from speaking! Learn what you like and what you don't. If you don't like something, just fucking scream!"

Then a noise: Genie behind the pastry table, wailing. The scream wasn't as powerful as Carly's, but people were nodding. A Chi Om

girl squealed—thin and treacly. The Cathouse girl shouted. Three
cops walked down the center of the Lawn toward them quickly. Still,
the screams picked up. Clouds blocked the sun. Carly screamed
again, and the smaller voices sawed beneath her. The British guy
stood by with his bike, eating another muffin. At the back of the
crowd, Leda opened and closed her lips, thinking of her choir conductor shouting from the top of his desk: *What are you SAYING?*

The pods in the basement of the music department could fit an
upright piano, a music stand, and a person. The doors were made
of soundproof glass, which made the pods less claustrophobic, but,
when someone walked by, you got looked at. Being seen was usually
good for Leda's concentration (she stood straighter, rounded her
mouth, enunciated) but tonight she wished she could drape something over the glass. Even the harsh motion light couldn't be switched
off. This and the glass, it was rumored, were meant to discourage
what music majors called "pod-ual activity," though Leda knew it still
happened surprisingly frequently. Some girls in her choir wet-wiped
the pianos before playing, for fear of pubes and bodily fluids.

She started with scales, dropping into her lower register. The padded walls hugged. The ceiling stopped only a foot over her head.
Maybe it was strange, but she liked the warm, cramped quarters. In
here, she breathed deeply. She reached down and scooped out sound.
Whoever passed down the corridor would only see her mouth moving; she could sing as low and ugly as she pleased. Elephants, she had
learned recently, communicated at a frequency below human hearing.
What freedom, Leda had thought. Until recently, no one had even
known they were speaking.

Leda didn't play piano exactly, but she used it to plunk out scales or difficult points in her music—weird rhythms or unexpected dissonance, challenging her brain to sit with the discord, to hear her part in it. This was the lot of the alto: you never got to sing the melody.

Learn what you like, Carly had shouted. *Singing*, Leda thought. *Astronomy. Running. Parties. Ian.* These were a few things she liked, but she wasn't sure if that's what Carly had meant exactly. *If you don't like something, just fucking scream.* But, for Leda, the line between liking and not liking was so thin, so slippery. One minute, she and Ian were kissing against some garden wall (as she imagined it). And the next, she had fled (fled home, she guessed), taking wild, drunken steps through memory's odd flashes.

Fled. She didn't remember *fleeing*; the word had just come.

She tried to focus. She sang, assigning each note a syllable. The traditional *do, re, mi* felt natural. It was pleasant, not knowing what she was saying. The sounds came out like a mantra, like meditating. Every note was just a tremor: an elephant's vibration. Maybe Leda was like the elephant. Perhaps her "true" voice was so low that even she couldn't hear it.

A muffled tuba burped in the next practice room. Leda pressed her temples, opened her music. She filled her lungs and opened her mouth: "*Ora pro nobis.*"

Pray for us. The notes long and low. Was this her voice?

"*Peccatoribus.*"

A knuckle rapped on the soundproof glass. Leda wheeled, wearing her what-do-you-want frown. Then her breath caught.

"Buenos tardes," Ian said in bad Spanish, his voice almost muted by the door. He was smiling. Perfect teeth. Hair a little mussed. Leda stood for too long, color rising to her cheeks, looking. Ian gestured at the door handle finally, and she bonked her own head with her palm. She opened the locked door to Ian, who smelled like her red dress

had smelled Monday morning: wood smoke and—yes, now she recognized it—chlorine.

"Who taught you Spanish?" Leda said, simulating confidence.

"Nobody." Ian smiled. "That's the problem, maybe. I picked up
some Nahuatl in Mexico, though."

Of course she'd never admit it, but Leda knew all about Ian's trip
to Mexico. The Psi Delta volunteer leaders had shown her photos—
Ian balanced on makeshift scaffolding; Ian peeling yucca; Ian pointing to a fresh-looking scar where his appendix had been. Leda had
never been out of the country, and she had a hard time not romanti-
cizing even the appendectomy, even what must have been weeks of
recovery.

Now, she tried not to sound totally gaga. "Say something in
Nahuatl."

"Tipatica," Ian responded.

"Which means . . ."

"'Are you happy?' You would ask that instead of saying hello."

"Wow. I'm glad I don't have to answer *that* on the regular."

"Agreed." Ian put his hand in his hair, his T-shirt lifting, showing
the scar.

Leda pointed. "Ouch." She had to have seen it before (in the flesh,
not just in pictures), but there was something about it—about his
whole body, really—that disturbed and fascinated her. Something
about how you could get so close to another person and still feel like
strangers.

"Oh, yeah." Ian lifted his shirt, revealing the full incision. "It's an
ugly one, isn't it? You can touch it. People always ask me."

Leda hesitated. Surely, she had touched it before, hadn't she? But
Ian was acting as if they had just met, as if this were the first time
they had ever held a conversation. Maybe it was. She reached out two
fingers. Her hand felt cold on his low abdomen.

Her voice came out small. "Did it hurt?"

"You kidding?" Something under his skin flexed. "They knocked me out."

Leda shifted, her fingers still touching him. She would have mentioned what her sisters had told her, but she didn't want to admit that they had been discussing him and his appendix.

Still, he seemed to read her expression. "They have hospitals in Mexico, too, you know."

He let his shirt fall on her hand, and she retracted it. He was joking, but Leda felt a little naive, having believed the whole "field operation" story. She wished she were holding something—an instrument, a pencil. She wanted some evidence that she was not just standing in this tiny room like some Disney damsel, waiting for true love's first kiss. Or, well, *second* kiss. The first, she couldn't recall.

"Anyway . . ." Leda was embarrassed now. "I have rehearsal soon."

Ian gestured back at the hall clock. "Ten minutes, no?"

He was right. Leda said, "How did you—"

"I just assumed you probably start on the hour." Ian smiled, shrugged.

"Right." Leda picked up her sheet music, as if it might protect her. There was no reason to be nervous. It was just that all she wanted to know, suddenly, was what had happened on Halloween. It seemed strange not to acknowledge it, as if it (whatever *it* was) had never happened. At the very least, it felt odd not to mention Charlotte. Especially since Leda was pretty sure she had seen Charlotte and Ian at the Cathouse, talking.

She took a breath. "Ian—"

A group of boys in tuxes squeezed past Ian, down the narrow hall. Behind them, a girl wheeled an enormous harp on a dolly. Ian had to step into the pod to get out of the way. Their bodies brushed.

"Leda." Even though the hallway was clear, Ian didn't step out of the pod. Gently, he took Leda's music out of her hand. He leaned his forearm on the doorframe—perfect arm, perfect body—dangling the score over her head. He said, "Am I allowed to kiss you again?"

Leda opened her mouth, but had no idea what to say. She felt like she was in high school again. A kiss—she could barely picture what Ian meant by it. Her heart flopped. He leaned in, and his cheek touched hers for a moment. Then, under the blue fluorescents, their lips met. Leda's body went still and corpse-ish.

Around them, footsteps clicked. A soprano hummed the first notes of what Leda had just been singing: *Ora pro nobis.* The same tuba honked. Ian paused, his lips on her lips. *Honk, honk, honk.* Leda's face cracked. Was this a nervous or a real laugh? She felt as if she were driving her truck into ice, feeling the tires' weightless swoon. They parted. The world swam, leaving only Ian in focus. It felt like a first kiss. Though it was now perfectly clear that it wasn't.

Leda heard the stage door to Bell Hall open. A trio of trumpets jotted down a brief, sticky harmony. Nearby, her conductor lectured somebody, animated and scolding.

Ian handed Leda's score back. "If you want, stop by on your way home, Leda."

He said her name as if it were more than a collection of syllables. *Do, re, mi* . . . Leda's chest sang. She held on to the doorframe as he walked away, as if to keep from falling.

In ten minutes, she took her place on the risers. She sang more scales, this time with sixty other voices. *Mi, me, ma, mo, mu.* Usually, these particular nonsense syllables struck her as sad, but today she was fortified against them. Sopranos dropped out when the notes got too low. Mezzos, too. Leda followed the sound down. She pulled it out like dirt by the handful. The notes got lower, quieter, reaching elephant frequencies. She kept digging, the last woman singing.

The velvet auditorium chairs were empty but for three students seated separately in the wings, laptops open, opting for a live home-work accompaniment. Some people were lucky, she thought. Then she corrected herself. *She* was lucky—the domed hall; the hushed chorus; the kiss, still on her lips. Though she wasn't happy, not exactly. She was exhilarated. Tense. Something.

Her conductor's baton lifted. Leda touched her own lips, as if she might understand the kiss more fully by touching it. Instead, her fingernail grazed the cut, and she winced. The baton pulsed, jabbed, and Leda's eyes refocused. The chorus breathed on her conductor's command, but Leda missed it. Suddenly, she was a measure behind. She caught up, but her conductor had already heard the mistake and let his hands drop.

B y the time rehearsal was over, it was dark. Stars showed over the Rotunda, down at the far end of the Lawn. Leda came down Bell Hall's front steps, humming Amy Winehouse (she had somehow gotten in Leda's head, even after two hours of Middle English and Latin). She stepped out onto the broad sidewalk, barely enunciating the word *love* just as she collided with someone. The guy mumbled, didn't look up. It was the dude she had danced with at the bubble party. He was walking away already, as if he'd hardly noticed they'd touched.

Today in astronomy, Leda had learned that when asteroids crash, they mark each other. They leave traces of their composition—their carbon, their silicate, their metal. Just like people, she thought now, forever knocking into one another, leaving dents and chemical memories.

Again, she thought of Charlotte, touching Leda's elbow for not even a breath before spinning off into the universe.

Far off, a group stood before the Rotunda with candles. Together, they made a sound like a moan. Leda approached, burying her hands in her pockets. Overhead, stars clung in a lactic net. Leda walked between big, blown-up photos of Charlotte and homemade posters— TAKE BACK THE NIGHT and MAKE OUR CAMPUS SAFE and YOU HAVE A VOICE. Carly's phrase was catching on already. A little ways off, in the midst of all the closed doors on the Lawn, she saw that Ian's was open. She stopped in the middle of the vigil, candles smoldering around her. She could see Ian, sitting at his desk, his back to her. Leda took a step toward him, brushing a girl holding a large image of Charlotte. But she stopped, remembering the strange cold of his skin, the shock and swerve of his kiss. She remembered how she had wanted to say Charlotte's name, and how he had stopped it with his lips.

Around her, the vigil began a low chant. Ian shifted, turning at the sound of the rising murmur. He was looking for her, wasn't he? Waiting for her. But before he could look back, Leda fled, hoping her body was masked in darkness.

4

Something large and red stared up at Leda from beside her bed. She gasped, knocked a bookshelf, and covered her eyes with both hands. What kind of childish reflex was this? *Quick, cover your eyes! It can't see me if I can't see it.* She could just remember her mother sweeping her up once, covering Leda's face, and walking quickly. Leda still didn't know from what, in that moment, she had been protected.

Now, Leda lowered her hands. Her mother's dragon had slumped out of the closet like a shed snakeskin. Fallen books surrounded it. She sighed, picked up its head. Its dull teeth parted. The doll eyes blinked as she crammed it back in the closet. Now her hands smelled of the dragon: the Nag Champa incense her mom used to burn plus, weirdly, artificial strawberry.

SAVE YOURSELF, the postcard shouted from the desk, where she'd propped it. Leda's empty red boots sprawled flatly beneath it. These, too, she stuffed in the closet.

Outside, Naadia vaped on the porch, wrapped in a Psi Delta blanket. She raised an eyebrow when Leda came out. "Are you okay?"

Leda blinked. "What do you mean?"

"You screamed." Naadia lifted a steaming mug to her lips. She sat next to an empty bottle of champagne.

"It was a bug."

Leda turned to go back in, but Naadia called after her.

"Did you find Charlotte's place?"

"Yeah." Leda paused. A front loader started up at the demolished home next door, drowning out the morning birds. "I met Flora."

"Flora . . ." Naadia tapped her knee. "Is she an international student?"

"I don't think so. She's got pink hair. Glitter on her face." Leda's leg jiggled. She needed coffee. Food. "You'd remember."

"I only knew Charlotte through some international club, though she's not even foreign."

Naadia vaped, drumming her fingernails on the empty bottle of champagne. Naadia's boyfriend had probably been over—this guy who seemed to study half a dozen languages, Sanskrit, Urdu, Farsi, French—and, like Naadia, he had expensive tastes. They had been together for a year, which, in Leda's world, was basically married.

The front loader revved, and Leda raised her voice over it. "Isn't Charlotte's mom Chinese?"

"Charlotte's white, basically." Naadia drew her blanket around her, watching the machinery. "You think they'd be looking so hard for someone who wasn't?"

Leda shrugged. She would have liked to think so, but she didn't know.

"Anyway. She's a pretty girl," Naadia said. "They'll find her."

Somehow, Naadia didn't sound too concerned. And maybe she was right not to be. Whether or not Leda told somebody what she'd seen, whether or not she contacted the police, Charlotte would be found. Everything would be okay. Eventually.

Leda headed downstairs to scavenge for breakfast. The kitchen was empty, but Carly was up, feeding Glock Cheerios.

Carly said, "Was that you?"

Leda grabbed a granola bar from someone else's bulk box. "Was what me?"

"Upstairs. It sounded like the ceiling fell."

"Oh. It was my dragon." Leda tapped her phone's locked screen. "I mean, my bookshelf."

A Pop-Tart sprang from the toaster, and Carly retrieved it. "You're going to have to explain 'dragon' to me."

Leda opened and bit the dry granola. "It was my mom's old dragon. Like, the ones you see in parades." Leda chewed. She didn't want to talk about the dragon. She'd had nightmares about it when she was a kid—color saturated, strawberry smelling.

"That's *normal.*" Carly bit the Pop-Tart—pink icing and pink filling. "How come I've never seen it?"

"It's in my closet. I don't have anywhere to put it." Leda slid her thumb across her phone's screen. No calls, emails, or texts. No Ian. Had he forgotten he'd invited her over? Had he noticed that she'd stood him up after choir?

Anyway, whatever. It was Thursday, and Leda had class soon.

"Why don't we hang it down here? Glock would like it." Carly used her baby voice, calling the cockatoo. "Wouldn't you, sexy boy? Wouldn't you?"

Leda ignored her. There were more reports on Charlotte in the news, but Leda didn't have time to properly comb through. She clicked on one about Charlotte's car, though there were only a few new details. Charlotte's phone and wallet had been in the glove compartment. A pair of white knee-high boots had been found in the trunk.

"You didn't scream, Lee," Carly said, interrupting.

"What?"

"You screamed upstairs, just a second ago. But I watched you yesterday, and you didn't scream."

"I'm in choir, Car," Leda said, almost without thinking. "Screaming fucks up your vocal cords."

It wasn't a lie, exactly. Still, Carly squinted at her.

"Google it." Leda put down the half-eaten granola bar. "Sorry. Class." Leda and Carly air-kissed. "Love you."

In Advanced Spanish Grammar, Leda hid her phone in her open textbook and read more articles about Charlotte. She thumbed around a map of the area that police and volunteers were searching: a green circle around the reservoir, the National Forest, the pastures, and Leda's childhood home, which was too small to see. This article concluded: *The public is still encouraged to call or email with any information regarding Mask and/or her whereabouts.* The sentence seemed to point straight at her.

Another article, posted recently, was titled, NEW INFORMATION IN MASK CASE.

At once, her professor's voice muted. The room around her ceased to exist. Apparently, one of Charlotte's neighbors had seen Charlotte on Halloween. Sometime after midnight, a car had dropped her in front of her house. Alone, she'd gone inside. The car had driven off. As of now, this neighbor, not Leda, was the last person to have seen Charlotte.

The vehicle in question, the article went on, belonged to Charlotte's roommate, Angel Carter. The third name on the letterbox, Leda remembered. One of the night's many skeletons. Carter, it seemed, had finally stepped forward and talked to the police. Apparently, he'd played only a minor role in Charlotte's evening. He'd given her a ride home in his own car, and then driven himself to another party, where his boyfriend and a number of friends confirmed he'd stayed until the early hours of the morning.

Charlotte's car had been parked on Nalle Street. No one had seen it leave.

It should have been a relief. Leda had not come face-to-face with Charlotte's abductor. Her involvement had been, at most, peripheral. Still, somehow Leda didn't feel much better.

She turned a page in her textbook, as if she were listening. She imagined Charlotte's house on Nalle Street—the blue Victorian with its dark windows, its messy garden and lopsided porch. She tried to picture Charlotte walking in, glittering in her swan costume. And then what happened?

The classroom stirred. Leda looked up. Apparently, they'd been asked to get in small groups. Obviamente, Leda hadn't been listening, so she had no idea why they were doing this. They were discussing, a classmate informed her, their greatest fears. She joined a group talking about spiders, airplanes, and pop quizzes. Nearby, two girls spoke haltingly about Charlotte, one describing her as perdida (lost) and the other, ausente (absent). Neither word was quite right. But what *was* the word for "missing"? Leda still couldn't think of it. But before she could look it up, it was her turn. She hadn't prepared anything to say.

"Les tengo miedo a las casas vacías, porque en ellas yo también me siento vacía." Then, too late, she realized what she had said: "I'm afraid of empty houses, because in them I also feel empty."

Sometimes, speaking in Spanish sabotaged her like this. Sometimes she and her classmates ended up being *more* honest than they would have been in English. They had to concentrate so hard on grammar and vocab that the truth slipped out of them.

After class, Leda had a half hour to kill before Chilean Lit, so she walked around grounds, avoiding the Lawn (Ian still hadn't texted), detouring through the gardens hidden behind the Lawn's pavilions, thinking of yesterday's kiss. She followed a circle of ash trees, touching the bark—silver and wrinkling. Hadn't she and Ian come here on Halloween? She paused, trying to think. Maybe he had pushed her up against one of these trunks. Maybe her breath had knocked out of her. Maybe the impact had, for an instant, woken her.

A crow barked from a pavilion roof. Her mother had always counted crows, assigning the numbers some meaning. But Leda couldn't remember the specifics. She opened her mouth at the bird, wide, as if to scream or sing.

It was possible that she was afraid of Charlotte's house. Maybe that was why she'd said that thing about emptiness. Though really the place had not been empty. Flora had come out, like a glittery ghost, bawling. And, no, Leda wasn't just scared; she was also curious. It was horror-movie shit; it was the reason that all those spooked protagonists go into basements and look under beds and open closets. Leda had never known that this was a real feeling. But now she felt compelled to swing back by Charlotte's. Even drive out to the road where Charlotte's car had been abandoned.

Maybe she would visit her mother's grave, if she were really feeling brave.

In the next garden, sugar maples shattered their last red leaves freely. The pebble walk cracked under her feet as she passed between stiff hydrangeas and smoke trees. Then she stopped. Someone stood beneath one of the maples, holding a leaf. She considered backing up slowly, but he had seen her already. He spoke her name, as if it meant something. He wore a glacier-blue jacket that made his eyes so bright they were frightening. Already, without thinking, she was crossing the grass, drawing in.

"What are you doing here?" she asked him.

"What am *I* doing? What are *you* doing?"

"I don't know." Leda smiled. Her thoughts rushed by like clouds in wind. "I don't know," she said again, forgetting about her class in fifteen minutes, thinking, *You tell me.*

T he only substantial thing Leda had inherited (besides, she guessed, the dragon) was her mother's truck—an old Nissan covered in patches of rust. She didn't drive it much. Compared with the other vehicles parked around the Psi Delta sorority—hybrids, BMWs, Volvo SUVS—it was embarrassing. So when Leda finally admitted to Ian in the garden that she had been thinking about driving out to the country, and when he invited himself along as company, she tried to make excuses, tried to think of any other activity. But he was so sure, so ready to join her, that she decided to skip Chilean Lit and walk to her Nissan with him. Now, they were speeding down a small highway, Ian flipping through Leda's old CDs as Leda began to slowly relax into the idea of being liked by somebody.

It helped that the Nissan was no longer out of place in the country. Out here, everyone had trucks. Out here, there was no such thing as nitro coffee or vinyasa flow or cake pops. Here, black cows bordered the roads like gravestones. Gas stations advertised Skoal and Grizzly. The churches had already set up their nativities. It was comforting to pass these familiar, immutable things, even if there was no home, no family to introduce to Ian.

"So," Ian said. "You *lived* out here?"

"Is it that hard to believe?"

Ian rolled down the window a crack, and the wind tossed his hair. "I just wouldn't have guessed it." It was weird, him sitting beside her. "Do your parents still live here?"

It was a harmless question. Still, Leda couldn't do anything more than shake her head and fix her jaw. She hadn't told Ian that she'd planned on visiting the cemetery. She also hadn't mentioned that she wanted to see where Charlotte's car had been. Her plans had dissolved the moment she'd seen him. She had lied, saying that (despite the cold) she was thinking about swimming.

When they came up on Leda's old house, they passed without slowing down, glimpsing it at fifty miles per hour. The driveway had been paved. The house had been painted white instead of red, and the lawn was smooth where before there had been explosions of garden.

It was fine. What did she expect? The house and nearly everything in it had been sold three years ago, the summer after senior year. Clarence, Leda's mom's then boyfriend, helped with logistics. He'd rehomed the chickens. He'd reduced the prices in her mom's rented spot in the antique mall. What didn't sell there was then sold at the estate sale: blue cutout squares taped everywhere, marking five-dollar shoes, the one-dollar bin (reading glasses, a button bracelet), the free grout and broken china that her mom had used for mosaics. The price tags weren't the only things that bothered her. It bothered her that this was the kind of sale that Leda and her mom would have attended themselves. Leda couldn't remember if any other antique dealers—her mom's friends, she supposed—had come to the sale. She only remembered standing in the front yard alone, watching strangers' heads move in the windows.

She'd been eighteen. An adult, technically.

In the trembling side mirror, she could still see her home. She pointed to the next house. "That's where I had my first kiss."

"What?" Ian laughed.

"Nick Pemberton." Leda slowed past the trim lawn and enormous flag. "Growing up, he was always a brat. Then he turned Goth in high school, and I kissed him."

Compared to the Pembertons', Leda's house had always looked like a weed—the mimosa in the backyard crazy with pink, her mom's chickens appearing in the grass like fleas. She and Nick had kissed in that long grass, knocking teeth. She had checked off a few bases with him. It was fun because it was different. She hadn't known it was supposed to feel like anything, or that she had any say in what they did or how they did it. It felt natural to be acted upon. That's what life did, didn't it? It threw things at her, and she lay there and took it.

Leda drummed the truck door, got back up to speed. She fell quiet, wishing she could remember that first kiss with Ian. She thought of the strained dress seam. Who had tugged it off—Leda or Ian? And what about the missing condom? They might have used it, or it might have simply fallen out of her boot.

She turned the pickup off the small highway onto Reservoir Road. When Leda glanced over at Ian, he didn't look bothered. Did *he* remember? she wondered. Had he *known* that she'd been unconscious?

A hill rose to their right, crested with flat graves and polyester flowers. She glanced away before she could recognize her mother's. The sun flashed through her window, bleaching out the close blue mountains. Then Reservoir Road sloped down, and the graveyard slipped into the background. They passed a stiff field—baled hay, crying cows.

Ian said, "It's beautiful out," as power lines soared over, as a net of birds threw itself at the sky.

But then there were cars blocking the next bend, blinking their hazards. Leda slowed and stopped behind them. Sun fell through the trees like confetti. It *was* beautiful out. Even so, Leda found herself squeezing the steering wheel, her knuckles pale. A man in an orange vest approached and waved them on. The traffic crept between more orange-vested men and women.

"What's going on?" Leda said, though she knew the answer as soon as she said it, as soon as she glimpsed a man and his lanky scent hound cutting into the forest.

The search party's parked cars lined the road for a while. Neither she nor Ian mentioned Charlotte. They drove for some minutes in silence.

Eventually, Ian asked, "You okay?"

Leda nodded, accelerating, while at the same time wondering if she *should* be okay. Wouldn't it be strange if she *wasn't* disturbed by the sight of men and women searching for a fellow student—a girl who could have been a classmate, a friend?

Ian, however, had barely noticed the search party. Either that, or he was wholly unaffected by it. It was strange. Even if Ian hadn't been a friend of Charlotte's, wouldn't he remember chatting with her at the Cathouse pregame? Already, Leda had heard a dozen I-saw-her stories. Wouldn't *this* be the time to tell his?

But, to be fair, Leda wasn't saying anything either. If she admitted that she'd spoken with Charlotte outside the bubble party, then she'd have to acknowledge that she didn't remember much else after that moment. She'd have to admit that she wasn't sure what she and Ian had done together. She wanted to seem confident around Ian, and confessing all this would achieve just the opposite.

The paved road ended in picnic-area parking. A gravel track continued into the mountains, its gate open, but it was too rough for the Nissan. Leda parked beside another pickup, facing a dirty camper and two child-sized tents—one pink and one red. Leda had never seen anyone here actually picnicking, but this family had the grill going. When she opened her door, dogs started barking.

"The reservoir's not far," she said over the noise. "I promise it's really pretty."

A thin woman appeared in the camper's screen door. Then two children pushed past her, running for the crated pit bulls. A chunk of something smoked on the untended grill.

Beside the gate to the fire road, a park kiosk featured a trail map of Bear Grass Creek and a hunting calendar. It was almost bear season. Men would be running their dogs soon, Leda knew, filling these woods with their hounds' crazed bugling. Then, pinned beside the dates for muzzleloaders and bows, there was Charlotte, holding a duck:

AGE: 22

RACE: ASIAN

TATTOOS/DISTINGUISHING CHARACTERISTICS: NONE

Ian didn't seem to notice the poster. He was already walking ahead.

Leda caught up with him. "So, I guess you've been here before?" Her voice came out knotted.

"Me?" Ian glanced back at her. "Nope."

They followed a deep rain gulley running down the middle of the fire road. They approached what looked like surveyor flags, then a yellowish rectangle of grass. Leda knew Charlotte's car had been found out here, somewhere off Reservoir Road. She eyed the yellow imprint. She glanced back at it even after they'd passed. Back by the camper, one of the children dashed for her pink tent and zipped herself in.

The reservoir chopped with wind when they came to it. Leda tried to let her thoughts flap—the search party, the MISSING flyer, her mother. She tried to let them go, let them be taken. She tried to put herself in the moment. Here she was, returning to a place she loved.

She'd come out here as a toddler, a child, a teen. She'd come with and without her mom. Only twice had she climbed the white sycamore—there, just as big as she remembered, where the river met the reservoir. When Leda was ten, she'd clambered up and refused to get down. At eighteen, she had shouted down to her friends from the canopy, *It ain't scary*. She had been too high up to hear her friends' reply. Only the wind had cried. Her branch had buoyed, the world below one great eddy. A raven had landed a few feet from Leda's hand, glossy and croaking. She had shouted again, and the raven had taken off, circled, and landed back beside her again.

It ain't scary, she thought, barely even recognizing herself in the phrase, though she knew she had spoken it. She had said it only a few weeks before her mom had died, though, of course, Leda hadn't known what would happen at the time. Her mom had been sick, yes, but that didn't mean that Leda had considered the word *death*. She had still been climbing trees like a child, never once considering that she might slip.

Somehow, the reservoir, the mountains, the whole park looked empty. Leda and Ian went out over the spillway, the walkway protected on either side by high chain link. They stopped halfway across the dam, at the end of the walk. Looked beyond. Bare mountains circled the reservoir, the water flat and empty save for one concrete tower. The tower was far off, sticking out of the depths like a plug. Only a narrow catwalk connected it to where Leda and Ian stood on the crest of the dam. Ian stared at it—the crown of radio antennae, the sepia windows cracked behind their bars.

Finally, Leda pointed past the tower. "How long would it take you to swim this whole thing?"

Ian blinked hard. He unzipped his coat and laced his fingers through the chain link. "Not long."

The wind pressed his T-shirt against his chest, and Leda felt a spark of warmth, of attraction. She wasn't sure what to do with it. She pulled off her sweatshirt. She wanted to feel the wind. And she wanted (only semiconsciously) to feel Ian's eyes on her skin. Her white shirt had a diamond-shaped gap between the shoulders, showing most of her back. The wind reached under it.

"I used to swim here all the time," she said. Her teeth chattered, from either cold or nervousness. "Me and my friends would go night swimming."

"Sounds a little scary."

"That's the fun," she said, thinking, *It ain't scary.* She tried to hold her jaw steady. She hadn't changed so much, had she? She was still young, still brave.

"I'm no expert," Ian said, "but even I wouldn't want to swim around this kind of machinery."

"There's no machinery. Silly."

"Are you kidding? That's an intake tower." Ian pointed at the isolated concrete thing. "They create these weird currents. Your body would get sucked down, and it wouldn't come out for weeks."

Leda lifted one eyebrow, trying to flirt. "But you could save me."

Ian shrugged, blushing.

Big birds whooped on the far end of the reservoir, flew up, and landed again. *Swans,* was Leda's first thought. But they were just geese, of course—honking, singing. Water slapped the dam. She listened. She tried to let herself be happy, standing there with Ian. Though, somewhere in the woods, she couldn't help thinking, were those orange-vested men and women.

"Leda," Ian said. "I was wondering."

When Ian didn't go on, she looked at him. He was staring at the tower again. "You were wondering," she prompted.

Ian cleared his throat. "Do you remember everything from Halloween?"

Unconsciously, Leda touched the gash in her lip. The geese, so far off on the water, looked like debris. She lied. "Sure. I think."

"I know it sounds stupid." Ian looked over the other side of the dam, where the water seethed over and plunged into an otherwise calm creek. "But I just don't remember all of it."

Leda picked up a rock from the gangway and dropped it into the water, where it disappeared under a skin of leaves. "Nothing bad happened, if that's what you mean."

"No," Ian said, though maybe he sounded relieved. "That's not what I mean."

Leda watched where the rock had disappeared. She didn't know how deep it got here; she didn't know how many layers of slimed things might be buried. When she glanced back, Ian was watching her.

He went on, carefully, "I just don't want you to think that that was me."

There was something odd in his tone. Leda held her sweatshirt against her belly, glancing back toward the parking area. This was how bad things happened, she realized. Going off unannounced, alone with someone you barely know. She scanned the trees on the shoreline, took in the high walls of chain link. If she shouted, she wondered, would anyone hear?

She said, "That *what* was you, Ian?"

Beside them, water plummeted down what seemed like one hundred feet. The air swarmed with something—bats maybe.

"I don't want you to think . . ." Ian looked down at his knuckles, his nails. His cheeks were flushed, but it was hard to tell if it was embarrassment or anger. "That *I* think that this was just some kind of fling."

Relief shot across her face—relief that Ian wasn't about to confess to forcing himself on her or taking naked pictures of her; relief that he wasn't about to bring up Charlotte's name (even though, just minutes before, she had wondered why he hadn't mentioned her). And relief that there was confirmation, finally, that they had had sex. Or something like it.

"Okay, Ian." The wind blew her hair into her face. When she brushed it away, she could see that they were not bats, but swallows, pitching around the dam's cascade. "I won't think that you think that."

"Maybe we can come back here when it's warm," Ian said, after a moment. "And go night swimming."

"And if I got sucked under . . ." She smiled, broadly now, the wind whipping her hair around her face. The crack in her lip twinged. "You'd save me?"

"I'd save you." Ian's eyes flicked over her lip. "Maybe."

Leda play-punched his shoulder. She was probably blushing, too, as he lifted a hand and touched her cheek. His thumb traced a cold line down to the soft impression at the base of her neck. She thought he might kiss her—she *wanted* him to kiss her, actually—but he didn't. His thumb squeezed slightly before he let his hand drop. The sun sank. Only the very tips of the trees were still golden. A big bird cut in and out of the mountain's shadow, either an eagle or a vulture. Ian turned back toward the fire road, and Leda followed.

Her old house was lit and brimming when she and Ian drove past it again. She pointed it out to him. It was a rush, telling him even this little bit. What she didn't tell him was that she had the urge to pull over when she saw it, that she almost believed she could go in and collapse on her twin bed, stinking of reservoir water. She almost believed she could lounge, dizzy from all day in the sun, while her mom turned faucets and boiled tea and picked up or put down the phone, and then Leda would be sleeping. In the morning, her window would show bright clouds. She would hear the ruffle of the chickens in the dust under the eaves. Her mom in the kitchen. The kettle whistling. And she'd toddle out, her face fat as a baby's.

But just the one admission—*that's my old house*—had not been easy. Especially since she was still thinking about Halloween, thinking now about her mother bringing her to the university to trick-or-treat. Even as a teen, Leda had been a good daughter, basically. Now, she knew what her mom would have thought about her blackout. *You are precious*, she might have said. *You have to keep yourself safe. You have to keep your eyes open.*

But what if it's love? Leda countered silently, surprising herself with the sting of this fantasy.

Forty minutes later, Leda found a parking spot close to the Lawn. She pulled in and let the engine idle, not sure if she was coming in or dropping him off. She turned to him, thinking that he would also be turned toward her, but Ian was already getting out of the car. He said good night from the curb. He was kind, of course. But he didn't invite her in. When he left, she looked after him, thinking, *That's it?* She opened her mouth, wanting to say something. To initiate something. *What do I want?* she asked herself, but she couldn't answer the question.

She pulled out quickly, angrily, only to stop at a red light some feet away. Her arms felt hot. Blocky boys in polos flocked the crosswalks. Out the passenger window, bright fraternities rimmed the dark playing field. The field was recessed—the Bowl, some people called it—and occasionally a drunk student or two collected at the bottom and sides like bugs, unable to scramble out of it.

In idle, the gearshift shook. She tried to steady it with her hand, but it did no good. Now, holding it, she trembled, too. Maybe she had gotten her hopes up. Maybe she had thought this was it: that savior, love. Love, that makes everything good—even a blackout, even a disappearance. Or maybe she'd thought something would happen tonight that might replace that gaping hole in her memory from Halloween.

She glanced into her rearview mirror, hoping that she'd see Ian coming after her. Instead, she tasted blood. Her lip. She cursed, dabbed at it. Maybe this, she realized, was why she was angry. There had been an opportunity to question Ian, and she hadn't. She hadn't said, *What happened to my lip? Did I fall? Did someone hit me?* She hadn't come any closer to knowing. *Did we have sex? Did you know I was unconscious?*

And then there was Charlotte. All day, she'd been telling herself that she should feel some relief. She *hadn't* been the last person to see her; she *hadn't* witnessed the pivotal moment that had decided her disappearance. But loss was not so reasonable. Now, she felt only more confused, more disturbed. She had struggled with something like this when her mom died. It hadn't helped to remind herself that every child will lose his or her parents. It hadn't helped to rationalize, to tell herself, *I should be fine.*

A moth smacked Leda's unmoving windshield and left a dusty smear. She considered pulling over and running after Ian. She thought about finding a party with him, forgetting about her mother, about Halloween, about Charlotte.

But he was gone. The truck shook. The stoplight glared red. Leda watched high-heeled first-years amoeba beneath it. Maybe she could go to Mary's place. She could tell her, finally, that she had almost no memory of her night with Ian. But the truth was that she already knew what her friend would say. She would say that an unconscious person cannot consent to sex. She would say that Leda had been raped.

This was the thing about Mary. She would say the things that no one else would . . . the things that Leda didn't particularly want to hear. To Leda, the Ian situation did not feel that simple. It—he—was all tied up with the bubble party—the spiked punch that had tasted like Juicy Juice, Moonie's corn chip kiss, the naked girls covered in foam. And now, somehow, with Charlotte.

An SUV passed her, its bass blaring, *mourn-ing, mourn-ing.* She realized she was stopped at a green. A guy in an open suit jacket slammed a case of Coors on her hood, to wake her, maybe. He thought she was drunk. She thought of Carly's emotion chart—all those melodramatic smileys. How was she feeling? Pissed? No. Maybe, more accurately, she was lonely. She thought of her childhood home, filled now with someone else's family. She thought of how badly she had wanted Ian to touch her, kiss her, love her . . . *something.*

She shot out a Psi Delta group text: Any action?

It was only Thursday night, but in seconds, her sisters had blasted her with tonight's readout. The pros and cons of this and that party. In and out of her windows, a breeze came rocking. She accelerated just as the light turned yellow, and pulled onto Memorial.

It was raining by the time Leda got to the party. She fluffed her hair in the front hall as Psi Delts descended on her, hugging her and kissing her cheeks. *Lee-Lee! Hey, beauty. Hey, gorgeous. Hey, lover.* It was cold in the foyer, but someone took Leda's fracket. She quickly lost track of the person who had taken it. Whoever it had been, she couldn't help thinking, it wasn't Ian.

Still, it didn't take long to find somebody who looked a bit like him. That is, he was blond. Leda couldn't see his eyes; he was wearing sunglasses, even though it was night, and they were inside.

When he passed her in the kitchen, Leda asked him, "Can you *see?*"

"Yes." He didn't look at her. "Thank you for asking."

The music was loud, and she had to shout. "You're wearing sunglasses."

"I'm aware." He was cute, basically, even if he was a bit arrogant. He wore frat formal—a pink bow tie, a suit jacket, khakis. Not Ian's style, exactly. He said, "Would you prefer I took them off?"

"I don't know you." Leda shrugged. "I don't care."

"Good. I don't care about you either."

"Good."

It was elementary, Leda had to admit, but sometimes it worked to use grade school tactics. Sometimes it worked to be mean to the boy you wanted. Not that *this* was the boy Leda wanted. Was it?

He poured himself a bourbon and drank it. He poured himself another, and then handed the bottle to Leda. Somewhere, she heard her sisters squeal.

Leda took the bottle, leaning her lips close to his ear. "I thought you didn't care about me."

"I don't." He drank, impassive.

"Then why are you here?" Leda took a swig—her first of the evening. She wasn't planning on getting drunk. She just wanted to fill the night in. Like gauze in a wound, she wanted to pack any holes, any residual aloneness.

The boy looked at her. "Here?"

In his sunglasses, Leda saw that despite the rain, despite Ian's rejection, she looked pretty. She pointed at the floor. "Right here."

He looked a bit startled. "Why are you?"

Leda shrugged, smiled.

He was no Ian, of course. His hair was too neat. His body wasn't as good. He didn't have that lopsided smile. But something in Leda needed this; she needed to forget her stupid hope and, ultimately, her embarrassment.

When Leda lost her virginity her first year, her whole dorm had chanted, Jerry Springer–style, *Cherry! Cherry!* They threw pillows, called her a slut, and poured celebratory orange juice shots that they cheersed and toasted: *To getting fucked.* The celebration had been more fun than the sex itself. Someone had given her a point on a whiteboard. *P in the V,* someone else called it, like a carnival game that could win her a large, cheap prize.

She still wasn't sure what the prize was, exactly. But she didn't have to be drunk to be curious. The boy in the indoor sunglasses invited her upstairs, and she went with him. She didn't even have to think about it. He was like the sun, shining on one path and not another. He shone on the steps, so she climbed them.

Of course she would have gone with Ian, but he'd kept his light to himself tonight. He had not invited her anywhere.

Still, she glanced back as she followed this new boy's path. She glanced at the foyer below, as if someone might be there, watching her. Who was she expecting? Mary, shaking her head? Carly, making some lewd hand gesture? Was she expecting Ian to be there, rushing up the stairs after her? Was she expecting (hoping for) her mother?

You are precious, her mother might say. Or, *You are grounded forever.*

In that moment, Leda wished someone would ground her. She wished that someone might care enough to try to deflect the world from her.

But nobody was watching. A boy in a fedora topped off everyone's drinks. Two girls took a selfie, one touching her tongue to her friend's cheek. There was balled caution tape under the girls' feet. After the pic, one shouted that it was snowing.

Upstairs, Leda spotted her fracket at the top of a fracket mountain. She grabbed it. A half-inflated balloon drifted across the floor of the empty hall.

"It's *snowing*!" the girl below shouted.

The boy showed Leda into an empty room. When the door closed, when the boy placed his hands on her hips, Leda was alone.

She had lost her virginity in a room like this. The sex hadn't been bad . . . but it hadn't been good either. It had felt like friction. And though she had known what *orgasm* meant, in theory, she had not come to know what it meant in practice. To be honest, she still hadn't. She thought about Ian. The condom. Would she remember if it had been good? Or, on the other hand, would she remember if something awful had happened?

Unlike Ian, this guy talked a lot. Leda perched on the side of the bed while he talked. She learned that he was in an elite honor society. She learned that his parents lived in the Midwest. Soon, he stood her up and took off her clothes. He talked while he undressed her. He said that he hated winter.

"I hate bourbon, too," he said as he finished off his drink.

Leda wasn't sure what to say about herself. But, then again, he hadn't asked. She said, "Is this your room?"

"Nah. I'm not a slob."

He offered no more explanation than this. He undid her bra easily, as if he'd unhooked hundreds of similar clasps. Then he took his own clothes off, though he left the sunglasses on. He had a lot of blond hair on his chest and down there. He touched her crotch and pushed a finger inside her.

Leda said, "You haven't even kissed me yet."

"Don't worry." With his free hand, he took his sunglasses off. He had small eyes. "I'm getting there."

There were clothes on the stranger's bed that smelled like neither one of them. He laid her down. There was a pinup overhead. The boy kissed her gently, and she thought of her and Ian's kiss in the music department: the sudden swoon, the feeling that she might slip. Now, she kept her eyes open. She caught glimpses of the girl in the poster.

Not long after that first kiss, the boy used his hand to move into her.

Leda stiffened. "Do you have a condom?"

He didn't seem to hear her. Fear fizzed in her throat as he moved in deeper. Was this how it had been with Ian? Perhaps she'd taken the condom from her boot, and he hadn't wanted to use it. She repeated the question, louder.

"Oh, shit." He pulled out, reached for something. "Sorry. My mother would be so disappointed."

He had a condom in his wallet. He fumbled it, put it on. He was drunk. Leda watched him. This was the first time she was really seeing his penis. It was not huge. "Your mother?" she said. She tried laughing.

"I'm serious," he said, laughing more freely than she. "What about you? What would your mother think?"

She opened her mouth, stung. He drove into her before she could respond. It was sudden. Already, he was thrusting too fast and too hard. Leda tried to forget what he'd said, tried to have fun.

She asked, "Can I touch your hair?"

"You can do whatever you fucking want."

She pushed her fingers through it, but the gesture felt insincere, awkward, so she stopped. He hovered over her, thumping his pelvis against hers, smelling like strange sweat and bourbon. The skin around his eyes looked pale without the sunglasses. Without them, he didn't look like Ian at all.

He was not unkind, but he was stronger than he looked. His penis felt like a nail being driven in. Soon, the only sensations she felt were slight pain and numbness. It didn't help that there had been no fore-play, no lead-up. Still, she wasn't disappointed. Though she had hoped, she hadn't *expected* the sex to feel like much.

Leda had seen a gynecologist only once, end of first year, and from behind her little mask the woman had asked if Leda was having orgasms.

"I don't know," Leda had admitted.

And the woman had responded in that unhelpful adult tone, "You would know."

Now, Leda moaned, as if to convince herself that she was enjoying this. She moaned and watched the ceiling. The woman overhead did not look real. It wasn't her body that made her seem fake, but her eyes.

Would her mom have been disappointed? Leda re-formed the question in Spanish, to take the sting off it. *Mi mamá hubiera sido . . .* with an upside-down question mark in front, because it was a question. She found this tense, the pluperfect subjunctive, difficult. It was often used, she had memorized, in conditional structures that re-ferred to impossible situations—*she would have been.*

"Fuck." The boy flipped her over as if she were a doll, and she looked at the pillow, down on her elbows. "You're going to make me fucking come."

Why did boys say this sort of shit? Maybe girls did, too. Maybe she was the only one unable to lie, to perform like this. She moaned in a way that could have been interpreted as sexy, though already she was beginning to hear herself more clearly. She sounded more squashed than pleased, trapped under something heavy.

Suddenly, she couldn't keep up the act. She wasn't drunk enough, perhaps. What had changed, from one moment to the next? She didn't know, but she wanted to leave. Had it been this way with Ian? Had she felt him, a stranger, shudder inside of her? Had she felt his eyes look through her?

But she didn't leave. She waited—sore and embarrassed and scared. She couldn't stop what she had started without making a scene. All she wanted was to slip out quietly.

If the boy had been paying attention, he would have felt her go still and cold. But he wasn't. He smacked her ass. And then everything stalled. He pulled out of her. His hands left her hips. *That was quick*, she thought, relieved, about to turn over and look at him, when warm liquid hit her back and ass. She was confused for a moment. From her elbows, she pressed up to her hands.

"Wait," he said, out of breath. "Stay like that."

She froze. She understood now what had happened. He had taken the condom off and ejaculated on her back, as if she were a wall or a floor. She heard a package open. She waited, afraid of where the semen might drip, watching the wall as a cold wipe cleaned it up with delicate swipes. Had this also been in his wallet?

"Okay," he said. "You're good."

She stayed like a table for a moment. He slumped next to her in the stranger's bed and pulled her down, put his arm around her, throwing the wipe and the condom. She lay, jammed uncomfortably into his armpit, staring at his diminishing dick.

Soon, the boy started to snore. The music from downstairs made the window glass groan. Leda got up to see if it was snowing. It wasn't. The alley below the window was wet. Nothing moved in it. She touched her sanitized back and buttocks. She touched her crotch, worried by the slightest wetness. Back in the bed, the boy with his small eyes slept. She felt like a little girl again, standing at her mother's bedside, wanting to be tucked back in.

Her clothes were in little knots around the room. She got dressed. There had been two bobby pins in her hair that she'd placed on the dresser when she'd come in. She found these. She scanned the room for anything that was hers, making sure not to let any little piece of her go missing.

Desaparecida. The word came to her suddenly. *That* was the Spanish for "missing."

She noticed the boy's open wallet, from which he had extracted the condom and, she guessed, the sanitary wipe. She flipped through a metro card, cash, a business card from a florist, a bakery receipt. She read the first and last name on his ID. She replaced the wallet. She considered crawling back into this strange bed, snuggling in, getting over it. But he would only rouse and look baffled for a moment, because he didn't know her, and she didn't know him.

The condom had landed on Leda's fracket. She picked it off and dropped it on the boy's own pile of clothes, next to the wallet. When she tapped her phone, she saw that she had missed zero texts, zero calls. Again, she looked at the penis, like an empty balloon. Why shouldn't she have made a scene? she thought. If she didn't like something, why shouldn't she scream?

Instead, she left, easing the bedroom door open and shut. She buttoned her fracket, touched the pins in her hair, and disappeared down the stairs.

5

The Float Yoga lobby was crowded with college students and fit, middle-aged women. Incense burned. Prisms spun in the big windows. Half-ounce bottles of flower essences lined gold trays. These and other delicate yoga merch surrounded Leda, Carly, and Genie as they waited in line to pay.

Coming to Float on Friday mornings had become a thing—a healthy Psi Delta routine followed by gossip and smoothies. It was a refresh, Carly often said. No matter what happened during the week, you could hit restart and get ready for an awesome weekend.

So: Charlotte, Ian, Indoor Sunglasses. She could just let it all go. That was the idea, at least. Except, already Leda found herself trying (and failing) to remember the name on Indoor Sunglasses' ID. Already, she could hear a few underclassmen Delts chatting at the cubbies.

"I haven't gone out after what happened at Moonie's," one said, toeing cashmere socks off her feet. "I don't feel safe."

Another girl nodded. "Whoever took Charlotte is still out there, obviously."

Leda stopped herself from pointing out that it wasn't from Gamma Kap that Charlotte had disappeared. She did her best to tune out the conversation, watching the prisms revolve in gusts of central heat until a rainbow stabbed her eye.

"Fuck," she said, blinking.

At the iPad, Leda and her sisters each paid twenty dollars—the student price, unbelievably. The cashier wore dream catcher earrings, which matched the larger ones dangling all over the ceiling, their tiny price tags twirling. Leda thanked her, and the girl responded, "Peace."

Leda didn't normally do yoga. She didn't like it, if she was being honest. Her hamstrings were tight (because running), it cost money, and she couldn't help but mentally critique yoga instructors' spiritual doublespeak. Plus, there was just something about exercising in place: trapped in a hot room with twenty other people and no air movement. The sound was fed through speakers. The windows were clouded with gauze curtains, making it feel as if you'd been removed to some loft-style heaven with exposed brick, to which the rest of the world hadn't been admitted.

Running was the opposite: You pushed through mud and windshield granules and spilled food. You saw mint growing through sidewalk cracks. You tripped on plastic bags and random shoes. Out there, it felt normal to sweat and stink. In here, everyone smelled like lavender and car leather.

Not to mention that, today, Leda felt like shit. Her head hurt. Her mouth tasted funny. Last night, she'd walked home alone in the rain. Then she hadn't been able to sleep as scenes from Halloween revolved inside her brain, her visions of Ian now blended with glimpses of Indoor Sunglasses. The come on her back. The way that touching his hair had felt not intimate, but unpleasant. At some point in the night, she'd sensed the spark of epiphany; she'd thought some memory had surfaced, shedding light on those blank hours spent with Ian. But, in the morning, she remembered nothing.

"Yoga is great for hangovers," Carly assured her now, though Leda wasn't hungover. She was just exhausted, moody. In front of the cubbies, the women around them chatted about this weekend's couples' yoga retreat, holiday shopping, babies. Leda unlaced her running shoes and escaped, waiting in line for the bathroom beside a corkboard of flyers. One poster advertised a yoga workshop with the phrase *Bring your sexy back, on and off the mat.* Below this poster, another had been partially covered, showing only the words MISSING: CHARLOTTE.

The woman in front of Leda wore a strand of white, religious-looking beads and a Bluetooth earpiece. She reminded Leda of Faye, the woman that Clarence (her mom's longtime boyfriend) had ultimately married, two years after Leda's mom's death. It was fine that Clarence had married. Leda had never called him Dad or anything. She had never met her father; her mother had been single-momming from the beginning, though she'd had multiple boyfriends. *I'm sick of men*, her mom had said, over and over again.

But Leda had liked Clarence, unlike her mother's other boyfriends, partially because he had stuck around the longest. Now, she basically liked Faye, too, and her two young children, even if she sensed something artificial in Faye's kindness, as if compassion were a club that could be joined, or a membership purchased.

"I love your necklace," Leda told the Faye-ish woman, who turned around, smiling. "Is it pearl?"

"It's a mala. And it's bone, actually."

"Wow. A mala." Leda reconsidered her compliment. *Mala suerte*, she thought. "What kind of bone is it?"

"You know, I don't know." The woman parted her mouth as if to laugh, but the bathroom had just opened.

Leda looked through merch while she waited: crystals, sandal-wood "malas," and natural mat spray (fragrance: the Way). She looked at a colorful chakra poster while the Beatles played sitar-ish ditties over the sound system. The woman popped out of the bathroom, leaving an incense match smoking from a rice-filled bowl. Leda peed, and then inspected herself in the mirror, looking around big white letters: *Love sometimes wants to do us a great favor: hold us upside down and shake all the nonsense out.—Hafiz.*

The word love was huge. *Love, love, love,* she thought to the Beat-les tune. The Beatles sometimes sounded bored of their own chorus. After so many repetitions (*love, love, love; yeah, yeah, yeah*), the words might as well have been, *Blah, blah, blah.*

In the mirror, she touched her lip, lifted her shirt, inspected her breasts and belly. In her eyes, she recognized a particular look: a pursed, critical look that her mother had also put on when looking in a mirror, that had made her mother look not at all like her mother. As soon as her mom turned away from the mirror, the sourness van-ished, as if it were a special cruelty reserved only for her.

In high school, Leda had spent long mornings in front of the full-length mirror, pinching and prodding her body. These days, she didn't worry as much. She didn't curl her eyelashes, didn't wear lip-stick or foundation. She also pictured Charlotte this way—natural, confident. But, then again, here was Leda with her shirt lifted, touching the softness around her hips, checking whether or not to be disappointed.

Someone knocked on the door. A quote stenciled behind the toilet read: *Don't forget to fall in love with yourself first.* Love, love, love. Last night, after dropping Ian off, Leda had found somebody to love. But actually, no. She hoped that wasn't love.

In the studio, she unrolled a borrowed mat between Carly and Genie. She did a few cat-cows and breathed. She saw Ian's fingers tracing the line of her throat, stopping at the base of the neck—that tender hollow. She felt herself on her hands and knees, feeling warm ejaculate splat on her body. She sat up to extinguish the image. Her head pulsed. Outside, a bus screamed. For the eight millionth time, she wondered what Ian remembered from Halloween.

It couldn't have been like last night, could it? Yesterday, he had said, *I just don't want you to think that that was me.* Clearly, he remembered something. Something that didn't reflect well on him, necessarily.

The instructor entered—one of two men in the room. The class sang *om*, the sound of the universe, supposedly. Why? She didn't know. Perhaps there was scientific evidence that all sounds combined would create *om*, just as all the colors of the light spectrum combined created white, just as the average color of the universe turned out to be beige (which Leda had found disappointing). But what about *om*'s pitch? Wouldn't it be suspiciously lucky if the universe's song fell within the human ear's range?

The instructor said, "If you would like to dedicate your practice . . ."

It was possible that he mentioned Charlotte. Last night, those orange-vested search parties had also invaded her sleep. Now, she tried not to listen too carefully.

The class performed sun salutations. Then: peace fingers around the big toes, lengthen, look up, and fold. Leda tried not to think about the instructor prowling the room with his defined pecs and white-dude dreads. She tried not to think of the covered-up poster in the lobby: MISSING. From chair pose, she lodged her left elbow on the outside of her right thigh and twisted toward the ceiling. She listened to her knotted breathing.

Then there was a hand at the small of her back, and her headache melted. She tried to keep her breathing regular, tried to keep her quads from shaking. His touch was so gentle, so convincingly loving, that her eyes welled. It was embarrassing. But, as soon as the touch had come, it receded. The instructor was off touching somebody else, saying, "Float up between your hands. Look beyond your feet."

In yoga class, *float* meant "jump." In the jump, she was supposed to feel antigravity, feel her own body's weight relieved. But Leda couldn't float from here; she had missed an instruction, maybe. She untwisted, jumped, and her feet boomed, the whole floor vibrating. Her toes clutched, not helping.

"Inhale . . ." The instructor paused. "Then let it go."

Let it go. All class, he had been saying this.

Toward the end of class, they practiced headstands. The instructor said that life was just a negotiation with gravity, and it seemed both true and ridiculous. Leda tried to kick up through gravity, though he had told them not to kick. By the end of the class, Leda was only half listening. His touch had felt so affectionate, so genuine, that she knew she couldn't trust him.

When they all lay on their backs, Leda tried to keep her hands unclenched. She tried to feel the earth press back at her with the same speed and force that she pressed down on it. Soon, a pair of hands touched her head, cradled it, hefted its weight. Leda's eyes pinched shut. She felt Ian touching her hair.

She didn't notice when the instructor's hands released her head. She thought she could still feel his fingers, when, on the other side of the room, he recited, "Light will someday split you open . . ."

Whose hands were they, then, holding her head? Her eyes fluttered at the sound of more *om*s. She was alone on the floor. The rest of the class was seated. She closed her eyes again, trying to remember what the instructor had just read.

In astronomy, her professor had said that any lump of matter bent time and space. It was like the chakra illustration in the lobby: the human body rippling the air as a pebble ripples water.

The yoga instructor's voice echoed. "If you chose to dedicate your practice . . ."

Her prof had also said that when two masses collide, they spit off waves of energy. That is, when two things crash (cars, asteroids, black holes), energy shoots off. So, did this rule also apply to people? Were there traces of energy floating in the atmosphere, produced by Charlotte's hand touching Leda's elbow? By that first forgotten kiss with Ian? Could Leda find these scraps of energy? Could they teach her anything?

Then her arms got chilly. Her feet twitched. When she opened her eyes, the studio was almost empty, and Genie with her black mermaid's hair was smiling down at her. Leda rubbed her eyes, blinked. She tried smiling. Her headache was gone, at least. And now she had her friends around her, pinching her cheeks, teasing her for falling asleep.

In the lobby, Genie bought a sheet of silver temporary tattoos. She used water from the bathroom sink to press a fern onto Leda's temple and stars under Carly's ear. For herself, Genie chose a peacock feather. They appraised their new markings, looking past the nonsense quote on the bathroom mirror. Leda's friends, even after an hour of sweating, looked amazing. Their hair had stayed neat; their faces were not red or splotchy. They, unlike Leda, did not stink. *These tranquil bitches*, she thought. They even smelled enlightened.

Carly drove them to a hippie grocery store that served smoothies, talking in the car about ways to enhance her scream. Already, she had gotten a lot of publicity. The student newspaper had written a piece. She'd posted a YouTube tutorial called "How to Scream," arguing that a well-calibrated scream was as good as any other self-defense technique. She had however many thousands of followers on Twitter, where she was promising Flash Screams, in which she would show up in random, organized locations at random, organized times, and scream. The local news, after only two days, called it a movement.

"What if we did the whole thing naked? Wouldn't that be neat?" Carly accelerated through a yellow light. "Or maybe I could wear *just enough* to not get arrested. Like a bikini." She swerved around a guy on a bike, rubbernecking.

Leda said, "It wasn't Benjamin."

"Where *is* Benjamin?" Genie asked. "Why have I not officially met him?"

"He's wherever. He's a dream, and he's totally hooked on me. We're exclusive now, officially; it's no worries."

"When's he gonna take you to England?" asked Genie.

"Oh my god, he said right before the lavender harvest. Whenever that is." Carly blew a stop sign and pulled into the lot. "All I want is to hear him say my name. That's it."

"Cah-ly," Genie mocked. "CAH-ly!"

From the backseat, Leda studied Carly's face. She seemed pretty nonchalant about the whole thing. She wasn't freaking out, wasn't second-guessing. Leda could probably just ask Carly what was normal to feel in situations like these. Instead, she changed the subject. "So, what would a naked protest have to do with Charlotte?"

"Well, it only works if Charlotte was abducted or raped." Carly parked, and they got out. "The idea would be that just *being* a woman with a voice and a body is inherently unsafe."

"You could get guys, too," Genie said. "Naked dudes."

"No." Carly pulled up her spandex. "Ew."

"But it would level the playing field. Make everyone vulnerable." Genie skipped between parked cars toward the grocery. "Anywhere a guy looks, he gets to see breasts. Even if they're not naked, he sees their shape and, like, fullness."

"So?"

"If you cover your nipple, then you can show any amount of boob. Cleavage, string bikinis, sports bras—all cool. Chick's jogging; shit's bouncing. Right? Guys get to see boobs."

"So what?" Carly pressed.

"Imagine a world in which we saw as much penis as boobs." Genie led the way through the automatic doors of the grocery. It smelled like coriander and curry. "Now we're talking revolution. Penis on the big screen. Penis on the news. That's where you would come in, Carly. The scream wouldn't just be a bunch of vaginas and boobs."

They passed an ashen man in one of the aisles, loading his basket with dehydrated soup.

"I hate that word." Carly said *excuse me* to the man, and then continued. "'Boob.'"

"I want to go to the IMAX and see penis," Genie mused. She stopped in front of the smoothie counter and looked at the menu. "Maybe it wouldn't effect social change immediately, but I'm just saying that when a guy turns on a movie, he gets to see titties. I imagine it's incredibly relaxing."

A guy in a green apron stood on the other side of the counter, not knowing exactly how to intrude. Leda ordered blueberry something. Carly and Genie got exotic-sounding things—flax oil, turmeric, protein. The smoothie guy didn't even shrug, as if it were part of his job to let people order weird shit without being judged. He was cute, even in that green, too-small apron. He wasn't ropy like so many hippie guys. He looked like he ate meat. Leda wasn't into thin guys, really. When Ian had kissed her on Halloween (for the first time, she could almost recall the feeling), she had liked his grip on her arms, the force of his body. Now, recalling this (the feeling of his skin on her skin) made her heart jerk, as if she had just been dead for an instant.

The blenders whined and jolted. On the inside of the smoothie case, holding nut butters and frozen fruit, was another MISSING poster. Carly and Genie chatted inaudibly at the end of the milk and cereal aisle, only an arm's length away. Their silver tattoos winked. Leda took a step toward them, about to speak, when suddenly they were catching her, as if she'd fainted.

She *had* fainted, actually. They made her sit down on the tile, and Leda sat blinking up at a line of cereal boxes: gorillas on vines, koalas holding spoons, and bags of panda granola repeating the word, in all caps, BEAR, BEAR, BEAR.

"I'm fine," she said eventually, finding her feet. The blenders were still going. "Actually, can I tell you guys something?"

Her friends nodded excitedly, shuffling Leda farther down the cereal aisle, where it was quiet. Carly produced a bottle of water and made her drink, asking, "What is it, Lee?"

"I think . . ." Leda sipped the water. She decided not to mention last night. "I think I had sex with Ian."

Her friends hesitated. Exchanged a look.

"Leda, you *think*?" Carly laughed then, loud, and tweaked Leda's cheek. "You are so cute. *I* could have told you that."

"Everybody knows," Genie said. "We *love* Ian. We one hundred percent approve."

"But . . ." Leda kneaded her hands. "How did you know?"

"*Lee.* He was all over you at Moonie's." Genie dragged her black hair over one shoulder. "It was sort of obvi."

"Ian is a fox," Carly added unhelpfully.

Genie started braiding a strand of her hair. "He's on the swim team, isn't he?"

"But the problem is . . ." Heat stood in Leda's eyes. How could they be so nonchalant about this? "Is I don't remember it. I'm not really sure what we did."

The boy in the green apron called out their smoothies.

"Well, whatever you did, it worked." Carly drifted toward the juice counter. "I heard he came to the house last night, like a lost puppy."

"He what?"

"Yup." Carly beamed. She seemed to have taken Leda's budding panic for excitement. Though maybe—Leda had to admit—there was some of that mixed in. "I think some younger girls turned him away," Carly continued. "It was like three in the morning. He'll be back, though; I have a feeling."

"Blackouts can be so not fun," Genie said sympathetically, retrieving her smoothie and slurping. "But look at you. At least you didn't end up like you-know-who."

The phrase echoed in Leda's mind as they headed for the exit. *At least you didn't end up like you-know-who.* She guessed this was true. She was here, buying post-yoga smoothies with friends. She was fine. But something told her that what had happened on Halloween wasn't over. Charlotte was not dead, but missing. And Leda couldn't just ignore the signals her body had been sending—the chill that had followed Ian's thumb as it traced her bare throat, the paralysis of that kiss before chorus.

But maybe that was just the thrill of . . . what? Infatuation? Love? Carly and Genie didn't seem worried. And maybe the fact that he hadn't kissed her yesterday, hadn't invited her in, meant that he wanted to be serious. She should be happy, shouldn't she?

Just inside the automatic doors, a voice shouted after them. It was Charlotte's housemate Flora, wearing a green apron. She came at Leda, seized her shoulders, and hugged her. Her pink hair was in pigtails, her face caked with even more glitter than when they had met on Monday. Without looking, Leda could practically feel Carly's and Genie's eyebrows lifting.

"Hi, Flora," Leda managed. "You work here?"

"I thought you knew!" Flora released her. Was it possible that Flora bear-hugged every vague acquaintance? "I saw you when you came in, and I realized I never even asked your name."

Leda told her. Then, for lack of anything else to say, she asked, "Have you heard anything about Charlotte?"

"Oh, we've had police in and out, asking questions. Our housemate Angel talked to them—he was so nervous! They took some things from her room. Her parents came . . ." Her eyes went glassy. "You know, all I can do is try to love her every day and hope that she feels it, wherever she is. Have you?"

"Have I . . . ?"

"Have you heard any news of Charlotte? Any clues?"

"Oh—" *Clues?* Who did she think Leda was? "I haven't really been looking into it."

Behind her, Genie and Carly were pretending not to listen. But whatever. It wasn't like Leda was hiding anything. She had met Flora accidentally, delivering those ugly roses. She wasn't snooping around with a magnifying glass, wasn't compiling evidence. Although, if Ian hadn't been with her yesterday, she might have talked to those men and women in the orange vests. And then there were those postcards in Flora's front hallway. If she were Flora, she would have read those a long time ago.

"My one friend," Flora was saying, "thinks that Charlotte took off in a dissociative state. You know, where you're conscious and functioning, but you don't remember your identity?" Flora's voice sounded calm, but her eyes darted.

"You mean she was drunk?" Genie cut in, sucking her smoothie straw. "*My* friend said *she* saw Charlotte stumbling around Gamma Kap. She was obviously wasted."

"Valid." Carly shrugged.

"Maybe." Flora nodded. "But to me, that's like saying it was Charlotte's fault. And anyway, Charlotte just wasn't like that. We were like sisters. She was so together. She was an *artist*, with this infinite capacity for other people's stories and suffering . . ."

This would get out of hand, Leda knew, if she let it continue. "Of course it wasn't," she interrupted. All three girls looked confused. "Of course it wasn't Charlotte's fault," Leda clarified. "Was it?"

Flora's eyes had gone huge. But Leda headed this one off. She made an excuse—class or something—and peeled her smoothie-slurping sisters away from this weepy, glittering girl. Leda was beginning to feel light-headed again, but it helped to go outside—the sound of milk crates stacking, a yeasty smell from the nearby bakery. Behind her, the automatic doors seized shut.

"Who *was* that?" Genie and Carly spoke simultaneously.

Leda gave a vague explanation to satisfy her friends, concluding, simply, "Flora's totally bizarre."

The sun rippled behind a cloud and then came back out. Leda blocked her eyes. *Light will someday split you open*, the yoga instructor had read. It sounded ecstatic, joyous. But it also sounded like a mess. Once you're split, what next? Do you put yourself together, or stay broken?

At least, Genie had said, *you didn't end up like you-know-who*. Meaning Charlotte. If Leda *were* to split, she thought, perhaps she would be more like Charlotte—dissociative, boundaryless. It sounded freeing, didn't it? But it also sounded dangerous.

On the drive back to campus, Leda found herself stuck on something Flora had said. The police and Charlotte's parents had come to collect some of Charlotte's belongings. Of course, there wasn't anything odd about this. Flora had probably told them every-thing she knew. She'd probably shown them the postcards and the SLR with (maybe) Leda's picture stored on the memory card.

Now that the photograph was beyond Leda's reach, she couldn't help but think that seeing it might have shown her something im-portant. Had Charlotte seen something in Leda that Leda herself couldn't? *You look familiar*, Charlotte had said. Would Leda have said even that much when, knee-deep in foam, she'd mistaken her reflec-tion for another red-haired student?

They passed the flower shop where Leda had bought Charlotte's roses. They passed the Baptist church and stopped at a red. If Carly were to take a left, they'd be headed toward Charlotte's. Leda looked down the hill, spotting that same Barbie car, making circles now in the middle of the road.

On a whim, she interrupted Carly and Genie, who were still brainstorming ideas for how to spread "world penis." She opened the car door, saying, "I'm gonna hop out here, actually. I forgot that I have to do this thing."

"Lee!" Carly turned in her seat, shocked. "What *thing*?"

But Leda was already blowing air-kisses as she slipped out onto the sidewalk, and the light had already turned green.

It didn't hurt to look, Leda thought, watching Carly speed away down West Main Street. Flora was at work, she knew. What did Leda have to lose? It was just that same vague impulse she had had on Monday—to walk by, to look. She crossed the street, the train tracks, approaching the dirty, Barbie-pink machine. A girl with purple hair bobbles drove it in tight, careful circles. Leda smiled at her, but the girl didn't return the look.

Deeper into the neighborhood, the same shirtless man sat on the same curb. Ahead of her, the university hospital towers winked red against the normal blue day. She wondered briefly if Carly and Genie had dedicated their yoga practices to Charlotte, as the instructor had suggested. Not that it mattered. Who cared if Leda hadn't dedicated her practice? Though it felt a little like not visiting her mother's grave; her refusal meant something.

A group of men on a porch watched her walk past them. She could sense their gaze without looking directly. She frowned the sun from her eyes, trying not to look lost. Behind her, she heard a high whir. She glanced back. The Barbie car was following her.

It was cute at first. But soon the pink car, about the size of an ottoman, followed Leda at only a few feet, its plastic wheels clacking. Leda tried to ignore it. She could see Charlotte's house now. The yellow roses on the porch had browned, but now there were candles and other fresher flowers. When she reached it, Leda didn't even stop in front of the house. She went straight down the walk, as if she lived there. She could hear the Barbie car halt in the street behind her. Leda glanced back at the girl, who returned her gaze, unsmiling. Then Leda climbed the porch steps. Without knocking, she took the doorknob, hoping that Flora had been telling the truth when she'd said they never locked it. She turned her wrist. The door opened, and she went in.

No one answered when she called hello. This was too much, she thought—trespassing, snooping around what might be considered a crime scene. Though Flora herself had told her that the house was always open. A community house, she'd called it. But what did that mean? Let anyone in, no matter what had happened? No matter what could *still* occur?

Really, Leda suspected the unlocked door had more to do with Charlotte. *If Charlotte comes home,* Flora had said, *I want the door to be open.*

Behind her, through the clouded glass of the shut front door, Leda could still see the little pink car. She would stay until the girl left, she decided. She would just show herself around the house. No biggie.

The stairs groaned as she climbed one at a time, pausing on each step.

"Hello?"

On the landing, she tried the first door she came to. The room was small, but it had nice windows. The bed was neat. Its frame looked to be made of pallets. Was this Charlotte's room?

The floor was mostly empty, aside from books. A nice ink pen sat on a side table next to what looked like an animal horn. Some clothes lay on the floor near the closet. Leda almost moved on to the next room; this one felt too lived in to be Charlotte's. But before shutting the door, she glimpsed a few white feathers on the windowsill, and she crossed the room. They glittered artificially, too soft to be real. They might have fallen loose from Charlotte's swan costume.

But no postcards up here. No camera. Leda opened the closet using her sleeve, only mildly aware of things like fingerprints and evidence. Most of the clothes were monochromatic—white, gray, and blue—save for something large and purplish zipped in plastic. It seemed like a prom dress, Leda thought, feeling the imitation silk through the plastic.

Aside from the feathers, there was nothing of interest—no notebooks, schoolbooks, journals. All of Charlotte's belongings must have been combed through.

Back downstairs, Leda could still see the pink Barbie car stopped in the road. She hovered in the entry, waiting for the toy car to drive on. On the hall table, the little woolen goat was still toppled over. Leda turned it upright. She remembered how Flora kept glancing over here—at either the camera or the postcards. Or perhaps she'd been looking at the closet under the stairs, on the other side of the table. Leda opened the narrow door, pushing aside skis and overcoats. The house creaked, and Leda listened for a minute before continuing her dig. There was a tote bag in the back of the closet. The camera and the postcards, rubber-banded together, were the only things inside it.

The camera's memory card was full of flushed cheeks, empty bottles of Mad Dog, and Natty Light shotguns. They were all dated October 31. Most were close-ups, magnifying pores and sweat and chipped teeth. People's eyes crossed or sagged shut. One girl shouted into another girl's ear. One male torso dangled a cigar from his fingers, an erection pressing his khakis. Leda clicked through—two scraped, feminine knees; a girl inspecting an open lipstick tube; masculine fingers releasing a Ping-Pong ball into the air with a jump shot's precision.

There were no selfies. No group photos. There were a few dark pictures, though—ones where the flash hadn't gone off, she supposed. She squinted at these, wondering if she could be hidden somewhere in the tiny black screen.

Eventually, she put the camera back in the tote, and the tote back in the closet. The postcards, however, she slipped into her big North Face pocket, reading only the card on the bottom of the stack—the first one that had been sent, Leda guessed.

> *Dear Charlotte, I arrived safely. It was a long drive—three hours into the mountains. Now, after only one day, I feel awkward around myself. It's as if I'm standing beside someone who hasn't been introduced to me yet. I don't know what to say to make my own introduction. "Hi, I'm . . ."*
> *Who? What? Going away sometimes feels like meeting a new person. Love, Pia*

The most recent postcard, of course, was not there. It was on Leda's desk. It seemed that no other card had been written since.

Before leaving, she passed through the living room, then the kitchen with its communal farm table and old, paned windows. White sheepskins cushioned the farm table's benches. Then she glimpsed movement in the windows and shrunk from the room. There was a man in the backyard, standing beside a yellow tent. He stood at an angle, facing away from her. He was bearded, wearing only yellow Crocs and boxers. A community house. Anyone who wanted could come pitch a tent. The man raised his hands in a sort of sun salutation. Then he pissed in a fire pit.

Leda zipped her coat and slipped out. In the front of the house, the girl with the hair beads was still there, glowering from her vehicle.

What? Leda wanted to shout at her. *What?*

But the girl seemed to look past her, focusing on something (someone?) just behind her. Leda looked back. There was movement in Charlotte's blue house—a flicker in the front door's glass. Quickly, Leda crossed the porch into the sun, resisting the urge to run.

6

T he problem with *Hafez*"—Naadia said, pronouncing the name differently from the yoga teacher yesterday—"is that the most popular English 'translation' is dog shit."

Naadia was leaning in the open bathroom door while Leda got ready at the sink. Apparently, Carly had written out a Hafiz quote on the whiteboard downstairs, and Naadia needed to complain about it. Leda scrubbed at her silver temporary tattoo, listening. It was Saturday, and because she had not heard from Ian, she was planning on going to the library to distract herself with actual homework and actual essays.

Leda dragged her nails along her cheek, the silver flaking. "I think Carly got it from yoga yesterday," she said. "The quote was something like, *Light will split you open . . .*"

"I don't even want to know. Hafez was a Persian Sufi. He didn't even do yoga."

Leda was tempted to confess that the poem had stuck with her, too, even if it wasn't authentic, even if she didn't fully understand it.

But Naadia was still going. "The problem is that Americans don't travel," she was saying, tapping her impeccably white sneakers. "They don't have a *global* perspective. Most of them don't even have passports. Their world has no context; it's all small potatoes."

Leda made noises of agreement, even though she herself had never left the country. She couldn't just expand her life on command; for one thing, she didn't have the money. For now, she was contained in this one life, one body.

Naadia followed her onto the porch, ranting while Leda brushed her teeth. To be honest, Leda was only half listening. After her encounter with Indoor Sunglasses (and, more obviously, Ian), she'd hoped she would get her period today. It had been, she estimated, about thirty days. But no such luck. She tried not to worry about it. This and other dramas inside the Psi Delta sorority were small potatoes, Leda supposed, compared to, well . . . the sky. The galaxy.

And what about Charlotte's disappearance, she wondered now. Was that also small potatoes?

A plane sliced the sky just over the Psi Delta roofline. Leda resisted the urge to wave, as she did to hot-air balloons and the conductors of trains—quaint habits leftover from childhood. Of course, no one was looking. And even if they were looking, Leda was too small to see.

She spit toothpaste over the railing, into the weeds below. Back in her room, it took a minute to find all her textbooks. She put on her coat, its pocket heavy. She hadn't taken out the postcards yet. Of course, she hadn't forgotten about them. She'd just been spooked by the impulse to steal these personal, potentially important documents that may or may not reveal something about Charlotte.

Now, she glanced back at Naadia, vaping on the porch, gazing into her phone. Leda took the rubber band off the postcards. There were maybe twenty of them. The fronts showed normal Appalachian scenes. They were all from the same person, and they were all addressed to Charlotte.

Dear Charlotte, Today I heard voices when I was in the old
vegetable beds—everything grown up, gone to seed, cottony.
I couldn't see who was talking. I thought they were talking
about me, and for a long time I stood in the elder weeds,
listening, though I couldn't understand anything. While I was
listening, a rabbit came to look at me, and then walked off. It
seemed unimpressed. Snapped me out of it. Love, Pia

The earliest cards were dated back to the first week in October. One of these described the markings of a bird Pia had seen. These, too, were small, Leda saw. Naadia would probably roll her eyes at the thought of reading such inconsequential musings, much less going out of one's way to steal the things. True, they offered no global perspective, no centuries-old philosophies. But, after reading the first few, Leda couldn't help but think that they, in their own way, opened a window onto a discrete and yet expansive world. A world that happened to include a now-missing girl.

Dear Charlotte, That feeling of newness I described the other
day has gone away already. There's that saying—wherever
you go, there you are. Only now do I realize it's true.
Somehow I had thought I could get around it. It's infuriating.
Love, Pia

Wherever you go, there you are. This seemed to be the opposite of what Naadia had just been saying, and the opposite of the postcard Leda had read yesterday: *Going away sometimes feels like meeting a new person.* Only three postcards in, and Leda was already confused.

. . .

The library's front lobby had a train station feel, clattering with coming and going. From there, you could reach the building's wings, all of which were immediately silent and, for Leda, inevitably sleepy. She usually chose the front hall for studying. Today, however, all the tables were full and the big armchairs taken. More students than usual concentrated around the TVs. Two of the screens shuffled through pictures of Charlotte: Charlotte in front of the Rotunda in feather earrings, Charlotte holding a duck, and then Charlotte posed beside a chair before a hazy lavender screen. A scrap of security footage enlarged over these three, showing a distorted figure in white. This, too, was supposed to be Charlotte.

A description of her costume appeared in bullets: dress, necklace, boa, ring. According to the text running along the bottom of the screen, Charlotte's parents had offered a reward, and the police department had matched it. Charlotte's parents had issued a statement, and as they appeared on camera, words crawled across the bottom of the screen: TIMELINE RELEASED.

It was Saturday, November 7. A week had passed since Charlotte went missing. For a moment, Leda paused in the lobby, watching her classmates watch the screens where Charlotte's father spoke between two flags under a low ceiling. He wore a wrinkled shirt. Leda read the closed captioning:

WE ARE HERE BEGGING FOR HELP FROM ANYONE WHO KNOWS WE WANNA TALK TO ANYONE WHO KNOWS WE WANNA TALK WE WE WANT TO TALK ABOUT HIS OR HER INTERACTION WITH OUR DAUGHTER.

The captions were incoherent—reproduced by a machine trying to understand human speech. Leda moved away from the TVs as Charlotte's father covered his eyes, his shoulders collapsing. She took out her phone and tapped the screen. She'd been trying not to check it since it had last vibrated, dreading the moment in which she'd see that the text was not from Ian. But, in some strange twist of the universe, it was him.

Would you like to have dinner tonight?

Her first thought surprised her: *No.* If he had said, *Come over* or *Let's go to such-and-such party*, she might have reacted differently. But there was just something about the *would you*, with the capital *W*. There was something about dinner. It was so formal, so serious. It meant that he liked her. It meant that he wanted their relationship to be more than blacked-out sex. Or whatever.

She decided she wouldn't respond yet. She would think about it.

Just as she started to put her phone away, Mary texted: I am being sexually harassed by a librarian.

Leda tried not to laugh out loud. She typed, Explain?

Keeping her phone in hand, she headed to a quieter wing of the library, where she logged in to one of the school computers and searched for the Charlotte Mask timeline. Meanwhile, Mary explained that a guy from the library desk (whom Mary had given her number to call when some seventeenth-century lit anthology came in) was now pelting her with gross-romantic texts.

Leda texted, I am at library now!

YOU? Plz.

Leda stepped back into the lobby to glance at the guy behind the circulation desk. Walking back to her stuff, she wrote, Hipster glasses? Too-vertical hair?

omg yes! Thinks "I need a copy of paradise lost" means "sext me"

Girl, Leda typed, you ain't THAT fallen.

She didn't mention her Ian dilemma. She continued to ignore his text for the moment, sitting back at the computer and scrolling through Charlotte's timeline instead. She had been planning to print some short stories for Chilean Lit, but now there was little chance she'd get even that much done.

The timeline started at 8:00 p.m., when Charlotte was seen at the Cathouse pregame. She left the Cathouse around eleven (some hours after Leda). At 11:20 p.m. she was seen on surveillance video at an ATM, where she withdrew two hundred dollars. Then a campus safety call box saw her, scanning and time-stamping, not knowing the difference between one girl and the next. It gave the address, and Leda recognized it: the blue light Leda had seen outside the bubble party. It was strange to think that there might be images of Leda, too, stored in its memory. Leda with friends. Leda with Ian, standing between tikis, Leda with (was it possible?) Charlotte.

Then the timeline incorporated the neighbor's and Angel Carter's new testimonies. As of now, no one had seen Charlotte since she'd walked into her house.

At the end of the article, there were more headlines, more links: VANISHED. 22-YR-OLD CO-ED VANISHES AFTER COLLEGE PARTY. CHARLOTTE MASK VANISHES. HOW SAFE ARE OUR UNIVERSITIES? HOW *CHARLOTTE MASK* COULD HAVE BEEN PREVENTED.

This last opinion piece recommended that women not go out after midnight, that they carry UV-staining Mace, and that they choose their outfits with "particular care." Reading this, Leda kicked the wheels of her chair. A group in an adjacent study cubicle startled and looked at her. The two girls in the group wore matching Scream shirts.

Leda searched for the surveillance videos, but they hadn't been released. The group next to her continued their conversation in a loud whisper.

"I mean, how many times do I have to ask for consent?" a guy in a baseball cap said. "I'm looking for a number. Is it two times? Or is it ten?"

"Feelings can change," a girl said. "You've got to keep checking in."

"But, I'm saying . . ." The guy agitated his cap. "Is it two times or ten?"

"I would say," the girl in the cubicle responded, "you should ask as many times as you need to make your intentions clear, and to ensure that those intentions line up with your partner's."

Leda scrolled through banal particulars, detailing Charlotte's day. Charlotte had gone to the library, then the Lawn to watch the trick-or-treaters. Leda's day, on paper, might have looked pretty similar. Although she had not gone to Bank of America, she'd run past it. It was across the street from the anthropology building with the limestone grotesques—the tapir, the walrus, and the fanged beast.

Then, somehow, Charlotte's car ended up parked along Reservoir Road. Somehow, she'd ended up within a few miles of Leda's childhood home.

Leda sat back in her chair.

The whisper of the guy in the study cubicle got louder. He turned his hat in his hands. "So I should say, like, 'I'm kissing you, but that's because I want to have sex, too. Like, not now, but soon. Is that cool with you?' But shouldn't that be implied? The sex?"

"Nothing should be implied," one of the Scream shirts said. "Everything needs to be explicit."

"Oh, shit. All right. Explicit. I can do explicit."

On the computer, Leda closed the timeline. She poked her phone, opened Ian's text, and then closed it again. Was it unfair that Leda was not being explicit with Ian? She was letting him hang; she was not saying what she was thinking, not saying, *I like you. I want to have dinner with you. But I also can't stop wondering what happened on Halloween. I can't help but feel afraid of you.*

"It goes without saying," one of the girls in the neighboring cubicle said, "that an unconscious or otherwise impaired person cannot give consent."

"At some parties," a different guy chimed in, "it can be hard to tell who is and isn't conscious."

Leda opened Facebook, only half listening to the adjacent conversation as she scrolled through pictures and messages posted on Charlotte's account. Some of them addressed Charlotte as if she might respond, as if acting normal might trick God, the universe, or whoever was in charge.

There was also information about how to volunteer, posted by a girl named Monica Suárez. Leda recognized the name, but it took a minute to place her. She had gone to Leda's high school, a year ahead of Leda. Now, she was organizing parties to search the National Forest. On a whim, Leda sent her a message.

After Facebook, Leda opened Google Earth. She found her house. She found Reservoir Road, the National Forest. She found the river that feeds the reservoir. With her cursor, she followed it to the headwaters as she had done once in ninth grade, hiking for hours after a fight with her mother. She'd seen a man who had just caught a fish. He had called Leda over, and she, trusting him, had soaked her Chuck Taylors wading over to him. The trout had been the size of a pocketknife: dappled purple and flushed bloodred on its belly and fins.

Leda scrolled and zoomed in. She half expected to see her own twig-sized silhouette still out there: that blur there, that flaw in the image. Leda in the sycamore. Leda in the clearing where hunters baited deer. Leda at the apple barn. Leda in the Bear Grass picnic area. There was the camper and the two tents—one pink, one red.

"And then," the guy in the ball cap kept going, "what if she *says* yes, but doesn't mean it?"

Where, in all of this, was Charlotte? If she zoomed to the top of Bear Grass Mountain and followed the Appalachian Trail, would she find something? If this was what she wanted, she could join one of the search parties that left from the basketball stadium every morning. Or would finding something—going into the woods and stumbling against a bump in the leaves—be too scary? Was there altogether something else that she hoped to encounter?

A shadow crossed the glass of Leda's computer screen. Someone was standing behind her. Leda turned around, heart vaulting. She almost said Ian's name, but it wasn't him. It was just some impatient chick.

"Are you done?" The girl nodded at the computer.

"Yeah." Leda logged off. "Sorry." Now, she could see the girl in the screen clearly.

The girl pointed. "Your lip is bleeding."

"What?" The tip of Leda's finger came away red. "Fuck."

In the bathroom, she dabbed her lip with wet paper towel. It didn't take much to stop it. What could have happened, she asked herself again, to create such a persistent wound? If she asked Ian, would she have to ask about the rest of the night, too? *Hey Ian, did we use a condom last week?* Or, *Hey Ian, I still haven't gotten my period, in case you were wondering.*

As soon as Leda left the library, Mary called. She said she was studying at Sweetie's Cupcakery. Leda knew what this meant— "studying." You didn't invite another person to come study if you actually wanted to learn something.

. . .

For an hour, Mary and Leda made a show of flipping through their textbooks on the Cupcakery patio. Sweetie's served beer now, and by hour two, wet glass rings had started to appear on the pages of Leda's astronomy book. Her feet were propped on the patio table, her eyes trained out above Wild Wings, where the sun was already beginning to sink. Mary, who always wore layers, had given Leda her fleece, and Leda was cozy, cradling the last few inches of her second IPA.

Mary nibbled a caramel stout cupcake and stuck mini Post-its throughout *Paradise Lost*. She had acquired the seventeenth-century lit anthology through alternate means and was still resisting the urge to write the librarian a long, lecture-y text re: sexual harassment. Mary showed Leda a couple of his "inappropriate" texts, but they weren't as horrendous as Mary had made them out to be. Still, Leda drank her beer and nibbled Mary's cupcake, listening. Her pencil had fallen onto the patio brick a long time ago, and she still hadn't retrieved it.

Eventually, Mary got up for coffee. Across the patio, a girl in a tube top played cornhole with a guy in American flag shorts. Leda watched the game. The girl looked cold. Leda could see her nipples poking at the sky-blue tube. Maybe this was intentional; her cornhole partner didn't appear prone to subtlety, judging from his shorts.

Mary came back with an elaborate heart poured in her decaf latte. "Now is my barista harassing me?"

"Uh-oh." Leda inspected the design. "Call the police."

"Oh, I forgot that you *like* being harassed, don't you, Lee?"

Leda shrugged, watching the cornhole couple miss each other's holes. "Your librarian was just clueless. What if he's just bad at flirting?"

"You call this flirtation?" Mary pointed her cell phone screen at Leda—a swarm of desperate, unanswered texts.

"Okay, he's *really* bad at it," Leda said. "Just tell me this. Tell me where the line is between flirtation and harassment."

"Easy." Mary dipped her pinkie in the latte foam before sipping. "Wanted and unwanted."

The tube top girl pelted beanbags at her partner's shins.

"So, is the idea that a person should check in?" Leda said. "Like, 'Is this okay? Do you *want* me to be flirting with you?' And then the flirtee checks back with the flirter—'Yes, it's fine, but do you want *me* to be flirting with *you*?' And then they should review their short- and long-term goals . . ."

"Consensual flirtation. Sure."

"So, the barista should have asked if it was okay to pour a heart into your drink."

"Yeah . . . but even him asking might have felt like flirting," Mary admitted.

Leda mashed a mini fork into cupcake icing. "Maybe instead of asking, we should all just pay attention."

"In a perfect world." Mary nodded, though she didn't seem fully convinced.

Anyway, who was Leda to be waxing philosophic re: wanted and unwanted flirtation and then (it naturally followed) sex? *It goes without saying*, one of the girls at the library had said, *that an unconscious or otherwise impaired person cannot give consent.*

The tube top girl stopped attacking her partner with beanbags. She got another bag in his hole. She did a victory dance.

"Ian asked me to dinner tonight," Leda said, watching them.

"Ah. Is this some new 'fuck first, woo later' policy?" Mary batted her blue-glitter eyelids. "Okay, sorry. *How romantic.* Is that what you want me to say?"

"I don't want you to say anything. I'm not there now, so I'm not doing it, obviously."

"Don't get pissed, Lee. Why'd you say no?"

"I didn't say anything. I just—I don't know." Leda pinched the bridge of her nose. For a breath, she considered telling Mary. She considered telling her that she had blacked out on Halloween. That she couldn't remember having sex with Ian, though everyone else seemed to take it for granted. That she had also slept with a random guy who looked like Ian, because she had been lonely, or because she had been trying to jog her memory. She considered telling Mary that she, Leda, might have been one of the last people to see Charlotte. But she feared that Mary would escalate things. She would want Title IX. She would want the police.

"I just have this bad feeling," Leda said finally. She thumbed her astronomy textbook. When she looked up at Mary, Mary's brow had cinched. Leda added accusingly, "Why do you look so worried?"

"I don't."

"Your eyebrows are all bunchy."

"It's just . . ." Tiny bubbles formed on the marred heart of Mary's latte. "It's just the same thing I wanted to ask you on Wednesday, when you were tabling."

"Well." Leda opened her arms, as if she had nothing to hide. "Ask me."

"Lee . . ." Mary's voice lowered. "How well do you remember Halloween?"

Although Leda didn't particularly want to answer this question, it was also a relief to be asked, finally, by a friend. By someone who would love her regardless of what she said. She tried to make herself speak, but her jaw only flexed.

"Do you remember leaving the bubble party?" Mary pressed. "Or . . . how you got home?"

Leda stared at the flaccid beanbags scattered around the patio. She managed, "No."

Mary waited. "Can you be more specific?"

Leda was relieved, yes, but she still didn't want to admit what she'd been worrying about all week. She didn't want to say that her last full memories of that night were with a now-disappeared person. She didn't want to say that she suspected Ian had known how drunk she had gotten and that (perhaps) he had taken advantage of it.

In response to Mary's question, Leda shook her head.

"Well, I started wondering about it," Mary said, "because I didn't think it was like you to leave the party without telling me." Mary's tone was surprising. She didn't seem angry or hurt. It was just . . . care. Concern. "And then you came to my door later that night. Like, really late. I was already asleep."

"I did?" Leda didn't remember this.

"Um, yeah. Are you kidding? You were sobbing, Lee." Mary glanced at the cornhole couple, who could probably hear what they were saying. "I couldn't make out anything you said. I tried to make you come inside and stay with me, but you wouldn't. You, like, dashed off. You went running."

Leda remembered Mary's cryptic text the following morning: Are you alive? And Leda's own impatient reply: Why wouldn't I be?

"I think I blacked out," Leda admitted. "Briefly."

The cornhole couple went in, looking sideways at Leda and Mary, leaving the beanbags where they had fallen.

"And then you said," Mary kept going, "that you really liked Ian or something. Remember, when I saw you before Shakespeare? So I told myself the crying must have been, like, drunk-girl drama. No offense or anything. But it still bothered me. You don't remember coming to my door? *At all*, Lee?"

"I mean . . ." Leda touched the little wound on her lip unconsciously. "I would remember if something bad had happened, I think."

"I think so . . ." Then Mary changed her mind. "I don't know."

Leda looked up toward the darkening sky, but was blinded by twinkle lights. Somehow, the sun had set. She fingered her astronomy textbook in the dim light, skimming information about planets: average distances from the sun, temperatures, densities.

Mary said, "You've got to figure it out, Lee. You were scary-weeping. And your lip was, like . . ."

Leda provided, "Bleeding."

She didn't remember weeping. She didn't remember the last time she had cried, actually. She did, however, know about the blood. She discovered it on her face and pillow when she'd woken Sunday afternoon.

For all of high school, Leda had imagined that "adulthood" meant nights like Halloween: drinking and staying out late and answering to nobody. It meant sex. It meant actions without consequences—no grounding, no go-to-your-rooms, no guilt trips. But, really, the opposite turned out to be true. Consequences got worse in adulthood. You woke up lost, alone. Bloody. You realized that a girl had gone missing.

Mary asked, "Are you *sure* you don't remember?"

Where's the line, Leda had just asked Mary, *between flirtation and harassment?* So then, she wondered now, where was the line between sex and rape? She tried to extinguish the thought as soon as it came.

She said, "I remember leaving the party with Ian."

Mary reached for Leda's hand. In the astronomy book, Leda saw that Saturn's average temp was −288 degrees Fahrenheit. She read that Jupiter had at least sixty-three moons, four of which were large enough to be considered planets, though they did not orbit the sun. She kept reading, filling her head with words, any words but the ones that immediately concerned her.

"I don't know what it means," Leda said, staring at the page, finally making herself speak. "I still *like* him for some reason. But my body . . . has this different reaction. It's like, even if my brain doesn't, my *body* remembers something. And then I keep thinking about Charlotte."

"Me, too," Mary said.

"How did this happen?"

Leda hadn't meant to say this out loud. Or, no, she'd wanted to say *something*, but she hadn't been sure how to put it. She'd wanted to say that the more she thought about Halloween, the more confused she became. She had blacked out, obviamente. That, in and of itself, wasn't such a big deal, usually. Case in point, Carly and Genie had treated her blackout as an occupational hazard. And little more than a week ago, Leda would have agreed. But this one, to Leda, had come to feel distinct. And it was scary to see that now somebody else—Mary—agreed.

"Leda," Mary spoke gently. "Do you want to tell somebody?"

It took Pluto, Leda read, 248 years to orbit the sun. From the surface, the sun looked like a bright star. Leda stared at the illustration of the recently demoted planet: cold, distant.

Mary nudged her. "Lee."

When Leda looked up, she found Mary's hand was still squeezing. She shook her head, squeezed back. "I think I should talk to Ian."

Mary opened her mouth, but Leda's phone interrupted, blasting its ringtone, "Dancing Queen." They both jumped in their seats. *Ian*, Leda thought immediately (she still hadn't texted him about dinner). But the screen read CLARENCE. She let it ring. Eventually, the screen faded. Then it lit up again.

Leda slipped her hand out of Mary's as she went to stand, apologizing. "It's Clarence."

A tiny scream pierced the speaker when she picked up, and she took the phone away from her ear.

"Hi, Lee! Sorry. Gino is screaming."

"Hi—"

"Sorry for calling twice. I got worried, with all that's been happening."

Clarence called about once a month, and she saw him even less, so she felt weird when he said things like this. Yes, he and her mom had dated for years. He had cleaned the gutters. He had built the garden fence. But if he really were worried, wouldn't he call more often?

Behind Clarence's voice, there were kitchen sounds: the sink, the boys, Faye's voice. The boys—Faye's from a previous marriage—were now nine (Jonah) and six (Gino). Clarence was a good dad, Leda imagined. He and her mom had fought every so often, but mostly Leda remembered him playing guitar, Dylan or the Grateful Dead or Neil Young, and she remembered dancing.

These days, his family seemed happy. They lived in a big house near the old graveyard downtown. The house had a blue door, old trees, and perennials mapped along slate walkways. The neighboring houses looked very much the same, some with raised beds, some with backyard chickens. It was an expensive part of town, though Leda supposed that the whole town was getting that way. Clarence was a contractor. Faye was a real estate agent and seemed to have plenty of money. Leda had never asked if the boys' father was living.

"Faye thought you could come over for dinner—" Then Clarence interrupted himself, talking to one of the kids. He came back. "I'm sure you have plans, but I thought I'd check. You haven't seen the boys since school started."

Leda walked to the far side of the patio, hugging Mary's fleece around her. She watched Mary flip through *Paradise Lost*, her eyebrows still cinched. She thought of Ian, waiting for a text from her. At least at Clarence's, she'd have the night to think things over. She'd have time to decide what she'd say to Ian without the risk of him showing up, unannounced, at her room.

"Okay," Leda said, surprising them both. "I'll walk over."

"Do you want me to pick you up? With everything in the news . . ."

"I'll be fine. I've got my running shoes." Honestly, it did feel a little good that Clarence was worried. If Leda were to disappear, at least one person would notice.

"Damn it." Something crashed. "Gino dropped the colander. Sorry, Lee. There are pasta wheels all over the floor. I've got to go. We'll see you over here?"

The line cut as the streetlights flicked on down West Main Street, illuminating a tall man pushing a brimming shopping cart. Leda walked back toward Mary. She braced herself for what Mary might say. About Ian. About Charlotte. About what exactly it meant to "tell somebody." Either way, Leda was an adult, she reminded herself. When she dropped a colander, she had to pick up the pasta wheels herself.

"I've got to pee," Mary said, standing up as soon as Leda was back in her chair again.

Leda wanted to say, *Wait*. But this was life, Leda guessed. Your family and friends made wobbly orbits around you before spinning off, sometimes returning, sometimes not: blinked into nothing, or spiraled into another galaxy, or broken up—the particles re-forming into some other unrecognizable body. And there you were (there Leda was) sitting in the same place with whatever remained—the empty beer glass, the wide-eyed dragon in the closet, the memories.

The tall man struggled to get his shopping cart over a little bump in the street. It took him a minute to manage it. When Mary returned, Leda said she should get going.

"Come here." Mary pulled Leda up and hugged her fiercely. Leda relaxed slightly, though Mary's silence scared her more than anything. Mary didn't have any ready solutions. She was no different from Leda; she didn't know what to do.

When Clarence married Faye, he got a haircut. Or, more accurately, a dad cut. After the dad cut, he no longer ate red meat. His wardrobe changed; he wore socks that supported your arch (supposedly), breathable polos, khakis.

Case in point: tonight, when he opened the door, Leda pointed at his feet. "Nice loafers."

Clarence hugged her. "Nice to see you, too, Lee."

Leda went to stash her backpack in the side room, but all the furniture had been removed. She tried to act normal, jokey. "Who stole your sitting room?"

"You haven't seen this?" Clarence rapped the doorjamb of the mostly empty room. "Faye can't jog with her knee, so she's turned into a yogi. Where've you been, Lee?"

"School." Leda tried to be nonchalant, even as her brain whirred. "Things."

Faye appeared, wearing patterned yoga tights and a gauzy blouse. She hugged Leda too hard, pinning her against her chunky necklace.

"The room looks great," Leda said when they parted. On the wall, a sharp Ganesha stencil offered a lotus. Beside a stack of green foam blocks, a beeswax candle proclaimed OM.

Faye threw out her arms. "It's my labor of love."

"Mom," Gino called from the kitchen.

"Mom," Jonah, the oldest, repeated.

"Speaking of labors of love—boys, come say hello."

The boys stomped in from the kitchen. Jonah held a bouquet of forks. Gino, behind him, pinched a cloth napkin between gummy fingers.

"Hi, guys." Leda put her hands on her knees. Her jaw felt stiff when she smiled. "Did you have an awesome Halloween?"

"No. Mom wouldn't let us go trick-or-treating," Jonah reported. "We dressed up, but that was it. Also, Gino wasn't allowed to be a Indian."

"Most sugar's not vegan, sweetie. Remember we talked about it?" Faye gave Jonah time to say something. He didn't.

"I ate a marshmallow!" Gino shouted and fled into the kitchen, knowing he had committed a major sin. Jonah sulked after him.

Faye rolled her eyes happily. "Kids."

Clarence modified the sentence. "Don't ever have them."

Faye placed her hands on Leda's shoulders. "Leda, I'm so glad you're *here*." Again, Faye hugged her. Sometimes she did this—she blindsided Leda with these sudden, profound moments, and Leda (tonight, in particular) had a hard time transitioning so quickly, meeting Faye's intensity with equal, wholehearted feeling.

"Thanks for inviting me," Leda managed, still hugging.

"I know I say this all the time, Leda. But if you ever need anything, just ask, okay?" Faye pulled back, holding Leda's shoulders. "We're family."

Leda nodded. Faye did say this constantly. On the one hand, it made Leda want to cry. On the other, it rang like her classmate's Spanish apologies: just a memorized phrase.

They separated. Clarence flipped off the yoga room lights, saying, "Faye just started her teacher training."

"It's mind-blowing!" Faye cried, leading them into the kitchen. Leda's cell phone shuddered in her butt pocket as she followed. She slipped it out. Ian had texted, Is that a no?

"It's become like church," Faye was saying.

Clarence agreed. "It's a wealthy community."

"Spiritual wealth, though," Faye said. "Right, honey?"

"Right as always," Clarence said, rubbing two invisible coins together when Faye wasn't looking. Leda smiled distractedly, her thumbs hovering over her phone. She typed quickly, im so sry! didn't see this. I have a family thing!

"Leda, have you been to Float?" Faye was saying. "I *love* it. Head over heels. Even Clarence is into it."

Faye turned around when Leda didn't answer, and Leda feigned sudden interest in the microwave. She pressed a button and the door popped open. Inside, a naked burrito sat on the glass plate. "Uh, yeah," she said. "Clarence, I didn't know you even did yoga."

Clarence unwrapped a package of light bulbs, humming, *Om.*

Ian texted, no worries ☺ tomorrow then?

Leda slipped the phone into her pocket without responding. Beside her, Faye flopped pasta onto white plates. Leda moved out of the way. The kitchen was big, but there still wasn't enough space. Back in front of the microwave, she distracted herself, looking at a photograph of a village nestled in big mountains. Beside this, another photo showed squat, gaudy women with gold teeth and colorful necklaces.

"Aren't those precious?" Faye reached past her for the salt and pepper. "It's the studio's sister village or . . . monastery. I can't remember which. There's an annual donation class that sponsors it. Which reminds me—did Clarence tell you? We have a houseguest."

Leda shook her head, getting stuck on that word—*precious*—and thinking of the woman in Float who didn't know whose bones she wore as a necklace. Leda's phone buzzed again, but she didn't check it. Faye didn't go on, distracted by Gino, who was making a booster seat out of yogic texts and Grateful Dead songbooks. Clarence, Leda knew, had followed the band after serving in Vietnam. When she was a teen, Leda had grilled him on motorcycles, free love, PCP, and whether people had actually worn those little hippie headband things. He had answered her honestly, and Leda, who had been used to the adult world's bullshit (again, she heard Faye's word: *precious*), had been surprised by it.

Leda took a place at the table. Clarence brought kalamatas and oven-warmed plates. Jonah smacked his hands flat and shouted, "Thank you!" Gino followed suit. Then they shook nutritional yeast onto their pasta and jabbed in, holding their forks in their fists.

"That's grace," Faye explained, laughing. "You don't have to do it, but it never hurts to thank the universe."

Small potatoes, Leda could hear Naadia say. What did the universe care whether or not Leda thanked it? Though somehow her life now (Mary's hand squeezing hers earlier; these texts from Ian trickling in) didn't feel like small potatoes.

Faye thanked the air as Clarence went to the stereo in the connected living room. There, a silent gas fireplace licked its glass with blue. It was cozy. Leda was glad to be here. But, at the same time, she could feel the world press in on the doors and windows. She could feel the walls bow in.

Faye twirled her fork. "So Leda, how's school?"

"Oh, good." But then Mary's question rose up and replaced it: *Do you want to tell somebody?* Leda said, "A little weird now with . . ."

"Yes. Unbelievable." Faye slow blinked. "I've dedicated some of my practices to her."

Leda bit a forkful of noodles. She was glad to be here, yes. But talking about Charlotte, she felt weirdly edgy, possessive.

"Prayer." Faye lifted empty hands. "It's all we can do."

Leda said dumbly, "You can still post on her Facebook wall, too."

Clarence came back to the table as a harmonium's drone filled the living room.

"To me . . ." Faye watched the blue fire across the room. "It seems implausible that a *student* could have done this. Isn't that what people are suggesting? I just can't imagine that someone who was able to get into such a competitive school would be capable of . . . I don't know. Do you? And they're so young."

"You can enlist at seventeen." Clarence swallowed his whole glass of water, glancing at the children. "And you don't need to be dumb to kill somebody."

"She's not dead," Leda said, too quickly. She tried to peel the intensity from her voice. "At least, that's what they're saying."

Seeing her face, Clarence was about to make some gesture toward her, about to say something. But then the stairs creaked in the front hallway. The boys looked up, red sauce on their faces. In unison, they shouted, "Vinnie!"

A bald monk in crimson robes stood in the arched doorway. He pressed his palms together and lifted them in front of his face. Krishna Das sang from the adjacent room, *Hare Ram, Ram, Ram . . .*

"Namaste, Vinnie!" Faye used her fork to push her pasta to one side of her plate. To Leda, she explained, "His real name is hard for the boys to pronounce. Well, honestly, it's hard for all of us."

Gino brandished his fork. "Vinnie, Vinnie, Vici!"

Vinnie went to the stove and put pasta wheels on a plate. Leda had stopped chewing. She was surprised, obvi. But, she also couldn't get her own voice out of her head: *She's not dead.*

"We're all absolutely thrilled Vinnie's here." In her lap, Faye repositioned her napkin. "That photo you were looking at? He's *from there!*"

The monk brought his dinner to the table and sat across from her, his back inhumanly straight. Slowly, Leda resumed chewing.

"Float sponsored him to come to our studio," Faye continued. "To lead a meditation retreat. We've discovered that he can't speak English, but in the end, it's all about the energy. Can't you feel it?" Faye wafted her hands toward her body.

Vinnie looked at Leda. Or, no—he looked *into* her.

Leda swallowed. "Totally."

What did he see? she wondered, as if he could mind read. Forced calm? Muted anxiety? Could he see Ian's last text, twitching around her brain? Whatever he saw, it seemed to strike him as funny. He looked as if he were about to burst out laughing.

"He's a solid dude," Clarence said. "He helps me in the yard if I need it. He sits with Faye in the yoga room. He doesn't do yoga, as far as we can tell. But that's cool."

"His journey is so beautiful." Faye pushed back her gray-blond hair, pink rising in her face. Leda couldn't always tell if her blushes meant that she was happy or nervous or angry.

Leda asked, "How long has he been here?"

"Oh gosh." Faye's eyes rolled up, her hands refolding her napkin. "Two weeks?"

"I like him," Jonah said.

"I like him, too," Gino agreed, swinging his feet.

Leda said, "So . . . you're hosting him?"

"He's really become part of the family." Clarence passed the olives, and Vinnie spooned what remained in the tub onto his plate. "It's been a really nuanced experience."

Faye nodded vigorously. "And, yes, practically speaking . . ." She straightened her fork. "We don't really know when he's leaving."

Vinnie ate, mopping up sauce with his right hand.

"The studio just doesn't have the facilities for him," Faye continued. "There's water, but there's nowhere for him to sleep. Initially he did stay in the studio for a few nights, and he seemed happy . . ."

Under the table, Leda flexed her fingers. She had been squeezing her hands together unconsciously. *Did* she want to tell somebody?

Did she want to speak that word that had lodged in her mind, though neither she nor Mary had spoken it?

Rape.

Leda touched her lip. Blinked. She had stopped eating.

"It wasn't sustainable," Clarence was saying. "We agreed to take him in. The studio's been helping with food and things. It's no trouble having him."

"He was scheduled for a few workshops. A long-weekend kind of thing. But then he just *stayed*. Which is great . . ."

"He *really* likes those frozen Amy's burritos. I gave him one, and he was just—" Clarence snapped his fingers. "Sold."

"And other than that, he just sits." Faye watched Vinnie, her mouth fallen a little bit. "The yoga studio bought us a case of those burritos, and that's it."

The gas fire licked at the glass. Wind pressed the windows. The Krishna Das CD ended. When Vinnie finished his pasta, he smiled around the table, lifted the hand that was not covered in marinara sauce to his chest, and stood. He rinsed his hands, put his plate in the dishwasher, and walked back to the stairs. At the last minute, he turned and gave Leda a funny, two-handed wave. It made her smile, actually, despite her slow, gathering worry. Vinnie went up. Faye asked the boys to take their plates.

"To tell the truth . . ." Clarence scratched his neck. "We didn't know when we started hosting Vinnie that his visit would be permanent."

Faye corrected him. "Indeterminate."

The dishwasher rattled as the boys jammed in plates. The Krishna Das album started over as the boys ran upstairs. The song twirled, the tambourine galloping. *Hare, hare Ram, Siva Ram, Siva Ram.* Faye balled her napkin.

Clarence stood and gathered the rest of the dishes. "Vinnie and the kids get along great."

"Whether he can be trusted babysitting is another thing," Faye said. "Someone comes to the door in a face mask, he'd probably make them chai or something."

Leda stood, too, drifting into the living room. "Do you mind if I change the music?"

"Plus, monks don't have a great reputation with fire safety," Faye was saying.

Clarence tried to calm her. "Sweetie . . ."

Faye's voice raised an octave. "You don't hear of anyone else self-immolating."

"He's not going to self-immolate, darling."

"I can babysit," Leda called, standing on tiptoes and fiddling with the stereo on its high, built-in shelf. She did something that made the speakers buzz horribly. She felt around the back of them, found the loose wiring. She flipped one speaker around, jostling a row of Buddha figurines positioned on top, wishing she had a step stool or something, and then freezing. At eye level, behind the Buddhas and the mess of wiring, she faced the nose of a gun.

Faye was saying, "You know CPR, don't you, Leda? Heimlich maneuver?"

The gun sat on a silk pouch. Without thinking, Leda reached for it. Picked it up. It was light, toylike. But seeing it in her hand made her reel. What was she doing? In the other room, Clarence offered a round of chocolate tofu mousse. In the window, his reflection approached. Leda panicked, replaced the gun, and spun the speaker back around. A Buddha wobbled. She about-faced just as Clarence rounded the corner.

"What happened to the music?"

Leda tried to sound calm. "It was making me dizzy."

"I'll change it." He ruffled her hair, as if she were a kid. "Go get some mousse."

In the kitchen, Faye handed Leda a crystal dessert cup of mousse and a tiny spoon. Leda brought the spoon to her mouth without tasting much. She told herself that she shouldn't be so shocked. Clarence was ex-military; he'd always had guns. Or maybe Leda was more surprised by her own impulse to pick the weapon up.

Clarence turned on some sort of sitar hip-hop in the other room.

Faye sat on the counter, eating tiny spoonfuls of mousse. "After what happened to that girl," she said to Leda, her voice lowered, "I get nervous harboring strangers."

"He's not a stranger," Clarence called, hearing her.

Faye ignored him. She asked, hushed, "Do you mind if I ask if you knew her?"

"I didn't really." Leda moved her spoon around the chilled tofu. "But I saw her."

"You what?"

Leda looked up. She didn't know why she had told Faye even this much. "It was only for a second. We were at the same party."

"Did you tell somebody? Did you contact the police?"

Leda looked at the floor tile. She was thinking of the gun, thinking of Ian's last text—tomorrow then? Why had she chosen now to open up?

"Leda, you have to," Faye pressed.

Leda's spoon scraped the crystal. "A million people saw her."

"But, you just never know"—Faye got down from the counter—"what information they have or don't have. You don't know what could be important. *You're* the kind of person they want to hear from, Leda."

"It's just not . . ." Leda looked at the open trash can, full of cooked pasta wheels. *It's just not that simple*, she thought. "I don't want to get involved."

Faye's face reddened—anger this time. "If you saw her, you are *already* involved."

But Leda could be angry, too. She spoke quickly, without thinking. "What does it matter to you?"

Clarence came in from the living room. "Is MC Yogi better?"

Faye looked lost for a moment, looking up at Clarence. Two long wrinkles had appeared next to her eyes. Clarence went and kissed the top of her head. She held a fist in the center of her stomach.

Leda said, brightly, "This mousse is delicious."

When she finished, Leda insisted on walking home. She needed the air, needed the silence, even as Ian still loomed in the back of her mind, even as Mary's and Faye's voices now eerily combined. *Did you tell somebody?*

Parked cars flashed red, pin-sized lights from their dashboards. They were all equipped with alarm systems, engaged even when the night was calm, even when every house in the neighborhood seemed to have every light in every room on. Somewhere, laughter murmured. Movement cast against curtains. A cat mewed, and a door opened for it. Solar lanterns illuminated paths. A jack-o'-lantern sagged, like a sick woman. There were mums on doorsteps, their colors mere variations of darkness. Leda could detect the chemical smell of them— like synthetic plant food, like a hospital room.

Leda tried to ignore the smell, tried to breathe. Her mother's room in the ICU had always smelled this way—sanitizer and store-bought flowers. When Leda had visited, she often fingered the packets of plant food, staring at the packages' pictograms. She hadn't known how much time her mom had left. She hadn't thought about it. Not one alarm bell had rung in her head, even though her mom had been eating very little then. Of the plant food, her mom had once said that she thought it was cruel to preserve flowers that were already essentially dead.

A rat crossed the road and disappeared into a garden. A motion sensor floodlight snapped on, revealing nothing. Leda's eyes flicked, landing on shadowed, innocuous yards. Like the floodlights, like the car alarms, she was vigilant. Nervous. Even if she didn't need to be, she couldn't turn it off.

In two blocks, the graveyard spilled darkness. For some reason, it looked safe in there behind the thick stone wall stretching on and on. At the first gate, she went in, surrounded now by dark boxwoods and obelisks. A car turned onto the road where Leda had been walking. Absurdly, she imagined it was Ian, looking for her, as she slipped deeper into the darkness. When it reached the cemetery, the car stopped, and Leda found herself dashing away, stumbling over uneven ground.

Only when the car moved on did she let herself slow to a walk, squeezing her waist, breathing heavily in the middle of the cemetery. Though it was chilly, she was sweating. Her eyes adjusted. She saw what had made her lose her footing. Little graves, the size and shape of Rubik's Cubes, stuck up in two- or three-inch stumps. They were everywhere, filling narrow slots between larger graves. Many more were sunken flush with the earth. The one nearest Leda was marked with a *B*. Leda stepped away from it. She tried to walk more carefully.

Voices glimmered and hushed on the other side of the cemetery. Leda listened until she was sure that none of the voices belonged to Ian. Of course it wasn't him. She was being ridiculous. When she got closer, she saw that they were just teens, huddled beside a mausoleum. They were about the age Leda was when her mom had died, their voices still fresh and untried. Everything was being done and said for the first time. A lighter flicked and illuminated a girl's heavily made-up eyes, her mouth on a pipe, and then the flame died. The girl became an outline.

You are already involved, Faye had said. She was right. Leda *had* been one of the last to see Charlotte. But . . . this was just one of those things that happened, wasn't it? Flames sparked and then faded. People lived and then didn't. Even the girl with the lighter, no more than a few yards away, had, to Leda, disappeared forever.

Something flew over Leda's head. Its body blinked into sight and evaporated. Leda caught her breath. It had been so fast, she questioned whether or not it had actually happened. The ground became a little more even. The streetlights, beginning at the far edge of the cemetery, revealed her hands when she looked at them. A girl giggled back beside the mausoleum, but the sound ended just as abruptly as it had started. Leda struggled over the wall, onto the sidewalk, and into the light.

7

On Monday, Leda's astronomy professor projected multiple-choice questions onto the screen. Leda and her classmates (which today included Ian Gray, about 1.3 parsecs away) answered on their remotes. With these, Leda could see almost instantaneously when she had gotten a question wrong, plus, a bonus: she could see what percentage of the class had not. When *everyone* got something wrong, Prof took some time to re-explain the concept. But, more often than not, Leda was in that bottom 4 percent that didn't know, for example, how planetary interiors create magnetic fields, how to calculate parallax, or how the solar system would be different if Jupiter had never existed.

It was strange to like a class in which she performed so consistently poorly. But she did like it. She liked seeing images from the Hubble Space Telescope. She liked the star labs, even though they'd interrupted many a Friday night. And though she had a hard time using the star chart (often holding the photocopy overhead, trying to wrap her head around the perspective), she liked trying to make sense of the sky's weird web. She also liked learning about observatories, about the people who studied this baloney. Usually, the places had their own extraterrestrial landscapes—Arizona, New Mexico, the very tip of Chile. She liked seeing their little offices, their lives shrunken to the size of a cot and a desk, but at the same time expanded to encompass the universe's meshed, glittering depth.

Lately, that observatory life looked more and more attractive. But Leda obviously wasn't good enough at astronomy for the cot-and-desk scenario yet. She punched *B* into her remote, guessing. That life probably wasn't so great anyway. Probably, Leda had been fooled by those romantic space movies that made you believe that your dead loved ones were just a wormhole away or were aliens trying to touch you with their clammy fingers or were caught in the strands of space-time, plucking the creaks and groans in your home to create some kind of intimate code. A code cracked only by love (if she remembered the plot correctly).

Love. Since her mom died, Leda hadn't been interested in love. Then, this morning, she'd found flowers sitting in front of her bedroom door. She'd blinked, thinking that she was still asleep, still dreaming. But there they were: flowers. Snapdragons, actually. And between the blooms, a tiny card.

For Leda. And then, on the other side: *Yours, Ian.*

She'd glanced around her, but there'd been no other Psi Delts around to explain how the flowers had gotten there. She'd rubbed her eyes, thinking, *Pinch me.* The blossoms were like tiny sunrises—yellow, orange, and pink. She'd squeezed the cheeks of one flower, and its jaws had opened.

The snapdragons had done something. They'd dissolved Leda's doubts, somehow. Before this morning, she hadn't known that these things truly happened—surprise flowers, love notes. *Love.* Was that going too far?

Maybe the snapdragons explained her performance on this morning's quiz. She was, well . . . distracted.

After the quiz, Prof kept the window shades drawn, the lights dim. He showed an illustration of the sun and the planets to scale "for some perspective." He said that if the sun were a grapefruit, the Earth would be the tip of a ballpoint pen. He said that the sun's mass outweighs that of all the planets combined by a factor of more than one thousand. In the illustration, the sun was pocked with yellow suppurations. It looked hungry. It reminded Leda of a children's book she and her mother used to read, in which Quetzalcoatl (the Aztec god), in the form of a green bird, plucked the sun from the sky and ate it like a berry. Ciao, humanity.

Leda glanced at Ian. Currently, he was looking up at the Milky Way galaxy. From the outside, it looked like a glittering purple Frisbee: the exact colors of the gown in Charlotte's closet. Leda's high school guidance counselor had owned a poster of this very image, the words YOU ARE HERE pointing down at space dust. Leda had wanted to tear the poster down every time she saw it. She hadn't cared if she was technically microscopic. She *felt* enormous.

Prof changed the image. There was the sun again, sending up a solar flare. Apparently these eruptions—not huge, Leda thought, compared to the rest of the sun's body—measurably disturbed the electromagnetic fields on Earth. Leda picked up her pencil and let the tip move on her open notebook, one quarter of her brain taking notes, one quarter seeing Quetzalcoatl with the sun in his belly, and one half thinking, *Ian.*

Focus, she told herself. *Focus.*

The Aztecs had believed (she'd learned this last semester, in a class on Mexican history) that Quetzalcoatl would return eventually. Montezuma, the last king of the Aztecs, had suspected Cortés in his Spanish armor to be this long-absent god to whom they had been sacrificing thousands of men, women, and children. Maybe, Leda thought—why not?—maybe Cortés *had* been some sort of god, come to complete the sacrifice, destroy the empire, and then fade again to formlessness, indifference. Because maybe God, like man, gets bored. Gets restless.

She glanced at the back of Ian's head. From her bag, she extracted a postcard from Pia to Charlotte—one she hadn't looked at yet. She wasn't reading them all at once. The cards were strangely overwhelming. The best she could do was read them one at a time, studying each as if it were a riddle or a puzzle piece.

Dear Charlotte, Somehow, the Earth produces life from rot.
How can I, while I live, possibly emulate this? Love, Pia

Although the message was short, Leda reread it, tilting the postcard toward the big, projected sun at the front of the lecture hall. Meanwhile, her professor explained that (according to the grapefruit scale) the ballpoint Earth would be about fifteen meters away from the grapefruit. Another projected image illustrated this. The Earth looked lost, tottering around that colossal mother that had (Prof was saying) a diameter of about 865,000 miles and an interior temperature of 27,000,000 degrees Fahrenheit. Earth's diameter, for comparison, was a little under 8,000 miles. Tiny.

Then the window shades lifted, and everyone shielded their eyes and blinked. Class was over. Sunlight wobbled through sycamores outside. *It ain't scary*, Leda thought, watching the branches swaying. She put the postcard away and closed her textbook. When she glanced up, Ian was turned around in his chair, staring straight at her. She froze. Then she got up and walked out of the lecture hall. She couldn't help thinking (pleading) as she had as a child, *Chase me*. The fear made it fun. Your brain knew that it was all just a game even while your body pounded, screaming, *Run!*

Of course, her fear had been real Saturday night with Mary. But then there had been something about finding that gun at Clarence's, picking it up, and then realizing how stupid that was. It was not Leda's safety that was in question. It was Charlotte's. Of course it was.

Not to mention that a whole quiet Sunday with no word from Ian had gotten her thinking. Thinking of him. Again, it was the law of scarcity: you take something away (even if that something scared the shit out of you yesterday), and suddenly it's the only thing you crave.

And then, needless to say, there were the snapdragons this morning.

The front doors to the building passed hand to hand as hundreds of students (Leda included) flooded out into the dappled light. For all its millions of degrees, the sun didn't feel hot, especially. She slowed, the crowd pushing around her like water around a boulder. Overhead, wood smoke wafted through sycamore branches from the Lawn's chimneys. She took out her phone, giving Ian time to catch her. She scrolled. Over a thousand volunteers had taken part in a search party on Saturday. The girl who had organized it, Monica, had already responded to Leda's Facebook message. To Leda's question—How did you know Charlotte?—she'd responded:

Are you kidding? Did anyone NOT know Charlotte?

Then she'd pasted a photo showing six girls in prom court sashes holding ice cream cones. Leda recognized Monica relatively easily, but it took her a second to locate Charlotte—her face paper white, lips red, smile immaculate. She looked completely different. The picture had been taken in front of Dice County High—a building Leda could immediately identify.

It had been obvious. Or at least it should have been. If Charlotte had grown up in Leda's county, then she and Leda had attended the same high school. Why hadn't Leda thought of this? She zoomed in on Charlotte's face, trying to place it—before college, before Leda had had sex for the first time, before her mother died.

Was this why Charlotte had recognized her Halloween night?

A text message appeared at the top of her screen, blocking Charlotte's forehead. Mary.

Did you talk to Ian?

Leda shut her phone off instinctively. She didn't know how she'd sensed him; she just turned and there he was. That half smile. That smell of chlorine and fire. She opened her mouth. What was she going to say? *Hey, I got your flowers.* Or, *Hey, did you rape me?*

But Ian spoke first—so calm, so normal. "Your parents in town?"

"What?"

"Saturday. You said you had a family thing."

"Oh, right. Sorry." She slid her phone into her pocket. "It was sort of extended family. Or . . . family friends. I was with them, and I missed your text." Leda didn't want to give any more than this. No dead mom. No Clarence.

"No worries." Ian shrugged. "Now you just owe me."

Leda touched her lip, worried it might be bleeding. "And what do I owe?"

"Another dinner, maybe."

They started walking. Leda wasn't sure if she had led or followed. She glanced at him quickly. *Did you know I had blacked out?* she could say. *Did you know I was unconscious?* But something in his face—his eyes, his lips—calmed her. He was not Indoor Sunglasses, she told herself. There was little evidence that he had been cruel to her. There had been no hints of underlying indifference. And now here he was: the boy who had left her flowers. A gentleman asking her to dinner. Maybe what happened on Halloween didn't matter. Maybe this was them, starting over.

Whatever you did, Carly had said, *it worked.*

They passed the fried dumpling truck, which gave off sour, porky heat. Leda skirted the truck for the warmth only. Semiconsciously, she touched her healing lip repeatedly.

She looked at Ian and, finally, answered him. "Okay."

"Really?"

Leda smiled a little. "You seem so surprised that I could be capable of eating a meal."

"I'm surprised that you're capable of eating a meal *with me*."

They angled between ponytailed girls using their chopsticks like spears. The sauced dumplings smelled both sweet and spoiled.

"I'd like to." Heat rose in her face, her heart skipping. *I want this*, she told herself, thinking of Mary's line between flirtation and harassment: *wanted and unwanted*. At least, she *thought* she wanted it. "Really."

"Well, okay." He was blushing, too. "Great."

He didn't touch her when they parted. *He's a gentleman*, Leda thought again, watching him go. *He's a fox*, Carly would have added.

But then there was Mary's text: Did you talk to Ian?

"Hey," she called after him.

He turned, students coursing around him.

"Thanks for the flowers," she said.

One half of his face dimpled. He lifted a hand. *Yours, Ian.*

The answer to Mary's question was no; obviously Leda had not "talked to Ian." But maybe she had been silly—getting herself worked up over nothing. Now, she felt giddy. It was no small thing. No small thing to feel as if the crush of gravity had lifted (if only just for a minute). The sidewalk felt like the belt of a treadmill. The lunchtime crowd of students parted like particles of mist, barely visible, barely even noticed.

She didn't text Mary back. But, in Poesía Moderna, she surreptitiously chatted with Monica while a classmate presented on an incomprehensible Neruda poem. Monica sent more prom court photos. It always took Leda a moment to recognize Charlotte: Charlotte in pearls, fingers laced primly at her belly; Charlotte in a sundress and pink-tinted sunglasses, laughing with her mouth wide open; Charlotte receiving a crown, cradling roses, wearing what could only be the glittering gown that Leda had seen in her closet.

She won? Leda typed to Monica.

Monica responded, Did you take the year off or something?

Those years were a blur, to be honest. If Charlotte had been a senior, then Leda would have been a junior. Her mom would have been sick. Leda had probably been aware of the dance, but she hadn't attended it. Between visits to the hospital, teenage milestones had felt trivial. A part of her regretted it—her tendency toward solitude then. But she was making up for it now, wasn't she? She had friends—*sisters*—who cared about her. And now, somebody liked her. *Ian*. And she was pretty sure she liked him.

She tuned back in to the Neruda poem, making an effort to listen to her classmate's presentation. But, by the time class was over, she still didn't get it.

We're gonna have dinner! she texted Mary after class.

Mary responded, so you didn't talk to him.

. . . no

When's din?

Leda frowned. idk.

It was true—they hadn't set an actual time or place. Whatever. She still felt big, walking home, thinking of those flowers in her bedroom window, thinking of what the grim reaper had asked at the Cathouse pregame. *Are you the girl with Ian?* Yes, she thought now. *Yes*. She wanted to shout it.

Of course, today's astronomy lesson had told her just the opposite. YOU ARE HERE, i.e., you are tiny. You are just a few decimal points away from nothing. She had never even noticed that poster in the guidance counselor's office before her mom passed away. Afterward, for the rest of her senior year, she'd found herself staring at it—alone. Undeniably so.

Ian, she reminded herself, turning in to her neighborhood. Why couldn't Ian be her person? *I like you*, he'd said on Halloween. Or was it *I love you?* She couldn't remember exactly. Regardless, maybe it would play out that way: true love. Every day, he would save her from loneliness. Every morning, she'd revive in his arms, like a dead princess.

Then a voice interrupted, and Leda blinked, jolted out of her fantasy.

"You look happy." A girl with thick, ponytailed braids was coming toward her at a run. "Just kidding." The girl stopped before her, panting. "But you should see your face. Seriously."

Leda squinted. "Do I know you?"

"You don't remember?" The girl wiped sweat from her forehead. "I live in the Cathouse. You came to our party."

"Sure," Leda said, not remembering.

"You're Leda."

"Yeah . . ." Leda glanced toward Varsity Field, where she liked to do her stretching. Between the columns, a new strand of panty flags had been erected.

"I swear I don't have a crush on you; I just know names. I'm Tamara. We're neighbors."

"Okay. Cool." Leda did her best to keep her face neutral, though it was hard to feign friendliness after she'd overheard so many Psi Delts bad-mouthing the Cathouse and its inhabitants. It wasn't that the Cathouse girls were bad people, her sisters said. They were just *different*. And yes, the word *different* was like the word *weird*—it marked a permanent condemnation, an ultimate judgment.

"Well," Leda chimed, finally. "Nice to meet you."

Leda made to leave, but Tamara didn't move. Her face shone with sweat. Her mouth glinted. It took Leda a minute to see the tiny rhinestone glued to the girl's incisor.

Leda filled in the silence. "Are you having a good run?"

"Ha. No. I hate running, but I get off balance if I don't subject myself to some amount of daily suffering." Tamara twisted her T-shirt into a knot, just above the belly. There was a dark tattoo there—a wolf or dog or something. "Plus, I would get fat, probably. My diet basically consists of beer, bread, and cheese." Tamara rolled her eyes. "My birthday was last week, and I literally ate an entire wheel of Brie."

"Oops," Leda said. "Happy birthday, at least."

"Thanks. It's so weird. I'm twenty-one. Nothing else to look forward to after this. Except, I guess, renting cars without the fee. Running for president. What are you doing?"

"Walking home."

"Sweet. As you can tell, I'm totally procrastinating. It's funny—I saw you earlier today. You probably didn't see me. You were walking with Ian."

When Tamara didn't go on, Leda asked, "How do you know Ian?"

"Oh, he and Charlotte were in my psych class. But that was forever ago; that was first year." Tamara flapped her shirt. "Is it just me, or is it hot for November?"

Leda repeated, "Charlotte?"

Tamara's eyes basically shut when she smiled. "Anyway, I heard that you and Ian are maybe dating? Exciting!"

"Well, not really." A shirtless dude came out onto the porch at Kappa Chi, stretching in the midday sun. He looked like he'd just woken up. Leda clarified, "I mean, *we're not*, really."

"By the way, I saw that thing on the Lawn." Tamara put her thumbnail between her two front teeth. "The scream? That was terrifying. I tried screaming with her, that girl, and I didn't come close to, like, half her volume. Carly, right? Crazy. It was fun, though. Who called the police?"

"I don't know." Leda's temples were beating. "Were Charlotte and Ian friends or something?"

"Oh, I think—" Again, Tamara put her thumb to her teeth. "They dated. Briefly. Well!" Tamara clapped her hands once. "Gotta keep running!"

Already, Tamara was trotting away. For some moments, Leda had trouble forming any one coherent thought. Was this a joke? Perhaps she'd misheard.

"Hey!" Tamara shouted back at her. She'd turned around, jogging in place half a block away. "Do you play Scrabble?"

"What?"

"Wednesday's Scrabble night," Tamara called. "It's really lame. You should come play!" Then she waved and kept jogging without waiting to hear what Leda would say.

Leda didn't have to think hard about whether or not she would go. While she wasn't planning on making regular Cathouse playdates, she needed to know exactly what Tamara knew about this. For one thing—the information was just starting to sink in—she and Ian had driven through a search party together. They had passed a MISSING poster on the way to the reservoir. He had *dated* Charlotte, and yet he'd said nothing. He'd betrayed zero reaction.

She walked slowly, trying to get her head around it, trying to decide if it changed anything. Tamara hadn't seemed worried. Should Leda be?

At home in her room, Leda brought her face level with the vase of snapdragons, as if they might tell her what to think, what to do. The Neruda poem mumbled in the back of her mind as she pinched one blossom's cheeks. She'd always thought Neruda was supposed to be easy. The grammar wasn't complex. The vocabulary was basic. But the poem had gone far over her head. It had unsettled her, seeing her classmates' comprehension and still just not getting it.

The little flower roared, then puckered its lips.

What was so complicated? What was Leda missing?

8

All at once, the birds seemed to wake. Tuesday morning was bright and cold and filled with singing. Leda listened, the windows open. It was like an orchestra tuning, warming up snatches of the day's song. A marvelous chaos.

Leda pulled her blanket from the bed and wrapped herself in it. It had rained last night. The windowsills were wet. Even the snapdragons dripped. She moved the flowers off her window and onto her bedside table, stepping around the floorboards that were shiny and wet. The card was saturated; the penned words smeared and bled.

From her porch, Leda could see new trees waiting to be planted in the neighbor's clay pit. Their roots were bound in burlap. Their crowns leaned against one another. Geese swept over them in wild, flying geometry. The moment in which they were loudest was also the moment that they began fading.

NPR escaped from Naadia's window. Leda hugged her comforter around her, listening. Politics shifted from national to local. The weather was pronounced like a prayer.

"Sunny and clear with a high of fifty-six . . ."

The weather comforted her. But then the newscaster switched, interviewing someone saying, "Do parents really want to be sending their children into environments in which . . ." and, "no accountability. No supervision," and, "Charlotte Mask has been missing since . . ."

Was that what Leda was—a child who needed to be supervised? Was that what Charlotte had been? Leda went inside, away from the voices. She visited the stack of postcards on her desk instead of poking through emails or skimming the news.

Dear Charlotte, Sometimes I suffer these little flashes of my so-called old self. I had thought that changing my routine would change who I was—"You are what you do," someone said, somewhere. But my "self" doesn't change, really. It just gets murkier, more swamp-like as I get older. Love, Pia

Downstairs, Leda made coffee. The muted television had been left on in the common area, filling the otherwise dim room with spasmodic movement. Genie and a handful of Delta newbies could be found here most nights in this kind of light, watching reality shows or the Home Shopping Network or sitcoms about typical families doing typical things that only seemed typical within the hyper-reality of the TV screen. Another way to lose consciousness, Leda thought briefly.

Glock the cockatoo bobbed at the screen. He'd probably been up all night, bobbing and dodging.

"Super," he said, and then stuttered, mimicking the coffee machine.

Leda hit the lights. An anonymous note had been scrawled on the whiteboard, surrounded by hearts: *LOVE YOU, bitches!*

When Leda had first joined the sorority, her sisters used to slip notes like this under her door. Well, slightly more sincere versions.

I'm glad we're friends or *Girl, you got this!* She'd get texts from twenty different girls on Friday nights, asking where the bejesus was she? There were mass group hugs. There was this party to go to; there was that party. There were comments all over the pictures she posted online: You are adorable. Love. Utter perfection. Beauty. None of it had seemed forced or cheesy. She remembered walking to class down Memorial Road—the fraternities stoic and backlit with the sun rising, the Rotunda puffed, a few clouds smeared like cake icing across the morning. It had taken her breath—not just seeing all this, but being a part of it.

And she was still a part of it, she reminded herself. Still loved. Still lucky. On her phone, she typed a message to Ian.

Good morning . . .

A fragile blue bubble appeared in their conversation, holding her text. Then she immediately regretted sending it. Her pulse felt like a fly on her skin—giddy and nervous. It was that feeling from childhood, when you laughed too hard or when you had bad dreams or when everything was just too much—when you simply couldn't hold it.

Could Ian really be Charlotte's ex?

She grabbed a cold Pop-Tart and went upstairs with it, flopping onto her bed, squeezing her snapdragons again. Her phone vibrated somewhere in the fabric, and she dug around for it on her hands and knees.

Can I see you?

She hesitated, then typed, Yes, before flinging herself back into the blankets. She squealed, literally, but she wasn't sure if it was out of excitement or nerves. Was she in control? She didn't know.

For the rest of the morning, Leda did her best not to agonize over whether or not to send Ian a second text. She did her best not to think too much about what Tamara had said. She worked on her Poesía

Moderna presentation, deciding to switch from a Borges poem to a Neruda, reading the new lines over and over. She considered whether she had left her phone on ringer or silent. She got up and checked. Ian hadn't texted. She checked Facebook, read the new messages dedicated to Charlotte, and then, on a whim, clicked on the list of Charlotte's friends. In the search bar, she typed, Pia. There was no match, not out of almost eight hundred friends.

Then she typed, Ian Gray, and there he was.

Just as she returned to Neruda, her phone buzzed. She threw her pencil and snatched it up. It was Clarence, asking if she could babysit this Friday. Leda clamped her tongue between her teeth, typing, Sure, and thinking, *Shit. There goes a potential Friday with Ian.*

The kids would be easy, Clarence wrote. All Leda had to do was heat up dinner and put everyone to bed at eight, including Vinnie.

Ian still had not texted. A bubbled ellipsis wavered at the bottom of their chat. It was supposed to mean that he was typing, but no text appeared as she stared at the screen. The ellipsis pulsed: fading, glowing, fading. She put the phone down eventually.

A fter Advanced Spanish Grammar and Chilean Lit, she ran, leaving her backpack at the gym. Every boy she saw looked like Ian. Ian with his hair mussed with chlorine, Ian wearing chinos, Ian slightly shorter, or slightly chunky. Her pulse jammed every time she thought she glimpsed him. The fantasy thrilled her—that strange combination of fear and pleasure.

She ran erratically, around neighborhoods where upperclassmen lived, passing brick houses with stubby porches, passing restaurants that smelled like tortilla chips, passing Ians. The ellipsis of his unsent text trailed behind her, as if he were everywhere, about to say something. What would he say? And then, in turn, what would she?

Would she "talk to him," as she'd promised Mary? Would she pursue what Tamara had said—that Charlotte and Ian had dated? How much control did she have over the situation?

The questions heaped, never coming to anything. It felt like when she fell asleep doing Spanish homework; the letters, punctuation, and accents just piling, never hardening into words or meaning. She passed the language houses, their yards turned up by backhoes for some reason. One magnolia remained standing—the last tree before the hospital.

She could have turned around, but she didn't. *I should be fine*, she told herself. *I should be.* The road slipped under a clear skywalk, which connected the hospital's wings. Through the glass, Leda glimpsed a woman pulling oxygen, a doctor walking quickly, a balloon tugging behind a lost-looking family. Leda saw them all in one breath before passing under the building. It was a brief tunnel—loud with traffic, sticky with exhaust. Leda put her sleeve to her nose and mouth.

When she shot out from under the skywalk, she was surrounded by hospital: eight floors of reflective teal windows. She and her mom had wandered so many different parts of these buildings, seeking doctors, blood transfusions, radiation. Once, her mother had collapsed in a hallway. Once, Leda had seen the white mesh mask that had been sculpted for her mother's face. The purpose of the mask was to hold the head in place during radiation. Her mom hadn't wanted Leda to see it, perhaps because the mask had looked human—like her mother. Or perhaps the shell of her.

Leda sprinted with her sleeve over her face. She tried not to look, tried to pass quickly, but at the last minute she craned her neck, staring back at the hospital's entry. There, after receiving a quart of blood, her mom hadn't been able to go down the three stairs that led to the parking lot. Leda wasn't sure how long they had waited there, holding the handrail. Why hadn't Leda done something? she wondered now. Why had she just stood there, waiting for help that wouldn't come?

Now, three years later, Leda stumbled on the sidewalk and reached out as if to catch that railing. Of course, it wasn't there. She knew that she would fall—that she *was falling*—even as cars and buses heaved past her, as the stoplight blinked, as people (one after the next) continued on.

She would've liked to tell her mother about Ian. She would've liked to ask, *What is this feeling? Should I be excited or frightened?* She could've used the advice—from someone who loved her. Who wanted the best for her. Leda hit her palms hard in the fall, but she quickly got herself up. A man at a crosswalk reached out as if to catch her.

"Are you okay?"

Leda heard his voice as she ran past him. She didn't look back. It made her angry that he would ask her that. Anger was easier than embarrassment—that was part of it. But she was also just mad at a world that pretended to care, but didn't.

Above her, smog billowed from smokestacks. A helicopter took off from the hospital roof like an insect. She dashed under a narrow bridge, which shrieked and rattled with a train. Her palms were bleeding. Girls in peacoats, waiting to cross the street, looked at her. Her face must have looked strange, because they quickly looked away.

Heading back toward grounds, she passed students carrying paper bags and boxed lunches. Two gray-faced men stood outside of CVS with their dogs—homeless and young. One of them watched Leda run. She ran faster. She wanted to run so fast that no one could see her. First-year girls came out of a doughnut shop, not looking. Leda veered off the curb and into the street. A guy with a ponytail swerved and biked around her, cursing. The asphalt was littered with gravel, and tiny pebbles hit her ankles. On a restaurant's patio, alumni ate burgers, their fingers and wrists brassy with class rings and crossed-saber cuff links.

Peccatoribus, she heard. *Ora pro nobis.*

A seated woman put a fry between her pink lips. An Indian guy wearing blaze orange stepped into the crosswalk, and she got so close to smashing into him that she could smell the mouthwash on his breath. He had earbuds in; he didn't even notice. She kept running. Her breathing was fucked. Two lanky hippies smoked in front of the bank where Charlotte Mask had, apparently, withdrawn two hundred bucks. There were missing posters on the bank windows. A Honda emerged from the side street that dipped into fraternities and sororities. It was like the one Leda had seen the skeleton driving on Halloween. It stopped for her. Leda glimpsed the hand on the steering wheel, waving her on, when a girl shouted, *"Perpetua!"* At least, that's what Leda heard as she smacked bodily into her.

A latte flew from the girl's hands. Luckily (or not), it was Carly.

"The fuck, Leda?"

By some miracle, the latte had sailed away from both of their bodies. Carly inspected her outfit—white canvas shoes, pale jeans, lavender blouse. Nothing looked ruined.

"Sorry," Leda panted. She wanted to hug her friend.

The Honda honked. They were still in the middle of the road. When they moved, the driver passed them, laughing.

Carly pointed a finger at her. "You got very lucky."

The adrenaline or the surprise or the pain in her palms had Leda shaking. She managed, "I'll buy you another drink."

She wanted to tell Carly about skinning her palms at the hospital, about Ian, about how she had gone from feeling loved and lucky to almost crying in the street. If not her mother, then she had friends—*sisters*—who cared about her, who would listen.

But Carly kept pointing. "Is something wrong with you?"

"I think—" Leda was still breathing heavily. "I think I'm confused. About Ian."

Carly inspected her own hands, as if they might be stained. She sighed. She wore an expression that Leda didn't recognize. "That's cute, Lee."

"No, really." Leda gripped her own hips, taking little steps in place. A pod of girls in matching tees passed them with bagels, stepping gingerly around the spilled drink. Leda kept going, hardly thinking about what she was saying. "He left me flowers yesterday, but then my body, when I'm near him . . . it has this, like, weird reaction—"

"Lee, seriously?" Carly's eyes grazed Leda's palms, but she didn't ask what had happened. "You're probably just PMSing."

"Listen." Leda's heart rate wouldn't come down. Her palms burned. "I ran into our neighbor, this girl—"

"Honestly, have you guys fucked again?" Carly cut in, glancing at her manicure. "Or can you not remember?"

The hurt must have shown in Leda's face.

"Don't be pathetic. I'm kidding." Carly flicked her wrist. Her eyes clipped past Leda's face as if Leda were a tree trunk or a phone pole or an empty space. "Anyway, class. Love you. Thanks for spilling my latte."

Leda tried to stop her. "Car—"

But Carly already had her phone out, texting and walking away.

In the gym lobby, Leda refrained from kicking a waist-high pyramid of tennis ball canisters. Why did she feel so weird? Shaky, giddy. Nervous, elated. As if she'd had too much caffeine. Had that conversation with Tamara changed so much, really? Okay, Ian and Charlotte had dated. It was a little unsettling, but it wasn't a game-changer necessarily.

Of course, the hospital hadn't helped—reminding her of the body's vulnerability, compounded now without her mother. She'd smacked into Carly, feeling alone, helpless, and her Big had treated her like little more than an annoyance. It would have been one thing if Carly had looked at Leda's splotchy face in horror, like those pea-coated girls near the hospital. But, somehow, indifference was worse.

She thought of her old guidance counselor's poster. YOU ARE HERE.

The wall clock showed that Leda was a half hour early for her work-study. She showed her teeth to the current girl at the desk before cutting through the fitness center, buzzing with moving machines and bodies. Ellipticals churned on blue carpet, straddled by girls letting their fists be pumped by handgrips. Treadmills whirred hot belts. Beeps announced changes to the machines' incline and speed. The runners were wild-eyed and, for all practical purposes, motionless, like people being chased in a dream.

The treadmills faced large interior windows that looked down onto the pool. Above the windows, muted televisions flashed colorful screens. The first TV showed a crocodile with its mouth open. On the next, a Psi Delta favorite: a reality show in which undercover police lure pedophiles into a house, using the promise of sex with underage tweens. On the last screen, a man and woman stood beside a flag and a podium. It was Charlotte's parents again, giving a press conference. The closed captions scrolled under her mother.

WE ARE HOPING TO BRING CHARLOTTE BACK HOME
CHARLOTTE IS ALSO OUR LITTLE GIRL SHE
SHE'S ENORMOUSLY PRECIOUS.

Charlotte's father's mouth hung a little loose from his face as his wife thanked law enforcement and the university. She called Charlotte a "conscientious young woman" who was mature, reliable, and "highly organized." Both parents looked a bit like the treadmill joggers when they broke for questions—the wild eyes, the saturated exhaustion.

Leda turned away from the screens. On a mat in the corner, two girls did crunches, looking angrily at their knees. Some guys lifted weights in front of a mirror, mooing. There was swim practice today, Leda knew. The swimmers had to walk through here to get to the locker rooms.

I'm gonna talk to him, she texted Mary, feeling less confident than she sounded. Tell me I'm not crazy.

But Mary didn't text back. Right when she needed her friend, she was busy.

Leda glanced back at the pedophile show. The weeping perpetrator hid his face behind a bouquet—flowers he'd brought, Leda guessed, for the underage girl.

A group of swimmers appeared, sauntering through the weight machines, their shower shoes flopping down the long ramp leading to the locker rooms. Leda followed discreetly, but they were out of sight before she could get a good look. She paused there, alone in the humid area outside the showers and pool. Leftover lunches lined the one bench in the room: white bags stapled shut next to individual servings of chips.

Shower spray hissed behind the closed doors. The carpet felt soggy. Shapes moved through the porthole window that led to the brilliant pool, the glass flicking between black and Listerine blue. Leda stood beside the chips. She looked back up the empty hall, putting her hands on her hips before letting her arms fall. Then, with no time to anticipate it, the locker room door swung open and ten silver-capped men came in.

"He accused us of forced imprisonment," the loudest voice said. "And hazing. The guy's a loser, and I don't use that word; it's an ass word. But in this case, it's true."

The guy speaking pulled his cap up off his ears, giving him a pin-head look. His body was immaculate; he had bright blue eyes, like Ian. The men filed past. It was a little difficult to tell them apart between the goggles and the caps and the defined abs. So, Leda let her eyes drift to their bellies, looking for the pink appendix scar. When none of them appeared to be Ian, she let her eyes drift lower to their Speedos—metallic-looking, with discreet (or indiscreet) bulges.

A bulge stopped before her. "Can I take some chips?"

Her eyes flicked up. She picked up the box of chips. "Yes."

He took Fritos. Another guy took Sun Chips. Then they pushed through the door to the pool, the loud voice still going. ". . . he said that he was *forced* to drink milk, beer, and prune juice. Like, I'm sorry, dude."

The door swung shut. Leda stood holding the box. That guy wasn't Ian, she reminded herself. *Hazing. Forced imprisonment.* Up the hallway, a TV commercial brayed, "You don't need to be *good* to be a great guy!"

After a minute of no Ian, she put down the chips.

The women's locker room was quiet—no shower noise or blow-dryers or stringy singing. The vents in the ceiling hummed disso-nance. Leda washed the blood from her palms at the sinks, trying not to wince. She hadn't skinned anything since she was a kid, and she didn't feel any braver than she had back then. She wanted to close her eyes. She wanted someone—her mom—to kiss each palm. *All better.*

She needed a shower, but she found herself leaving the room, pushing out the emergency exit into scraps of clouded sun. Stunted shrubs scratched her ankles as she walked along the building. She stepped on the wax paper from a panty liner's adhesive strip. The pool windows were too blurred to see in. At the corner of the build-ing, she picked up a cloudy pair of child's goggles. She carried them through the parking lot toward New Dorms, away from the gym.

What was she doing, lurking around, getting all worked up? She was just worried about speaking to Ian, she guessed, about being vulnerable in front of him. But, after her conversation with Tamara, she had to ask. *What happened between you and me?* and *What happened between you and Charlotte?*

Though that wasn't how she'd frame the second question. She didn't know how she'd say it. Of course nothing had *happened* between Charlotte and Ian. Just because they'd dated first year didn't mean Ian knew anything about Charlotte's disappearance.

A voice called out. Ian—the real Ian—crossed the parking lot toward her. This was the culmination of her Ian fantasy, but she felt unprepared for it, standing here at the curb, wandering in the opposite direction of where she should have been headed, clouded goggles dangling from her fingers.

"So, I *do* get to see you," Ian said. He wore a light blue button-down, ironed. A big black bag hung over his shoulder.

Leda tried to make her mouth light. "I said you would, didn't I?"

She couldn't help but think of what she'd just tried to put into words—*my body, when I'm near him, has this weird reaction . . .*

"Yeah," Ian said, "but you never said where or when."

"Right here." Leda tried to still her hands. "Right now. I'm glad you made it."

Ian dropped his gym bag and looked at her. She recognized the look; it was always the same, no matter whose face was making it: fear peeled away for an instant to reveal attraction, curiosity. It was the way a magnet might look if a magnet had a face, if it could show the pleasure and surprise of sucking into some invisible field and finding the sudden, hard source of it. Seeing it felt good. It made her want to forget her plan to ask the question.

"Ian—" How much control did she have? Could she just open her mouth and ask about Halloween? About Charlotte? "I wanted to give you these." She handed over the kid goggles awkwardly.

"Wow . . ." Ian managed to put them on, smiling. They were too small for his face, not to mention that the lenses were completely opaque. "That was so thoughtful." When Ian pulled the goggles off, he saw her hands. He took them and touched the raw, red place. "What happened?"

"I fell." Leda dragged her shoe along the curb. "It doesn't hurt."

Ian's thumb shifted. He pressed a little too hard. "Are you sure?"

Leda held her jaw, nodded. Ian kept holding her hands, magnetized. Did he feel how hard he was squeezing this tender place? She flinched—she couldn't help it. It was microscopic, this little jerk away from him, but he noticed it. His eyes searched her face. He looked genuinely confused, and she wished then that she hadn't drawn back, hadn't registered the pain. She wanted this to be easy. She wanted him to pick her up, kiss her, carry her away. She wanted him to stop her from saying what she was about to say.

"I heard," Leda said, "about you and Charlotte."

As soon as she said it, she regretted it. She wished that she had said anything but this. She wished she had said, *Fuck me* or *Let's get married* or *It's cloudy*. She didn't care what Tamara had said. She just wanted to feel her life leading up to this. She wanted to feel twenty-one years of inertia building, pushing, and releasing her here, into this moment: a declaration of love; a head-in-hands kiss.

But she'd said it, and now it was his turn to pull back. "What do you mean?"

"I mean, I guess . . ." Leda hesitated. "That you and Charlotte Mask dated."

"That was a long time ago," Ian said, with a sort of forced calm. "What about it?"

"I guess I wondered why you didn't say anything . . ."

Ian touched one side of his belly, as if some pain had registered there. The scar, maybe. Some muscle in his cheek tensed. "What should I have said?"

"I don't know," Leda admitted. *Shit*, she thought. *Shit*.

"I haven't asked about any of your past relationships."

"No, you haven't." Leda took a breath. "But Charlotte . . . came up."

"Charlotte's *gone*," Ian corrected.

It was a strange word to choose, Leda thought. One that had not yet occurred to her: *gone*. It had been ten days. She tried to think of something to say as his face became strange—maybe hurt, maybe angry.

Leda asked, "Did you see her that night?" And strangely, she wanted to go on, wanted to know everything. *Did you speak? Did you see her before or after you saw me?*

"I did." Ian didn't elaborate.

Scary-weeping—Leda heard Mary's voice in her mind. She tried to remember it . . . and suddenly she could. Some, anyway. Maybe it was having Ian here, right in front of her—so close that in his blue eyes she could see flecks of gray.

She tried to push into the memory, tried to walk herself through. She tried to look back at the tikis, lit and gleaming, as Charlotte and the skeleton drove away from the party. She moved back between the torches, damp and drunk and ready. As she walked, details filled in. Hipsters smoked on the patio. The Chiquita Banana girl pumped an empty keg. Inside, she saw two more skeletons, talking to each other. Genie danced in the heart of the crowd, swinging a forty wrapped in beads. A boy found her sister's mermaid hips, and Leda watched her rhythm shift to match his. A ghost dragged a full keg past Leda down the hall, and then she saw him—Ian—eating that strange, misshapen candy. When he saw her, he took her hips in both hands, saying that he'd been afraid she'd left already.

"Afraid?" Leda had teased, pulling away. She could see the pile of clothes behind him, an eyeless mask staring.

"I love you," Ian said, his toga slipping.

She laughed at him. "You don't even know me."

"I do." He nodded. His face was too close to see properly. He was just as drunk as she. "I can't let you get away."

Leda, still laughing, pulled her head back but let her pelvis draw into his. "But what if I *want* to get away?"

The whole house, though full of people, felt gutted, quiet, even as bass lunged from man-sized speakers, as dancers twined like mating snakes—wrapping and binding, kissing and biting. Before her, Ian looked godlike, even in his punch-stained toga. His skin glistened. She let her hands feel his shoulders, his collarbones.

He lifted her against the wall, and her breath knocked out of her. "I won't let you," he whispered.

There were bodies around them—witnesses (why did that word come to her all of a sudden?)—but the faces were eyeless and rubbery, fading in and out of her periphery. He kissed her. For the first time, she remembered it. It was a good kiss. He was strong; she could feel it in his arms, his chest. It had felt good to be held up under him, helpless.

Across almost no physical distance, Leda had asked, "What if I don't love you?"

And he'd countered, "And what if you do?"

And then what happened? she both wanted and did not want to ask, just like she wanted and did not want to know why it had taken him so long to contact her after Halloween, why he had missed so much class, and why he had never mentioned Charlotte, never said, *I knew her. I dated her. I fucked her.* It was relevant, wasn't it?

Now, standing before Ian, Leda felt her body brace in the same instant that Ian backed away.

"I'm sorry." The kid goggles dangled blindly from his fingertips. "I don't know what you want me to say."

Leda stalled. Maybe it was her turn to apologize for bringing Charlotte up, for being insensitive about a sensitive subject. It was possible that she was being conceited, assuming that what happened to one girl must have something to do with her. *Here's Leda*, her mom might have said, holding up one finger, *and here's the world*, her second finger orbiting the first.

Or maybe Carly was right. Maybe Leda was just PMSing.

Regardless, Mary had seen her sobbing, bleeding. The morning after, the condom had been gone, her red dress strained at the seam. Now her period was late. No, she didn't remember what had happened with Ian. But she couldn't help filling in details from her night with Indoor Sunglasses. The fizz of fear in her throat as he'd pushed his naked cock in. How no one had even noticed she'd gone upstairs with him. No one had asked where she'd been. It was Leda alone who would live with these memories. And these consequences.

Ian looked into her face. "Are you okay?"

"I'm fine." Leda nodded, trying to convince herself of it. She stared down at her skinned palms, remembering how Carly's eyes had flicked over them. She thought of her mom.

Really, Ian hadn't said anything wrong. It was just that her head suddenly felt very far from her feet. It was just that the great, overcast sky had become so heavy and bright, she worried that she wouldn't be able to keep standing here, resisting the weight of it.

"I have to go," she managed, and she started walking, quickly, as something ugly rose up from her chest and into her throat. She slipped between moving cars in the street, trying to hide whatever was coming. She didn't want him to see her cry, though somehow her eyes were still dry.

Ian called out to her as she climbed the green hill, pushing between backpacks, lunch boxes, briefcases. She cut through a ring of cyclists in bright jerseys. She dodged laughter. She saw a woman who looked like her mother, and moved after her, veering off the sidewalk, her pink shoes smashing the saturated grass. Her walk turned into a jog, then a run, but Leda wasn't fast enough. Charlotte stepped inside her dark home. Her mother's eyelids closed.

When she glanced back, Ian was no longer in the parking lot. He must have gone in, given up. She had embarrassed herself, and she knew it. She passed the woman who was not her mother, who did not look even remotely like her. She ran faster. At the last dorm on the top of the hill, a defunct garden reached up empty stakes and balled leaves. Shriveled, inedible tomatoes littered the mulch. Overhead, the white sky gagged. Leda stopped running, the wind knocked out of her, the sudden punch—regret, grief—pushing her down to hold her own knees.

9

Tamara kept three cats at bay with her feet while Leda squeezed through the open front door. Once she was in, the cats took off, paunches swinging, and Tamara showed Leda past a dark staircase where Leda could hear more cat collars jingling. In the living room, a sectional couch gave off a minivan smell—years of sticky things being spilt on upholstery. The rest of the house smelled like weed, as it had on Halloween.

Tamara paused beside the brick fireplace. Her box braids were piled on top of her head, and she wore lipstick so red that the Psi Delts probably would have outlawed it.

"You don't need the grand tour, right?" Tamara said. "You came to the party."

Leda nodded. But now that the space wasn't full of weirdo college students, it did feel different. Now, she could actually see the room— the windows covered with thin block-print hangings, the coffee table littered with rolling papers, used tea bags, and Hershey's kisses. There was a bong and a lawn flamingo on the mantel behind Tamara. Something metal poked out of the fireplace.

Leda said, "It's so cozy."

"Aw, you know." Tamara hugged herself. She wasn't wearing a bra under her unicorn cami. "It's home."

In the kitchen, three girls sat around a Scrabble board under wheezing fluorescents. When Leda entered, the room cast its eyes on her. She tried to smile even as her own eyes watered in the harsh light, feeling as pitiful and exposed as she'd been yesterday under those bright, dense clouds, dashing away from Ian, from everything.

"I would introduce you, Leda, but I already told everyone about you. Sorry. Do you want a drink?" Tamara opened the fridge. Either she was oblivious to Leda's discomfort, or she was trying to take the pressure off. "Or a joint? Or, like, iced tea? I think Shanti made iced motherwort and barley. It's pretty okay. No offense, lady."

"None taken." Shanti was pale with long dark hair. Leda recognized her as the girl who had been doing tai chi at the party. "There's vodka in the freezer, too."

Somehow, Leda always forgot this—that non-Greek-life women of drinking age could have alcohol in their homes. No big deal.

Leda tried to sound casual. "I'll have a beer if you have any."

Tamara nudged a cat out of the way and rummaged. A Viking helmet and a variety of jars cluttered the top of the refrigerator. Then, beneath the helmet, Leda remembered Tamara: she'd been the Viking playing Jenga with Charlotte.

At the Scrabble board, a chubby, pink-faced girl with a lip piercing turned CHILL into CHILLAXING. No one challenged it. A girl with half of her blond hair buzzed calculated the word's value and cursed. It was Tamara's turn.

"Oh, shit." Tamara held the fridge door with her foot and consulted her letters. From the existing word LEON she placed the word PLEONASTIC.

"I'm not gonna challenge it," the pinkish girl said. "I don't know what it means, but I am not challenging."

The girl with the shaved head looked angry. "It's a word," she confirmed, tallying. The dark-haired girl, Shanti, leaned back and sipped from a mug of tea. On the nearest counter, yellowing wheatgrass shot out of a tray. Behind this, a cookie jar was labeled NIGHTMARE CAT DRUG.

"Do we *have* beer?" Tamara asked everybody. "Every day someone new is not drinking. Today it's me. Yesterday it was . . ."

"Shanti," answered everybody, looking at the pale girl, who didn't look up from her tea.

"Baby needs to start drinking again," the chubby girl added.

"Fuck you, too," said Baby, the blonde with the half-buzzed head. The grim reaper from Halloween.

Tamara said, "Mine won't last, probably. But I swear, the sheer volume of alcohol I drank on my twenty-first birthday might have turned me off the sauce for good. It's like when I turned eighteen, I stopped smoking. I smoked a whole pack, and then I was like, 'Okay, I'm stopping.'"

Leda said to Baby, "I think I met you at the Halloween party."

Baby shrugged.

"Of course . . ." Tamara was still going. "Now I've started again. Smoking."

Baby had shown Leda to the bathroom, where that boy had been on the floor, hallucinating. That boy that no one had known.

Finally, Tamara found Leda a beer. Shanti placed an –ALLY on the end of PLEONASTIC, and everyone howled.

"Jesus fucking Christ," Baby said, scoring. Then she turned to Leda. "Don't you have to be rich to live in a sorority?"

"It's a little cheaper than a dorm and meal plan." Leda hesitated. "Plus, I have a work-study."

"Baby, you're such a bitch." Tamara called from the pantry, taking out boxes of herbal tea: PMS Tea, Yin Yogi, Radical Raspberry Leaf. "Do you even *know* how much your dad pays in tuition?"

Baby grunted, placed the word ORANGE, and added up her points. Leda drank her beer, watching her reflection in the window over the sink. It was nice, actually, to drink without feeling like she owed anything. She was beginning to feel surprisingly safe, even in this room of strange, cursing women.

The water boiled, and Tamara poured her tea. On the Scrabble board, she placed the word VICARIOUS while she bounced the tea bag, waiting for it to steep. Leda glanced at the photos and magazine clippings on the fridge. In one picture, Tamara had her arms draped around another girl's neck. From the look of the kitchen table— ashtrays, Solo cups, cheap liquor—they were having a party. The group looked drunk—flushed, hugging one another. Leda recognized Shanti, her long hair crazy, hoisting one of the cats in the air.

Leda asked, "How many people live here?"

"Eight," Tamara said. "But it always feels like more. We keep that door locked, but folks always end up weaseling their way in, eating our food and smoking our shit. Not you, though, Leda. You're cool. By the way, Shanti, where's the weed?"

Somebody upstairs shrieked, but no one reacted. The scream gave way to hiccupped laughing. Shanti took a joint from behind her ear and handed it to Tamara.

"You're sweet." Tamara hugged Shanti from behind. "I get vertigo," she explained to Leda. "Marijuana is the only thing that helps me see that I'm *not* falling down some bottomless pit."

But Leda wasn't quite listening. She had recognized another face in the photograph. She spoke without thinking. "Is this Charlotte?"

Baby looked up from her tally.

"That was second year." Tamara dipped and redipped her teabag. "You knew Charlotte used to live here."

"No." Leda's voice had changed pitch. "I didn't."

In the picture, Charlotte was laughing. Her hair was longer than when Leda had seen it, as long as it had been in those prom photos. Her T-shirt was dark and shapeless. Her cheeks were flushed. Smiling.

The girls at the Scrabble board focused on their letters. Tamara turned to Leda. "You want to smoke this upstairs?" The rhinestone on her tooth caught the fluorescents. "I'll whoop y'all next time," she said to the Scrabble players.

Compared to the kitchen's hard light, the rest of the house felt cave-like. Tamara lit the joint in the living room, smoked, and passed it. Leda inhaled at the base of the stairs and coughed. She hadn't smoked weed in a long time. At the Psi Delta house, this form of intoxication wasn't exactly encouraged. But the past few days had been so odd already that Leda didn't have the energy to resist. Drunk, stoned—what was the difference?

Invisible cats brushed Leda's ankles, jingling up and down the dark stairwell. She followed Tamara up, wondering if this moment made her more or less of a lemming, to use Mary's word. On the one hand, she was smoking weed with a tattooed, non-Greek girl. On the other, she was following Tamara's lead just as she might follow Carly's. Following ensured that people would like you. It guaranteed you a tribe, a family. So she had thought, at least.

Leda held the joint against her beer, touching the handrail that Charlotte had once held. Upstairs, Tamara's room smelled like tea tree. The table lamp had a purple scarf over the shade. The floor was strewn with clothing. The closed Venetian blinds glowed with orange streetlight, striping the far wall and its uneven posters: the

Stooges, Black Sabbath, and some movie called Princess Mononoke, featuring that same wolf thing tattooed on Tamara's belly. Beads and bras hung on the back of the door, clacking when Tamara pushed it closed.

"I'd say that I'm doing laundry," she said, "hence the lack of sheets and the complete chaos of everything . . . but I would be lying. Also, you don't have to smoke that. I just thought you might want to talk privately."

Leda passed the joint. She admitted, "I don't usually smoke weed."

"Maybe you should." Tamara toked, and then pointed the joint at Leda's hands, which were trembling. "Helps with anxiety."

Leda shook her head. "I don't get anxiety."

Tamara shrugged, exhaling. "It's nothing to be ashamed of. I'd be freaked, too. I sort of blindsided you. I assumed you knew about Charlotte and Ian. But, regardless, I'm glad I told you; *I'd* want to know if my maybe boyfriend once had a relationship with a maybe-murdered girl."

Maybe boyfriend. Maybe-murdered. What was Tamara suggesting?

Leda sat on the bed, trying to sound calm. "How long were Ian and Charlotte . . . ?"

"I don't know. A semester?"

To Leda, a semester was like forever. Again, how had Ian not mentioned this? A whole semester certainly wasn't a fling; it was a relationship. So, what did it mean that Ian had said nothing when his ex-girlfriend went missing?

"I don't know why they ended things. She didn't talk about it." Tamara leaned on her windowsill, passed the weed. "Even right before they broke up, she was covered in hickeys."

Leda smoked and passed it back, staring at a vanity cluttered with makeup and glass figurines. She remembered her own necklace of hickeys blooming after Halloween. She remembered feeling oddly proud of the little injuries.

"Don't get me wrong," Tamara said. "I'm not saying Ian 'did it' or anything."

Leda let the smoke escape her lungs. Her hands, balled in her lap, trembled visibly.

"Charlotte was tough," Tamara was saying. "She just didn't always have the best judgment."

"What do you mean?"

"You could say she was a bad judge of character. Or, to put a more positive spin on it, she saw the best in everyone. She wasn't skeptical. Of course I don't *know* that Ian is a bad guy . . . but I know that if he were, Charlotte wouldn't have seen it. She saw potential where someone like me sees evil."

Leda blinked at the word. "That sounds like a good quality," she tried.

"You're right; it's a virtue. But it's dangerous, too."

The radiator ticked. Outside, blue headlights struck Tamara's window blinds. That same scream-laugh came through the wall. Leda asked, "When did Charlotte move?"

"A year ago? Year and a half?" Tamara pinched the roach to her lips, inhaled, waited. "I think she knew some people there. Recall what I said about bad judgment." The joint was cashed. Tamara dropped what remained into an old water glass.

"What's wrong with the place?"

"Nothing, technically. I think Charlotte thought it would be a different scene. She wanted to get away from the whole college thing. The Cathouse is great, but a lot of shit goes down. We're probably no different from you girls across the street. A lot of flying estrogen."

Leda nodded. She knew what Tamara meant, though her sorority sisters would not agree with the comparison.

"And Charlotte always liked the idea of a co-op. A community house," Tamara said. "Where anybody's welcome, I guess. I just have a feeling it wasn't as different as she thought it'd be."

Leda thought of Charlotte's roommates. There was Angel, dressed up as one of the university's many skeletons. And Flora. The fading pink hair. The glitter.

"I found it creepy," Tamara went on. "Though I only went there once. Some people don't detect creepy. Once, I met a guy whose *smell* tipped me off. He just didn't smell right. It's like an animal instinct. I try to go with the gut."

How had Flora smelled? She hadn't seemed so bad, had she? And Ian, of course, smelled like wood smoke and chlorine. Leda liked it, honestly.

"I saw them talking," Leda said. "I saw Ian and Charlotte talking at your party."

But Tamara waved this off, silhouetted in the weird light cast by those headlights outside. "Yeah, and you and me are talking, too. Doesn't mean I'm gonna off you."

Leda watched the blinds, picturing Charlotte balancing on the curb, camera dangling. Charlotte playing Jenga—tugging a block, the tower twisting. She considered telling Tamara what Mary had told her about Halloween. The blood, the sobbing. She considered saying that she didn't remember most of what had happened that night with Ian. And then there was his reaction yesterday, when Leda had spoken Charlotte's name.

"I like you." Tamara broke the silence first. "But you remind me of her."

This wasn't exactly a compliment, Leda could see. Flora had said that Charlotte had no boundaries, as if it were a good thing. Now Tamara was saying the same thing, but slanted differently—Charlotte had been trusting to a fault. Her openness had obstructed her judgment.

Outside, the headlights swiveled. Tamara cracked the blinds and looked out. "Damn cops."

"Huh?"

"You haven't noticed? They're always shining their spotlights around here now." Tamara turned away from the window, cast in full silhouette. "You'd think they'd have something better to do."

Under her butt, Leda's phone buzzed. When she pulled it out, the ringtone emerged. "Dancing Queen."

"Oh my god. Are you serious?" Tamara laughed. Leda envied it— that easy laugh, just when you think you might vomit. Leda thought Tamara had seen who was calling. But instead, she said, "I sort of love that song."

Leda silenced the ring and blackened the screen that read IAN.

The Scrabble game had ended by the time Leda got going. The house was dark. Tamara wrote her number down for Leda and walked her out. The cops were still there, sitting in front of the Psi Delta house in their dark cruiser. Halfway down the porch steps, Leda turned again.

"Have you talked to anyone who lived in that house with Charlotte?" she said, thinking of Angel and Flora.

"Nah." Tamara glanced between Leda and the cruiser. "Not to sound superstitious—though my mom is Haitian, so it's unavoidable, to be honest—I try not to get messed up in bad spirits."

Tamara sounded like Leda's mom, reading the world for hints and omens. Even normal things—leaves in a puddle, crows flying overhead—had seemed to tell her something portentous.

Leda said good night and crossed the street to her sorority. A black cat lay on the asphalt in front of the police car. It took off running when Leda got close, its gut swinging. She heard Tamara calling the cat behind her, "Nightmare! Here, kitty."

The cruiser flicked its brights on, and Leda shielded her eyes. Cops aside, she hoped no one in the sorority house had seen her chatting with Tamara. Not to mention that if any of her sisters were in the common room when she came in, they'd smell cannabis. It was part of an implicit Psi Delta agreement—no ugly drugs, no shady boozing. Remember that, wherever you go, you represent the Psi Delta sorority.

Of course, it was this mentality that had driven Mary out. But even after Mary left, Leda had never even considered testing her boundaries. For her, pledging a sorority had been like selecting a family. When Leda had accepted the bid from Psi Delta, she'd been ushered into this very house and showered in confetti. There had been initiation rituals (not hazing), in which the girls stared into each other's eyes for five minutes, or wept together, or sat knee to knee in a circle with candles and shared their "biggest secrets." Weeks later, Carly (assigned as Leda's Big) had anonymously lavished her with gifts. It was tradition, yes, but that hadn't made it feel any less special. It had been surreal, witnessing the kind of love people were capable of. And then it came to feel real, miraculous even, so soon after losing her mother.

But now she felt guilty with the cops' headlights on her, as if she had committed some error, some infraction that even her sisters might not forgive.

Mercifully, the common room was empty. The kitchen, too. But on her way upstairs, Leda found herself pausing outside Carly's bedroom. It had been such a relief, in those early days, to whisper in each other's ears. *Tell me a secret*, Carly would say. But now, looking back,

Leda realized she'd never once mentioned her mother. She'd never said, *She died.* She'd never said, *I miss her.*

Why then had Leda chosen to mention her mom to Charlotte? Leda had acknowledged her (her death), and then something remarkable had happened in turn. Charlotte had *seen* Leda. Recognized something in her. *You look familiar.*

It was what anyone might want, in any interaction. To be seen. Heard.

Had Charlotte *seen* Ian like that? Or had her eyes been clouded, as Tamara had suggested? Had she not sensed the danger?

Ian—who had just called Leda. And Charlotte, his ex—maybe murdered.

Stoned, scared, and exhausted, Leda knocked on Carly's door.

10

By midday Friday, Psi Delts were telling Leda that they'd "heard about Ian." It was coming on two weeks after Charlotte's disappearance, and people were getting antsy for new info, new theories to suck like candies.

The rotation was swift, as if the planets had shifted somewhere in the solar system. It took only a few days for general Ian enthusiasm to turn to suspicion. For one thing, someone had spotted Leda and Ian's little argument between New Dorms and the gym. It didn't matter that no one had been close enough to hear the conversation; they'd seen her hurry away and they'd seen him let her. But, more than this, it was Leda's knock on Carly's bedroom door that had really sparked the rebellion.

Standing outside Carly's room the night before, Leda had told herself that she wanted to get the information out in the open— release it from the echo chamber of her skull. She'd told herself that she needed to get some perspective on the whole situation. But now, looking back, she suspected that she'd been trying to redeem herself after the latte incident, offering Carly a confessional morsel.

Still, Leda should have known what would happen. Word would spread. Carly couldn't keep her own menstrual cycle confidential. Now, the whole sorority was theorizing. Anything the girls didn't know, they invented. Sometimes they ran it by Leda, as if to test their idea's validity. But really, they just seemed to be having fun creating their own stories.

It shouldn't have been surprising. This was how the gossip wheel turned. First, Ian was a saint building homes in Central America; next, he was dangerous. First, Leda was stealing the heart of godlike Ian; now, she was his latest victim.

By lunchtime, Leda had heard all about Ian's history of aggression. Girls said he had been in fights throughout college—one with his RA first year, one with his swim coach, and one (apparently) last Wednesday evening. They said that an ex-girlfriend had said that he had put his hand on her neck once when having sex. They said he had spoken hatefully about women. They said he had emotionally abused Charlotte. They said he was jealous, and that he had isolated Charlotte for the six months they had dated. Then they said that Ian and Charlotte *hadn't* dated; he had actually stalked and harassed her. Threatened her. Only one girl used the word *rape*—saying that even if he hadn't raped Charlotte, he was certainly *capable* of it.

The word stuck in her head. Rape. *Was* he capable of it? Was that the word for what had happened to Leda? Had that been the word all along? And had the same thing happened to Charlotte?

Leda had known Ian for only a few weeks, and they had never talked intimately. So when girls asked about her experience with Ian, she wasn't sure what to say. She didn't know whether the stories were true. He had given her snapdragons. She had taken him closer to her childhood home than anyone else she knew. But this wasn't what they wanted to hear. They wanted to hear about Halloween, when practically everybody had seen them kiss and leave together.

Most of Leda's sisters sounded genuinely worried when they asked her about it. Though their faces communicated something else entirely. They looked expectant, excited.

"If something happened, Lee," Carly said, poised on the other end of the couch while Leda hunched over her astronomy, "you can tell me."

Leda had to stop herself from saying that she had tried already. She'd tried to tell Carly and Genie a week ago, after yoga, and they hadn't taken her seriously.

Look at you, Genie had cooed. *At least you didn't end up like you-know-who.*

Now, she didn't know what to believe. It seemed possible that she *could have* ended up like Charlotte. Stalked. Harassed. Threatened. Raped. And the danger, she feared, had not passed. If what her friends said was true, then she shouldn't yet count herself lucky, she knew.

It was a relief to go to Faye and Clarence's house to babysit. Suddenly, it seemed like a sanctuary. She packed her backpack, silenced her phone, and walked across town to their big blue door. She felt better after the walk, slipping her bag off her shoulders while she waited for Clarence to disengage the new security system. He apologized through the door (apparently the alarm had been Faye's idea) until he finally got it open.

"Leda's here!" Clarence shouted, overloud, and hugged her. The air in the house smelled burnt.

Faye spoke from within. "This is our *home*."

"*Leda's here*." Clarence repeated, still hugging Leda in a way that felt more like obstruction than affection.

Faye kept going. "This isn't some public space where anyone can come in and eat *our* food and interact with *our* children."

Clarence cringed, and Leda knew she had heard something private. Her instinct—as it had been when she was a child, overhearing arguments—was to assume that the conversation was about her. (*Here's Leda; here's the world* . . .) Already, she was stepping back. Already, she was telling herself that it had been foolish to think of this place as a sanctuary. She knew she and Clarence were not technically related, and she knew that she had no right to come here, mooching off somebody else's family. She took another step away from Clarence, her backpack suddenly heavy. Clarence mouthed a word to Leda: *Sorry.*

"I feel like I have no privacy. Like I can't buy something for myself without hiding it. Isn't that crazy?" In the kitchen, the oven slapped shut. "You saw my salted plums. *I just bought them*, and now there's only one."

Leda looked to Clarence, confused.

"I hear you, honey, but Leda's here," he repeated. "For babysitting."

"Oh!" Faye came into the hallway from the kitchen, struggling to fasten a necklace with one hand. She wore an oven mitt on the other. "I'm so sorry, Leda. I'm just talking." She held the clasp and gave Leda a one-armed hug. "Responsibilities. Commitments. It feels great to be involved and doing something for someone, for the community. And then at the same time it feels like you might combust at any moment."

"Self-immolate?" Clarence teased.

"No. *Combust.* Spontaneously. Leda, do you know what I mean? It's as if all you want is to take a long bath, and then you see that someone has used all the lavender salts and left a sopping towel in the basket." Faye let the hand in the oven mitt fall. "And then there's the girl in the news . . ."

Did the new alarm, Leda wondered, have something to do with Charlotte?

She tried to change the subject. "Are you baking something?"

"I made no-bake cookies." Faye lifted the mitt. "Would you believe I burned them? I just wanted to warm them a bit." She turned her back to Clarence, holding the necklace, and Clarence took the clasp in his big fingers and fastened the gold strands. "Anyway, the boys are upstairs playing their game. As far as I can tell, there's no shooting or blood violence. You know: spurting."

"Sweetie." Clarence touched Faye's elbow. "Why don't we do some legs up the wall before we leave?"

Faye looked at herself in the hall mirror, her lips squeezed unnaturally. "By *we* I know you mean *me*, and we're late as it is already."

Clarence removed Faye's oven mitt. "We're not late for anything."

Faye sighed, exasperated. Leda sloughed her backpack in the hall and took her shoes off while Clarence helped Faye place her back to the floor, scooting her hips close to the wall until her legs ran straight up. Clarence asked Leda to grab an eye pillow from a hall drawer.

It was sweet, like Ian touching Leda's skinned palms. Though he had squeezed a little too hard—the pressure of his thumb intensifying the sting.

After Faye had settled in, Leda followed Clarence into the kitchen, where a tray of blackened cookies sat on the counter. Clarence opened a drawer. "Do you mind if I smoke?"

"You still smoke?"

"Tobacco. Faye doesn't approve, but what can you do."

Leda said, "You used to get high, didn't you?"

"Sure." Clarence shucked a cigarette out of a crumpled pack. "But, baby, I'm on the straight and narrow."

"You guys would get stoned while I did my homework."

"Hey." Clarence pointed the cigarette at her, opening the back door. "I helped you with your homework."

"You did not." Leda dug her hands into her college sweatshirt.

Clarence shrugged his big shoulders. "I even helped your mom bake a fraction pie. You just don't remember."

They went to the edge of the patio, where an ornamental waterfall fed a small koi pond.

"Math gave you a hard time." Clarence cupped the cigarette and lit it. "You would cry and cry."

Leda grunted. She was being unnecessarily testy, but it was hard to make Clarence angry. She could say anything, really. She had tested this theory as a teen, saying, *I think I'm going to try heroin* or *I might have an STD*. But since her mom died, Leda hadn't wanted to joke. Since her mom died, it was hard to talk about anything.

"What about the dragon?" Clarence said. "Sometimes we would ask him for answers."

Leda shrugged. The koi swam in place, their glassy gills flexing.

Clarence said, "I know you don't like to remember those things."

"What things?"

"Your mother. It's painful for me, too. I know you don't believe it, but it's true."

There went Leda's sanctuary. Again, she was exposed.

Clarence said, "There was a while when I couldn't talk about it. If someone tried to approach me, or tell their own story, it would piss me off. Just like you're pissed at me."

"I'm not pissed at you."

Though he was right, and he knew it. She didn't want to be reminded of what had once been. It was too painful to stare at a hole and know that she had nothing with which to fill it. But somehow she had felt okay taking Ian to her old house. Somehow, with him, she had believed that she could withstand the pain of it.

"What I mean is that everyone has their own shit going on," Clarence said. "It's not just you. So, sometimes people can help, despite how much you don't want them to."

The water distorted the fish.

Leda didn't want to talk about this. "You mean that there are people out there with their own shitty lives who want to help me with mine."

"Having a shitty life and having shit going on are two different things. Your life isn't shitty."

"Clarence, you have your own family to worry about." Her tone was sharper than she had intended. But who was Clarence to tell her about her own life? To Faye and Clarence, Charlotte was just part of the news cycle. He didn't know what her friends were saying about Charlotte, about Ian, and about Leda, too.

Sunlight struggled through clouds and hit Faye's boys' trampoline. Beside it, dead hydrangea blossoms illuminated occasionally.

"Just because your mom's gone," Clarence said, "doesn't mean you're not my kid."

Gone. Out of the corner of her eye, Leda looked at him. It was the hardest word. The harshest. But perhaps the most accurate.

"People talk about moving on." Her voice strained a bit. "And you did."

"Sure. But I also can't pretend that the love I feel for you and your mom . . . I can't pretend that doesn't exist. I've buried a lot over the years, but burying doesn't get rid of anything. It just festers until, years later, you're sick."

Leda flexed her fingers. She nodded, though she still didn't get it. Didn't *want* to get it. "Did you get sick?"

"Yes." Clarence dropped ash into the grass. "Even Faye, though you wouldn't believe it, has not had an easy time of it."

Leda made a sound. It wasn't a scoff exactly. At least, she hadn't intended it to be.

Clarence said, "What does that mean?"

"From the outside, it looks like she has things pretty easy."

"From the outside, anyone can look like anything."

The pond water dashed against the rocks and cycled into the pump. The fish looked cold at her feet.

"You know, that dragon was surprisingly good at math," Clarence said, going back. "And we deferred to him with other things, remember? Dragon, what should we have for dinner? How long should Leda brush her teeth? And we couldn't argue. He had the last word on everything."

"She," Leda correctly quietly. She was annoyed again, though she shouldn't have been. She just didn't like having her memories claimed. Stolen. They belonged to *her*, her reality.

Or maybe that wasn't it. Maybe it just hurt to remember what was gone.

Clarence ground what remained of the cigarette into one of the waterfall's rocks. Ash fell on the pond surface, and the fish tried to eat it. He was about to walk in, about to rouse Faye, but now there were other things Leda wanted to say. She wanted to tell him about Charlotte and Ian. She wanted to talk about reality, too—how difficult it was to decide what was true.

Instead, Leda said, "I was always afraid of the dragon."

"Really?"

"I still am." Leda kept her head down. "A little."

The back patio door drifted open, the house's warmth spilling. "It doesn't mean you're weak," Clarence said, "if you feel something."

The wind sucked the back door shut. A keypad glowed red over the knob. Clarence pocketed the cigarette butt and punched a code in. Inside, the house still smelled burnt. Leda lingered before the charred cookies while Clarence went to get Faye. A laptop glowed on the kitchen table, a paused news report on the screen. A red banner beneath the video read CHARLOTTE MASK SEEN?

In the video, a female newscaster spoke facing the screen. "City police have now put together an almost complete accounting of Charlotte Mask's whereabouts on October 31, leading up to the moment that Mask went missing."

Leda paused it. That was stupid. Charlotte hadn't been "seen" then, had she? Of course people had seen her *before* she'd gone missing. They should be interviewing Leda and everyone else at the Gamma Kappa bubble party if they were interested in this kind of thing. They should be interviewing Ian.

This last thought gave her pause. Did she really believe that the police should be speaking with Ian? Did she believe that Ian could have done something to Charlotte?

Beside the cookie sheet, dinner was set out on the counter for Leda to heat. Tofu wieners stuffed with vegan cheese. She uncovered a bowl of Broccolini and stared into it, fingers tapping. The computer screen glowed in her periphery.

Faye looked stoned when she came out of the yoga room. Keys in hand, Clarence jotted down a few things—the internet password, the front and back door codes, instructions on how to engage or disengage the security system. Before they left, Faye pushed a book into Leda's arms—bedtime reading, in case the boys had trouble sleeping.

"Don't open the door for anyone, and if there's *anything* you need . . ." Faye was saying as Clarence shut the door, leaving Leda holding *A Year with Hafiz*. These yoga bitches, she thought, and their Hafiz. She opened the book to its bookmark.

O look again within yourself,
For I know you were once the elegant host
To all the marvels of creation.

This was the translation that Naadia had called dog shit, probably.
But the words made sense at least. Upstairs, she could hear Jonah and
Gino playing their video game: a whoosh and some kind of creepy,
minimalist music. She looked back at the book, at her hands holding
it. *Look again within yourself.* She tried. Her hands. Her feet. Her
belly. Already, she realized, she had gotten used to the smell of
burning.

Leda played the rest of the news report before checking on the
boys upstairs. Only a minute in, Flora appeared in front of her house.
It was weird, seeing her—her faded pink hair, her eyes starry with
tears. Two microphones hovered before her.

"The last time I saw her, it was probably two or three in the afternoon on Halloween." Flora's voice wavered. "Charlotte came to the
house. She'd been around the block taking pictures."

An invisible reporter spoke. "Did she seem distressed?"

Flora shook her head.

"Did her behavior strike you as out of the ordinary?"

"No, I mean . . . she wasn't wearing shoes, but that was just Charlotte. She'd often walk around the neighborhood barefoot."

Leda thought of the glass and gravel on Nalle Street. Thought of
the bearded man she'd seen in Charlotte's backyard, pissing in the
ashen fire pit.

The reporter continued. "And the shoes that Charlotte was last
seen wearing—a pair of white knee-high boots—were found in the
trunk of her vehicle. Is that your understanding?"

"Yes." Flora's face stayed oddly still. "Apparently."

Of course, Leda had heard this disturbing detail before, but hearing it now, for some reason, brought to mind something she'd forgotten about—the mud on her own feet, Monday morning. She'd slept practically all day the Sunday after Halloween, so it wasn't until Monday that she'd noticed these little things—the missing condom, her dress's stretched seam, and, yes, her feet. They'd been filthy.

The MISSING flyer appeared in the corner of the screen.

The reporter kept going, her voice nasal, authoritative. "Investigators say that your area may not be safe, particularly for young women. Are you taking any security measures or other precautions?"

"Our house is a community house." Flora gestured behind her at the blue Victorian. "It's a roof for anyone who needs it. So, no. Our doors are still open. No matter what happened . . . we've got to keep that vision alive. We've got to keep living."

The video cut off, and the next one in the sidebar opened automatically. The bottom of the screen read REPORT A SIGHTING ONLINE . . .

What would Leda say if she were to report something? *Charlotte was barefoot, and I think I was, too?* They'd laugh at her—the police or whoever. Leda shut the laptop, still hearing the reporter. *Precautions. Security measures.* She glanced toward the bookshelves that held Faye and Clarence's sound system. The line of miniature Buddhas stared and laughed and offered incomprehensible hand gestures. Leda shifted the speaker so that they turned their backs to her.

Clarence had taught her how to handle guns. He'd taught her to treat every gun as if it were loaded, and to pick one up only if she were ready to accept the responsibility of inflicting irreparable damage. Now, she knew she was being reckless. She didn't *need* this gun. But, at the same time, there was something about the shape of it. The way it fit in her hand. So solid. And if her friends were right, whispering rumors of stalking and abuse, then maybe she could use the extra protection.

The dark windows reflected her and the pistol as she faced the room. Upstairs, a door opened. Leda spun and put the pistol back on its purse, listening for the creak of the stairs. Instead, a toilet flushed. A sink ran. No one came down the steps. She padded toward the front hallway. Some tinny sound effect chimed upstairs.

Leaving the gun, Leda went up. It was carpeted and clean up there. One door had the boys' names spelled out in wooden clowns. Leda knocked and pushed it open. Inside, the bedroom was its own universe. It smelled like hot plastic and Goldfish crackers. Light from the hall streamed in, and she could see Jonah and Gino glaring at the television. Jonah, the elder, held the controller. Gino sat cross-legged, holding his knees. Vinnie sat between them in lotus, also watching the dark screen.

"Hey, guys." Leda was surprised by her own voice. Vinnie looked up and smiled broadly. Leda smiled back and then felt guilty, as if she'd just lied openly.

The boys didn't glance away from the game, saying, "Hi," and, "Hi."

The game, to Leda, looked like a black screen. "What's going on?" She could hear wind and a distant bell ringing.

Jonah said, "Playing this thing."

He hit a button, and the screen illuminated. Leda expected to see a gun or sword in the character's hand, but there was only a tunnel. Gino squirmed, seeming to anticipate something worse, but the screen went dark again.

Leda asked, "What's 'this thing'?"

"*Lucks*," Jonah and Gino responded in unison.

She watched from the doorway as the character felt his way through darkness.

Jonah asked, "Could you close the door, please? I can't see."

Leda closed it and sat on the floor next to Vinnie. She stuffed her hands under her thighs. "I still can't see anything."

Jonah said, slightly exasperated, "That's because you're not look-ing."

Leda looked. Eventually, she could make out the vague outlines of a wall. A bell rang, far off. Charlotte stood on the curb in the dark. Someone lobbed a disco ball onto the lawn.

Leda asked, "Where are you trying to go?"

Jonah responded, "Dunno."

And then what? Charlotte went home. Charlotte drove or was driven out to Reservoir Road? And then where did she go?

Leda said, "You have to have some idea, though."

"It's a *liminal* setting." Jonah employed his *duh* voice. Obviously, he had read the packaging. Or maybe he had just seen the game's intro sequence so many times that it was teaching him vocabulary.

"*Liminal.*" Leda pretended to ponder. "So what does that mean?"

"It means you don't have to *know* where you're *going.*"

Good enough.

Unprovoked, Gino lunged in his seat and screeched.

"What?" Jonah turned the character around skeptically.

Gino said, excited, "The floor was different."

Jonah went back, walked around. Gino was right; the floor sounded more like gravel than dirt. Plus, the ringing was louder. Then, at the top of the screen, Leda saw something. There was a crack in the tun-nel, and stars—tiny pricks of foil—were suddenly visible.

"Oh—" Leda said. "Look."

It was her mother's voice. *Look.* She'd said it to Ian, Halloween, her back against an ivy-covered wall. She could barely remember it . . . but he had looked, she thought. The more they'd looked, the more stars had spilled like sugar from the darkness.

Jonah turned the character away. "It's just stars."

The floor became dirt again. The bell faded. The tunnel remained the same. The longer that nothing happened, the more disconcerting the game became. Leda got why Gino had been squirming. It was uncomfortable to walk blindly in the dark.

The character picked up an object, signaled by the sound of a rustling pack. The bottom of the screen read: *Inventory—Umbilical Cord.*

"Eat it," Gino said.

"No." Jonah didn't.

Leda asked, "What else do you have in your inventory?"

Gino rocked in his seat, using a mad scientist voice to list the things. "He has a rosary, three teeth, and jewels of unknown origin."

"*Gems*," Jonah corrected. "And I have a dagger, but I haven't used it."

"And a blank scroll," Gino added.

"Well." There was Jonah's *duh* voice. "*Everyone* starts out with that."

"Why won't you eat it?" Gino whined.

"You can't eat a umbilical cord."

"But you ate the gold bezel!"

Leda snuck a look at Vinnie, who seemed to be enjoying all of this. *This is our home.* It had been the first thing Leda heard when she walked in. Faye didn't want to share. Was that it? Or was it Vinnie's silence, Vinnie's aimlessness that creeped Faye out a bit? Or maybe a better word for aimless, Leda considered, was *peace*. No striving. No struggling for . . . what? What did Faye want? Safety. Control.

That's what holding the gun had felt like, Leda realized.

The TV flashed white, illuminating Vinnie. His face broke, and he burst out laughing.

"God damn it!" Jonah shouted.

"Jonah," Leda said. "Please don't say that kind of thing."

Jonah tossed the controller onto the carpet. "I died."

"Why?" Leda asked.

"Sometimes," Jonah said, "you just die."

The four of them stared into the white screen. Charlotte shimmered her white boa above dancing bodies. Jonah passed the controller to Vinnie.

Leda asked, "Vinnie knows how to play?"

"Yeah. But he plays it really boring. He stops and looks at *everything*. It takes a *really long time*." Jonah drawled his words to emphasize slowness.

Vinnie waited for the white death screen to go away. Faye, Leda supposed, might call Vinnie's peace laziness. And what did Leda know? Maybe Faye would be right. Maybe it was an undeserved privilege to live so carelessly, a privilege to hide nothing behind your Buddha figurines. She pictured Charlotte, shoeless, wandering around Nalle Street.

Three fluorescent letters appeared on the already-white screen: LUX.

"Oh," Leda said. "*Lux*. It rhymes with . . . kooks."

Gino giggled, but Jonah looked skeptical. "Looks?"

"It means 'light.'"

Jonah frowned. "Well, that's stupid."

Leda shrugged, humming. *Lux aeterna luceat eis . . .* The song was so dissonant, so crooked when Leda's chorus performed it. The chords diverged; the harmonies bent and blurred. But, sung alone, the tune sounded simple.

"What does light," Leda said, "have to do with the game?"

"Umm." Jonah considered, looking alarmingly adult. "It's too complicated to explain."

Leda wanted to agree. *It's* all *too complicated*. Ian kissing Leda against the brick, her head merry-go-round dizzy. And Charlotte . . .

where had she been? Had she seen those same stars? Or had she already been taken? Perhaps she'd been home, waiting for her unnamed fate. And when that fate arrived, where was Ian?

When Leda stood, the carpet fell away from her feet. For a moment, she was suspended in the darkness: the body heat, the floury smell of children, the static from the television. When she found the door, light rushed in.

"Can we order pizza?" Gino spoke bravely.

Leda steadied herself on the doorframe. She frowned back at him. "Pepperoni or cheese?"

The boys gave a resounding chorus. "Hawaii!"

Downstairs, one of the Buddhas had fallen off the speaker. Leda dialed the pizza place, the greenish figurine at her feet. The skin on her palms stung, but the pain was almost comforting. She had felt torn up before, but invisible pain felt silly. Made-up, maybe. If there was no evidence of something, people said, *You're imagining things.* And maybe they were right. Maybe she got herself worked up over imaginary things. *Love. Loss. Memories.* It would be easier if the symptoms were visible—bleeding, hives, lesions, swelling . . .

When she hung up, Leda returned the Buddha to the top of the speaker. With a slight tilt, there was Clarence's gun. At least, she'd assumed it was Clarence's. But when Leda took the gun down for the second time that night, she felt again how small the thing was. It fit perfectly against the heel of her palm. It was a woman's gun.

Faye *was* a bit paranoid, Leda supposed. Faye had spoken of self-immolation as if it were a legitimate worry. She'd beefed up their security system, as if whoever had disappeared Charlotte might next target their home. But keeping a deadly weapon on a bookshelf seemed like a whole different level of delusion. Though perhaps this wasn't fair. Leda hadn't been surprised at the idea of *Clarence* owning a weapon. Why should the image of Faye holding a gun seem reck-less, hysteric?

From the outside, Clarence had said, *anyone can look like anything.* Even Faye, he'd suggested, had not had it easy. So, Leda supposed, Faye wanted to feel as if she had some control.

It took some fiddling to release the magazine (it had been years since she had done this kind of thing). Eventually, it dropped into her palm. It was full. She pulled the slide back to see if there was a round in the chamber, and one kicked out and landed on the carpet. One tiny bullet.

In the kitchen, Leda placed the pistol and loaded magazine on the counter. Of course she wasn't going to do anything with the gun. She didn't aspire to Faye's level of paranoia. But maybe it was possible to trust the world too much.

She checked the chamber again: empty. Upstairs, a door squeaked. Leda stuffed the gun and the loose magazine in her sweatshirt. Empty, she reminded herself. Still empty.

You remind me of her, Tamara had said. Had she been calling Leda open or stupid?

No one came down, but Leda didn't take the gun back out.

On the other side of the kitchen island, a construction-paper hand with a crayon-drawn wattle covered the November calendar. Until this minute, Leda had forgotten about Thanksgiving. Maybe she re-lied on this too much—this not remembering. These little sucking holes in her memory where her mother should have been, where Charlotte should have been. Ian. *Maybe we should all just pay atten-tion.* She herself had said it. In a perfect world, everyone (Leda in-cluded) would be 100 percent conscious.

On Halloween, everything might have gone differently if Leda had been attentive to herself and her surroundings. But she didn't even know when she'd blacked out. It was like trying to pinpoint the exact moment in which you fell asleep, to examine that transition between realities. After losing consciousness, she had to rely on what others told her. According to Mary, she'd shown up crying, bleeding, as if she'd escaped something. Escaped Ian. After she'd left Ian, he could have gone anywhere, could have seen anyone, could have done anything.

I'm not saying Ian "did it," Tamara had said, though just voicing this thought seemed to imply the opposite.

Would Halloween have gone differently if she, if *Charlotte* had been carrying a gun?

She shook herself. She needed air. She decided to wait for the pizza outside. Following Clarence's written instructions, she disengaged the security system and went out the front door in her sock feet. What did paying attention even feel like? Did it feel like this— taking a seat on a stoop with a concealed weapon? Was she being delusional . . . or vigilant?

She put up her college sweatshirt's hood, stuffing her hands in the pouch along with the pistol and magazine. Despite the cold, Leda slipped her socks off and examined her bare feet, watching the delicate tendons flexing. Inside, her phone vibrated. It had been in the hall on silent for the past hour at least. She padded in, retrieved it. Her entire sorority was flipping:

Where r u, Lee!? We r worried!

Please check in! Ian came by and asked about you and everyone is freaking!!

U okay?

Where are you?

Where u at, LEEE? Ian was here and HE DID NOT LOOK GOOD.

Everything OK?

Still, these voices followed her—the panicked cacophony. *Was* she okay? She didn't know. *Couldn't* know. Nobody could know what was coming.

When she was a kid, Leda used to get a creeping feeling. The hairs would perk up on the back of her neck. Her heart would drum. Right when she got it, she would dash to her mom, feeling the thing at her heels. A monster. At the time, she'd figured that the monster never got her because she'd outrun it. Either that, or it was afraid of her mother. Of course, it never occurred to her that the monster didn't exist. Because it did: she felt it. That had always seemed like enough evidence.

Now, she closed her eyes for a minute. She tried to sense that old monster. And there it was—right on her.

Her phone trembled in her hand again. She opened her eyes: Ian.

Sorry for being so fucking awkward yesterday. And I'm sorry if I upset you. You make me nervous, Leda. You do know that you're beautiful, don't you?

Instead of feeling flattered, Ian's text spooked her. But, without her mother, where could she run?

A set of headlights approached, and Leda shut off the phone. *Don't open the door for anyone*, Faye had told her. And here it was, gaping. Her hand slipped back inside her sweatshirt, her fingers finding cold metal. With the pistol, she realized, she didn't have to dash inside. She didn't have to hide. She could stand right here and face the monster. It was a new feeling, this power.

The car slowed and stopped short of Faye's house. It parked. The trunk popped. A man got out, slow. Leda's hand lay on the gun in her pouch.

From the trunk, the man removed a twelve-pack of toilet paper and two grocery bags. Leda let her breath out. It was just a neighbor.

He glanced sideways at her. He was probably just as suspicious of her—a hoodied, barefoot stranger.

A motion light blasted his yard as he went up his walk. In the light, Leda recognized him.

"Professor?" She took her hands from her sweatshirt and stood. "I'm sorry. This is so weird. I'm in your astronomy class. I'm Leda."

"Oh—" Her professor paused with his groceries, not exactly smiling. "Hello, then. Hope the class is going all right."

"Yeah, it's great." She took down her hood, trying to appear less menacing. "I mean, I don't think I'm doing very well grade-wise, but I like it."

"Well, good . . . I think?"

"I'm not a math person." She went down the steps into the yard. "Those quizzes sort of demolish me."

Her professor squeezed the groceries. "It's not for everybody."

"Seriously." Though this wasn't what she had wanted to hear, exactly. "I'm doing the homework," she added, which was almost true.

"You're always welcome to ask questions after class," her professor said. "It's important to understand the origin of certain equations, so you're not just plugging in numbers."

"Okay," Leda said, nodding, her hand drifting back to her pocket, fingering the magazine.

"It's a beautiful night tonight, in any case. Gives some perspective, I think." Her professor pointed past the bleary streetlights. He loved this *perspective* thing. "You can just catch our Milky Way."

He was right. There was the foggy edge of the galaxy, home to more than one hundred billion stars. In illustrations, the galaxy (*our* galaxy, she thought, almost smiling) looked like a soft Frisbee. From the inside, it was hard to see one's own shape clearly. Though, of course, there were other ways of "seeing." There were equations to calculate mass and distance and velocity. The visible-light spectrum could reveal sulfur, neon, hydrogen . . .

He took a step away. "Well, it was nice to meet you."

"Actually, Professor?"

He stopped, waited.

She wanted to tell him she appreciated it—the whole perspective thing, even if it was corny. She appreciated how, in class, he sometimes got her to see outside of herself for an instant. But then his front door opened. A woman stood in the threshold. The brass numbers on the wood door shone.

"Never mind," she was saying. "I'm sorry to bother you. It was nice to see you. Or . . . meet you."

And already, he was walking away. Already, he was greeting the woman in the doorway. A baby cried inside. The door closed. The motion light extinguished. Overhead, a jet blinked. There was no moon, or the moon hadn't risen, or it was hidden.

The pizza came, and Leda took it in. She reengaged the alarm system as the burnt smell came back, now mixed with hot pineapple. She texted her friends, saying she was fine. Ian's message went unanswered.

You do know that you're beautiful, don't you?

It seemed so random. The tone, the timing—it all seemed off. Though, she had to admit, she felt a little less spooked with the gun in her pocket.

In the kitchen, she nibbled the Broccolini and fed a few tofu dogs down the garbage disposal, though the whirring blades made her shivery. She would make the boys take oaths; the extra-large Hawaiian would never be disclosed. She was about to call the boys downstairs when she got another message. Carly.

I hope you are not with Ian.

Via text, the period was the angriest punctuation. What was Carly suggesting?

Leda responded quickly. Car, I'm babysitting. Do you want proof or something?

Flying estrogen, Tamara had called this. Leda wondered if Charlotte had ever had to deal with it—how your friends could swing from love to dislike and then (worse) disinterest. How you could feed them bits of gossip to get their attention again. And then there was this, Carly's most recent message that seemed to suggest that Leda was somehow to blame. As if she'd asked for this.

Was this really friendship?

But Carly seemed to ignore Leda's irritation. She wrote, I don't know what other people have told you but i think he is dangerous. Genie is downtown, and she said she just saw him come out of the police station. keep ur phone by u and text me when i text u. I am not pissed at u, im pissed at the world, and want to know u r safe in it. <3

Leda had never gotten such a serious text from Carly or anybody in her sorority. She reread the message. Maybe she had been wrong. Wrong to assume that all her friends wanted was gossip. Maybe they would face the monster with her.

Leda wrote, Thanks, Car. Really. I'll be home soon. She felt warm, writing it.

And she felt warm when Carly texted back, Luv you. Morning yoga?
Only bc I luv you too

Leda inhaled with her chest and belly. Again, she clicked on Ian's text. If what Carly said was true, then he had probably been in the police station when he sent it.

Still, she didn't need to be paranoid; she had friends. She had support. She didn't *want* to go the Faye route—installing alarms, stashing weapons. She didn't want to get to the point where even a Buddhist monk made her suspicious.

Perhaps all she could do was break things off. That seemed like a sane solution. She'd tell him she wasn't interested and then she'd distance herself from him. She returned the gun to its place behind the speaker. Fragments of song flashed through her: *Peccatoribus. Lux. Ora pro nobis.*

Sinners. Light. Pray for us.

"Pizza!" she shouted upward.

11

Carly was MIA Saturday morning. She wasn't feeding Glock his morning Cheerios. She didn't come to her door when Leda knocked. Leda tried not to worry. Carly was an earplugs and eye mask kind of lady; she was probably just sleeping through their yoga date.

Granted, yoga was not Leda's thing. But today, Leda could have used the distraction. She had gotten another text from Ian, late.

Can we talk?

After receiving the message, she hadn't been able to sleep. She'd huddled on her porch until morning, shuffling through Charlotte's postcards, scanning for a single word: Ian. He had been such a significant figure in Charlotte's life, she thought Pia might have known about him.

Hours later, when Carly didn't come to her door, Leda found herself back on the porch, staring at the cards' precarious cursive as the sun rose, her legs bare and cold beneath her dingy Psi Delta robe. By now, she'd skimmed every card . . . but she hadn't *read* them all. Not really. She both wanted and didn't want to read them. She felt this way about the dragon. Fascinated, but also frightened.

> *Dear Charlotte, I've noticed that you often leave your door open. Do you forget, or is it intentional? Maybe too much wood in the woodstove? Of course, there's no one out here but goats, but you never know. Love, Pia*

No Ian. No allusion to Ian. Honestly, the postcards confused Leda more than anything. Where *was* Charlotte? And who was this person, Pia, weirdly spying on Charlotte, and then telling her about it?

> *Dear Charlotte, I watched the snow blow into your cabin on your morning walk to find wood. The door was (again!) open. Did you hike all the way to the rim? There was so much fog, so I couldn't see far, but I imagined those warped pitch pines, the laurel. Then so much cloud moved in that I couldn't see your cabin at all. Love, Pia*

One after the next, she flipped through hazy streams, fall colors, sunrises over mountains.

> *Dear Charlotte, Why do I like the quiet, sensitive type? They're no different, when it comes down to it. Love, Pia*

"Hey."

Leda jumped, stuffing the postcards under the flap of her robe. It was Naadia, hair rumpled, rubbing her eyes like a child.

"Chill," Naadia said. "It's just me."

"Sorry." Leda did her best to pretend that she hadn't just jammed a stack of loose postcards into her robe.

Naadia didn't seem to have noticed. She was still half asleep. She took her vape pen out of her pocket and rubbed her eyes again. "Has anyone told you you've been acting a wee bit odd lately?"

"No." Leda thought of the gun she'd left at Clarence's. She glanced at her pale, veiny feet. "What do you mean?"

Naadia clarified, "Like, *jumpy*."

"Oh. No." Leda laced her fingers on her knee, like Charlotte when she was prom queen. "No one has mentioned it."

Naadia yawned. "Do you want to, like, talk about it?"

Somewhere, a glass bottle smashed into a bin of other bottles, and Leda felt the shock register in her spine. Birds shot from the backyard bamboo and into the neighbor's construction pit. The trees over there were still unplanted.

"I don't think so," Leda said as Naadia yawned for the second time. "Thanks, though."

Her sister only shrugged, moving back toward her room. She wasn't going to press it, and Leda was, oddly, disappointed.

"Naadia?" Leda said. "Have you seen Carly this morning?"

"Mm . . . I think she stayed over at Benjamin's."

Naadia went in, leaving Leda to stare at the neighbor's root-bound trees. Carly had stood her up. She had sent Leda that mothering text—as if she were really worried, as if she really cared—and then she had gone off to fuck her British gentleman.

I need to get out of here, Leda thought. She needed to step back, needed to get some perspective. Whatever that meant.

She texted Mary, You busy?

Mary responded after a few minutes. take home midterm in 1 hr. I'll txt after

Whatever. Leda silenced her phone, stood, and dug the loose cards out of her robe. Inside, she sat at her desk with the door closed.

> *Dear Charlotte, A new guy just arrived on the farm. He's been traveling around the country for months, sleeping in cars, in parks, in parking lots. He "finds himself" (his words) by trusting the world, trusting people. He hitches rides. He knocks on doors and asks for water. "Freedom"—another one of his words. I have tried asking the world for things. I have tried trusting people. I still try. But I'm beginning to wonder if it is possible to do this (a woman) and survive. Love, Pia*

Leda read the card a second time. Then she got up, found her running shoes, and knotted the laces. What was with the whole barefoot thing? she wondered. Was it trust (to use Pia's word)—trusting humanity, trusting that the world would take care of you—or stupidity?

She found the scrap of paper where Tamara had written her number. Do you know if charlotte went somewhere last summer? she texted, glancing at the postcard she'd just read. Like a farm . . . or some place in the country?

She would have texted Flora, Charlotte's roommate, who had already mentioned that Charlotte had been out of town, but Leda didn't have her number.

Just below Leda's conversations with Tamara, with Mary, there was Ian's text from 4:30 a.m.

Can we talk?

She stared at the gray letters until the screen went dark.

It was chilly out, but she warmed up quickly. She ran to the Lawn. She sprinted, actually, taking the bike lane so she didn't have to deal with pedestrians. Her phone bobbed in the zip pocket of her leggings. Cars rushed by at her elbow. She passed Indoor Sunglasses' frat, dub reggae inside, echoing. She passed some Theta girls, hauling what appeared to be an oversized horn of plenty. And then there were ginkgos and sycamores overhead. White columns blinkered in her periphery. The grass on the Lawn had frosted. Leda could see her breath—white, hot—when she stopped in front of Ian's door. She tried to return to that mental state she'd achieved yesterday, holding the gun. Control. Calm. She lifted her fist and knocked.

Nobody came. She waited. She was holding her breath, she realized, when she went in for a second knock. She let it out. What was she expecting? A scream? A gunshot?

As soon as she turned away—relieved, in all honesty—the door swung.

"Oh—" Obviously, Ian had not expected to see her. He squinted, his eyes bleary and bloodshot. "I mean, sorry. Hey. Are you okay?"

"Huh?"

"You're sort of . . ." Ian scratched his head. "Gasping."

She was, wasn't she? "I was running."

"Last time I saw you, you were running away from me. Now . . ." Ian might have been trying to smile, but the expression looked painful. "You want to come in?"

"I'm okay," Leda said, though she was cold. She glimpsed his loft bed, unmade, behind him. The room smelled familiar—the sheets, the fire—though she couldn't actually remember having been inside. "I saw your message this morning."

Of course, that wasn't the real reason she was here. She had come to end this—whatever *this* was.

"Great," Ian said with what was certainly forced enthusiasm. "*Yeah*. Well, let me put on my coat."

He closed his door, and Leda waited, watching her breath steam. The Lawn was oddly empty. A bundled girl—maybe three years old—pedaled through the silver grass on a tricycle, her mother jogging alongside. The girl wore kneepads, elbow pads, and a helmet. Better safe than sorry? Was that the philosophy? But, then again, the girl probably couldn't feel the wind in her hair or on her skin.

Leda checked her phone, perhaps to feel slightly less alone.

I think Char's aunt has a farm, Tamara had texted. But it's far . . .

Leda thought of the sheepskins in the communal kitchen. The woolen goat figurine. Or had it been a sheep? She typed, How far?

Tamara responded, 2 or 3 hrs? Name of farm has dog in it

Thx, Leda typed as Ian's door rattled open.

Tamara shot back, How's Ian?

"You're sure you don't want to come in?" Ian said. "I just got the fire going."

"I'm sure." Leda stuffed away her phone. They paused, looking at each other. Leda said, "You look . . ."

"Tired," Ian supplied, closing his Lawn door. "I look tired, I'm guessing."

"Right." Yes. He looked like someone who hadn't slept. Like someone who had been (as Carly had suggested) at the police station, being questioned. Interrogated. Was there a difference? Leda said, "You texted me pretty late."

"Sorry. I don't think I realized how late it was." Ian zipped his coat, glancing toward and away from Leda's face. "I guess I'm apologizing a lot. But, I am sorry if I upset you the other day. I guess it's a sensitive subject."

"What is?"

"Charlotte." Ian swallowed, as if the word dried his throat. "You're not the only one who has brought it—her—up. And I don't want you, of all people, to think . . ." He trailed off.

"Think what?"

Ian cleared his throat and started over. "I understand why finding

out about my relationship with Charlotte might make you uncomfortable." He spoke now in a soft monotone, as if he had rehearsed the
wording, the tone. "So, maybe if you can think back . . . you might be
able to clear up, in your own mind, what happened that night."

I can't remember anything, Leda didn't say. She tugged her long
sleeves down over her fingers, glancing back at the deserted Lawn.
She said, "Why did you send me that text yesterday?"

"Which one?"

"The beautiful thing." The scrapes on her palms itched, as if Ian's
thumb were still pressing the raw skin.

"I don't know." He looked embarrassed . . . and something else.
Spooked. Edgy. "Because it's true."

She opened her mouth, but her phone interrupted. It was Carly
calling, as if she had sensed Ian's presence. Leda let it ring.

Ooh, see that girl . . .

When "Dancing Queen" stopped, Carly texted. Where ARE you?
It's an emergency!

Leda didn't write back. Most likely, Carly was being melodramatic.

"Listen." Leda took a step away from Ian. It had been a bad idea,
coming here. "I've got to get going."

"I can walk with you."

It wasn't a question, and she didn't stop him. She didn't have to be
anywhere, obviously. She had come here to talk to him, to finish
things. It was all getting too weird, too nerve-racking. But actually
opening her mouth, actually speaking proved harder than she'd
thought it would be. If only she could speak to him in Spanish, so she
could focus on grammar instead of meaning.

He followed her down the brick walk along bone-white columns.
There was no more evidence of Halloween—no balloons, no streamers, no candy.

Ian said, "Will you try to remember?"

She thought of the stretched seam in her dress, the missing condom. She thought of the dried blood on her lip and her period that still hadn't come. How could she possibly say any of this?

Leda said, "It's been two weeks."

Ian ignored this. "I know that people are talking to you." His blue eyes landed on hers. "I know what they're saying, and I only want . . . I don't know. I like you, and I want you to trust me. I don't want you to think something terrible about me."

I like you. It still squeezed her heart a little. But she couldn't just *remember*, on command. She could recall only scraps, flashes. She remembered that these bricks had been cold on her bare feet. She had been holding her boots in her hands. A torn black streamer had flagged toward the dark center of the grass, and she'd been startled by it—as if a strip of the night had unraveled. She had walked a ways before she'd stepped in Silly String. How had she forgotten this? Leaning on a pillar, she'd tried to jam her sticky feet into her boots. On the brick, she'd left a wormy streak of hot pink.

Ian said, "Do you remember what time you left my place?"

"No." Leda shook her head. "I just . . . left."

She went silent again. A strong wind sailed over the quad.

"Look," Ian said. "This isn't easy for me."

"And you think it's easy for me?"

If something horrible had happened, would Leda remember it?

"That's not what I mean." He was getting impatient. "It's just . . . maybe I'm not being clear. I woke up, and you weren't there. I'm wondering why you left. I'm asking you to remember if I made you upset."

"Mary . . ." Leda started. "Mary said that she saw me."

"When?"

"I don't know."

"That's it? She just saw you?"

Wind slid in from an alley, the cold seeping into the sheltered quad. When sun finally hit them at the end of the colonnade, it was no warmer than the shade. There was no one in front of Bell Hall. It was early. A Saturday. Leda headed for a random building, hoping the doors wouldn't be locked.

"Think of it this way," Ian said, his voice a little stiffer than it had been. "If someone were to ask you about that night, with me . . ." Even in the chill, Ian appeared to be sweating. "What would you say?"

Suddenly, Leda felt sick. "Is that what you want to know?" She walked faster, but he kept stride. She pushed into a building, the dry warmth tight, enveloping. "You want to know what I'm going to say about you, about that night, *if someone asks me.*"

They were in an open, empty stairwell. There were empty classrooms beyond them, down an empty hall.

"I just mean that if I can clear anything up," Ian lowered his voice, avoiding the echo, "if I can convince you that nothing happened . . ."

"Mary said—" Leda's voice shifted octaves. "She said I came to her door that night, crying."

"Okay. What else?"

In earnest, Leda tried to think back. But it was as if she had fallen in a hole for eight hours. "Ian, I don't know," she admitted, exhausted, embarrassed. "I blacked out."

"But . . ." Ian stalled. Leda had thought that this admission would change everything. Now Ian, at the very least, would owe her a real apology. But it became clear that for Ian, this was not a revelation. He didn't look surprised. He had known she'd been unconscious. His voice came out small and pressurized. "Can you remember if something upset you? Specifically."

"Why don't you tell me?" Leda spoke quickly. "Did you *do* something that might have upset me?"

Ian fell silent. Leda turned and went down the wide stairs, steadying herself on the handrail, though she still felt as if she were falling. Falling down some bottomless hole. The hole in *Alice in Wonderland*, say, where at the bottom there wasn't just blackness, but a whole new reality. There were rules you had to learn, and consequences if you didn't. Things that appeared friendly were not always so. Though the same went for things that at first appeared evil.

Ian followed, too close.

Leda said, "I've got to go home." But what she meant by *home*, she didn't know. She went down another flight of steps. "I think we need to stop this."

"Stop *what*? This is not just about you." Ian hissed. "*Something happened* that night, and I'm trying to understand what happened."

"Right." Leda stopped when the stairs ended, and turned to him. She thought of what Indoor Sunglasses had said in those ten minutes they had known each other before they'd had sex: *I don't care about you either.* "You're worried," Leda said, "because after I left, you could have been anywhere."

Ian opened his mouth, but she lifted a finger.

"For all the police know," she said, "you could have been with Charlotte."

You're beautiful, he had texted. What bullshit.

Ian's mouth was still open, but he said nothing. She'd expected him to react. Why wasn't he denying it? She turned from him—disturbed by this new silence, this blankness—and he reached a hand out, as if to stop her. His fingers grazed the inside of her wrist.

"Ian." She looked him dead in the face. She wasn't afraid, for some reason; she was pissed. "Don't touch me."

He fell away immediately.

She walked, quick and steady, her footsteps echoing. She was his alibi. She saw that now, clearly. He'd counted on her being sober enough to confirm that they had been together, but drunk enough to not remember the particulars.

The basement hall was dim and empty. No students or professors were around today. She glanced behind her only once; she was alone. Only silence followed. She passed bulletin boards filled with YOU HAVE A VOICE and MISSING posters, including one she had never seen before: MISSING: LINETTE JOHNSON. She paused, looking at this girl she'd never seen, never heard of. Underneath her photo, there was that same bullet point list: Eyes, Age, Race . . . It had been three years since the girl (brown eyes, eighteen, black) was last seen. She had been fifteen when she went missing.

A door shuddered, and her mind snapped back to Ian. A figure came out of one of the classrooms at the far end of the hall and hurried toward her. Leda glanced back to where Ian had been, but the stairwell was empty. She waited, tensed, until she got a good look at this person.

"Flora?"

Flora halted. She must not have recognized Leda either. Her pink hair stuck up at all angles. She looked shocked. Guilty. But what had she been doing?

"Hey!" Flora ran a hand through her hair, succeeding only in making it crazier. "I didn't see you there. Off in my own world. All good, Leda?"

Leda frowned, because it was Flora who did not look "all good." Her glittered cheeks looked puffy, as if she'd been crying.

"I'm good," Leda said, though her body still rushed with adrenaline.

"Great!" Flora's voice sounded strained. "Well, see you!"

Leda had been about to say something else, but Flora was already hurrying away.

When Leda reached the other end of the long hall, she stopped at the classroom Flora had seemed to come out of. The door was marked with a piece of paper: *Intro to Photo.*

The room was not locked. The lights were still on. It wasn't so different from any classroom, except for the black revolving door on the opposite wall. She remembered this kind of door from her high school's darkroom, which had been a popular place for couples to kiss, even among non-photography students. A week ago, Leda might have taken note, thinking of Ian. But so much had changed in the last few days.

She went to the door and stepped in. The experience felt something like a magic trick—you entered in one state, spun the door, and then you came out different.

The red-lit darkroom was like a warm closet. Leda hushed, glancing around the room, though there was no one here. She wasn't even sure what she was looking for. There were five enlargers and a basin of dribbling chemical baths. A few developed prints hung from a string. Under the string, there was a tall shelf of narrow cubbies. Each cubby corresponded with a student name. There was Flora Blackshear, toward the top. And there, in the middle, was Charlotte Mask.

A folder stuck partway out of Charlotte's cubby. Had Flora just been here, Leda wondered, looking through Charlotte's portfolio? It was possible that she'd panicked, hearing Leda and Ian's voices in the hall. And yes, the photos inside the folder faced every which way, as if they'd been hurriedly put away.

The first images were similar to the ones Leda had seen on the SLR's memory card. A shirtless boy hooked his thumbs through his front belt loops, showing a dark pubic shadow. Two hands held a girl's nearly naked ass, wearing only wedgied underpants. A boy wept into a large jar of Jif peanut butter.

Charlotte had written her name on the backs of these, along with what must have been a title—*Innocence/Experience*. They were good, Leda could see, though she wasn't sure why exactly. They were neither romantic nor judgmental. They were exploratory—as if Charlotte were simply trying to understand something, understand this world in which straight-A boys and girls let themselves unravel. Or were they *men* and *women*? Or something in between? Neither adult nor child, maybe.

Again, Leda remembered the picture Charlotte had taken of her—Leda at the Cathouse, accepting a condom from a gorilla. Had Leda been exploring her hidden parts, too? Her fantasies? Her vulnerabilities? In the world being documented—this world called College—self-exploration seemed to occur only in moments of extreme debauchery. It was as if confronting the self were too dangerous, too daunting a task to undertake sober.

Leda stopped again on the boy holding his belt loops. It *was* dangerous, she decided. You could get hurt if you explored too deeply. You could step into traffic. You could fall off a roof. You could trust somebody you shouldn't. And you could cause harm, too. Because it wasn't just about you; other people were exploring their tender wildness, too.

So, was it possible to be vulnerable and careful, too?

After a dozen college photos, Charlotte seemed to swap that world for another—one of mist and trees and quiet. First, a sharp cliff with only fog beyond it. Next, a tattooed hand hauling a bucket, a human form reflected in the bucket's bright liquid. Then, an animal's horizontal pupil reflecting another human silhouette. Leda turned this one over. There was Charlotte's name, and under it, the photograph's title: *Pia*.

The word slipped out of Leda's mouth like a curse. "Pia."

She flipped the photo and stared at the image. That silhouette. She turned back to the tattooed fist carrying the bucket, the liquid reflecting that same mottled human image. This one had no title, but this, too, must be her.

Leda checked the backs of more photos. When she flipped back to the cliff, the writing was so narrow that she had to squint: *The Rim at White Dog Farm.*

This was all she needed. Leda pushed the photos back in their folder, returned them to the cubby marked *Charlotte*, and stepped into the revolving door.

An online search for White Dog Farm yielded contact info and an address. The place was a little over two hours southwest. She could make it a day trip tomorrow and get back in time for Monday's classes. In the meantime, Leda would lie low with her door bolted.

She wrote the owner of White Dog Farm—a woman named Daria, who must have been Charlotte's aunt. The place had a volunteer program; Leda considered saying she wanted to learn about permaculture or something. Instead, she tried to be honest, admitting to her vague connection to Charlotte. However, she didn't comment on how she'd found out about the farm. And she did not mention Pia.

At her desk, Leda searched Pia's postcards for more mentions of *the rim.* She'd come across one this morning, but she could have sworn Pia had referenced it more than once. She skimmed cards detailing birds—the beak shape, the color. There were descriptions of trees and another comment on Charlotte's open door.

> *Dear Charlotte, Did you get that wren out of your cabin? I don't know what you expect, leaving your door open again. Who are you trying to let in? In my experience, someone will always take advantage. Love, Pia*

Leda glanced at her own bolted door, thinking of the girl she and Ian had seen on their way to the reservoir, dashing for her pink tent and zipping herself in. It was funny how a flimsy tent flap, a locked door, the blinking light of an engaged alarm could all create the same illusion of safety.

Then, she found the rim—little, brief mentions. Some sort of cliff, Leda guessed. A rock. A mountaintop. These postcards ended like all the others: *Love, Pia.* If she could find Pia, Leda vowed, she would show her this stack of cards. Then, somehow, she would convince Pia to show her Charlotte's end of the correspondence. Though it would be foolish, Leda supposed, to trust the girl too quickly. There was no guarantee that Pia was blameless.

The next postcard in the stack was longer, the cursive squeezing to fit.

> *Dear Charlotte, The harmonica guy always plays the same rhythm. I asked him if he hears that sound in his dreams, and he asked me what was my reason for asking. I didn't know. I think I made him angry. Here on the farm, I still ask questions, but there's no one to answer. You'd think this would force me to answer. Love, Pia*

When Leda next looked up, an hour had passed, and she was hungry. She hadn't eaten anything all morning. She dragged herself down to the deserted kitchen. A crusty log of cream cheese sat in the fridge door, and she extracted it, looking for mold, when she heard a whimper. Leda looked up, facing Carly's emotion chart—blank today. The room appeared empty. She went back to the cheese, but again she heard the whimper, then a sniff, coming from the common room couch. Or, more specifically, a quivering blanket mound.

Leda peeled away the blankets and found Carly underneath,

ugly-crying. Until now, Leda had forgotten about Carly's emergency text, though she still didn't feel too bad about it. She was still pissed at her Big, to be honest.

Even so, she tried to speak gently. "What's wrong, Car?"

Carly mumbled something directly into the cushions.

Leda's phone rang. The screen read UNKNOWN. She silenced it. "I can't hear you, Carly."

Carly showed her face, her cheeks like raw chicken, and then buried it again without saying anything. This was just like Carly. Always needing to be the center of attention. No matter what happened to anyone else, she'd turn it around and make it about her.

Of course Leda didn't do this. Did she?

Between sobs, Carly whispered, finally, "He's not British."

Leda didn't get it. "Who isn't?"

Carly dug a tissue out from the couch cushions. "Benjamin." Her lip trembled. "If that's even his name."

Leda rubbed Carly's back halfheartedly. "Carly, you're going to have to explain."

But Carly was crying again, her whole body trembling. Leda tried to be compassionate, but she also couldn't forget the put-on mothering, the disingenuous texts, the way Carly's eyes had sliced through her after the latte incident as if they barely knew each other, as if they weren't even friends.

Glock, in the corner, whistled and flexed his crest. "Superman." His feet tacked on the metal bars. "Bitches."

Maybe I should be crying, too, Leda thought. *Maybe this is a normal response.* She rubbed Carly's back. "Why is your emotion chart erased, Car?"

"I erased it," Carly said forcefully.

"Bitches."

"Shut up, Glock!" Carly shrieked. "Benjamin lied to me about everything. He's not British."

Leda did her best to speak gently. "Well, is he, like, Australian?"

"He's a liar," Carly said into the couch. "I heard him."

"What did he say?"

"That's not what I mean." Carly sat up, a fistful of Kleenex blocking her face. "I *heard* him. *Talking*." She blew her nose and then leaned against Leda with all her weight. "On the phone with his *mummy*. He thought I was asleep."

"So, he's not . . ." Leda looked back at her friend, finally getting it. "He's not British?"

"He's from Kentucky. At first, he wouldn't admit it. But I *heard him*. His voice is borderline *country*."

"So is he not a student? Does he not study philosophy?"

"I don't know." Carly clutched her tissue, blew. "I don't know who he is. I don't know anything!"

In the grand scheme of things, this discovery did not seem earth-shattering. But Carly wasn't looking for perspective. Leda said, "Car, that is fucking creepy."

"I felt like such a crazy bitch," Carly said, encouraged. "Freaking out in front of his *flat*mates." A wrinkle line stood between Carly's eyes. Even so, her breathing was beginning to slow. "I tried to fill out my emotion chart, actually, but it didn't have the right smileys."

The girls sat shoulder to shoulder for a beat before Carly started laughing. Leda looked at her friend. She was disturbed, suddenly, though perhaps she shouldn't have been. She should have been happy that Carly was moving on, snapping out of it. Instead, she felt manipulated.

"We had sex," Carly hiccupped, "and he used the word 'shag.' How can you trust someone after that?"

Glock mumbled, "Super."

"It's like he took notes from Austin Powers." Carly stood, brushing flecks of tissue from her U-neck. "Ugh. I'm so hungry, Lee. Do you want something to eat?"

Leda followed Carly into the kitchen, though she'd lost her appetite. Carly and Benjamin had been *shagging* when Carly had supposedly been so worried about Leda's safety. Right when it seemed like Leda had her Big's support, her protection, here she was weeping over Benjamin.

From the pantry, Carly dug out what looked like a jug of laundry detergent—Bisquick. Anytime Pancakes were one of her favorite things. Leda knew this from their Big-Little get-to-know-you quizzes. She also knew Carly's favorite color: yellow. She knew her favorite animal, which was also the same as what Carly had wanted to be when she grew up: a monkey. Why? *Because they're loud*, she'd shouted.

Had these quizzes helped Leda *know* her friend? Had these little details, this trivia, really told Leda anything about Carly? At the time, Leda had thought so. But now it all felt frivolous, irrelevant compared to, well, a different kind of Q&A: *Weight, Hair, Eyes, Age, Race.* Charlotte Mask. Linette Johnson. And how many others went unreported? Leda would have been a freshman when Johnson went missing. And there had been no vigils. No search parties. No news coverage. No reward money.

In the Psi Delta house, the Benjamin incident would get more play than Linette Johnson's disappearance. It would trump the building evidence that Ian had *known* that Leda had been unconscious. He had, quite possibly, *planned* on it. And there was a good chance that, at least for the day, this not-British crisis would eclipse even Charlotte.

Carly forward folded with the Bisquick to get the couch kinks out of her back. She came up singing Amy Winehouse, bumping butts with Leda as if no tension could possibly exist between them. Big and Little. Sisters.

Carly whisked lumps out of the batter, singing tunelessly. (*And I wake up alone . . .*) The Bisquick smelled like butter and plastic.

"I need a shower," Leda said.

It was just an excuse to get out of there. More Psi Delts were trickling in, as if they had smelled the drama the way sharks smell blood. Already, Carly was rehashing the Benjamin report.

"He never slipped up," she was saying. "I think a part of him believed it. He had constructed *actual* memories. Holidays to the North Sea, eating custard with Gran or whatever they call the elderly . . ."

Upstairs in her room (dead bolt in place) Leda saw she had missed two "unknown" calls. There was also a text from a number she didn't recognize.

Hi, Lee! Going out for pizza at 6—usually I wouldn't, but boys have been driving me CRAZY. They've revolted. They won't eat ANYTHING. Would love for you to come if you're not busy?? xoxo Faye

Okay—Faye. Not too scary. Leda glanced at the clock. She had plenty of time, but right now she couldn't face Clarence and Faye. She couldn't face Carly. Even Mary was occupied with her own concerns, her own life.

But could she really blame her friends? What could be done about Linette? About Charlotte?

She checked her email. To her surprise, she saw that the owner of White Dog Farm had already responded. Daria said that if Leda had four-wheel drive, she could come whenever she wanted. On impulse, Leda emptied her backpack, dumping pencils, Neruda, her astronomy book. Out of the depths of the closet, from underneath the dragon, she found her mother's hiking boots. She rubber banded the postcards. She packed a simple bag.

Before leaving, Leda dragged her mother's dragon out of the closet and hung it from the ceiling. She hammered nails into makeshift hooks, snaking the body across the ceiling. When she was finished, the dragon's jaws faced the door. She shouldered her bag, telling herself that she'd be back in time to catch up on homework.

Downstairs, the Psi Delta house was loud with girls. They snacked on marshmallows and chocolate chips. They hovered their faces inches from the bathroom mirror, applying mascara and dabbing wedge sponges across their skin. Blow-dryers whined. Only an hour had passed, but already it smelled like Saturday night: the Anytime Pancakes, the holding gels and straightening irons.

At first, no one noticed Leda gathering a few bottles of water from the kitchen. Carly did handstands in the hall off the common room, telling her story, looking like the Venus of Willendorf after a summer of Pilates.

". . . I'd rather believe he's sick in the head instead of just a total skeez trying to get into my skinny jeans." Carly pointed her toes against the wall, her big calves flexing. "Which he did."

The bathroom asked, "Was he good at least?"

"Not really." Carly stretched one leg to touch the opposite wall with her toe. Her shirt slipped, showing pale belly. "A big you-know-what only goes so far, honestly."

The microwave dinged. A bag of popcorn teetered within, but nobody retrieved it. A girl tried to pick up Glock, but was surprised when his claws were sharp. Leda scavenged some road snacks from the kitchen. She took a handful from the open bag of chocolate chips, glancing at the swarm of smileys newly circled on Carly's chart: Brave, Hopeful, Optimistic, Determined, Stubborn, Pissed . . .

"Lee!" Carly had come down from her handstand and spotted Leda in the kitchen. She sashayed around the kitchen island, snatched the popcorn out of the microwave, and hugged Leda too tightly. "Let's be buddies tonight, Little. Can we?"

"Lee!" the other girls shrieked. It was like the old days when everyone, even the girls you didn't know, cried your name. They were not even tipsy. They were just keyed up; they were ready to party. It took a certain amount of Zen to enter this mental space in which you were ready to forget the past, disdain the future, and become a creature of immediacy. Zen or amnesia, maybe.

Carly opened the popcorn, and it smoked. Girls crammed hot handfuls into their mouths.

One pointed at Leda's feet. "What are those?" Her mouth was full. Leda looked down at her mother's boots.

But Leda didn't have to answer. Someone had switched on Eminem and turned it up, loud. It was "Superman," Carly's *song.* The girls shouted Carly's name, dancing with one another, looking back at their own asses. Carly shimmied toward the music, and Leda, unnoticed, slipped out of the room.

The pickup was parked on the street between Psi Delta and the Cathouse. Its engine took a few minutes to warm. Leda watched her mother's boot on the clutch. She checked the time. A little after five. She thought of Faye's invitation—pizza at six. The gearshift shivered in the palm of her hand.

Before leaving, she glanced back at the Psi Delta house. A curtain was parted, and a pale, cherubic face stared out. It wasn't hard to recognize Carly's white-blond hair. Eminem carried into the evening. Then the music faded as Leda pulled out.

12

In the last hour of the drive, Leda was glad when her phone service went out. Now, even if they tried, no one could contact her. She navigated using Daria's written directions, scanning for landmarks and mile markers. It was calming, actually. This was how she and her mother had spent their weekends, finding estate and yard sales according only to directions written in the newspaper. They'd look for handmade signs or a row of oddly parked cars. They'd keep their eyes peeled for clues the ad might have mentioned: *look for horses on your left* or *follow the yellow balloons*. They'd have to decipher it, like a treasure map. And sometimes there was treasure, sometimes there wasn't.

Now, she was out of practice. *Keep your eyes peeled.* It had been years since she had heard that expression. Did that mean people were paying less attention?

It didn't help that it was dark. More than once, she had to backtrack, turning eventually at an abandoned school bus onto a rough dirt road. Now, she drove between walls of stiff honeysuckle and prehistoric vehicles. The school bus, it turned out, was the first of many. Some appeared to have been lived in, with woodstove

252 · *Anna Caritj*

chimneys and moth-eaten curtains. Some may still have been inhabited. Once, she caught a whiff of cigarette smoke. In one vehicle, a naked light bulb glowed.

As the track climbed, there were fewer and fewer signs of humanity. She was nervous, navigating private property with only her headlights, bidden by a stranger online. But—she moved her backpack slightly, to see it—Faye's pistol on the passenger seat was a small comfort. Light as a toy, and loaded.

It had not been difficult to get into Clarence and Faye's home. Leda had simply waited in the truck until she saw the whole family leave (Vinnie, too), on their way to get pizza. Luckily, she'd found Clarence's handwritten note in her jeans—the security instructions and door codes. She'd simply punched the correct numbers and walked in. The gun had been right where she'd last seen it. *If you need anything*, Faye had said, time and time again.

It was a little insane, she admitted—taking the weapon. But she didn't want to be like Charlotte right now. She didn't want to step out of her house barefoot.

For a long time, the truck rumbled through steep woods. Her backpack jostled in the passenger's seat. The few times Leda had run away as a child, she'd always packed a bundle. A sweater, a sandwich with slightly more J than PB, and some toy—a plastic dinosaur, a bouncy ball. Then she'd tie it all up in a kerchief and attach the kerchief to the end of a stick, though this process was never as easy as the cartoons made it seem. Once she'd run away—walking for all of five minutes—she'd eat her sandwich in the woods. Then, when she had finished the sandwich, the sun would inevitably dim. A cloud always moved over. The wind always went cold. Suddenly she'd feel as small as a leaf, listening for her mother's call, desperate to be caught. She'd never wanted to go anywhere. When she vanished, she'd just wanted to see if the world noticed.

This time, Leda had brought a gun in her runaway bundle. So why did she still feel so scared? So small?

Leda cracked the window. She thought she'd heard something—bells, maybe, though she couldn't be sure. She rolled it shut, just as a figure stepped out of the dark.

From this distance, the person seemed to have enormous hands. But, as Leda drove closer, slipping the pistol into the pocket of her coat, the figure resolved: a woman carrying bunches of greens, blocking her eyes against Leda's headlights. Her gray, electrified hair was nearly waist length. Her jean shirt was worn and muddy. Somehow, she looked like Charlotte—that same open face.

Daria introduced herself by opening the passenger door and getting in, pointing ahead of them into more black wilderness. "I wasn't expecting you so soon," she said. "But I saw your lights at the bottom of the road, and I figured it had to be you."

In the distance, the bells kept going. Leda drove, glancing at the woman with the pile of greens in her lap. There were so many things she wanted to ask, but they had only just met. Right now, the name Pia felt too risky, too delicate.

Eventually, the woods opened up to cold pasture and meadow. Daria showed Leda where to go. There were a number of cabins on the property, she explained, for interns and volunteers. Right now, only one cabin was unoccupied. She hadn't had the heart to clean it yet, she said. No one had stayed there since Charlotte.

"I hope you don't mind," Daria added.

Leda shook her head, though she wasn't sure. Regardless, she didn't seem to have a choice in the matter.

"You'll probably see the barn cat Charlotte adopted," Daria said as they pulled up to the cabin. "She keeps getting in. No one opens the door for her anymore, but she still finds her way in."

"I don't mind cats," Leda said, distracted by the dark shack in her headlights. It was not at all the quaint cottage she'd been picturing. "How long was she here?" Leda finally asked.

"Three weeks."

Leda nodded, though it seemed an impossible length of time. After seeing the place—small, dilapidated—Leda was already anxious about staying a single night.

Daria got out, taking her greens from the truck's passenger seat. Leda shut the engine off, grabbed her backpack, and followed, stumbling in the dark. It couldn't have been much past eight, but the sky was black already. The stars seemed to wobble and pulsate. It didn't help that her legs were shaky after two hours of back roads. Plus, she couldn't quite see the land—couldn't orient herself with trees or hills or buildings. Fields of stars seemed to extend both underfoot and overhead.

Just in time, her eyes adjusted enough to decipher the small reflective surface. A pond. She hurried along the edge of the water, out from under the weight of all those stars.

"No electricity," Daria explained, casting a dim flashlight around the single room. "No plumbing. But there's heat if you build a fire. At the main house we've got solar and, in theory, wifi."

Leda's eyes followed the dull beam, illuminating a dusty woodstove and a bit of stacked wood. There was also a desk, a chair, a bed. The outhouse was only a short walk through the woods, Daria said. She tried to indicate the structure with the flashlight, but the beam was overwhelmed by night.

Eventually, they stood in the threshold in silence, looking into the room. "My brother," Daria said, "Charlotte's father, came out here, too. Sometimes it helps, coming back to these places." Daria stepped away from the cabin door. "Sometimes it doesn't."

These places. Haunted places, maybe. Places loaded with someone else's memories. Thoughts. Worries.

"Why don't you rest?" Daria said.

Though Leda hadn't been tired before she said it, she was exhausted upon the suggestion. Her sorority sisters often said that this happened to them when they returned home on vacation. They would shut down, sleeping for days while their parents cooked their meals, did their laundry, kept the world turning.

Now, for some reason, Leda felt a similar release. She could see folded quilts in the flashlight beam. She could see some sort of herb bundle hanging from the ceiling. Daria said good night and left Leda in the dark. The cabin door, Leda realized, did not lock.

When Leda woke, she didn't know where she was. She heard dubstep—the lurches and squeals that so often woke her in the early hours of the morning, coming from a fellow Psi Delt's room or some nearby party. The music echoed, stamped into her brain like a nightmare or a memory. A deer antler dangled over her head like a pointed finger. She blinked. A pale cat sat at the foot of the bed.

She had dreamed of Ian. Though now she couldn't recall one scrap of what had happened, couldn't even remember if the dream had been good or bad.

The dubstep faded, replaced by that phantom sound she'd heard last night—bells. Leda sat up, disoriented. By this time on a Sunday morning, she would ordinarily be running. Campus would be full of girls like her, listening to the slap of their tennis shoes. Why wasn't Leda there, too?

The cat at the end of her bed looked at her. It looked blind, its eyes glazed white.

It's as if I'm standing beside someone who hasn't been introduced to me yet, Pia had written. *I don't know what to say to make my own introduction. "Hi, I'm . . ."* Who? What?

What Pia hadn't mentioned was that this sensation of waking up in a new place was also a bit like kissing a stranger: feeling a new taste in your mouth, feeling new hands—a new frame—shaping your body. It was usually fun for a minute, fun seeing your reflection and not immediately recognizing it. *Who is that? What is she doing? Why is she doing it?*

On campus, Leda didn't ever attempt to answer these questions. But now, she found herself wanting answers. Who *is* that? That verb had always given her trouble in Spanish class. *To be.* In Spanish, there were three different ways to say it. But before taking Spanish, she had never even thought of "am" or "is" as verbs. She had never thought of "being" as an action.

The cat scattered when Leda's feet touched the dusty cabin floor. Charlotte's cabin. Her woodstove. Her window. Charlotte had slept in this bed, sat at this desk. And where had Pia been?

Leda found clothes, a jacket, and, yes—the pistol. It looked strange here. Out of place. She slipped it into her backpack. Safe.

Outside, there was fog. Leda looked out the door, but she couldn't see far. She couldn't see beyond the small pond that she had mistaken for more sky last night. Now, the water stirred with white ducks. Leda shut the door again, though it did not lock.

There was kindling in a basket beside the woodstove, plus a newspaper dated mid-October. If the paper was any indication, Charlotte had come here in the middle of the semester. Was it possible that what Leda's sisters had said was true? Charlotte had been stalked and harassed, they'd said. Threatened. Perhaps it had been so bad that she'd needed to leave school. But *wherever you go, there you are.* There was no guarantee that, off campus, it had been any better. There was no guarantee it hadn't followed her. Pia, Leda couldn't help thinking, was also a kind of stalker.

Leda opened the woodstove and started a little teepee of paper and twigs. When was the last time she'd built a fire? As a child, probably, with her mother's help. Or with Clarence. She found a matchbook, fed the flame as it grew, and eventually added some wood that Charlotte must have chopped and stacked along the cabin's back wall.

The fire took. She crouched there, watching it, and then felt light-headed when she stood. Her hands found the desk and leaned there, waiting for the world to fizz back into focus. Maybe Charlotte would write Pia here, at the desk. But that didn't make sense. Why would Pia and Charlotte write each other while they were both here? And even if they had, why would Pia have mailed her side of the correspondence to Charlotte's town address?

The room resolved. Three blue bottles stood on a sill above a white sink. Leda turned the sink faucet and stuck her hands under nothing. Of course. The sink wasn't connected to anything.

From her backpack, Leda took the postcards and placed them on the desk. The cabin warmed. The antler revolved from the plywood ceiling, as if responding to the heat. Beside it, red-brown feathers had been meticulously threaded onto a string. Turkey feathers, maybe. Had Charlotte made this? Leda wondered, thinking of the white feathers she'd found in Charlotte's room, possibly loosed from the swan costume.

The bony cat curled up before the stove. The bells banged somewhere. It was possible she was imagining it—just as the dubstep had slid into her ear, as if she were back on campus. But these bells were getting louder. Then there were footsteps, too, right on her porch. There were knocks and scuffs at her door. Leda tensed, glancing at her backpack, where she'd hidden the pistol. When the feet moved off, more feet replaced them. Leda crept to the window.

Brown, cream, and black goats jangled up the road, wearing bells around their necks. Thick white heads emerged from the herd every now and then—a dog back or tail cresting before ducking under again. Great Pyrenees, the White Dog Farm website had said. They lived with the goats and shadowed them as they went out to graze on the farm's three hundred acres, keeping them safe from coyote and bear and whatever else was out there.

A goat jangled onto the porch, its udder shrunken and rosy. It had just been milked, probably. It rubbed its horns on her door. With just this small bit of force, the door popped open. The goat looked up, mildly surprised. Before continuing on, the animal met Leda's eyes.

Despite the cold, Leda lingered in the open door, watching the goats pass with their alien eyes and flopping udders shaped like grapefruits, or icicles, or wineskins. The animals were at once proud and dainty, severe and ridiculous. Some skipped onto Leda's porch and leapt from it, while others lumbered forward, dogged. Some jostled the others, like bullying children. Others dodged or bore the blows.

The fog had not lifted, though the sun was climbing. Still, Leda could see no composting toilet, no other buildings, so she squatted in the hoarfrost to pee as the goats filed past. She wasn't sure if there were other cabins nearby. Since Daria had left, she'd heard no human voices. It was both peaceful and lonely. Last night, trying to stem this loneliness, Leda had tried to text Mary and found her phone dead, with no way to charge it.

Some jay called sharply, and Leda pulled up her jeans. She felt that prickle on the back of her neck. She felt watched. Could Pia see her? Or what about the man who slept in parking lots, who asked people for water? Even the harmonica guy—the one Pia had angered accidentally—could he be out here on the farm?

She tried to shrug it off. It was unlikely that someone was watching her pee. Who would want to, really? She was alone with a bunch of goats, making their morning commute toward a low line of forest. For now, the cabin was hidden—cloaked in fog and backed by woods.

Though there was a stretch of sky visible at the top of the incline. Was it possible that the rim—so named by both Pia and Charlotte—could be just uphill of Charlotte's cabin?

Grabbing her coat, Leda started into the fog. Soon, everything around her was frozen—black-trunked maples and silver poplars, stones and unidentifiable bones. She nearly collided with a pitch pine, lunged forward like a dancing woman. She ducked under, feeling lucky for a moment—lucky to be out here breathing the cold. And then she felt lucky that she had been expecting the rim, because she reached it as another blanket of fog swept in. It was lucky that she had sensed the air opening up, sensed the swirling wind, right before she stepped over the cliff.

When she stopped, pebbles scurried and dropped. Beyond the rim, there was nothing. Even Leda's body, when she looked down at it, seemed to be a few particles shy of disappearing. More fog moved in, mouthing her legs and torso. Leda hugged herself, arm clutching arm. Tiny flurries touched her face, though she couldn't even see the flakes; they were just white rushing out of white. Under her feet, the Earth rocketed forward, twirling over one thousand miles per hour.

Crouching, Leda felt with her hands until she came to the cliff's lip. She couldn't tell how high up she might be, the fog had gotten so deep. She couldn't tell if she was in danger, or if she was just being silly. So she sat, inches from what felt like the edge, feeling the wind. She watched a hole open in the clouds overhead—a blue skylight, illuminating Leda before burying her in fog again.

Overhead, the distant jays sounded like a phone line ringing. For a long time, she listened. Once, she had dialed her dead mother's cell phone and listened to it ring. Her whole heart had started stupidly beating, ear pressed against nothing. She listened now, ear to air, as if something might answer. And then, as if in response, a body entered the fog behind her.

She felt it long before she saw anything. She felt it, and then she remembered that she had left the cabin door open. Pia had dwelled on this habit of Charlotte's, a habit that Flora might have called carefree. Tamara, on the other hand, would have called it careless. And now Leda had left that same door open. Now something or someone approached.

The air danced like television static as she waited. She might as well have had her eyes shut, listening to the hiss, like the empty space between telephone rings, like a buzzing radiation machine. She had only ever heard the machine, never seen. She had never seen her mother's head screwed into position. She had only picked up some lead things in the hospital hallway while she waited—lead blanket, lead hat, lead gloves.

A voice rang out. "Leda!"

But the shout was more distant than this presence, here on the rim, here where she could easily slip off the mountain and never be heard from again. She could hear it, in fact: this thing, this person. When she twisted around, she could see it materializing—white moving out of white.

"Leda!"

The shape was on her before she properly saw it: a white dog lumbering out of the fog, its black nose in her face, its eyes brown-gold galaxies. The animal's body touched hers before receding. Leda crawled herself away from the rim. Why had she gotten so close? She stood only when she was sure she was well away from the edge, and then followed the big animal back down the mountain.

The haze melted as she walked. Below her, in a shallow valley, she could see the farm—the old vans, water tanks, and windmill vanes. The main house was a patchwork of scrap woods, corrugated metal, and solar panels. There was a barn beside the house, surrounded by a few fenced enclosures and garden plots. She saw no other cabins.

A river rushed somewhere—or was it wind? She smelled wood smoke but, looking back toward her cabin, realized that it came from the fire she had built not long ago.

Leda stopped, watched the cabin for a moment. A steady trickle rose from the chimney. Watching the smoke, she could just trick herself into thinking that someone—that *Charlotte*—might be in there. She could just imagine that, in taking this trip, she actually found Charlotte. Found her and brought her back home. Back to life. Until now, that idea hadn't been at the front of her mind, but now it almost seemed possible. What if, in searching for Pia, she actually found Charlotte? Now, she could almost see Charlotte pushing open the cabin door, Charlotte pausing in the threshold . . .

But, of course, no door opened.

When Leda finally turned back toward the farm, she saw someone: a girl hauling buckets across the dirt track. Leda glanced back at the cabin one last time—the rising smoke—and then hurried up the road.

The girl looked to be Leda's age or slightly older, wearing jean shorts over torn leggings with a patched black sweatshirt. As Leda approached, she had a hard time not speaking the one word on her lips: *Pia?*

The girl spoke first. "Leda."

She put down her buckets, pulled off a glove, and extended her hand. She had gauged earlobes and a slightly chubby face. She had letters tattooed on her fingers, like the hand in Charlotte's photograph.

"Daria told us you were coming," the girl said.

Leda took the girl's hand, not knowing what to say, not knowing how to start. She hesitated, holding the girl's hand for too long, wondering what the letters on her fingers spelled out. Finally, she managed, "Us?"

"Me and the other interns."

"Oh." Leda tried to smile. "Duh." She was still a bit dazed from the rim, from watching Charlotte's cabin with as much delirious hope as she had when she had called her dead mother's phone.

"Anyway." The girl pulled her glove back on, took up a bucket, and nodded to the second. "Grab that for me."

Like that, the moment in which the girl should have spoken her name had already passed.

The bucket was heavy, sloshing with gallons of yellow liquid. Leda struggled after the girl—*Pia*. Surely, this was the girl who had written Charlotte.

"What is this?" Leda asked once they'd come to an animal pen.

"Whey." The girl stepped onto a rickety stool, hauled her bucket up, and poured the stuff over the fence into a recessed trough. "It's leftover from cheese making. Pigs love it. But, then again, pigs love anything."

A dozen spotted piglets hurtled out from a dark enclosure, each no bigger than a loaf of bread. A mountainous sow emerged behind them—their mother, Leda guessed. She must have weighed three hundred pounds. When Leda stepped up on the stool, as the girl had done, the sow put her front feet in the trough. Leda managed to lift the bucket toward the top of the fence, but then she paused.

"Just pour it on her," the girl said.

"On top of her?"

"Sure."

The whey slammed down on the sow. The animal turned her face up into the stream and opened her mouth, her babies clambering around her. A bright tang mixed with the pigs' sourness. When the bucket was empty, Leda stepped down. For some reason, her arms were shaking. She couldn't help but think of Carly at the bubble party, parting her lips as another girl shook amber beer down onto her face and into her mouth.

"I think I was just on the rim," Leda said, to get her mind off this image, testing out the term, wondering if the girl would recognize it.

"I'm surprised you could find it in this fog."

"It was sort of scary up there," Leda said.

"No shit." The girl took the empty buckets, moving off toward a low barn. "We almost lost a goat to it."

"Hey—" Leda called after her, as if she, too, might disappear. "I don't know if I caught your name."

"Oh, my bad." The girl stopped in the barn door, pausing just before the dark enclosure swallowed her. "Zoe."

The girl went in. For a moment, Leda stood alone. *Zoe.* There was no way Leda had misheard. She took a heavy breath, and then another, no lighter than the first. *Why am I here?* she wondered. *What am I doing?*

Overhead, the sky looked greased and pale, like the white of an eye. No one was looking—no God or whoever. No one even knew she was here. To her friends, to Clarence, she could easily disappear. Out here, Leda was a distant galaxy: so distant that, to the naked eye, she would appear as a smear. Even if you looked straight at her, you might mistake her for nothing, nowhere, nobody.

Had anyone wondered where Leda was last night? This morning? She hated to agonize over it, hated to care, but of course she did. She couldn't help it.

A pair of hands took Leda's shoulders from behind, and she shuddered. It was Zoe again, who had emerged from the barn, bucketless.

"You here?" Zoe smiled. Her teeth were small. "You want to breed some goats?"

It was a tone you might use with a child, but, strangely, it didn't bother Leda. She nodded and followed. Right now, she didn't mind being reminded that she was visible, standing here in the lifting fog. She thought of the dog that had found her on the rim, picking her solid body out of all that nothing. She thought of her mom.

"Zoe?" Leda tried the name out loud. "Did you hear somebody calling earlier? I thought I heard my name."

"Hmm . . . nope." Zoe glanced back at Leda and grinned with her small teeth. "Sometimes the wind—it sort of speaks."

How was this not Pia?

What if I just asked? Leda wondered. *What if I just said something?*

Instead, Leda stuffed her hands in her pockets and felt one cold, heavy bullet. Her hands felt dirty against it—sticky with whey. She followed Zoe between barns and outbuildings, fingering it. Chickens prowled the winter-brown grass, splattered with orange morning sun. Zoe stopped at a fence labeled *BUCKS*.

The animals inside looked nothing like the female goats that Leda had seen this morning. *Does*, Zoe called them. The bucks were twice the does' size, with stiff backs and bulging eyes. Their hair was slick. They smelled both perfumed and rotten.

Leda said, "So, I'm guessing 'buck' means—"

"Bro." Under *BUCKS*, two more handmade signs read *Dionysus* and *DiCaprio*. One of the bucks rammed the gate while Zoe struggled to get it open, warning, "Get ready to be doused in pheromones."

But Leda was already holding her nose. She didn't know quite what the plan was. These animals were too big to handle, too wild to control. The one who had rammed the gate had broken his horn. His head was bleeding. Leda pointed this out cautiously, but Zoe waved it off.

"He's been ramming the gate all day."

"Why?"

"He knows what he wants." Zoe smirked. "Not so different from some guys I know."

With one last shove, the bolt holding the gate came free, and the bucks charged from the enclosure.

"Come on." Zoe walked after the loose animals. "Charlotte hated this part."

It was the first time the name had passed between them, though it had been in the air all along. It was strange to hear it dropped so casually, strange to hear the instinctual past tense, as if Charlotte were already gone.

Gone. That was Ian's word, wasn't it?

Up near the farmhouse, the bucks were doing their best to break into another enclosure. Behind it, another intern had rounded up some does. Zoe introduced them. Lewis. Lewis had a mustache and wore an Incredible Hulk T-shirt that didn't fit right, as if it were a large child's size. He had a notebook—a log, Zoe explained, of family trees, to avoid inbreeding. But Leda was only half listening. The bucks' moans were deafening. They bawled and jerked and lifted their glossy lips. One extended his pink, finger-length penis, craned his neck, and peed in his own mouth. Leda put a hand to her face, but no one else appeared shocked.

Lewis grappled with one of the bucks, dragging him to a sort of holding pen while Zoe released one doe with the one free buck. The buck sidled alongside the doe, twitching, tongue out. He moaned. The breeding took less than a minute. Zoe dragged the animals apart when it was done. Lewis noted the act in the log.

"The girls are so much smaller," Leda said. "How do they not get hurt?"

"Sometimes they do." Lewis released a different doe to the same buck. "Unfortunately, that's part of it."

More pee in mouth. More lip lifting.

"What did I tell you?" Zoe crouched down to tie her boot. "Typical dudes."

She was joking, of course, but the comparison was worrying. "What did you mean earlier?" Leda asked her. "When you said Charlotte hated this part."

"Well, it's not that I *like* it." Zoe scratched her cheek. "But, I guess Charlotte didn't like the, um, *natural* violence."

One of the does, a bit smaller than the others, almost collapsed under the weight of the buck. After it was done, she limped back toward her enclosure.

"She's a little young," Zoe said, frowning. "But she's in heat. She'll be okay."

Zoe explained how to tell when a doe is in heat, pointing out the signs. They shake their tails. They get loud and rowdy. Leda watched the does push and jostle one another at the gate. They were interested, clearly. Still, Leda couldn't help but touch the mostly healed dent in her lip, watching the small doe hobble away. *She'll be okay.*

The does seemed barely satisfied after breeding. The bucks never were. But, Leda supposed, if animals were totally satisfied by sex, there'd be a lot less of it. If it totally satisfied them, then they wouldn't expend so much energy seeking it. Maybe humanity, she thought, was no different: its brute cycles of passion and disappointment.

In an hour, Zoe and Lewis had bred almost twenty does. Though Leda hadn't helped at all, she'd been lightly brushed by one of the bucks, and now her entire arm smelled of him. Every so often, she couldn't help but sniff her pheromone-coated arm, both fascinated and disgusted. Meanwhile, the two bucks were still lunging toward the does. Many of the does that had already been bred were shaking their tails again. Together, Zoe and Lewis struggled to get the bucks back to their pen.

"You hungry?" Zoe said when she came back, stinking of buck.

"Not really," Leda admitted.

Still, they went in. In the kitchen, strips of dough lattice lay on the floured table. Daria sliced apples, her apron blasted with flour, her hair worn in two long braids. A woodstove popped and gushed in the corner, heating two big vats of water. A bearded young man—another intern, Leda guessed—tended the fire. Leda eyed him. She couldn't help being suspicious. But when he noticed her looking, he smiled.

Zoe and Lewis washed their hands in a tub of gray water. Zoe's brown hair looked stiff-dirty. Her clothes would smell like buck for weeks, she was saying. Still, she and Daria laughed, quick and hard, at something Lewis had said. They were an odd sort of family, and Leda was having a hard time placing them in the world Pia had created through her postcards. The traveler. The harmonica player. The quiet, sensitive guy who had turned out to be "no different" from any other.

As Leda watched them, Daria started telling a story about Charlotte, perhaps for Leda's benefit. Charlotte had once let the pigs out by accident, and she'd spent a whole day cursing and chasing piglets. The others laughed, remembering, and Leda felt lost suddenly, as if she barely knew the person in the story.

13

L eda kept waking throughout the night, thinking that a light was shining in her eyes. A pair of headlights approaching the bubble party. The wink of a smashing disco ball. A search party. But when she opened her eyes, there was no light—just the jiggling stars outside. Eventually, she got up. Outside, she found herself surrounded by stars, wild in the bright black air and in the earthbound pond.

Now it didn't seem so strange that the stars had woken her. For one thing, the sky no longer looked like sky. It wasn't smooth and high. It drooped, warping with the weight of all those distant suns. Leda stood for a long time with her head tilted up. Looking at this sky was like looking through deep, clear water; she could see shelves and layers, mottling the usual constellations. No more Pleiades. No more Orion. Just the swollen universe around her: everything bright and booming.

Last night, this same sky had overwhelmed her. *Scared* her. What had changed? Now, she couldn't pull herself out from under it. She looked up and up, her eyes finding new folds and profundities, thinking nothing.

. . .

Then Leda's own personal star rose. She had gone to bed with everyone else when the sun had set. Now, despite the restless night, she woke up with it. She had not dreamed of Ian, though she thought of him now as she unzipped her backpack to check on the gun.

It was Monday. Somehow, two days had passed. She poked her phone to check the time, out of habit, but of course the battery was dead. She'd forgotten. She had been planning on packing her backpack and leaving this morning, returning to campus. But now she simply opened the cabin door and looked at the morning. A litter of white feathers clung to the surface of the pond. No ducks. Somewhere, the goats squalled, almost human.

There was no fog this morning, so Leda decided to find the rim again and follow it toward the main house. The view was undeniably beautiful. Beyond the cliff, winterized mountains sketched the horizon. With distance, the gray branches somehow blended into blue. If Leda looked back over her shoulder, through the bare woods, she could catch glimpses of the rest of the farm. She could make out the broad meadow behind the main farmhouse and a faint path cutting through the stiff, silver grasses.

Still, the rim scared her—that sense that she could slide over the edge and, like that, be gone.

One of the dogs greeted Leda when she approached the main house, pushing its square head under her palm. Chickens bathed in the dusty shadow of the building. In the kitchen, the bearded intern made breakfast. Potatoes and eggs hissed on the woodstove as he added hunks of butter to both cast-iron pans. Apparently the goats had already been milked. There was a jug of fresh milk on the table, though Leda wasn't sure if she wanted to taste the warm, raw liquid.

Zoe twisted a hand grinder, milling beans for coffee, saying, "Can you believe Daria lived out here for years, alone? No running water. No electric. Just the dogs and the goats."

Leda was only half listening. She was still tuned to the hens' babble and the woodstove's pop. The bearded guy turned the eggs. Zoe pried the lid off a honey jar and stuck her finger in, still talking. She poured herself a glass of milk. When she passed the jug to Leda, the warmth felt good between her palms.

If Leda closed her eyes, she could be home. She could be on the porch, hearing kitchen sounds. Cooking. But, like most of her memories of home—of her mother—the image ended there. She was stuck on the porch; she couldn't go in. It was like bumping into a video game's invisible barrier—the scenery seems to continue, but you can't walk through. Lately, it seemed like Leda was often stopped in thresholds, facing invisible walls.

But here, she'd stepped through easily. She'd been welcomed and seated at a long communal table. She'd been treated warmly, as if it made sense that she'd be here, asking questions about a girl they'd all known—a girl who had disappeared.

Leda put down the milk without pouring herself a glass and stood from the table. Still, she couldn't relax, couldn't settle in. Perhaps she'd imagined that all the answers would just be here, lying around in the open. The truth was, now she felt less sure than ever.

Daria came in from outside and took chèvre and butter from the crowded refrigerator. They'd gotten a bunch of expired whipped cream for free, Daria was saying, and with it they'd made more butter than they knew what to do with. Then the eggs were ready. Potatoes, too.

Leda felt stupid, sitting down to breakfast. What had she been expecting, coming here so impulsively? She was beginning to think that this whole farm trip had just been a fantasy, an escape from reality. She'd tricked herself into believing that she might come to understand why Charlotte had gone missing. As if only she, Leda, could have the power to find her. As if Charlotte were the only thing Leda was looking for.

In reality, nothing would change. Charlotte was still gone, whether or not Leda found out why she'd come to this farm midsemester. Whether or not Leda found out who Pia was. Back in town, Ian was still on campus, texting her probably. Her sisters were undoubtedly asleep, still hungover, not even aware that Leda's bed was empty.

But of course Leda was not missing. She was right here. She looked down at her hands, holding cutlery. Wasn't she?

"I was wondering . . . ," Leda said, thinking, *Fuck it.* She put her silverware down. It was already too late to get back in time for her first class. She might as well ask the question she had come here to ask. "Does anyone know someone named Pia?"

But despite all the buildup in Leda's mind, Daria and Lewis didn't even seem to be listening; they had started looking at Lewis's breeding notes. The bearded guy shrugged, saying he'd only been here a week. Zoe, however, looked at her.

"Someone named Pia . . ." Zoe rubbed her neck. "I mean, sort of. I guess."

"Oh." Leda tried to keep her voice level. "Who is she? Or, where is she?"

Zoe's expression was difficult to read. She looked amused almost, as if she thought Leda were telling a joke. "You want to meet her?"

Leda glanced at Daria, who still hadn't tuned in. "Sure."

"All right." Zoe stood from the table. "Let's go."

Leda left her plate and followed Zoe out, glancing back only once as if someone might stop her, as if she were no longer sure she wanted to know.

The goats wailed in the barn, waiting for something. Food? Freedom? Or maybe they didn't quite know. Leda and Zoe walked along their fence. A bitter, piney smell followed. A white dog lay on a table, damp with a few renewed flurries, though the sky was mostly clear this morning. It picked its head up when they walked by. Leda glanced back and watched it watch her. Was this the dog that had come to find her?

At the end of the yard, they turned down a row of outbuildings. The cloying manure was richer here and thicker underfoot. Zoe stopped at a low barn door, turned a wood panel that acted like a rudimentary bolt, and opened the door.

"After you." Again, Zoe looked amused.

It was too dark to see in, but Leda stooped blindly and entered. The floor was spongy with straw and dung. It took a long time before Leda's eyes began to adjust.

Zoe said, "You want a light?"

The doorway was too bright when Leda glanced back at it. She squinted. Behind Zoe, there was a straight line of sight to Charlotte's cabin. Zoe turned on her cell phone light and shone it in. The stall was small—ten by ten. In the corner, two eyes glowed green in the light.

"There she is." Zoe knocked her boots on the side of the small structure, and the whole thing shuddered. When Leda looked confused, Zoe clarified. "That's Pia."

Leda pointed at the animal. The goat. "*That's* Pia?"

"Does that answer your question?"

"Well . . . no."

Zoe shrugged. "This is the only Pia I know."

Leda opened her mouth, but no words came out. What could she possibly say? If she told Zoe about the postcards, then she'd have to explain how she got the cards in the first place, and how she'd been withholding (she guessed) what could be important evidence. And then even if she *did* explain everything, what sense could Zoe—could *anybody* make out of two dozen postcards written under a goat's name?

So Leda tried to act unsurprised, as if she'd expected Pia to have hooves and a beard. "Why is she in here?"

"Herd drama." Zoe scratched the backs of her knuckles. "Every now and then, the girls decide who to beat up on, and they don't stop. It's a pecking order thing. A way of establishing dominance. Usually, they work things out on their own. But in this case, we had to step in."

The animal looked basically healthy. She wasn't as small as the one the buck had injured. Except for acting a bit skittish, she seemed content.

"How bad did it get?"

"They might have killed her if we'd let it continue. We don't disbud—we let their horns grow, I mean—so a few well-placed head butts can do a lot of damage. And for Pia, it wasn't a few; it was constant. You know how I mentioned we almost lost a goat to the rim? Pia got pushed off. Broke her leg. I don't know how she survived it. We isolated her while the leg healed, and she sort of thrived alone. So we kept her apart."

"But . . ." Leda hesitated. "Aren't they, like, *herd* animals?"

"Not Pia, apparently." Zoe turned off her phone's light, and Pia disappeared. "Did Charlotte mention her or something?"

"Sort of." Leda didn't know whether to shake or nod her head, thinking of that photograph titled *Pia*. It was Pia's eye, she supposed. And the silhouette reflected in it had not been Pia, not Zoe, either, but Charlotte, holding the camera. "To tell the truth," Leda said to Zoe, "I thought *you* were Pia."

"No." Zoe laughed. "Thank god."

"So Charlotte came here a lot?"

"What? To see Pia?" Zoe stuffed both hands in her pockets. "I don't think so. I never saw her over here."

Leda looked at her. "Never?"

Zoe shrugged, not quite comprehending. "Nope."

Of course, Zoe wouldn't understand why this piece of information was so maddening. But, Leda couldn't help it—her confusion was starting to edge with frustration. She pushed out of the stall. Pia was not a person, first of all. Next, Zoe wasn't even aware that Charlotte had had any interest in this goat, so it seemed unlikely that Zoe or anyone else might have used the pen name as a sort of inside joke. Is there *anyone else*, Leda wanted to ask, named Pia? But she knew it would be unlikely, finding two Pias on this one middle-of-nowhere farm.

What was Leda missing? She tried to picture Pia looking out at Charlotte's cabin . . . or, no—it was *Charlotte* looking from her cabin across the farm to Pia's stall. Maybe it was Charlotte looking at Charlotte, as if the postcards were a kind of journal—an attempt to locate herself inside the girl who had been so many things to so many people. Perhaps she'd been struggling to see herself. Hear herself.

"I think about Charlotte really often." Zoe closed the stall door, interrupting Leda's thoughts. "She was hard to get to know, but we got along. I think she and I liked animals for the same reason."

"What's that?"

"They're predictable . . ." Zoe smiled, showing dimples. "And they don't talk."

Zoe moved back toward the kitchen, and Leda followed.

"So, Charlotte sort of kept to herself?"

Zoe shrugged. Nodded.

Leda asked, "Was she always like that?"

Zoe thought for a moment. "Charlotte was the only person I know that I'd call trusting," she said slowly. "She wasn't dumb or innocent. She just saw potential in people. She gave them a chance. A lot of people *need* that. And then some take advantage of it."

They passed the goats. This time, the dog didn't look up from its table.

Leda asked, "What do you think happened?"

"My guess is . . ." Zoe paused, her teeth chattering a little, though the snow had nearly let up. "My guess is she trusted someone who didn't fucking deserve her trust."

Zoe's eyes had gone glassy and hard. Behind her, across the farm, no smoke rose from Charlotte's chimney. The cabin was almost translucent in the glittering flurries. Leda found herself staring, stopped outside the main house. She lifted a boot, dense with manure, and found herself too tired, too overcome to move. She was hoping Zoe would go inside without her, but Zoe paused, too.

"Leda," Zoe said. "How well did you know Charlotte?"

Leda had never been asked this particular question, and it startled her. The truth was, of course, that she hadn't known her. She hadn't known Charlotte at all.

"I met her a few hours before she went missing," Leda admitted finally. "That's all. I know it seems crazy that I'd come out here. That I'd still be thinking about her. But she . . . recognized me, for some reason. She said I looked familiar."

"She *saw* people." Zoe nodded, stuffing her hands into her jeans pockets. She didn't explain further.

Instead of going back inside, warm with fire and food and laughter, Leda walked back along the rim toward Charlotte's cold cabin. The few clouds in the sky had rushed off, leaving only metallic sun. Again, she tried to picture Charlotte out here. Did a person seek these places out in order to feel fragile or powerful? Large or small?

The white ducks had gathered a ways down the rim, preening their feathers by the edge of the cliff. They didn't seem at all conscious of the precipice. Leda, on the other hand, could already feel her body react to it—a slight, swiveling nausea. She'd felt this way on the dam, with Ian, looking down that hundred-foot drop. Her gut had registered the danger, even when her brain had not.

At the time, Leda hadn't thought much of her nervousness. She'd been too busy wondering if Ian would kiss her. Too busy mistaking geese for swans. Ian, on the other hand, had been staring at the intake tower. He'd been thinking about the machinery underneath, speaking as if he had already researched these things.

Your body would get sucked down, he'd said. *And it wouldn't come out for weeks.* It sounded like a threat, in retrospect.

Leda stepped away from the cliff, touching her throat, touching the soft spot where Ian's thumb had pressed.

Back in the cabin, Leda spread Charlotte's postcards across the desk. This was Charlotte's handwriting, she knew now. This was Charlotte's voice. Did anything change, she wondered, knowing this? Would this knowledge illuminate something she had previously missed? She turned all the cards so that the images faced down, skimming the contents as she went. One of the cards, however, came apart as she flipped it. It appeared two cards had been stuck together. One of them dropped to the floor. Leda bent and retrieved it—a long, cramped message that she hadn't seen before.

Dear Charlotte, I wish you would believe me when I tell you that it's not your fault. That you weren't asking for what happened. That there was nothing you could have done to stop it. Just listen: you froze because you were in shock. Because you didn't want to believe that another person could be so cruel. You still don't want to believe it. So, for some reason, you've decided that it's easier to believe that you were at fault. Charlotte, just pretend for a minute that you are your own best friend. Would you tell her she deserved it?

At the end, there was no *Love, Pia*. There was no room left.

14

There was a poster taped to Leda's doorknob when she got home midday Monday—a screaming mouth on hot-pink paper:

YOu HAVE A VOICE
SCREAM FOR CHARLOTTE MASK
ON BEAR GRASS MOUNTAIN
GATHER AT PSI DELTA FOR CARPOOL
MONDAY NOV 16, 4 PM

It was an anniversary scream—two weeks since Charlotte was reported missing. In the top right corner was a handwritten note: *You're coming.* The words had been underlined twice. It was a command, not a question.

Leda went to check the time, but her phone was still dead. She left the poster on the knob and opened her door, facing the jaws of her mother's dragon. Her room smelled stale. Even so, she locked her door behind her.

She didn't want to go to the scream. For one thing, she no longer believed Charlotte could be found so easily. Charlotte wasn't *lost*. She wasn't leaving a trail of breadcrumbs in some forest. Something had *happened*. Ian himself had said it. And whatever it was, it had happened well before Halloween. Whatever it was, it had Ian worried. This was why he'd been hounding Leda, pleading with her, basically, to remember their night together, remember enough to prove that he'd been nowhere near Charlotte. But Leda had a hunch that he'd chosen that night—the night he'd had Leda, his alibi—to finish whatever he'd started.

She trusted someone who didn't fucking deserve her trust.

The second reason Leda didn't want to go to the scream was that she didn't want to walk downstairs and see everybody making hearts with their fingers. Everything hunky-dory. Though, at this point, would Leda's sisters still hand-heart her? She had ghosted Saturday, leaving Carly to be her own buddy after the Benjamin breakup. Carly was probably already saying that Leda had stood her up, had slipped out without saying anything, had not *been there* for her. Or, worse: she could be saying that Leda, like Mary, had gotten weird.

Yet the flyer on Leda's door suggested otherwise. *You're coming.* She'd been given a chance, it seemed. One more chance to be included, be a friend. A sister.

So, she'd go. And anyway, it would give her time to think about her next move. She didn't want to act too quickly, didn't want to risk her own safety. It would be a way to avoid Ian, too. There was no way he'd have the nerve to show for an event honoring Charlotte.

All the same, Leda took Faye's gun out of her backpack and zipped it into a small purse. Sure, Ian wouldn't show. Sure, she'd be surrounded by sisters and classmates. But it didn't hurt to play it safe.

Leda plugged her phone into its charger and unpacked the rest of her things. She placed the postcards in her underwear drawer, her eyes lingering on that crunched, tumbling cursive. It was strange. Some of the cards that she'd only skimmed previously now seemed loaded with meaning.

> *Dear Charlotte, The goats didn't come home yesterday, and I couldn't sleep. It looked like you were up, too. Your door closed and opened all night. Does it help being out here, after what happened? At least the goats came home eventually. The full moon was so bright, they must not have realized it was night. Love, Pia*

When had Charlotte started sending these messages to her own address? Had she started writing them as soon as she got to White Dog Farm? And was that before or after she'd been . . . what? Assaulted? Raped? There were no details anywhere. To herself, Charlotte hadn't needed to explain.

After, Leda thought to herself. These cards, she sensed, were a reaction to something. A coping method. An attempt to process what had happened. Maybe she'd been trying to listen to herself, to what she felt, what she wanted. As if she were a friend. Maybe knowing yourself wasn't as easy as it sounded.

Does it help being out here, after what happened?

Maybe going to the goat farm had been another grounding attempt. Maybe Charlotte had gone there for some of the same reasons Leda had—because she'd thought she could leave behind her fears. Because she'd thought this other world—a world of solar panels, goat milk, and poplars—would protect her. Or because she'd thought that in the quiet, she'd be able to hear herself better.

When Leda's phone powered up, she found a curt email from her work-study supervisor, plus another from a Spanish professor regarding missed work. She also found texts—Mary, Carly—and a missed call from Ian. She cringed, clicking away, checking the news. A few surveillance videos had been released, though Charlotte was barely recognizable on the screen. She appeared as a yellow highlight, a smudge, or a pixelated smear. The world around her looked wide and misshapen. In some recordings, human figures jerked in the periphery. Perhaps Leda stuttered by in one of those dark crowds, engaged in the night's proceedings.

In the last video, taken outside Gamma Kap from a campus security camera, white spots wiggled in the lens like ghosts. The night seemed to flake. *Moths*, Leda remembered, beating the camera with their wings.

Leda texted Mary to see if she was going to Carly's Scream.

Class, Mary texted back. Am I the only person that goes to class at this university?

And then, when Leda didn't answer immediately, Mary messaged, Ian came to my room this morning. Thought I should tell you.

Leda wrote quickly. Why? What did he say?

Mary seemed to be typing for a long time, but her next message was short. Lee, I'm getting a bad feeling.

Downstairs, the kitchen was buzzing. Girls in neon Scream tees were making trail mix, dumping peanuts and yogurt-covered raisins into gallon Ziplocs. One girl used her finger to draw a penis in the fogged window's steam. Carly was in the common room, wearing spandex and a terry cloth headband, feeding Glock M&M's. Leda slipped into the kitchen, stole a bagel from a white bag, and toasted it.

Carly spoke without looking up. "Leaving in ten, Lee."

Otherwise, no one acknowledged her. No one asked, *Where've you been?* No one said, *We've been worried.* A few Psi Delts gossiped around Leda as if she wasn't there, brushing the salt off their manicures while Leda watched the toaster filaments glimmer.

L eda drove to Bear Grass Mountain alone. *Solus, solo.* Every word for "alone" felt like a hole. Of course, she wasn't 100 percent alone. Technically, she was flanked by Psi Delts, beeping at one another in their sports cars and SUVs. She thought of what Zoe had said about Pia, about the herd turning against her. *They might have killed her.* But why? Leda should have asked her. What makes one animal a target? Do the others simply sense that it's different?

They parked along Reservoir Road just before the orchard. Carly hopped out, directing cars, and Leda let herself be parked. The picnic area was still a few miles off, down where Leda and Ian had parked to go to the reservoir, where Leda had seen that girl dash for her pink tent as if it were a shield, a force field. Leda missed that—how, in childhood, there was always a base. A rock that you could touch. A tree trunk where everyone agreed you were safe.

A pickup drove by, spitting gravel. Followed by two others. Leda waited for them to pass in her own truck's cab, arranging her purse's long strap across her chest, checking in on the pistol. When she got out, the three pickups were still braking past Carly's crowd. Each had the same wooden frame on the back—a dog box built to fit the dimensions of the bed, with eight portholes for eight squirming hounds cut in. The dogs yodeled, loud. Scent dogs, Leda realized at once. Though the rest of the crowd seemed not to notice.

It was a strange sight: eighty-some college students winding into the trees, chatting and laughing, their feet shattering beds of leaves. Leda couldn't help scanning the crowd for Ian, though of course he wasn't here. She tried to relax. Tried to forget about him, thinking instead of those old prom court photos her classmate Monica had sent—Charlotte's wide laugh; the sprinkles on her ice cream cone. And then Leda thought of herself, before all this, before the night of Halloween. She thought of that word—*cunt*—thrown at her from the roof of a fraternity. She had saluted, hadn't she? She had yawned at those boys, so small on their rooftop. She had gone to the Lawn and crunched a lollipop before continuing her run.

Now, Leda looked down as she walked, watching her mother's boots step through mud and rocks. The next time she looked up, she found she'd outpaced everybody. She stopped and waited for the crowd, jangling forward like the herd of goats Leda had watched from Charlotte's cabin door. They bumped and jostled one another. They whined and tattled. Some thrived on it—the constant nips and butts. Some plodded through it. And others lagged, a few steps ahead of being left behind.

At the overlook, people stretched and milled, kicking aside leaves as if a girl were a thing that could be put down carelessly, as if a girl might be retrieved if everyone just retraced their steps and looked carefully. Beside the rock, goldenrod and milkweed released white-winged seeds. The seeds hung and spun like snow, drifting out over the rocks and into the open.

Carly handed out white candles, and people cupped their hands and lit the wicks. The flames stayed and then blew out when they took their hands away. Some people knelt and prayed over their cold candles anyway. Leda had never prayed. To her, it had always seemed like a fruitless effort, like all these floating seeds. It was amazing that humanity, that nature, kept trying.

She climbed higher on the rock. Her mom's boots gripped well and propelled her up. A raven gusted overhead, passing through golden windows where the clouds had broken. From here, the reservoir looked like liquid metal, interrupted only by that distant stub of the intake tower, plugged in the middle of the water. From here, she did not see Ian. Of course she didn't. The group was mostly girls—girls wearing neon Scream shirts, holding hands at the edge of the overlook while someone took a picture of their chests, reading YOU HAVE A VOICE over and over and over.

Leda unscrewed her water and shut her eyes against the setting sun. She felt wind. For a moment, she could sense the planet's torque under her. It was like sitting in the sycamore, where Bear Grass Creek meets the reservoir. She'd been ten when she'd spent an entire night in those branches, claiming she'd never come down again.

And her mother? Where had she been?

Water glugged onto Leda's fingers. She had squeezed the bottle too tight. She capped it, put her legs out in front of her, and slid down the rock. When she landed, she wanted to run. Run home. Run and find Clarence, digging holes for new garden fence posts. Run to her mother, nipping apart teacups and dessert plates for some new mosaic, blowing china splinters from her fingers as if all of life would forever be this simple, this safe.

The group assembled, and Carly gave a speech in which she repeated the words *together* and *grief.* Then other people stood up and said basically the same thing. They missed Charlotte's kindness, her smile, her contagious laughter. Fragments of Charlotte's postcard flared in Leda's brain. *Your fault . . . deserved it . . . shock.*

When the speeches were over, everyone lay down. Leda blinked. She had been zoning out. When Carly passed, Leda wanted to ask, *What do I do?* But she was sick of relying on her Big. Sick of seeking approval.

Carly instructed the group, placing one hand on her chest and one on her belly, demonstrating something. She said, "Yogic breathing." Leda was still sitting up. She met Carly's eyes as she told the group to shut them, to unlock from the "mind's habitual fear response." Carly,

Leda couldn't help thinking, had probably watched a YouTube video on this. She talked about breath: into the belly, into the chest, and then out. In-in-out. They would breathe this way for fifteen minutes, through the mouth. A gong hit, just as the sun touched the horizon, just as Leda saw him.

Ian sat at the edge of the crowd, his eyes on hers now.

"If you feel a building numbness," Carly was saying, "or tingling, or pressure . . . don't worry. It's normal. Just keep breathing."

By the time Carly screamed, Leda was already cutting down the mountain, glancing back to see if Ian was following. She didn't see him. She saw only white seeds, floating above the canopy. She listened for footsteps, for cracking leaves, but already more voices were starting to scream. It sounded awful. Worse than the crying goats, waiting to be bred. Worse than those that had just been finished, just been marked down in the breeding log—a notation not dissimilar to Leda's own records. *Indoor Sunglasses*, she had written, along with a date. And before that, a question mark beside *Ian Gray*.

When Leda looked back down, away from the scream, the head of a deer appeared amid laurels, made visible by the white satellites of her ears. One ear angled up. Leda blinked, and the animal was gone. The woods went dim. A twig snapped up the mountain.

Leda cut off switchbacks, taking the fastest way down. Back at the trailhead, she had trouble unlocking her truck. She couldn't make the key turn; her hands had gone numb. She cursed, squinting at the lock in the half-light, annoyed that she had come, had let herself be bullied into coming. The praying, the yogic breathing, the Scream—they were all just floating seeds that would never land anywhere, never take root in anything.

A pair of headlights hit her—the dropping night drawn back. She hadn't even heard the vehicle approaching. A face wavered there behind the dark windshield, reminiscent of Ian, then of the fanged beast emerging from the anthropology building—the human ears, the fleshy cheeks. But then, in an instant, she saw him more clearly— a man in full camo and a blaze-orange cap. More dogs in the back. *Hunting* dogs, Leda corrected her earlier thought. They were probably getting exercise or running bear before the hunting season started. Charlotte was missing, yes. But the whole world was not looking for her.

SAVE YOURSELF, Charlotte had written. She'd known that no one cared. Not really. Not enough. She'd known that no one else was going to do it for you.

But maybe there were exceptions. Maybe there was still some- thing Leda could do. She jammed the truck into gear and drove, glancing in her rearview mirror. She sped away from the main high- way, words and images flashing through her brain: Ian asking, *Do you remember everything from Halloween?* Ian staring at the intake tower at the reservoir, saying, *I'd save you. Maybe.* He hadn't been able to take his eyes off that tower. He had lost his train of thought, looking out across the opaque water.

There were no headlights in her rearview mirror. It didn't look like he was following her. Even so, she pulled onto the next orchard road and turned off her lights, crawling uphill between uniform trees. Fallen apples cracked under her tires. Eventually, she shut the engine off, watching the road. Five minutes passed. Ten minutes. No Ian.

The camper at the Bear Grass picnic area was dark. Her head- lights showed the pit bulls in their cages, but even after she'd gotten out of the car, they didn't bark. Leda took her phone, though she barely got service out there, and secured the gun in the back of her jeans. She still wore her mother's heavy boots, the soles dense with earth and manure.

Something had drawn her here to this place where Charlotte, she suspected, had been murdered. Maybe it was seeing Ian, now that she knew something had happened between him and Charlotte. Or maybe it had been those flimsy speeches before Carly's scream, bringing with them the realization that Charlotte would be forgotten ultimately. Even the people that championed her were already forgetting. Most had barely known her in the first place. Maybe Leda needed to face what had happened instead of closing her eyes and shrieking. She needed to believe that she could do something.

The fire road up to the dam felt longer than when she and Ian had walked it, following this knee-deep gully of washed-out clay and gravel. Overhead, the tree branches poised like fingers. At her feet, the gully looked like a scar.

It took a few minutes to cut through the woods toward the dam. She tried to be quiet, but it was impossible not to stir up leaves and branches. On the way, she passed under her sycamore tree—even bigger than she remembered it. Its branches hung out over the black water. Its roots hunched like the legs of a spider. Quiet, Leda touched the trunk. Looked up. The lowest boughs were well out of reach. How had she ever climbed up?

She hovered for a moment at the base of her tree, listening, looking out at the intake tower across the water. She tried to make out what she'd seen that day with Ian: the cracked windows, the color of bug wings; the white feathers in the metal screen, loosed from a white boa. The more she looked, the more she thought she could see their artificial glinting. Above her, the sycamore's limbs moaned, like the sound of creaking bone.

Was it possible? Leda asked herself. Could Ian really have brought Charlotte here? Lured her or followed her? Could someone Leda had known—someone she'd kissed, slept with—really have dumped a girl in the water?

The feathers might not solve anything, but they were a start.

Leda walked out onto the dam, stopping where she and Ian had looked at the mountains and smooth water, now indistinguishable from each other. The intake tower was only just visible in the falling dark—strange and isolated. Only a narrow catwalk connected the dam to the tower, elevated about ten feet over the reservoir.

The public walk reached halfway across the dam, ending in a high gate. A few yards beyond the gate, a black cascade replaced the walkway. Only this gate stood between Leda and the catwalk. At first, Leda thought she might be able to cling and shimmy around it, but the chain-link fencing extended a few feet to either side of the dam's crest. A fall would be dangerous. To her left, the overflow plunged into darkness. To her right, the still water would be frigid. And anyway, the water was not still, was it? Ian had described undercurrents and hidden machinery. She might hit something on the fall in; she might get sucked under. Then, whether by drowning or hypothermia, *she* would be added to the list of missing persons.

The structure trembled under the soles of her boots as millions of gallons of water pressed against it and as thousands spilled through. The cascade roared. Yet, somehow, Leda's mind was quiet. It was as if all the chaos and confusion of the past weeks had resolved into these simple tasks: climb the gate, find the feathers, don't fall in.

The chain link wasn't easy to manage in her mother's boots. Still, she climbed, trying not to look down the hundred-foot drop, where she and Ian had seen swallows pitching over a faraway stream. A few strands of barbed wire extended loosely across the top of the gate. It was like climbing a cow fence, she told herself. She'd done it hundreds of times as a child. She got her footing, steadied her grip on the wire, and swung her leg over.

"Leda—"

Wobbling, Leda glanced behind her, but the voice must have been in her mind. Below her, she thought she could see fragments of her mother hovering in the water: patterned skirt, brown bracelet, strong calves. Her voice was close, and then far. That day—eleven years ago, when Leda had climbed and then refused to get down from the sycamore—crept back to her. It had been a good day. There had been soda and sandwiches. Clarence had found a big crawfish. He had made imperfect skipping stones skip and skip. Maybe the day had been too good; Leda hadn't wanted it to end.

She hadn't realized then that all things end. Soon, Mom and Clarence were at the pickup. They were leaving, they said. The sky turned colors above and below the sycamore, from which ten-year-old Leda shouted something indignant. The truck engine started. The taillights ignited.

Now, Leda couldn't tell if she'd really seen this—this flash of red—or if she had imagined it, *remembered* it. She watched the woods, still straddling the barbed wire. She decided that she hadn't seen it, got her other leg over the barbs, and slipped down the gate on the far side.

The catwalk made a T with the dam. It took her away from the crest's overflow, spilling down in black foam. Her boots rang on the metal diamond tread. The narrow structure swayed. It seemed to, anyway. She steadied herself on the handrails, walking out across the calm water, doing her best not to think about what might be below the surface.

She let a hand rest at the small of her back, touching the gun. Clarence had told her to never carry a gun like this, in your pants, like you see in the movies. But this *was* a bit like a movie. Or a video game, maybe. She felt as if she had lost control of her own decision making, as if she were a character being walked across this catwalk by some unknown player. It was comforting to think of a player, a god, like Vinnie—careful, attentive to detail. Jonah as a god would be scary—impatient, impulsive. Though perhaps Jonah would be better suited to defeating villains, administering justice.

Or maybe it was just adrenaline pushing her forward. Maybe it was her heart, churning blood into her feet, her hands, her belly.

Behind her, there was still no light, no movement, no Ian.

A low concrete wall surrounded the intake tower, and she palmed it, trying to find her balance. A bit of white showed in the darkness: the feathers, caught in the window's metal mesh. She crept closer. Old spiderwebs trawled her legs. Then something warped the shape of the air just over her, and she ducked. A man, she thought, bearing down on her. But nothing touched her. When she looked up, she saw it: an owl had dived down from the tower. Now it slipped away, gliding noiselessly over the water toward the shore. There, in the trees, something moved.

She stopped, stiff as a deer. For a long time, nothing happened. Then a man walked out of the woods.

Leda dropped into a crouch behind the low wall. Her hand found the gun, though she didn't take it out. She waited, out of sight, eyeing the feathers. Eventually, she peeked over the wall.

The man had walked out across the dam and stopped at the chain-link gate. He didn't move for a few long minutes. Leda's phone quaked in her pocket, on silent, but of course she didn't look at it. The light of the screen would give her away. And anyway, no phone call could save her.

Her legs burned in the squat. There was no way she could reach the feathers without getting up. So, eventually, she came to stand, taking the gun in one hand, the chamber empty, the magazine loaded.

One-handed, she picked out as many feathers from the window as she could, sparing no time to inspect them. She stuffed them into her jeans pocket and then held the gun with both hands, pointing it down and away from her body. Still, the man had not moved. She took backward steps until she rounded the tower. The man slipped from sight. She felt the exterior wall, but it was just concrete. There was no door. No magic escape.

The next time Leda looked out from behind the tower, the man had moved. Her eyes darted, adjusting again to the rising moonlight. The catwalk leading back to the dam gleamed white. Somewhere, chain link rattled. It was an unmistakable sound—the flutter of link on link. With a cold hand, Leda pulled the pistol's slide and let it go. An active round released into the chamber. The gun felt heavier now.

SAVE YOURSELF, Charlotte had written. Was this what she'd meant?

The shadow broke the white of the catwalk. The man walked like Ian. Had he heard the gun's click? Could he see the weapon? He called out, but Leda couldn't make out what he said over the crashing water. Maybe there was anger there, in that voice. Maybe there was excitement. Fear. Whatever the emotion, Leda wasn't going to hang around and ponder it. The only way back to land was now blocked. She was cornered here by the man who had murdered Charlotte. She looked around her at the black reservoir. She was running out of options. She could stand her ground and face him, she thought. They could talk. But something deep in her gut pleaded, *Run.*

Squeezing the pistol, she stepped onto the concrete wall. She was in plain sight now—there was no way he didn't see the gun. Though, admittedly, she still could not properly see him. He was still just a shadow, a cutout. Her finger slid from the frame of the gun and pulsed on the trigger. Her heart seemed to swell across her chest and down her arm to fill that one single digit. She would not follow Charlotte.

The man called her name. Now, she could hear him.

Behind her heels, the water glinted. What would happen if she stepped off? She would fall. She would drop, not knowing when to hold her breath, not knowing when she'd hit the surface. And then, all at once, sound would rush in as she crashed through layers of shock and numbness. Maybe the water would cradle her, like a womb. Or maybe the impact would stab her.

And of course, even if she were to survive the impact, the cold, there was no way that she could outswim Ian. She couldn't help but remember him saying, *It's never too cold to swim.*

She squeezed the gun with both hands. The water below was moonlit, yet featureless. Some reservoirs, Leda knew, concealed whole towns. Houses. Cars. And how many bodies? Standing on the wall, she imagined her body sucking under. She could disappear right here, she knew, and no one would notice. After going to the goat farm, she knew now that it would take more than a few days for her friends to even register the loss of her.

"Stop," she tried to call out, but her voice came out shrunken. The man didn't stop. Did he not see her? Did he not see the gun?

You froze, Charlotte had written. *You were in shock.*

Had Charlotte run from this man? Had she *tried* to run? What does a person do if there's nowhere to go and no one but your own scared self protecting you?

The moon slipped behind thick clouds as Leda pointed the gun up at the sky and fired. She wanted him to hear her, see her. Fear her, even. And now, finally, he did. The blast split the night open. She had forgotten how loud a gunshot was. The man yelped, crouching down, his hands over his head. He groveled there, no more than twenty feet from her. For a moment, Leda panicked, thinking she'd hit him.

The moon came back out—cool, indifferent—illuminating Ian. Suddenly, she could see him clearly, cowering on the metal walk.

"It's me," he was saying, panicked. "It's just me."

But Leda only blinked, gun still pointed up at the air. Her ears throbbed. Ian started to back away, still crouched. He must have seen something in her face—something cold, unreachable—because he'd stopped speaking, stopped trying to convince her of who he was. That, she knew already. Or, she'd thought she had known.

Eventually, Ian scrambled up. Of course she hadn't hit him—she'd pointed the gun nowhere near him, she'd fired a warning shot—but still she was stunned. She only watched as Ian backed down the catwalk.

He is so cute, she could hear Carly say Halloween morning, standing in the green grass of the Lawn. *And he likes* you.

Around them, costumed children shivered swords and flung magic wands, their cries so wild that it had been hard to tell whether they were happy or frightened.

And what had Leda said?

Says who.

Thinking back, Leda hardly recognized the girl Carly had been talking to.

Ian left her alone beside the tower, the gun loose in her hands, her heels inches away from a drop into frigid water. He was running now. He dashed across the dam and vanished into the woods. Leda still had not moved. Moonlight glinted in the black weapon. Slowly, feeling returned to her skin and the muscles beneath it. Slowly, she began to understand that she had been wrong. It was not Ian she had to be afraid of.

Her hand groped her pants pocket. She took a feather out, held it up. It was a feather, yes. But it had none of the shine of Charlotte's boa. None of that artificial iridescence. Had that, too, been all in her head?

Hands shaking, Leda emptied the weapon. She put the magazine in one jacket pocket and the gun in the other . . . though really she just wanted to put the thing down, leave it on the ground. She retraced her steps. The fire road was empty when she came to it, but still Leda paused in the trees, trying to control her breathing. In the picnic area, the pit bulls were quiet. No danger. Not here. She stepped out onto the road. The night was getting cold.

Remembering the vibration in her pocket, she took out her phone.

Carly asked me to find you, Ian had texted. Are you okay? I see your car but idk where you are?

Find me, she thought now, as if this were some game. A game with no safe zone, no base. A game in which, no matter what, you keep getting chased. But Leda wasn't a child. Of course, it was too late. The parking lot at the base of the hill was empty. Ian had driven away.

15

L eda knocked on Flora's door and waited. She turned to face Nalle
Street, her breath coming out white. It could snow; the sky had
that weight to it. She would have stuffed her hands into her jacket
against the cold, but the pockets were full. Charlotte's postcards took
up a lot of room.

Charlotte had been missing for over four weeks, and people were
starting to talk about other things. Most of Leda's sisters had flown
home for Thanksgiving. They'd slept in their childhood beds. They'd
eaten turkey and biscuits. Now, it was almost exam week. Now, every
library, every coffee shop brimmed with bodies. Even Carly was
hauling around books. Lately, she and Leda hadn't spoken much.

Charlotte was still in the news, if you looked for her; but, these
days, Leda may have been the only one looking. She'd spent all of
Thanksgiving break studying and checking the news. She'd studied
her ass off, actually. It had been a way of distracting herself from the
humiliation of having shot a gun at (well, *above*) Ian. A way of distracting herself from her confusion. She had been so sure, so ready to
point a finger at him. Maybe it had felt good to have someone to

blame for that night—for everything that had happened to Leda, to Charlotte.

Sometimes there was everyone to blame. Sometimes there was no one. She should have learned this from her mom, her mom's illness. It was no one's fault.

But then sometimes, you didn't know. *Couldn't* know. Over break, Leda had done her best to sit with this, lying low. She'd taken refuge with Clarence and Faye. It was the first time she'd asked them for something, asked for help, and the experience had been remarkable only in how unremarkable it'd been. Leda had simply brought her overnight things and set herself up on an air mattress in the yoga room. Together, they'd cooked a vegan Thanksgiving. And although Clarence and Faye had lately been focusing their energies on getting Vinnie on a flight to New Delhi, they were also, somewhat contradictorily, learning Hindi.

It had felt good to stay away from grounds for seven whole days, to check her phone only to see if she had missed a call from the police station. Some days, she could trick herself into thinking that nothing much had changed. But then she'd hear the boys playing that video game. She'd glance at the row of Buddhas on top of the living room speakers. She had returned the gun weeks ago, minus one bullet.

Faye hadn't noticed that the gun was missing. Or if she had, she hadn't said anything. She had only told Leda, apropos of nothing, that Jonah and Gino's father had been killed when the boys were young. She didn't elaborate—didn't say what happened or who did it and with what purpose. As if it didn't matter. And perhaps, at this point, it didn't.

"After that," she'd said, "everything was different."

For Faye, Leda supposed, the gun was a coping mechanism . . . along with the door codes and home security system and her tendency toward suspicion. *Paranoia* was how Leda sometimes thought about it—this delusion that had transformed Ian into something that he wasn't, this defective sixth sense that had nearly done irreparable damage.

Of course, she knew plenty of women who carried Mace in their purses. A few of her sisters even had concealed carry permits. A part of her wanted to call them paranoid, sure. But many, like Faye, had lived through trauma. They knew what it meant to be vulnerable. They were preparing for the worst.

Still, Leda found that she didn't want a gun. She could have easily trained her weapon on Ian that night. She could have easily pulled the trigger. But then she'd seen his face. The moon had come out, revealing not a shadow, not a monster, but a person. Seeing him clearly, she'd no longer felt sure. Who was *she* to decide whether he was guilty or innocent? Who was she to decide who lives and who dies?

Of course she didn't *know* that Ian was innocent. But she couldn't get that look on his face out of her mind. He'd been scared of her— scared of her sudden, reckless power.

Now, it was December. It had been two weeks since Leda had fired Faye's weapon and two weeks since she'd submitted the feathers from the intake tower to the police, filing everything she knew in the Department of Justice's online system. As of this morning, she still hadn't heard from them.

Admittedly, she'd known that the feathers weren't quite right. Yes, they were white. But they were not soft like the ones from Charlotte's room. They were probably just bleached goose plumes. The police had probably written her off as another person obsessed with a case that had nothing to do with her, obsessed with the bleak spectacle of murder.

In a way, they'd be right. She'd blown the threat of Ian out of proportion. She'd let him go black and white in her mind, like a criminal composite sketch—a mash-up of all her anxieties. For all Leda knew, the police may not have even suspected Ian. Just because he'd been seen leaving a police station (according to her sister Genie) didn't mean anyone thought he was a killer. It was possible he'd gone there of his own volition, hoping to submit some bit of information that might help the investigation.

That wasn't to say that Leda thought Ian was blameless. Something *had* happened between him and Leda. That is, they'd had sex while Leda was blacked out, unable to consent. But Leda was also willing to admit that the situation had been complicated. *Sex* was complicated. It was possible that she had come on to him, that she'd said yes. It was possible that they'd both been unconscious.

Slowly, she tried to move on, tried to keep her distance. She'd changed her number since that night at the reservoir. She got to her classes late and left early, in case Ian tried to intercept her. Astronomy was obviously tricky, but so far he, too, had steered clear of her.

Once, Indoor Sunglasses had passed her on the Lawn. He'd seen her for an instant—recognized her—and she'd done her best to look through him. A few days after that, she'd gotten her period—that thick ball of dread dissolving as if her body, too, was ready to press on.

Leda stomped her numb feet on Flora's porch. Still, no one had answered. She reached to knock again, but paused with her fist hovering. The letterbox beside the door had been altered. *Flora Blackshear*, it read. *Angel Carter*. The third name, *Charlotte Mask*, had been Sharpied over.

The letterbox was empty. Of course it was. What had Leda expected? She let the lid slap shut. Even as she did her best to move on, she still returned to that first—or rather, Charlotte's *last*—card. Back when Leda had assumed that Pia was a girl, a person, she hadn't agonized over the meaning of it. But since then, she'd read and reread the postcard.

Dear Charlotte, I'm dropping out soon. Maybe I'll think more clearly after. Maybe I'll find something out there— down there—and someday I'll tell you about it. Take care of yourself, friend. SAVE YOURSELF. Love, Pia

These were Charlotte's last words, as far as Leda knew. Unlike the first time she'd read the card—exactly a month ago today—she now sensed that *dropping out* meant something more than just leaving school. Maybe protecting yourself, *saving* yourself, meant getting away. Stepping back. It meant living in a cabin with no electricity, no cell phone, no running water.

But, of course, Charlotte hadn't gone back to the goat farm. Leda had been there, and there'd been no sign of her. There'd been only Pia in her dark stall—a herd animal that was happier away from the herd that bullied her.

And then there was that odd interjection: *down there.* Leda couldn't make sense of it. *Maybe I'll find something out there—down there—*

Down where?

She knocked again. Her hope was that Flora could help her. Of course, she didn't expect that they'd crack the code, save the day, solve the mystery. She had shed those delusions. But maybe Flora could help her understand this final message. Her plan was to explain everything—from stealing the postcards to firing the gun—and then to admit, finally, that she didn't know, *couldn't* know, what had happened to Charlotte. Her plan was to bring them both some closure.

But no one came to the door. She touched the place where Charlotte's name had been on the letterbox. She pulled the postcards out of her coat. Perhaps she could simply place the cards in the box. It would be easier this way—to let it all go.

But then the door came open, and Flora saw the cards. Leda had expected her to start crying, but Flora's expression was stony, unreadable. She stepped back and held the door wide.

The few times Leda had been in the house, it had felt dim and drafty. But today it was warm. It smelled like baking bread. *We were like sisters*, Flora had once said. Back then, Leda had assumed it was an overstatement. In that first week of Charlotte's disappearance, everyone had been exaggerating. But she could see the truth of it now in Flora's face. In the few weeks since Leda had seen her, Flora had aged.

The kitchen was cluttered—vegetable scraps on cutting boards, dishes in the sink. Still, it felt homey. The radio was on. A tall man in an apron removed two brown loaves from the oven. The skeleton, Leda realized. The first man she'd suspected. Flora introduced them, though apparently she didn't need to.

"I saw you." Angel let the loaves tumble to the table. "I saw you standing with Charlotte."

At first, Leda didn't understand.

"I swear." Angel smiled, shook his head. "In my head, I've gone over that night eight million times. I *definitely* remember you."

Then Leda got it. He had thought about her as much as she'd thought about him. Maybe he'd hoped that she'd come forward with information. Or maybe he'd feared her—afraid of what she might say if she did.

"I guess I'm not the only one, then," Leda said dumbly, "who's thought about it."

Obviously, this was an understatement. But she didn't want to go back into it. Not with him. In the past few weeks, she'd been trying to focus on school again, trying to reestablish a relationship with her sisters—her friends. Of course, she hadn't forgotten. Even if she had wanted to, she couldn't have forgotten Charlotte. But she'd been try-ing to keep herself safe from her own mind; she'd been trying to live her life. And this, she hoped, was the final step. Return Charlotte's postcards to Flora. Lay this all to rest.

Still, being brought back to that night, even after all this time, Leda still couldn't control the expression that cut through her mouth, her eyes. Clearly, Flora saw it. Angel didn't. He began recounting that short drive home. How Charlotte had been totally normal.

Flora cut in. "Angel?" Her face, Leda noticed, was bare today—no glitter, no makeup. "Would you mind if we had a little, like, girl time? I hate to gender things—you know me—but seriously."

Angel shrugged. He didn't seem to mind. He left the loaves on the counter.

To Leda, Flora apologized. She fiddled with a rainbow barrette in her pink hair. Her eyes went to the postcards in Leda's hands, over and over again.

"Tea?" Flora finally said, putting water on without waiting for Leda's reply. Her fingers worried a dishcloth as the kettle hissed and rumbled.

"I'm sorry," Leda spoke up eventually. "Are you all right?"

"It's just . . . been a long time," Flora said. She took a breath. "She's been gone a long time."

The kettle heated. Flora went to the fridge. Saint candles rattled on top of the refrigerator as she tugged the door open—Frida Kahlo, LeBron James, William Faulkner.

"I honestly thought she'd come back," Flora said, looking in, drumming her fingers before closing it again, empty-handed. "I was stupid."

Leda didn't know what to say. The kettle started to whine. Flora turned off the flame, taking her time.

"I found those, you know." Flora pointed to the postcards in

Leda's hands. "I found them in her room after she didn't come back. I was trying to find her parents' names, phone numbers . . . something I could use to contact them."

Leda nodded. Her mouth wouldn't open. She hadn't expected this—the shame. She'd been planning to sit down and do most of the talking, but here she was, unable to say anything.

"Then, only a few days later, I couldn't find them," Flora said. "The postcards. I thought that the detectives had come back . . . or that maybe Charlotte's parents had found them. I didn't want to ask, because then they'd know that *I'd* known about the cards. They'd know that I hadn't told anyone about them." Flora took down mugs, shook her head. "I never thought that *you* . . ."

"I'm sorry," Leda said again.

"To be honest, I never understood them." Flora poured the tea, brought the mugs to the table, and gestured for Leda sit. "Did you?"

With some difficulty, Leda placed the postcards on the table and took a breath. She found her voice again. She told Flora about taking the cards. Reading them. She told her about Ian—what Tamara had said about him, yes, but also about her own experience with him. Then she told her about Pia, though she didn't go into the whole farm trip. She didn't say Pia was a goat. For one thing, she didn't want to complicate things. But she was also curious to see if Flora would provide the information for her. She wanted to get a sense for how much Flora had known.

"It was an alias," Leda explained. "It's sort of a long story, but I'm *sure* that Charlotte wrote these cards."

"To herself?"

"I guess."

"It would make sense," Flora said, after a moment. "It sounded like her—the tone. It sounded like Charlotte. I never thought to check the handwriting. But now that I see it again . . . it is. It's hers."

"Did you read all of them?"

Flora nodded.

"So . . . do you know what happened?" Leda asked. "Not when she disappeared, I mean, but before that. She said that she blamed herself. It sounded like something . . . someone . . ."

"I remember that card." Flora's face had gone slightly gray. "Whatever it was . . . Charlotte never told me about it. She never said anything."

"You never noticed some . . . change?"

Flora shook her head. "She could be private. Didn't talk much about herself. Asked a lot of questions. She . . . listened." Flora picked up her mug, but she didn't drink. Her fingers were white on the ceramic. "But it's weird, isn't it? Sending out secrets with no envelope. She must have wanted someone to know."

"Know what?"

"That something was wrong." On that last word, Flora's voice broke. Her eyes shut, but she was not crying. If anything, she looked angry. "I was so . . . stupid."

"Don't say that," Leda said, though she wasn't sure what Flora was referring to. "It's not true."

Flora spoke slowly, almost to herself. "Of course it's true."

Something chimed on the other side of the room. Flora stood. Her phone was on a countertop near the stove. She stared at the screen for a moment. Eventually, she came back to the table with it. She turned the phone to face Leda.

The image was blurry. Some parking lot. A black-haired girl, wearing a white, oversized shirt. Leda couldn't make out her face. She was too far away. Whoever had texted the photograph had also written, *C Mask? I saw poster.*

Leda's stomach lurched. "Did you just get this? Is this—?"

"No." Flora stopped her. "It isn't her."

"Then who . . . what is this?"

"That first week that she was gone, I made flyers." Flora picked up her tea, but didn't drink. "Every time someone came through the house, couch surfing or something, I'd ask them to take some. By now they're probably posted all over the country, and they've got my number on them. So, I get a lot of texts and calls from people saying they've seen her."

Leda stared at the grainy image. "Where?"

"That's not what I mean. A lot of them must have seen my interview on the news. I don't know why, but they latched on to the barefoot thing. Did you see it?"

Leda nodded. Under the table, she shifted her feet in her mom's hiking boots.

"Now it's like people message me whenever they see a girl, any girl, walking barefoot. It has slowed down a lot, but, every few days, I still get pictures. It'll be two in the morning, and someone will send me a blurry photo of a girl outside, like, an Idaho Walmart. I could show you a dozen pictures like that on my phone."

The girl in the image, Leda saw now, was not wearing shoes. On her leg, she had some kind of tattoo. It wasn't Charlotte. Of course it wasn't.

"I'd never thought there were so many girls, walking around barefoot," Flora said. "I mean, *of course* Charlotte isn't the only one. It's just . . . I was stupid. I could have, I *should* have—"

"Flora, it wasn't your fault."

"No, see, that's what pisses me off." Flora looked at Leda now, straight on. Her eyes were big with something. "Maybe it was."

Strangely, Leda recognized this look. It had struck Flora's face at the health food store, when Leda had run into her after yoga. At the time, Leda hadn't thought anything of it. Flora had just seemed emotional, weepy. But now, Flora wasn't crying.

"I lied in that interview." Flora swallowed. "I said that the last time I saw Charlotte was two o'clock in the afternoon. But that wasn't true."

"But . . ." Leda was confused.

"Charlotte—" Flora's voice spiked. "Charlotte was really generous, you know? With her time. She would *do* anything. If you invited her to, like, a sweat lodge, or a field rave, or your grandma's hundredth birthday, she'd just go. It sounds cheesy, but I think she had this real interest in people, to the point where, I don't know . . ."

Leda thought of those prom photos. That laugh—her mouth wide open. There were probably dozens of pictures of Leda like this, first and second year—the years she had devoted herself to her friends, her sorority. The years she had memorized all of her sisters' middle names and birthdays. The years she'd spearheaded fundraisers, logged volunteer hours, attended date nights wearing perfume and heels.

But then, briefly, her path had crossed Charlotte's.

Leda finished Flora's thought. "There was no room left for her."

Flora nodded. "She was always doing things for other people. Doing things for me. So when she asked me for something, I wanted to help."

Leda picked up her mug, swallowed tea. It didn't taste like anything.

"I haven't told anyone this," Flora said, quiet. She got up and stood by the sink, looking out the window as if seeing something, somebody. "I was home."

"What do you mean?"

"I mean that Angel gave Charlotte a ride from that party, right? Well, after that, Charlotte came inside. She walked into the kitchen and sat on that bench you're sitting on, right across from me. Angel didn't know I was home. Apparently he didn't even notice that Charlotte was upset. She sat down and told me she needed a break. Like a reset. She said she wanted to start over, fresh. She wouldn't tell me what happened, but whatever it was, it was tearing her up."

Leda waited.

"Then she asked me what I had." Flora's hands gripped each other. "I knew what she meant. I don't do hard stuff, but sometimes I microdose, like, natural drugs. I always have psilocybin. I gave her some. Maybe more than she needed. She tried to pay me, but I wouldn't take it. She'd never asked me for anything, and I was so sure the mushrooms would help. I wanted to *help* her. And then she got her keys—"

Leda cut in. "When was this?"

"Late. Probably two in the morning. She said she'd touch base. I didn't ask where she was going. I didn't think much of it. I thought I was being a good friend, giving her space, giving her what she needed . . . and then I got a bad feeling. I got worried when she didn't check in. I called her parents once I tracked down their number, but they hadn't seen her. I didn't tell them my name; I was sort of panicking. I think I didn't want to be blamed. I think I was afraid. Her parents must have reported her missing. Then, when someone found Charlotte's car, I went out there to the woods, and I looked for her . . ." Flora turned to face Leda, her face strangely still. Then her mouth widened—a grimace—trying to hold something terrible in.

Leda went to her, but she stopped short. She didn't touch her. It seemed that the narrative Leda had assumed—that everyone had assumed—was far from true. No one had abducted Charlotte from her home. No one had coerced her into doing something or going somewhere. Charlotte had left on her own.

"I should have gone with her." Flora covered her face with both hands. "I shouldn't have let her go, alone."

There was very little Leda could do, little she could say that would change anything. She went back to the stack of postcards. The most recent one was on top. Now she brought this card to Flora.

"There's something," Leda said, "that you haven't seen."

Dear Charlotte, I'm dropping out soon. Maybe I'll think more clearly after. Maybe I'll find something out there— down there—and someday I'll tell you about it. Take care of yourself, friend. SAVE YOURSELF. Love, Pia

Flora looked up a little, tears landing on the floor.

"It was in your mailbox," Leda explained. "The day I dropped off those flowers."

Leda was about to apologize again, about to admit that she'd had no right to take it, but strangely, Flora smiled.

Leda hesitated. "What?"

"It's just that Charlotte used to say that." Flora shrugged, that bizarre smile still on her face. "Drop out."

"Like, drop out of school?"

"No." Flora wiped her eyes. "One time, she told me that she has this place she goes when she wants to be alone—this, like, cliff where she starts from the top and climbs down. She said her favorite thing about it was that her phone always lost service on the way down. One by one, she'd watch the bars drop until, at the base of the cliff, even her GPS wouldn't know where she was. She said it was freeing. She said that watching her phone service blink out was like watching herself, watching her dot on the map . . . vanish. Anyway, that's what she called it. Dropping out."

"Does anyone else know about this place?" Leda asked.

"I don't know. I don't think so."

"Look," Leda said. "The postcard was in your mailbox Wednesday morning. She must have mailed it after you saw each other on Halloween. She must have been trying to communicate something—"

"To me."

Leda's calves twitched. She wanted to pace the room, wanted to move. Was it possible that Charlotte *had* tried to check in with Flora, just as she'd promised? She had tried, but Leda had intercepted the message. That last postcard, in a way, had told Flora exactly where Charlotte had gone.

"Except that I don't know where it is," Flora said, as if Leda had been speaking out loud. She handed the postcard back, her smile fading. "That cliff."

But Leda did. She stared down at the postcard, reading the words, *Love, Pia.* In a way, Pia had dropped out, too. The goat had been pushed off the rim. But she'd *survived* it. Afterward, she'd dropped out of the herd. Happier by herself, away from the world's natural violence.

Charlotte must have climbed down the rim, Leda thought. She'd dropped herself off the map. She'd let herself blink out.

Except there was still something Leda couldn't make sense of. Charlotte had sent that last postcard here, knowing that Flora would see it. A secret with no envelope. But if Flora hadn't known about the rim at White Dog Farm, about Pia, then how could Charlotte have expected Flora to understand the message? Had she hoped that her friend would put the pieces together? Or had she hoped that she wouldn't?

"I'm sorry." Leda said, chest beating. "Would you excuse me for just a minute?"

Leda stepped outside and paced the front yard. Was it possible that Charlotte was still out there—*down there*—at the bottom of the cliff? She thought of that feeling she'd had, standing on the rim. What if Charlotte had been there all along, trying to get her head

around things? What if this whole fiasco—the news reports, the pro-
tests, the screams—had been blown out of proportion? Charlotte was
just a person trying to cope, trying to move forward no matter how
painful, no matter how slow. Maybe it was okay to drop out for a
while, Leda thought, as long as you know how to climb back out.

But it had been a month now. Did Charlotte want to be found?

Shadows of a passing flock flecked the grass at Leda's feet. Down
the street, she could hear the electric whir of that Barbie car. Eventually, she glimpsed the girl, her hair done up with purple beads. She
wore a pink puffy coat. The wheels roared, crushing glass and gravel.
Leda shielded her eyes. The birds twisted up and over the girl's head,
effortless.

Leda looked back at Charlotte's old house—the dim windows, the
empty mailbox with her name marked out. *It's been a month*, she
thought. She looked down at her hands, still holding Charlotte's last
card.

Behind her, the Barbie car whined by, its plastic wheels clacking
on endless grit.

SAVE YOURSELF, Leda read. It was like a dare. But a dare to do
what?

Leda called the police after she left Flora's. She told them about
White Dog Farm, told them she had reason to believe that Charlotte Mask might be there, at the bottom of a cliff. No, she didn't
think that Charlotte had jumped, she said into the phone. Or rather,
she didn't know. She hadn't thought about it. She had tried not to
think about it.

When they asked her who she was, she said she was a friend of
Charlotte's. She gave her name. She tried to sound unafraid.

She did not say that Charlotte had probably been high, intoxicated.

Drugs, alcohol—it was all the same. They were both ways to let go, lose consciousness, forget. *Light will someday split you open.* That old quote came back to her again. It was a beautiful image . . . if you could survive it.

After she hung up, she plugged an address into her phone's GPS. Before she'd left Flora's, this had been Leda's last question. Flora hadn't blinked. She'd given the information freely. Charlotte's parents lived barely fifteen minutes from town. Flora had been there recently, helping them move Charlotte's stuff out of the community house.

Now, Leda coaxed her truck up smooth asphalt. It was already getting dark, and every house here was lit up.

The suburb was similar to the one on Leda's old bus route. (The fluffy towels. The peculiar absence of dust.) The lots weren't huge, but the yards were polished. The houses themselves varied only in the color of their siding: white or gray or cream. The streets had peaceful names, like Old Pond and Raintree.

Standing in Flora's front yard, Leda had made up her mind to come here tonight. Too much time had passed; something had not gone right. It was hard to say how she knew. She knew what it felt like, maybe, to want to black out your mind. To forget that something ever happened. To forget that someone ever existed, ever meant something to you . . . To drop out for a while—away from your friends, your family, your life.

Flora, it seemed, knew it, too. She had only nodded when Leda told her what she planned to do.

Leda parked in front of Charlotte's parents' house and walked to the door. She stood on the clean welcome mat, holding Charlotte's postcards in front of her. *SAVE YOURSELF* was on top. A dare, perhaps, to drop out. But, no, Leda couldn't believe that. Because, in Leda's experience, within every dare is an implicit challenge to defy it.

Keep going, Leda told herself. *Don't give up. Don't let go.*

Inside the house, she heard voices. The clink of cutlery. TV. Leda stood at the door like this for a long time, not knocking.

When she was little, Leda had sometimes hovered outside of her own home like this, watching her mom and Clarence. She had wanted to see how quickly they would notice her absence. The rule was: however much they seemed to miss her would be equivalent to how much they loved her. The problem was that she was impatient; she'd give up hiding before their grief ever showed. Because loss would look like something, wouldn't it? Crouching outside, looking in, she'd imagined that she'd be able to see it.

But at this house, there were no banners. No blown-up photos. There were no wails or sobs or screams. From the outside, you couldn't see that gaping hole, that missing piece.

In the shadow of the front door, Leda waited. But of course no one came to the door, because no one knew Leda was out there. Eventually, she knelt and left the postcards there.

16

The library was packed full of undergraduates who had been, for one reason or another, living on another planet all semester. Even though Leda hadn't exactly blacked out for three months, as the story sometimes went, she felt some kinship with these panicked, disoriented students—waking up to (surprise!) their lives. Leda had left Charlotte's postcards on her parents' doorstep last week, and now she was already on her way to her first exam this morning, deciding now between a twelve-ounce coffee and a sixteen. Already she was drilling herself on blue and red shift, magnetism, the solar wind. Already, Leda felt as if she were regaining consciousness.

The weird thing was that although Leda was awake now—ready for her test, soon to be caffeinated—the world felt off. The televisions showed college football scores and Gulf Coast floods while, at the same time, Charlotte was still missing. Charlotte was missing while one frat boy poked another with a spork. Charlotte was missing while a girl in a study carrel slept with her mouth open. Charlotte was missing when it was Leda's turn to order, to put a lid on her coffee, to move out of the way for the next person. The world should seem different, Leda thought, with Charlotte still gone.

The lecture hall was loud and chaotic. Everyone seemed to be sitting where they didn't normally sit, and Leda took a random seat, doing her best not to look around for Ian, though somehow she'd already sensed him. He'd taken a seat only two rows in front of her. She shifted her gaze to her hands, not looking up until someone passed her an exam. She wrote her name, opened her blue book, and began.

For an hour and a half, the room was silent save for turning paper. But by the time the first students gathered their things and turned in their exams, a murmur had built in the lobby outside the lecture hall. The students who were still working glanced back occasionally. Leda kept her eyes on her paper, even as a low roar built outside the double doors. She wrote out equations, described the process of nuclear fusion, identified constellations. Yet, at the same time, she couldn't help but think of the day Charlotte had disappeared—how everyone in this very room had kept checking the news, how even their professor had seemed distracted, and then how everyone (Prof included) had gathered around the televisions after class ended. Now, Leda sensed that something had happened. Some shift had occurred. Some news had broken.

One student pulled out her phone after handing in the exam, and her muffled inhale—not a gasp, not so conscious as that—seemed to linger even after she'd left the room. Everyone would know, Leda realized, by the time she left this lecture hall.

She went through the test a second time, dragging her feet, checking over everything. A part of her never wanted to leave, never wanted to step out of this warm space into the cold, noisy lobby. But this fantasy was dependent upon everyone else staying, too. Time had to stop in order for Leda to remain here—a student among students, hunched over pencils and papers and calculators. In reality, she had only a few more minutes. For a few more minutes, she knew the answer to every question—every chart, every equation. For a few more minutes, she was safe.

One by one, her classmates finished. Leda was one of the last to leave. Ian, she couldn't help noticing, got up shortly after she did. She turned in the exam at the front of the room, thanked her professor, and walked back up the middle aisle toward the double doors, keeping her eyes down as she passed Ian.

The doors hissed opened, as if some pent-up pressure had been released. Students crowded together beneath the atrium, practically shouting to hear one another in the echoing lobby. Most held cell phones. Many had let their backpacks slump to their feet. A sweater lay on the floor between three girls, each holding the other, their foreheads pressed together. Overhead, the solar system did not so much as quiver. Though this, of course, wasn't really true. Nothing ever stops. Nothing ever stays still.

The morning that her mom died had felt almost like this—a slip. But, at the time, she hadn't wondered how long she'd be falling or how hard she would hit.

Also, she'd been alone then; that was another difference. Now, Leda was surrounded by people like her, feeling the world quake and swerve. Now, a group of classmates beckoned to her, though they barely knew one another. Their phones lay face up in their palms, and though Leda's eyes had gone fuzzy—as if to protect her from seeing, from knowing—Leda saw the headline. She saw the word *body*.

Though she read that word surrounded by people, she felt no less alone.

Behind her, the doors to the lecture hall opened. She turned. She could conjure no expression with which to face Ian. They looked at each other as if they were complete strangers.

That night, it was announced that fellow Psi Delt Melanie would be living in the Psi Delta house in the spring. Naadia was graduating early, with a paid internship set up in Bahrain already, so Mel would take her room. There were two things Leda knew about Melanie. The first was that Melanie had broken her leg in a fall off a fraternity roof, not even a week into the fall semester. Leda had heard rumors of this incident long before she'd realized the girl in question was also her sister. Even now, months later, Melanie wore a black, orthopedic boot. The second thing Leda knew was that Mel had called Leda a slut on Halloween.

Regardless, Leda cheered with the group, and Mel took her pick of celebration venues. This or that fraternity? Already—only one day into exam week—there were plenty of end-of-semester parties from which to choose. No one said, *Charlotte*. No one said, *Did you see the news?* Mel chose the party with the heated pool, and, an hour later, Leda and her sisters had suited up: tiny skirts and dresses, knee-high boots. It occurred to Leda that this was as much of a costume as what she or anyone else had worn on Halloween. A cat or Nefertiti. A swan or Zeus. A skeleton.

Skeletal remains. Those were the words the newspapers were using. It was disturbing that a person could be reduced to bones so quickly. Five weeks in open air, exposed to nature's brutal efficiency. An autopsy had not yet been performed. A conclusive identification had not yet been determined. But everyone knew. Though the cause of death had not been identified, there was no mention of suspects, no mention of a criminal investigation. Charlotte had been found "at the bottom of a precipice."

Leda made an effort to think of her like this. Not as a body or DNA. Not as human remains, but as Charlotte. Tiny and wondrous. Same as Leda. Same as anybody.

That night, Mary was staying in, studying (even after Leda pressed her, even after she texted, Please?). It was unclear if Mary knew what had been uncovered. Did you hear . . . Leda started to type, and then deleted it. She didn't know how to say it. It was like putting words to an avalanche, an earthquake.

She did, however, text Tamara on the walk to the frat. I'm sorry. And then, I'm here if you need me. Really.

Carly started chanting Eminem before they even got to the party, shouting through the snow flurries that cycloned through car head-lights on Memorial. Leda had brought her winter coat, but Carly sang and strutted sleeveless. She spread her arms and challenged an oncoming SUV, which stopped in the middle of the street. The passenger window came down, and the back door opened. There were guys inside. They made room. They gestured, drunk and gentle-manly. The air inside the SUV steamed.

"Get in," the guys said.

A few girls did, giggling. Leda tried to keep the rest of them walking. A few guys got out and followed them.

Leda asked Carly, "Do you know them?"

"They're Tri Pi," Carly said, flippant, as if this were an adequate credential.

Ever since that night at the reservoir, things were no longer the same with Carly. It wasn't just that Leda had walked out on her scream. It was the fact that Carly had asked Ian to follow Leda, telling him she was worried about her Little. Of course, Leda knew Carly better than that; she and the entire Psi Delta sorority had been gossiping nonstop about Ian—his supposed mistreatment of women, his capacity for vio-lence. Surely, Carly hadn't believed that Ian would actually harm her.

She probably didn't believe her own gossip, not seriously. But, at the very least, Carly had wanted to frighten her sister.

Now, Carly linked arms with one of the SUV dudes. With the guys, their group didn't have to wait in line on the sidewalk to get into the party. They just stepped over a slumped section of orange construction fence as the SUV guys hit fists with the dudes at the entrance, as if exchanging currency.

The frat was nicknamed LOVE, owing to the four freestanding block letters in the side yard, glowing red through the falling snow. Other than the word, the frat's architecture mimicked the rest of the university's—the pediments and the portico and the mini colonnade set off along an impressively squishy lawn. It was convincing, except for the fact that everything was flaking. Paint chipped from the window frames. The front porch was powdered with brick dust. Inside, tall boys smoked cigars in the foyer, a bare light bulb dangling over their heads where there had probably been a chandelier once. There in the entrance, the gummed end of a cigar was presented to Leda like a welcome gift. Someone's phone flashed as she took it. Leda stopped, looking for whoever had taken the photograph.

A boy approached and showed Leda how to hold the cigar properly, but she no longer wanted it. Had never wanted it. She gave it back. Behind her, Psi Delts diffused across the threshold into unseen rooms.

The pool had long been drained. But, there was a big covered patio with a freestanding fire pit. There were jumbo marshmallows and (oddly) crawfish, which had apparently been delivered live. A beer pong tournament occupied the other end of the patio. An expensive-looking camera had been left among the Solo cups. Though Leda seemed to be watching the tournament, she was really looking into the camera's black lens. She steadied her drink on the head of a stone cherub, complete with penis stub, belly, wings.

Why do you do this? Mary had asked, forever ago. At the time, Leda had been slimy with dish soap bubbles and irreversibly drunk. At the time, she hadn't even pretended to answer.

Now, here she was again. Bodies coursed around her. Her skirt was uncomfortable, and she tugged at it. Why had she worn it? Someone danced into the back of her, and she shifted her eyes down to see a pair of red shoes. She stiffened, as she had stiffened on her hands and knees underneath Indoor Sunglasses, as she had stiffened when Ian kissed her in the music department basement. She remained still, like a deer or a rabbit, hoping that the red shoes would take the hint. They didn't, so Leda walked away. She stepped into the snow and stood with her toes at the edge of the deep end. A beach ball drifted in the empty pool basin. It was quieter here in the snow. But with the silence came thoughts, memories.

Last seen the night of October 31. Reported missing November 2 . . .

When, Leda wondered, had Charlotte really disappeared? Even after Charlotte had left Flora on Halloween, she'd given the world a test. That was how Leda imagined it. Charlotte had driven out to Reservoir Road, left her boots in the trunk, and walked off. She'd let herself be vulnerable. Perhaps she'd hitchhiked to her aunt's land—land she knew and trusted. Perhaps she'd gotten on the Appalachian Trail and walked. There was a trailhead near the reservoir, and it seemed entirely possible that that same trail—which followed the same mountain range up and down the East Coast—came close to Charlotte's aunt's property.

However Charlotte had gotten there, it was possible that she'd tried to live out there beyond the rim, alone and undetected. It was also possible that, eventually, she'd tried to climb back up again.

Perhaps a person didn't always vanish at once. Perhaps a disappearance could be incremental, slow. Had Charlotte sensed it happening? Had Charlotte known?

She passed away. More than once, she'd heard that awful phrase today. A phrase she'd always hated. She hated the way it smoothed over the violence of death, the pain. But now, standing in the blank dazzle of snow, she could begin to imagine that death, too, sometimes went in stages—as if the soul were just a dense fog that gradually breaks up.

The snow masked the party for a moment. Leda stepped back in. The just-boiled crawfish had been dumped onto newspaper, steaming. A polo-ed boy Leda recognized from second-year Shakespeare spilled the melted butter, and everyone dabbed bits of crawdad meat around the soaked paper. Pieces of conversation slipped in and out of Leda's hearing—reimagined dramatizations of Charlotte's death, and then accounts of where each of them had been the night that it happened. Meanwhile, they discarded crawfish shells and legs, throwing them into the empty pool, letting the snow conceal them.

"I think I slept with that awful guy Halloween night," Genie said. "The one with the blue zero on his chest."

"Moonie?" Carly cackled. "*I* slept with him! Like, *the day* after that party."

"You are not serious. He was so gross," said Genie. "He sort of . . . lowed."

"That was before I met that *arsehole* Benjamin . . ."

An obese cat took a seat at Leda's feet, and she scratched it, distracting herself with it. LOVE gleamed in the side yard, over near the freestanding colonnade leading to (apparently) nothing. Crawfish parts sailed into the backyard cavity, surrounded by stone angels playing stone flutes.

Carly cried, "Why didn't you guys *tell me* he was a creep-o?"

Leda thought, *Here we go.* Benjamin had been seen holding hands with another undergraduate, and Carly couldn't stop talking about it.

Now, Carly posed a question: Is it or is it not creepy for a thirty-year-old to date someone who's basically twenty? Somehow, no one seemed capable of answering.

The cat slumped onto its side and showed Leda its wide belly. Maybe it was a trust test, Leda thought—exposing the softest part of the body, as if to ask, *Will you kill me or pet me?* Leda thought of how her blood had always risen to her face around Ian, as if to announce her pumping heart—her most vulnerable part. But today, after the astronomy exam, that hadn't happened. His pale face had mirrored hers. Charlotte was dead. And something else, too, had been killed between Leda and Ian.

Someone at the crawfish table talked about Charlotte's parents, about closure, saying, "At least we know . . ."

But this was what disturbed Leda the most. This whole time, she had thought she might experience some relief through the discovery of Charlotte's body. But now that it had come, she felt worse, knowing that there was no longer hope. She felt worse because she realized now that the location of Charlotte's body wasn't what she'd wanted to know. She had wanted to know, maybe, who Charlotte had been, or what Charlotte had seen when she'd taken that picture of Leda on Halloween. She had wanted to know what had chewed Charlotte up in the end, and whether or not she, Leda, may also be threatened.

But Leda had done this, hadn't she? She'd brought about this discovery. *She'd* united these misshapen puzzle pieces; *she'd* pointed the police a hundred miles southwest of Charlotte's abandoned sedan. Of course, she told herself that the police could have already known about the rim at White Dog Farm. Or, if they hadn't, someone on the farm would have eventually figured it out. The dogs had probably known a long time ago—they'd known when Charlotte arrived and when she died, just from the smell of the air. Even so, Leda couldn't help but feel responsible, as if *she* had killed Charlotte, once and for all.

The guy in the red shoes came back, dancing on Leda again. This time, she pushed him off. Somewhere, a tinny boom box pumped what sounded like Girl Talk. A Beatles sample—a repetitive, *I love you*—interwove with a persistent chant: *Hey! We want some pussy!*

"I love you," Carly chose to sing. "I love you . . ."

At the crawfish pile, Genie said, "I heard someone say she killed herself."

The guy from Shakespeare asked, "Who?"

"I don't know." Genie sucked her beer through a twisty straw. "I didn't know her. She just said that that's what somebody told her."

"Nah." Shakespeare shook his head, dabbing a body in butter. "She was fucking murdered."

Leda walked away, into the snow again, past the drained pool. From here, she could see people taking pictures with the word LOVE, surrounded by frosty red cups. Beside the word, the frat house looked like a gaunt castle. It hunched and glittered. Everyone at the party seemed to glitter. There was a part of Leda that hated it, that hated all these people around her.

A girl climbed the illuminated *O*, and then turned her back, as if to trust-fall into too-few waiting arms. Maybe every day was a trust fall, Leda thought. Every day you stepped into the world, vulnerable, testing to see whether you'd be caught or dropped.

Moisture leaked through Leda's boots as she walked, crunching through the thin layer of snow toward the front yard. The line to get into the party had dispersed from the front sidewalk. Leda walked to the curb and looked down the empty street. Empty, that is, except for an approaching figure.

She was alive, Leda thought then. She had to keep living.

"Leda." The figure resolved out of the darkness. "You all right?"

He smelled like wood smoke, chlorine.

"I'm all right." Leda breathed. "You?"

"Me?" Ian sounded surprised. "I'm okay. I'm fine."

They stood there for a moment, staring at the bright, decrepit fraternity. There was too much to say—Charlotte, the reservoir, Halloween—so for a long time they said nothing. In her mind, Ian pushed her against a wall at the bubble party and kissed her. The room had spun like a carousel. She had thought, *This feeling. Finally.* Like being picked up. Like being carried.

"Can you tell me," Leda said now, "what you remember from Halloween?"

"Halloween," Ian repeated the word, as if he didn't know its meaning.

After the kiss, Leda stood outside Ian's room, bleeding. After the kiss, she'd peeled pink Silly String off her feet. She had felt something dangerous inside her loosen.

Leda said, "You haven't thought about it?"

"No." Ian stalled. "I have."

It was stupid, Leda thought. It was stupid how easy it was to *do*— sex and everything leading up to it—and how difficult it was to talk about it.

"I can't remember if we had sex," Leda said. "To be honest, I can't remember any of it."

"Right," Ian said, though his tone wasn't exactly confident. "Well, we did. Have sex."

Looking at him—knowing now that Ian had nothing to do with what had happened to Charlotte—Leda realized that, like her, Ian was nervous.

"You came over," Ian said, trying again. "And afterward, we fell asleep. *I* fell asleep, at least. Then, in the middle of the night, I woke up, and you were sort of sitting up over me."

Leda could almost remember this, watching Ian sleep. As a child, she'd woken her mother nightly, saying she wanted to be tucked back in, as if the quilts had just come loose, and she didn't know how to fix them. Really, it had just scared her to feel her mother sleeping—absent from the world suddenly—and the only comfort had been to break the spell, to make her mother's eyes blink.

Ian said, "Maybe you were half asleep, because you looked at me for a long time. And then you sort of bolted, like you were trying to stand up. You hit your head on the ceiling, 'cause the bed is, you know, a loft. I think I asked you what was wrong; I was sort of out of it. You must have bitten your lip when you hit your head, because there was . . . blood."

Thinking back, she knew she had hovered over Ian for a moment. She'd sat up, looking down at him. She'd been just as scared in that moment as when she had stood next to her mother's bed—the swift separation, the deep aloneness. Lying there, asleep, he'd looked dead. *Wake up*, she could have said to him. *Wake up*. And everything might have turned out different.

But it was too late, wasn't it?

"And then I left," Leda said. She didn't want to say, *I was thinking about my mom*. She was too embarrassed to say it, but she felt the truth in it.

"Yeah. You sort of fled. And then after everything came out about Charlotte, I guess I was nervous. I didn't know why you ran out like that; I didn't know what you might think . . . And then there were times that you just scared the shit out of me."

"Yeah . . ." Leda hesitated. Around them, the snow had all but stopped.

"You shot a fucking gun at me," Ian said suddenly. He didn't sound angry, exactly, but amazed, as if he'd never imagined having to say this to anybody.

"It was in the air," Leda corrected, though she heard how absurd it sounded. "I wasn't aiming . . . at you."

"*I* didn't know that," Ian said. "I could barely see you."

"I was freaked out. I thought you were following me."

"I *was* following you. Carly practically begged me to. She thought something was wrong, and there obviously was."

Yes, Leda believed it. She'd believed it the moment she'd squeezed the trigger. Just the sound of the blast had been enough to drop him. He'd cowered, his face gone pale with shock. But—of course she wouldn't say this to Ian—she also couldn't help but wonder if part of what had scared Ian was their role reversal. He was used to being in control. Maybe it had woken him up, too, to feel suddenly fragile.

"I'm sorry," Ian said then, and it surprised Leda how good it felt to hear him say it. Did she deserve it? She wasn't sure; she'd put his life in danger. But it was a relief to hear him acknowledge her pain, her fear; although it had crystallized in a single night, it may well have changed the course of her life.

"I'm sorry you thought I was there to hurt you," Ian continued. "I had no idea you actually believed . . . that you thought that I . . ." He trailed off. The word *Charlotte* was there in the air, but he didn't bring it down. He let it float there. "I liked you," he said. "Maybe that sort of blinded me to how you were feeling."

I liked you, Leda thought. Past tense, not present. For a moment, she had wondered if this was one of those stories that could be funny in retrospect. A story you tell people about when you first met.

It wasn't.

"Thanks," Leda said, ending it. "Thanks for . . . talking."

There was still a hole, obviously. Leda would never know what the sex had been like with Ian. She would never know who had initiated it. (Had he pressed into her or she him?) She would never know the physical *feel* of it. She wouldn't know if she'd suffered—it could have been painful or boring or awkward—or if she'd realized that it was a bad idea halfway in. Or maybe . . . it had felt good. Maybe she hadn't wanted it to end.

There was no one she could ask. She'd never know.

Leda and Ian went inside together, but they parted soon after. In the front hall, people were talking about the same things—Charlotte's body; whether she'd jumped or fallen.

Outside, the empty pool bobbed with dry heads. People had climbed down into the basin. Now, Shakespeare was declaiming from the pool ladder, still maintaining that Charlotte had been murdered. Many agreed, though there was a split between those who thought the killer was local and those who thought he was a drifter. Either scenario must have comforted these people, Leda thought. A murder was clear-cut. There was no gray area. It was evil that could be caught and sentenced and locked up.

If only it could be that easy, Leda thought. If only we could identify one culprit, like a rotten fruit. If only we could know that, without it, nothing would ever again go rotten.

At the crawfish table, one girl said that Charlotte had been drugged. One said a government plot. One spoke of dissociation, fugue states, identity swaps.

"I feel that," said a girl in a trucker hat. The front of the hat read *Blessed*. "Sometimes my weeks are so busy that all of a sudden it's Sunday, and I'm like, *Who am I?*"

"I don't know if that's the same thing." Shakespeare climbed out of the dry pool, popped a crawfish, and wiped his fingers on a napkin. "And that still doesn't explain how she fell off a cliff."

In response, Genie put a buttery finger-gun to her own head and pulled the trigger. Her sequin bikini was just visible under her micro puff.

The *Blessed* hat said, "I don't think there was a gun."

"Well, then she probably threw herself off." Genie looked suddenly ugly. Her face was wraithlike, smirking.

"I think she tried to run away." This was Carly, drunk. She sat at the edge of the pool, feet dangling into nothing. The guy in the red shoes sat behind her, massaging her shoulders. "I think she was just sick of this—class, parties. Girls. Dudes." Carly's voice tilted. "I think she was just sick of all of it."

"Or maybe . . ." Melanie fooled with the Velcro on her orthopedic boot. "Maybe it was an accident."

There was a pause, and then Shakespeare poured everyone shots. Leda felt sick, hearing everyone chew over Charlotte. Where had Charlotte stepped off the path? they all asked. Where had Charlotte gone wrong? As if they were blameless, as if they'd played no part— however small—in what had happened. But, at the same time, Leda had to admit that some of them were right. Charlotte *had* been sick of this. She *had* run. And, maybe, as Mel suggested, there had been some accident. Maybe she had just wanted a break. Maybe she hadn't wanted to die this way.

I spoke to Charlotte on Halloween, Leda didn't say. *But sometimes I wonder: If she hadn't disappeared, would I have even remembered her?*

She didn't say it, because no one was listening. She didn't say it, because it disturbed her. It made her wonder something similar about her mother, wonder if people could only be seen—*really* seen— through tragedy. She tried to figure out how to say this. *Si mi mamá hubiera vivido . . .* If she had lived . . . But what was the use in imagining impossible situations?

Am I just like you? That was another question Leda wanted to ask. Was Leda just another drunk girl that Charlotte had photographed? Another person Charlotte had been trying to see that hadn't bothered to see her back? But perhaps in trying to find Charlotte, Leda had come closer to finding herself. Perhaps she'd woken up a bit.

Shakespeare handed Leda a beer, as if just now noticing her. He said, "If you want to know what I think . . ."

No, Leda thought. *I don't.* She set the beer down, unopened. She was about to walk off, about to leave. But it had begun to snow harder, and, anyway, where would she go? A wall of haze approached Leda, pushed around her, and past her, as if she were entering that video game fog or passing through her memory's virtual wall. *It's a liminal setting*, she heard Jonah say, condescending. *It means you don't have to know where you're going.*

But how could a person trust a world, she wondered now, with no clear destination? A world in which the rules constantly change? But, at the same time, how can a person come to know the world without trusting it? So, the challenge was to both trust the world and survive it. To be both open and safe.

Back in the frat, shaking snow out of her hair and off her coat, she heard a sound. A pitch pipe, off in a different room. She followed the sound deeper into the fraternity, down an empty hall toward a big, trashed room. There was a ladder covered in toilet paper. There were cans and cups and bottles. And there was a girl, playing a pitch pipe app out of her phone. Some men and women gathered there hummed the notes, huddled in a tight circle. Leda recognized a few of them from choir or from various a cappella groups. Some recognized her, too. They made room.

A guy told her what they were singing. It was a song that didn't ordinarily require a pitch pipe—a drinking song that might as well have been an unofficial university anthem. Everyone knew the chords, the lyrics. First and second year, it hadn't been uncommon for masses of drunk college students (typically dudes) to end a Saturday night pumping their fists, barking the verses.

A shout rose up in the back of the house. Probably a beer pong fail or triumph. The girl played the pitch pipe app again. Everyone hummed their notes, Leda included. She didn't particularly like the song, but she was here. She was a part of this. Why shouldn't she sing it?

The girl marked time with her Solo cup—much slower than Leda had expected. Drinking songs were usually quick, always speeding up. The last verses typically spun out of control, to the point that it was hard to keep up. But tonight, no one protested the slow tempo.

The other people in the room weren't watching. They preened and teased and flirted, shouting into one another's faces as if they weren't sure which part of the other person would hear them. In the middle of all this, Leda and these dozen random students faced one another. One girl wore a faded Pantera T-shirt. One guy, a Vineyard Vines bow tie. There was someone in overalls, someone wearing all black, someone in pearls. There was red-haired Leda in her short skirt. They breathed together.

Typically, Leda didn't sing drinking songs. Most had been written by men, for men. But the way they sang now somehow transformed the tradition. The music became contemplative, mournful, and, more than anything, strange. At this speed, the words no longer made sense. The more they lingered—milking harmonies and pauses— the more abstract it became. Eventually, when Leda got over how *off* the whole thing sounded, she closed her eyes. Somehow, she'd needed this. She'd needed to hear her voice mesh with other voices. She'd needed to sing her part, to hear all the parts stretch and blend and pull apart.

And, oddly, she'd needed this song, these words. She'd needed something to both acknowledge and disrupt this world that had disappeared Charlotte.

Drink her down . . .

They repeated the final line, again and again as the room chattered and laughed around them. This was usually the chorus, but now it sounded like a death knell, a toll.

Down, down, down . . .

On Leda's first day as a Psi Delt, she'd climbed up on a table, placed her heels on the edge, and crossed her arms. With her back facing her sisters, she'd closed her eyes and let herself fall.

Drink her down.

It had seemed as if she'd been in the air, falling, for too long.

In astronomy, she'd learned that the universe is curved, like the inside of a snail shell. The planets, her professor had said, are just marbles coursing around in it, falling always toward a great magmatic star that had been the beginning and would be the end of everything. The end meaning a collapsed star. A collapsed star meaning a black hole. And whatever fell in a black hole . . . well. Leda didn't know. It was only an introductory class; they hadn't gotten that far.

Perhaps, Leda thought, everything is always in free fall. More of a float than a plummet. More of a drift than a drop.

When they finished, the final chord rang in the room even after their mouths had shut. No one applauded. Most people in the room had barely noticed the song. Still, the singers grinned around at one another. They glowed, shoulder touching shoulder, chests buzzing with that final note. Somehow, Leda had forgotten about these moments.

And then Leda saw that someone *had* been listening, standing in the doorway with her arms folded. Mary was not wearing party clothes—just a normal Mary outfit of jeans and a bulky, olive jacket. No makeup. Glasses.

"I just heard," Mary said, when Leda went to her. "I've been writing essays all day—I've been so out of it—and then I heard . . ."

Leda opened her mouth, about to respond, but Mary just took Leda's hands. Leda didn't need to say anything.

Mary had first done this not long after they'd met, when she'd first learned about Leda's mother. At the time, her mom hadn't been dead a full year. After that, they'd held hands often, like children trying not to get separated. They had probably squeezed hands ordering whipped cream on morning lattes, googling "fellatio 101," or walking to their first frat party. Now, Leda thought, they hardly looked any older. But things had changed. A girl—their classmate—had been found dead today. For the first time in a long time, Leda felt real tears escape. And for the first time in a long time, she didn't blink them away.

Mary hugged her, held her, squeezing harder. The singers broke up, going to get crawfish, drinks. Cold air swept into the house, gusting in from somewhere. Leda breathed into Mary's shoulder, thinking now that perhaps that world was real—the one of love, of safety—thinking, *We build those worlds for each other, maybe.*

Around them, of course, the party didn't stop. It flexed and belched and shimmered, same as always. Time seemed to hover just outside, in the falling snow. No one was getting tired. No one was going home. A dude howled. Carly, somewhere, started rapping again, managing to mimic the way Eminem changed voices. This song seemed to include four or five characters played by one person.

In the hallway, someone was saying, "How can they do an ID when there's no, like, body? Wouldn't it be rotted or something?"

"Or eaten by vultures," someone concurred.

"Lee," Mary whispered. "Is there any way, we can like . . ." Mary gestured around her.

A few guys struck warrior poses, wielding lacrosse sticks. Others guillotined the tips of new cigars beside a knot of girls, dumping blue and pink Pixy Stix into vodka. A girl climbed up the toilet paper ladder. Overhead, a wall of bucks and does stared with plastic eyes, not taking it in.

"Leave?" Leda asked, laughing now. "Absolutely."

By the time they left the party, it became clear that time had not stopped. It was almost morning. Steady, unstoppable, life had gone on.

Leda and Mary walked through slow, drifting flurries. They parted ways at Memorial, knowing they would get home safely. They were both sober, and there were still a lot of people in the street—some who hadn't slept, some who had woken early. Leda walked, humming tunelessly, looking out at the morning. The snow had begun to stick to the roads, even as a ripple of color—not light, exactly—cracked the clouds' dense screen. Leda kept walking, bundled and slow, not quite wanting to return home. So she turned around and walked toward the university. She could go wherever she wanted. She walked toward her exams, her choir concert, her holiday with Clarence and Faye. She walked toward friends and maybe love, one day. Bits of ice and glass and loose concrete crunched under her feet. Typically, she walked without noticing these things. But had she really expected that she would be able to go this long without feeling anything?

She smelled browned butter. She smelled cheap coffee. For a few steps, silky, yellow gingko leaves carpeted the icy concrete. A pool of black ice winked. Leda knew there was no path without glass and grit; such a thing did not exist.

Fraternities glowed across the street. Above them, a few morning stars still shone. It was old light, she knew. That light from those stars had to travel so far that it was possible she was seeing the glimmer of an already dead star. It could have been dead for a year, or hundreds. And yet its light still stretched, still touched her—a ghost, a spirit. Or no, maybe it was just *light*. Maybe that was the best way to understand it. Even after a body dies, its light keeps going.

She thought of her mom then. She *let herself* think about her. So often, she tried to smother these little flares of her. But this morning, she tried to walk with her—*Mom*—wondering if humans put out light, wondering if any of that light might linger after death. A kind of afterlife.

Ahead, a peeling sycamore dropped brown globes of seeds. Leda stepped around them and touched the trunk. She watched her white breath blend with the white of the tree.

The first time she'd climbed up that sycamore by the reservoir, her mom hadn't noticed immediately. She'd been ten, and she'd gotten in her head that she would never come down again. When she'd announced this from the branches of the tree, her mom had been nonchalant about the whole thing. When it started getting dark, her mom had called up that she and Clarence were going home. Still, stubbornly, Leda stayed in the tree.

Now Leda, standing across from the glowing fraternities, felt herself back in that sycamore tree, watching her mother's taillights recede. Usually, the memory stopped there. But, tonight, it kept going.

Up in the tree, ten-year-old Leda stopped crying eventually. Weeping seemed pointless if there was no one to hear. Night wrestled the branches. Stars overhead pointed at her like fingers. Time lay still. Her mother had left her, she realized, for eternity. Now Leda lived in a tree with arms that felt like string cheese, like a Barbie's dead arms that wouldn't bend around anything. Leda sat in the tree, small. She was sure she would fall. She was sure she would be covered in dew and spiders and bark. She was sure she would be alone forever.

Something in the night had made a strangled sound. Leda shut her eyes, remembering, placing her two hands against the sycamore on Memorial. But a noise startled her. A long groan. Then a voice. A boy.

"*Fuck.*"

Leda blinked—the Rotunda in view, as white and indifferent as the moon. She looked around the trunk of the tree. The boy lay face-down against the roots. He wore a dress shirt and orange shorts patterned with palm trees. A pair of Ray-Bans lay broken at his feet. Leda put her boot to his boot. Nudged it.

Even as a child, Leda had known she'd done it to herself. She should have climbed down when her mother asked her to. She knew it, and yet she was furious. Confused. She slipped on the branch once and screamed with the same voice as the strangled animal she'd heard. She found the trunk eventually and stayed there against it, breathing. Invisible insects climbed over her hands. She had to pee. She tried to pretend that she was an owl or a crow. In the dark, she hadn't been sure if her eyes were open or closed.

Finally, after nudging him again and again with her boot, the boy rolled over. He moaned. There was mud and light from the sunrise on his cheeks. His skin was smooth. His eyes opened, wide as a ba-by's. Blue. Her mother's eyes had been blue, too.

He said, "I love you."

Leda laughed out loud. "I love you, too," she said—he smiled when she said it—and then she left him, sprawled against those white roots.

Before her, the morning opened like a window.

Somehow, still on her branch, little Leda had dozed. The white tree had held her all night, it seemed. She climbed down, feeling the ghost touch of spiderwebs snapping, as if they, too, had been keeping her from falling. At the base of the tree, she found her mother leaned against the trunk, asleep. Seeing her, a feeling rose up. The sunrise bubbled with pink. The ground wobbled after so many hours in the tree. Her belly was full of heat. Leda had wanted to kick her mother. She'd wanted to scream. Instead, she'd collapsed beside her, feeling the exact point of pressure where her mother's sleeping hand touched her.

Now, Leda walked alone down Memorial, the dense clouds turning pink. Though the sun had still not yet risen, the morning gleamed. She closed her eyes, stepping carefully, feeling the light on her cheeks.

"Oh, darling," Leda heard her mother say above her. "My darling."

Leda roused and looked up at her. But her mother hadn't said anything; she was still asleep. The morning bulked and sang. How could her mom sleep through this? How could she? There was no way that Leda could sleep now that everything—life!—screamed. The Earth looked at the sun. Birds rioted. The reservoir under the sycamore dazzled like static, like memory. It all tugged Leda urgently. It was an impossible feeling for someone so small—the need to love, to live, to keep going. Still, her mother slept. Of course she slept. And of course Leda kept her eyes open. Uncountable crows shot at the sky, and she stood and watched them. The world woke. For once, she let her mother sleep.

Acknowledgments

I had a great deal of help in the making of this book from a number of deeply generous people.

My gratitude goes to everyone who read early drafts of this novel at Hollins University. To Carrie Brown for your kindness and heartfelt encouragement. To Richard Dillard, whom I admire so deeply as a writer and teacher. Without you, this book might have never left Fincastle.

I am forever indebted to my agent, Madison Smartt Bell, for championing my work at every turn, and to the team at Riverhead and Penguin Random House, including Alison Fairbrother, Delia Taylor, and especially Sarah McGrath, who was a delight to work with and whose infallible insight and intuition helped shape this book into the best version of itself.

My sincerest thanks to my family. To Liz Denton and Mark Edmundson, for your ready wisdom and bottomless generosity. To my father, William, and my brother, Paul, for believing in me and supporting me for as long as I can remember. And to my late mother, Elizabeth, who taught me to never stop moving my pen.

Thank you to my hometown and my alma mater, where I got my first taste of the writing life. Thank you to Mark Whittle for introducing me to the stars and galaxies, to Gustavo Pellón for challenging me to be precise in speech and writing, and to John Parker for showing me how thrilling and strange literature can be (and, I should mention, for bringing me and my now-husband into the same classroom).

Above all, thank you to Matthew, who read so many drafts of this novel. You are my most trusted reader, my love, my home.